THE UNRAVELLING OF JULIA

Praise for *The Unravelling of Julia*

'A compelling thriller with dashes of romance and excellent twists!'
New York Times and #1 International Bestselling author,
Karin Slaughter

'Scottoline deftly weaves a touch of astrology through this fast-paced thriller, and the result is a stunning novel that will leave you breathless' **Fiona Davis, *New York Times* bestselling author**

'Pulse-pounding, propulsive, and utterly unputdownable… another can't-miss masterpiece… [It] reaffirms Scottoline's status as the undeniable queen of the psychological thriller' **Kristy Woodson Harvey, *New York Times* bestselling author**

'All the hallmarks of the very best Lisa Scottoline novels and yet is also something spectacularly new. This might just be my favorite Lisa Scottoline book yet, and that's saying a lot!' **Marie Benedict, *New York Times* bestselling author**

'This is a thriller as twisted as an Italian road with high-speed car chases, visions, terrors day and night… Enthralling, intriguing and ridiculously entertaining' **Liz Nugent, internationally bestselling author**

'A delicious escape that blends suspense, atmosphere, and heart – this is Scottoline at her finest' **Danielle Trussoni, *New York Times* bestselling author**

Also by Lisa Scottoline

LISA SCOTTOLINE

THE UNRAVELLING OF JULIA

NO EXIT PRESS

First published in the US in 2025 by Grand Central Publishing,
an imprint of Hachette Book Group,
New York, USA

First published in the UK in 2025 by No Exit Press,
an imprint of Bedford Square Publishers Ltd,
London, UK

noexit.co.uk
@noexitpress

ISBN
978-1-83501-309-0 (Paperback)
978-1-83501-310-6 (eBook)

2 4 6 8 10 9 7 5 3 1

The manufacturer's authorised representative in the EU for
product safety is Easy Access System Europe, Mustamäe tee 50,
10621 Tallinn, Estonia
gpsr.requests@easproject.com

Typeset in 10.75 on 13.4pt Garamond MT Pro
by Avocet Typeset, Bideford, Devon, EX39 2BP
Printed and bound in Great Britain by
CPI Group (UK) Ltd, Croydon CR0 4YY

For my beloved daughter Francesca

I look quiet and consistent,
but few know how many women there are in me.
—Anaïs Nin

Astrology penetrated deep into the intellectual
and political life of the Renaissance. It was,
as it had always been, a spacious philosophical
structure, somewhere between a science and a
religion, offering a unifying perspective on
questions of cosmology and physics, medicine
and biology, and above all on human destiny.
—Peter Whitfield, *A History of Astrology* (2001)

Little Green, have a happy ending.
—Joni Mitchell, *Little Green*

1

Julia knew something terrible was about to happen. Her knowing wasn't conscious, but something she sensed and couldn't acknowledge, even to herself. It felt like dread, but she'd never dreaded anything like this. Reflexively she tucked her arm under her husband's as they walked down the street. It was dark and almost midnight, since they'd gone to dinner late.

Julia glanced over her shoulder, nervous even in the exclusive Rittenhouse Square neighborhood. No one was behind them. Twenty-First Street was lined with tall Victorian row houses converted to apartments, and TVs inside flickered like lightning strikes. Only a few people were out, hurrying home as they talked into earbuds, conversing with the night.

'You okay, babe?' Mike asked, leaning toward her. His hands were in the pockets of his overcoat, and he had on a suit since he'd been in court that day. His red hair caught a gust of cold wind, and freckles dotted his face like constellations.

'I'm fine, let's go.' Julia couldn't explain a feeling she didn't understand. Their street was only steps away. Home was just around the corner.

'What's the matter?'

'I don't know, I feel… scared,' Julia answered, and as soon as the words escaped her lips, she knew the terrible thing was going to happen *right now*.

Suddenly a man came around the corner, blocking their path. A blue hoodie shadowed his face. He had on a black down jacket and jeans. In his hand was a large hunting knife, its blade lethally jagged.

Julia froze, terrified. The man grabbed her shoulder bag, but the motion yanked her toward him.

Mike lunged between them to protect her. The man thrust the knife into him. Mike groaned in agony as his head fell forward. The knife protruded from his chest, stuck gruesomely in his white shirt.

'No!' Julia screamed. Mike wobbled on his feet.

The man yanked the knife from Mike's chest, and blood spurted from the wound. The man turned and ran.

Mike collapsed. Julia grabbed him and fell with him to the sidewalk. His blood sprayed them both, hideously warm.

Frantic, Julia covered his wound with her hands. Blood pulsed into her palms, then stopped abruptly. Mike looked up at her without seeing her, his gaze gone vacant. His blue eyes fixed like ice. His jaw eased open. He lay lifeless on her lap, leaking blood.

'Mike!' Julia shrieked, a primal wail echoing in the night, reverberating off the concrete.

Mike stared at the stars.

Seeing between them, forever.

2

Julia sighed, the only sound in the apartment. Mike's funeral had come and gone, and her in-laws were back in Massachusetts. She wondered how often she'd see them now. There were no grandchildren to bind them, since Mike hadn't wanted to try to get pregnant yet.

Babe, next year, I release the Kraken.

Today was the first day she'd made it to her desk. Every morning since his murder had been a unique sort of hell. She'd wake up, realize he wasn't there, and remember why. He wasn't at the office. He wasn't playing basketball. He wasn't in the kitchen making them both coffee, a kindness she was grateful for, every day.

Julia would remember things he said or did, having teary flashbacks. They'd met freshman year at Notre Dame, where he was a sports fanatic who took art history on a lark. He was clever and fun, and they clicked instantly. They married at the Basilica and moved to Philly, where she got an MFA in painting at Penn while he went to its law school. They became each other's family and were blessedly happy, most of their fights over stupid things like March Madness, which she regretted now.

Mike, it's only a basketball game. If we leave now, we'll be back for the last quarter.

Babe, that's the climax. Boys need foreplay, too.

Julia's memories would keep her in bed, where she was the most miserable, and the more she remembered, the more miserable she'd be and the more stuck in bed. Getting up meant starting another day without him in a life that was Before and After. She lived an Afterlife.

Mike's ashes were on the bookshelf in a brass urn, since he told her he wanted to be cremated in a conversation they both thought was hypothetical. Next to it sat a photo of him from his law school graduation, grinning in a mortarboard. It had been displayed at his funeral, but Julia thought no photo could capture Michael Aaron Shallette, who was so full of life, talk, and opinions.

He has the gift of the gab, her father always said.

Her truest feeling was a deep sadness for *him*, not for herself. Mike got only thirty-two years and twenty-one days on the planet, and she raged at the injustice. *Gone too soon* and *life cut tragically short* were too generic for him. Mike set goals and announced them, always planning. He wanted to be a father by thirty-four and he used to talk about their first child. He'd say, *I'll take a boy or a girl. Girls can hit three-pointers, too.*

He used to talk about the BMW Z4 he configured online. *Honey, I'm getting that car when I make partner. The website said so.*

He used to talk about his lawyers league championship. *Next year, Dechert goes down.*

But Mike didn't get next year. He didn't even get next week, and that was what she mourned. *Sorry for your loss*, everyone told her, but he was the one who lost everything, and *that* killed her. She didn't know if the word for that feeling was grief, or love.

Julia barely slept. She had nightmares that left her trembling. She'd see the man in the hoodie stepping from the darkness, the knife, Mike's blood. Some days she'd get up, brush her teeth, and shower, but working seemed impossible. She had a small business designing and maintaining websites, but she could barely concentrate. Meanwhile, the financial pressure was on. She made $75,000 to Mike's $250,000 a year, and his firm had already direct-deposited his last check. She had rent, student loans, credit card bills, and car payments. There was about $37,000 in savings, but $8,500 went for his funeral. Mike had only minimal life insurance because he was too young to die.

The police had no leads on his murder, and she routinely called the Homicide Division and the ADA. She'd given statements but didn't have a good description of the killer because it had been too dark. His face had been shadowed by the hoodie, so she hadn't seen his features and didn't know his race or age. He hadn't said anything, so she hadn't even heard his voice. The ADA warned her to be vigilant when she went out, since she was an eyewitness, and it disturbed her that the killer knew what she looked like but she didn't know what *he* looked like. She wouldn't see him coming, so she stayed inside.

The guilt was a gut punch, and a loop of second-guessing ran through her mind several times a day. What if she hadn't worn a designer bag? What if they hadn't eaten so late? What if Mike hadn't tried to protect her? Since the funeral, Julia had a constant stomachache. She thought it was something she ate until she realized it was pure, weapons-grade guilt, Catholic in origin. Mike had *died for her.*

A social worker had called, urging her to use Crime Victim Support. Julia ended up Zooming with a mother whose son was shot at a wedding, a man whose brother was stabbed in a bar, and a woman whose sister was strangled by a boyfriend. Julia listened to them in horror, crying with them. Her nightmares intensified, so she quit.

Her best friend Courtney made her see a therapist, Susanna Cobb. They had their first session, also on Zoom, and Susanna recommended a Zoom widow bereavement group, but that didn't work, either. The other widows had decades with their husbands, and all Julia could think was how lucky they were. Plus the facilitator talked about 'widow empowerment' and 'interactive self-help tools,' when Julia felt neither empowered nor interactive. They told her to expect the occasional 'griefburst,' but she lived in a griefburst. MOPING IS COPING read their slogan, but she coped way too much.

Since Mike's death, Julia thought of her mother more and more. They'd been best friends, and Melanie Mortssen Pritzker was a warm and funny woman, a former NICU nurse devoted to Julia and filling her childhood with happy moments. Chasing foamy wavelets at the beach. Exploring the smelly darkness of the reptile house at the zoo. Nobody loved to bake more than her mother, and making a Funfetti cake was her birthday tradition.

Julia would never forget her tenth birthday, when the two of them huddled happily in the kitchen, sprinkling Funfetti into the batter. Her mother always mixed with a wooden spoon, *old-school* she said.

Her mother smiled. *This is the happiest day of the year for me.*

My birthday? Julia asked, surprised. She watched the red, green, and blue jimmies churn by in the batter.

Absolutely.

But you didn't get me on my birthday. Julia had known she was adopted from when she was little. Her mother had told her with characteristic honesty, making it no secret.

True, but the world got you that day. Her mother's hazel eyes twinkled. *And I'm so happy you were born.*

Julia still had questions. *Do you ever wish I came out of your belly?*

Her mother shook her head. *No, not at all.*

Julia wasn't sure she believed her. *Why not?*

Other moms and dads don't get to choose, but I got to choose you. I waited for you for a long time, and you're very special. God wanted us to have you and He brought you to us.

Julia smiled, suffused with her own adopted specialness, but suddenly her mother frowned, her hand going to her forehead.

Ow, that hurts.

What, Mom? Mom?

Julia didn't want to remember what happened next. Her mother collapsed to the floor, her eyes wide open. The wooden spoon lay where she'd dropped it, dripping cheery Funfetti batter. Julia had tried to shake her awake, but her mother was already gone, dead of an aneurysm that very moment, on Julia's tenth birthday.

Her father died of a heart attack her junior year at college, but they were never close. Her mother was their family's chirpy driver, and her father its taciturn passenger. A structural engineer, Martin James Pritzker shut down after his wife died. Julia stepped into her mother's role, cleaning and making dinner, but she couldn't make him happy. He was a Sigher, and she didn't have to ask why. She knew he missed her mother.

Once a year, they endured the awful convergence of her birthday and the anniversary of her mother's death. They would visit her mother's grave, then go home and have lunch, talking neither about her mother nor her birthday. Her father would descend to his basement and watch TV with a bottle of Johnnie Walker Black Label, which he permitted himself this day only.

Finally, when Julia turned fourteen, she found herself teary-eyed in the kitchen, making a Funfetti cake and mixing the batter *by hand*, then she took it downstairs.

Dad, look, I made—

What the hell is that? Her father turned in his leather recliner, a crystal tumbler in his hand. The TV showed a golf tournament on mute, its bright green fairway filling the screen.

It's for her, Julia answered, instantly regretful.

Bullshit! It's for you! Her father scowled, slurring his words. *You made a cake, today? Your mother deserved better than you! Better than me!*

No… Dad, Julia tried to say, stricken. *I just thought—*

You're an ingrate! You should thank your lucky stars for her! All she wanted was a baby! And I couldn't give it to her! She never shoulda married me!

Julia edged back to the staircase.

You wouldn't be here but for her! You were her idea! The whole damn thing was her idea. I didn't want you!

Julia's heart broke that day. The Sigher had been sighing because he was stuck with *her*. She realized then that adoption gave you a family, but not necessarily a happy one.

Sitting at her desk, she realized how different her life was from other people her age. She was only thirty-two, but she'd already lost all the family she had. So far, her defining moments were marked by gravestones, not milestones. She wondered if grief acquired mass with loss after loss, like an avalanche rumbling down a mountain, gathering size and momentum, flattening everything in its path. Flattening *her*.

Julia came out of her reverie and glanced outside, since her desk sat against a window overlooking the street. Bundled-up men and women hurried to work laden with purses, messenger bags, and backpacks. Young mothers yakked on phones while they pushed strollers. Neighbors walked dogs, and runners ran by, checking watches.

Julia couldn't imagine going Outside, among the people and the phones, the designer bags and the knives. She was afraid, but mostly she didn't think she belonged there anymore. She belonged Inside, with her mourning and her memories, her voices and her ghosts.

But she had to get to work, today. She turned to her desktop, palmed her mouse, and opened her email account, which piled onto the screen. Her attention went to the oldest email, which came in on October 11, the day of Mike's murder.

Julia shuddered, thinking back to that morning, which was like any other, then snapped out of it and made herself focus. The email was her daily horoscope from StrongSign, which she usually checked. She'd become interested in astrology after her mother died on her birthday, a fluke of fate if there ever was one, like a freak accident in a family. She often wondered if her own birth was an accident, too, given that she was put up for adoption. Sometimes she even wondered if she was cursed.

Julia opened the email and read the horoscope:

You're a Cancer Sun, Sagittarius Moon, and Virgo Rising, and you love your home and family. Do not be alarmed but do be aware today. You or a loved one may be in jeopardy. Trust yourself today, and every day.

Her mouth went dry. The horoscope *predicted* Mike's murder before it happened. Dumbfounded, she read it again and again, then the guilt, second-guessing, and self-recrimination started. If only she'd read the horoscope that morning. If only she'd trusted herself that night. Could she have prevented Mike's murder? Would he be alive today? Was it her fault? Was it his fate? Was it hers?

Julia needed somebody to talk to, and she knew just who to call.

Every woman did.

3

Julia FaceTimed her best friend, and just the sight of Courtney Horan made her feel better. They'd met in drama club at their small Pennsylvania high school, where Julia felt weird being adopted and Courtney felt weird being biracial. They were on stage crew together, while Julia painted sets at a level of detail an amateur production of *Annie* didn't require, and Courtney came into her own as stage manager, even standing up for Julia when a mean girl in the cast called her Little Orphan Julie. On the show's opening night, Julia didn't cry during 'Maybe' because everyone was watching her, but she lived that song.

Their one mistake was giving up me.

After graduation, she and Courtney went to Notre Dame together, helping each other through bad boyfriends and Statistics I, and they got married around the same time, serving as each other's maid of honor in real Jimmy Choos.

No knockoffs for us!

Julia's phone screen showed Courtney in aviator glasses that emphasized her striking green eyes and prominent cheekbones. Her skin was a poreless light brown, her thick black hair pulled back into a short ponytail. She wore almost no makeup, naturally pretty in a navy Patagonia fleece and white cotton turtleneck and jeans. She was sales manager for an office equipment company, on the road constantly, a creature of the airport lounge, where Julia found her today.

'Courtney, do you have time to talk?'

'Totally, I'm on another delay.' Courtney smiled. 'How's my girl?'

'I have something to tell you. My horoscope predicted Mike's murder.'

'What?' Courtney's eyes widened. 'That's not possible.'

'Listen to this, from October eleventh.' Julia read her the horoscope. 'Well? I'm not crazy, am I? It says what I think, doesn't it?'

Courtney blinked. 'It really says "be aware"? A "loved one in jeopardy"?'

'Yes, and I told you, right before it happened, I knew something was wrong.' Julia remembered the feeling, the dreadful knowing. 'I had a premonition, straight-up, but I didn't say anything. I didn't trust it. The horoscope says I have to trust myself and—'

'Stop, hold on. Don't blame yourself.'

'Why not? I should've said something when I had that feeling. If I'd trusted myself—'

'No, Jules, that's wrong.'

'—I could've warned him.' Julia was upset all over again. It felt like a confession, but she was already guilty.

'What difference would it have made?'

'He could've moved aside. I could've screamed sooner. People could've come.' Julia's gut twisted. 'Anything could have happened. Anything *else*.'

Courtney scoffed, shaking her head.

'Plus if I'd read the horoscope, *I* would've made different choices. Not go out to dinner. Order in. Cook. He'd be alive today.'

'Mike didn't die because of a stupid horoscope.'

'Don't you believe in astrology? I thought you did.'

'Not like *this*.' Courtney's expression softened. 'Look, I believe there's a lot of things we don't understand. I believe in God, and He does work in mysterious ways. I know it's a cliché, but I believe it.'

Julia had gone to church when her mother was alive, but not since. She'd lost her religion on her tenth birthday.

'Everything happens for a reason. Another cliché, but it's true.'

Julia couldn't imagine the reason God would take Mike in such a horrible way.

Courtney frowned. 'Jules, you look tired. How are you sleeping?'

'I'm okay.' Julia glanced at herself on the screen. She used to be cute, but she'd lost weight and her face was too thin. Her blue eyes had dark circles underneath, and there was a reason her dirty blonde hair looked dirty.

'You're out of pajamas. Good for you.'

'Right?' Julia had on a house sweater and yoga pants that could use a laundering, but the washer-dryer was in the basement, which creeped her out these days.

'Anything new on Mike's case?'

'Not yet.'

'You can't be okay in the apartment with all his stuff.'

'I like his stuff.' Julia loved Mike's stuff. His headset and gaming console sat beside the monitor. His puffy coat and backpack hung by the door. His ChapStick tubes rolled on the kitchen counter. Most of their kisses had been Classic Spearmint. Last Thanksgiving, she bought him Pumpkin Pie flavor, which he didn't like.

What, no turkey flavor?

Courtney was saying, 'Let me help you pack it up. I can make a quick trip to Philly. We can put it in storage.'

'No, thanks.' Julia couldn't bear the thought of *storing* Mike. 'How are you?'

'I'm fine, but I worry about you.' Courtney cocked her head. 'Did you think about moving to Chicago? You could be near me. There's nothing keeping you in Philly.'

Julia knew it was true. Most of their friends were Mike's. He was the extrovert, not her. 'I live here. We picked this apartment together.'

'Come on, we'd love to have you. We could hang like we used to.'

Julia cringed. They'd been a foursome at school, not a threesome. 'You're never home anyway.'

'What are you going to do for Christmas?'

Julia didn't want to go there. 'Could we get back to the horoscope? I mean, it *predicted* his murder.'

'Let me see for myself.' Courtney started typing on her laptop. 'Okay, I'm on StrongSign. Oh look, a pop-up. It says I can ask the stars a free question.'

'So, ask.'

'Okay. When's my fucking flight?'

4

The morning sun slipped through the blinds, waking Julia up, and she groped for her phone to check her horoscope. In the past six months, she'd gone full astrology girlie. She always read her StrongSign horoscope, then checked three other astrology sites. She'd become Queen of In-App Purchases and she asked the stars ten questions a week. She did natal charts for herself, Mike, Courtney, Paul, Jennifer Aniston, and other random celebrities. She memorized her customized annual reading. She learned words like *sextile* and *trine* like they were SAT vocab.

Julia opened StrongSign and read today's horoscope:

Your luck is going to change today. You are stronger than you know. Trust yourself. It is only the beginning.

Whoa. Julia sat up, astonished. She couldn't believe what she was seeing. It was an amazing horoscope, and so specific. The last horoscope she'd gotten like that was on the day of Mike's murder. Too often they were generic affirmations, like *integrate past lessons* and *determine what belongs to you* and *don't be self-critical.*

Julia blinked, her mind racing. If her luck was going to change, then something really good was going to happen today. She wondered what, and her first thought was that the police would catch Mike's killer.

Yes! Her heart lifted with hope. So far there hadn't been any leads, and she'd been worrying they'd never find him, as if Mike didn't matter at all.

Maybe *today* was the day.

Julia *believed*.

Julia gulped breakfast, avocado on Ezekiel toast, and read her horoscope again and again, her brain afire. She could barely wait until nine o'clock, when she called her contacts on Mike's case to see if there was any news. Neither answered, so she left messages.

She slipped the phone into her pocket and tried to start the day. She had to get the mail because she was expecting a check for eight hundred dollars. Then she crossed to the door, got her key from the woven bowl, and undid the deadbolt. She stalled, nervous whenever she left the apartment. She'd barely gone out since Mike passed. She bought everything online, even groceries. She ordered takeout on Seamless so she didn't have to talk to anybody.

She braced herself, opened the door, and peeked into the hallway. No one was there. She stepped out and locked the door behind her. She hurried down the stairs, reached the ground floor, and opened the door to the entrance hall, propping it ajar with her foot. On the left was a panel of stainless-steel mailboxes, and their mailbox was the third; apt 2 PRITZKER/SHALLETTE, read the label in Mike's neat printing.

Babe, I put your name first. Happy wife, happy life.

Julia unlocked the box and pulled out the mail. The check hadn't come in. There was only a bill from PECO and a yellow plastic envelope from DHL. Weird, she never got international mail.

She closed the mailbox, locked it, then slipped back through the door, making sure it locked. She hurried upstairs, reached her apartment, unlocked the door, and went inside, locking it again.

She crossed to the table and sat down with the DHL envelope. The return address was Massimiliano Lombardi, Studio Legale, Via Santa Maria alla Porta, 5, 20123, Milan MI, Italia. She didn't know anybody in Italy. She opened the envelope and inside was a sheet of old-school embossed stationery, which read:

```
Ms Julia Pritzker:

I am an attorney representing the estate of Signora
Emilia Rossi. Client Rossi has left a significant
monetary bequest to you, in addition to a property
located at Via Venerai 282, Chianti, Italia, including
a villa, vineyard, and land.
   Please contact my office as regards this
inheritance. I have been trying to contact you via
email.
   Thank you for your prompt attention to this matter.

Very kindly yours,
Massimiliano Lombardi
```

What? Julia read the letter again. It sounded like one of those scams from Ethiopian princes. She didn't know who Emilia Rossi was. It *had* to be a scam. She rose with the letter, crossed to her desktop, and searched her email for Massimiliano Lombardi or Emilia Rossi. No emails from either.

She navigated to her spam folder, and two emails popped up from Massimiliano Lombardi. She opened the most recent, and it was the letter verbatim. So Lombardi *had* been trying to reach her. She opened his earlier email. It was a copy of the letter, too.

Huh? Julia racked her brain but didn't know any Emilia Rossi. She picked up her phone to call Lombardi, then realized she didn't know how to call internationally. It was a different time zone, too. She googled both answers.

Julia pressed in Lombardi's number, then remembered:

Your luck is going to change today.

5

'Mr Lombardi? My name is Julia Pritzker. I'm calling about Emilia Rossi.'

'I'm delighted to hear from you. I have been trying to reach you, Ms Pritzker.'

Miz Preet-zker? Julia thought Lombardi's accent sounded Italian, but she couldn't tell if it was real or fake. 'Are you really a lawyer?'

'Of course, yes. I am one of the most well-respected estates attorneys in Milan. I wrote to inform you that you are a beneficiary of my client Emilia Rossi.'

Yeah, right. 'So this is real?'

'Certainly. Why not?'

'I don't know Emilia Rossi.'

'Pardon me?'

'I have no idea who Emilia Rossi is. I don't know anyone by that name.'

Lombardi fell silent a moment. 'She has bequeathed you a very considerable sum, a villa, and property.'

'She can't have, I don't know her.'

'A distant relative, perhaps?'

'No, it must be a mistake.'

'Ms Pritzker, there is no mistake.'

This has to be a scam. 'What do you want from me? Money?'

'No. On the contrary, I'm obligated to send *you* a distribution after probate is complete.'

This guy is good. 'How do I know you're who you say you are?'

'Ms Pritzker.' Lombardi's tone stiffened. 'If you wish to review my bona fides, please consult our website, Lombardi & Palumbo, Studio Legale.'

Julia typed it into her laptop, and a website popped onto the screen, showing two older lawyers in a modern office in front of a cityscape. Still, she made websites for a living, so she knew it could be fake. 'This doesn't prove anything.'

'Ms Pritzker, I assure you, I am genuine.'

'But I don't know any Emilia Rossi.'

'There must be someone in your family you can ask.'

Julia blinked. 'My parents have passed, and I'm adopted. I don't know anything about my biological family.'

'So you cannot say you are *not* related to Emilia Rossi.'

'Well, no,' Julia said, realizing it was theoretically possible. 'But in Italy? How could I be related to someone in Italy?'

'In any event, I intend to see that distribution is made to you as soon as possible. Probate will take several months under Italian law, due to taxation and such. In total, your bequest amounts to three million, two hundred thousand euros.'

Wait, what? Julia gasped, stunned. She must've heard him wrong. *'How much?'*

'Your bequest is three million two hundred thousand euros, which is roughly the same in dollars.'

'Are you *serious*?' Julia's mouth dropped open. Her mind reeled. It was like she won the lottery if it was true, which it couldn't be. 'That's impossible!'

'Ms Pritzker, I have a meeting and I cannot be late.' Lombardi cleared his throat. 'You may take possession of the villa immediately, and I will draft the necessary papers. If you wish, I will have my assistant fly you to Milan and book you at a hotel near my office. You could sign the papers, then travel to your property. I could arrange a car.'

Oh my God. Julia's head was spinning. 'Where's the house again?'

'The villa is in Chianti, and the property is twenty hectares, about forty acres.'

'*Forty* acres?' Julia asked, trying to get a grip. 'Plus I thought Chianti was a wine.'

'Chianti is a province in Tuscany, outside Florence. Sangiovese grapes are grown in Chianti province. Authentic Chianti can be made only there. My wife is Tuscan.' Lombardi's voice warmed. 'Tuscany is very beautiful, and we go often.'

'I can't believe this.' Julia shook her head, unable to process it fast enough.

'Should you wish to sell the villa, I can engage a realtor for you. He can ascertain the value of the property better than I.'

'And I get a house *on top of* the money?'

'Yes, of course.'

'Holy shit!' Julia blurted out, dumbfounded. It was an enormous inheritance, if a total mystery. 'But I don't know Emilia Rossi.'

'I could also assist you to investigate your familial connection to her. I have a family investigator I use. I can include him in our meeting, if you wish.'

'I wish!' Julia felt a surge of excitement. The prospect of learning about her biological parents made her heart race. She'd wondered about them her whole life.

'Ms Pritzker, I must go now. Please let me know when you wish to visit. I'm available this week but not the next few.'

'Thank you very much.'

'My pleasure. Good evening.'

'Goodbye.' Julia pressed End in a sort of shock. She found herself rising and looking out the window. Sunlight flooded through the glass, so bright she couldn't see outside. She stared into the light, trying to get through her head what had just happened. She was inheriting millions of dollars, a villa, and land from a stranger who might be a blood relative.

Her horoscope said her luck would change today, and it was right *again*.

Still, for a lead in Mike's case, she would've given all the money in the world.

6

'Courtney, hi!' Julia opened the door in the entrance hall, and Courtney rushed in, bear-hugging her.

'Jules, you're a *millionaire*!'

'Can you believe it?' Julia hugged her back, still incredulous. She'd tried for days to absorb the news, but her thoughts kept returning to Mike. How she wished it were a break in his case. How he deserved to share her luck. How happy he would have been, should have been, deserved to be.

'Is this real life?' Courtney released her, alive with animation. Her hair was in its ponytail, and she looked classy in a tan linen pantsuit with a white silk camisole and nice flats. She'd been at a sales conference in New Jersey and had come over to celebrate. 'Let's go out! You're buying dinner!'

Julia stiffened. They hadn't talked about going out. She thought they'd eat in. 'I made us salads. Arugula, feta, orange slices, and walnuts, like you like.'

'Are you crazy?' Courtney rolled her eyes. 'We're *drinking* dinner! Champs! *Chianti! Both!*'

'But it's late.'

Courtney snorted. 'It's nine o'clock!'

'I'm not dressed.' Julia had on a white cotton sweater, yoga pants, and Birks.

'You look fine! We're going out.' Courtney grabbed her arm, but Julia pulled away, eyeing her street through the window in the outer door. It was dark, the only light from a fixture with a dim bulb. Mike had been killed five blocks away. She flashed on that night. The man in the hoodie. The big knife. The blood. Mike's eyes, staring heavenward.

Julia's mouth went dry. 'Let's stay in.'

'All right.' Courtney smiled begrudgingly. 'But you better have wine.'

Julia sipped the wine, a fruity Vermentino, which relaxed her. They'd finished their salads, put the dishes in the dishwasher, and shared a container of Cherry Garcia. They played Stephen Sondheim's *Into the Woods* and *Sunday in the Park with George*, since they were theater nerds. Night had fallen outside the window.

Courtney's eyes narrowed. 'Can I ask you something? When was the last time you were out?'

'I don't know,' Julia answered, hoping she sounded nonchalant. Courtney's mother was a therapist, and Courtney was an Esther Perel wannabe with Sandler training.

'Was it since Mike's funeral? That's what Paul thinks, but I told him he's wrong.'

Julia felt embarrassed they'd discussed her, even out of love. 'Court, I go out.'

'Oh really? Well, remember when we gave each other Find My Phone? You were worried about me, because I was flying so much? Well, after Mike died, I was worried about *you*, so I started checking the app.' Courtney got her phone, scrolled, then held it up. Its glowing screen showed Julia's profile picture over a grayed-out map of Philadelphia. 'Your lil' face never moves from that spot. I never see you leave the house. As far as I can tell, you don't go *anywhere*.'

Julia's mouth went dry. 'You *track* me?'

'Yes. You can thank me anytime.'

Busted. 'Look, I don't go out that much, but whatever. I work at home, and the prosecutor told me not to, remember? And it was winter.'

'It's been six months.'

'That's not long.' *In widow years.*

'I think you're self-isolating.'

Me, too. 'I'm fine. I'm working.'

Courtney pursed her lips. 'All the time?'

'I have to, I need the money, plus I'm a homebody. Typical Cancer.'

'Don't start with that.' Courtney shot her a look. 'Are you afraid to go out?'

'No.' *I'm afraid of what could happen when I do.*

'I'm worried you're agoraphobic.'

'I get a little nervous on the street, after dark, that's all.' *Can you blame me?*

Courtney cocked her head. 'What does Susanna say?'

'She says it's part of my "grief journey."' Julia hated the expression, which sounded like a trip nobody wanted to go on. 'You get twelve months before it's "prolonged grief disorder," so I'm crushing it, mourning-wise.'

'Do you have a diagnosis?'

Julia's cheeks warmed. She knew her DSM codes because she submitted them for insurance, which didn't cover much anyway. 'It's obvious, isn't it? Situational depression and generalized anxiety, with a dash of PTSD. Season to taste.'

'I'm sorry, honey.' Courtney made a sad face.

'It's okay not be okay, right?' *Or is it?* 'I hate the "D" in PTSD. I hate thinking I have a disorder. I'd rather just have stress like everybody else.'

Courtney smiled, sympathetic. 'So make the "D" stand for something good.'

'Deluxe?'

'Delightful, delicious, de-lovely?'

Julia chuckled. 'Anyway, it's not forever.' *I hope.*

'Agree, totally. Do you think Susanna's helping you?'

'Yes,' Julia answered, though all she did was cry through the sessions, at $250 an hour. She could've cried alone for free.

'Do you go to her office?'

'No, we Zoom.'

'Does she know you don't go out?'

'I don't know. We have more important things to talk about, like Mike.' Julia felt a stab of grief.

Courtney's expression softened. 'What does she say about meds?'

'Nothing. She gave me coping strategies, like box breathing. Breathe in and count to four, then breathe out and count to four.'

Julia didn't like feeling that she had a mental illness, but at the same time, judged herself for being so retro, newly sensitive to terms like *crazy, basket case, nutjob*. She wondered if people understood how easily you could cross the divide from normal, whatever *that* was, to whatever she was now.

Courtney met her eye. 'I gotta say, I think you need meds.'

'I gotta say, I think you sell office equipment.'

'Jules, sales involves a lot of psychology.'

'But I'm not a laser copier.'

Courtney smiled. 'Then how are you going to Tuscany if you don't leave the apartment? I'd go with you but I have work.'

'I'm not going.'

'What?' Courtney's lips parted in surprise.

'There's no reason to go, and I have work.' Julia sipped more wine. She wanted to go to Tuscany, but she couldn't imagine it, with or without Courtney. It simply wasn't possible.

'What about the money?'

'They can send me a check.'

'And the villa?'

'They can sell it.'

'Don't you want to *see* it first?'

'Why? I'm not moving there.'

Courtney blinked. 'What about the investigator? Don't you want to meet with him about your bio family?'

'We can Zoom.' Julia didn't use terms like *bio family* because she hadn't grown up with them. Maybe she was *old-school*, too. Meanwhile she'd always wanted to know about her biological family, who they were, where they were from, and why they'd given her up. But Italy?

Maybe far away or maybe real nearby.

'You're *Zooming* instead of going to Florence?' Courtney threw up her arms. 'Jules, you *have* to go! They have so much art! You'd love it, and you're rich! You can go shop till you drop!'

'I don't need anything.' Julia flashed on the last time she'd gone shopping, with Mike at Crate & Barrel, when they'd bought an end table. *Another end table?* he'd asked. *Can this be the end of the end tables?*

'But what're you going to do with the money?'

'Get out of debt, pay off my cards and loans, save—'

'Buy something, buy a Porsche! Don't you want a Porsche?'

'No, I have a car. Do you want a Porsche? I'll get you one.'

'Aw.' Courtney smiled, waving her off. 'I'm not taking your money.'

'There's plenty,' Julia said, meaning it. 'I'll pay off your student loans, too.'

'I'm talking about *you*, honey. Buy something! Don't you want anything?'

I want Mike back, Julia thought but didn't say. 'You know, my horoscope predicted this, too.'

'You mean your *horror*scope?'

'Joke all you want. I did a deep dive, and it even said I was expecting a windfall this month. The whole thing was all there. Plus Mercury's in retrograde in Aries, so don't make any contracts.'

'I make contracts every day.'

'Well, read the fine print.'

'Nobody reads the fine print.'

'Court, be that way, but we just had the solar eclipse, did you see it? It's a time of new beginnings, new directions, new starts. My horoscope predicted my luck would change.'

'What about the billion other times it didn't predict anything? Since when do you need a horoscope to learn about yourself, Jules? You know yourself. You're not one of those people.'

Maybe I am, now.

'What's with the astrology, really?'

'I just like it,' Julia answered, hoping it would suffice. Astrology gave her a sneak peek at fate, a fighting chance against the stars, and until this inheritance, her luck hadn't exactly been stellar.

'Whatever. Go to Tuscany. Go see your *villa*. Count your *euros*.'

'What if the police get a lead on Mike?'

'Tell them you're going on vacation. They have your cell and email.'

'What if they get a suspect and I have to identify him?'

Courtney waved her off. 'You can fly back. They'll schedule around you.'

'What if they won't? I have to remind them of the facts whenever I call. They act like he's a cold case. If I don't bug them, they'll forget about him. They're never going to catch the guy, are they?' Julia blurted out, realizing she'd never said it aloud. But she thought it every day.

'Yes, they will.' Courtney looked pained. 'We have to have hope.'

Julia reached for her wine, but the glass was empty. She'd been drinking too much lately, she knew that, too.

Courtney's bright eyes lit up. 'Hey, I just figured out why you *have* to go to Tuscany. You inherited everything in Rossi's house, right? Her personal belongings?'

'I assume so.'

'So, anything she touched will have her DNA. Her clothes, her shoes, her towels, even her furniture. You should collect her DNA and get it sent to a lab. Then *you* should take a DNA test.'

Whoa. Julia felt the realization dawn on her. 'Then I'd know if we're related.'

'Right, it's proof. You need to oversee the collection of her DNA and you need to get yourself tested.' Courtney leaned over, newly urgent. 'Not only that, imagine what you can find out about her, going through her stuff. Computers, files, bills. You can't do *that* over Zoom.'

Julia swallowed hard.

'So, are you going?' Courtney asked, triumphant.

7

Can I have some wine, please?' Julia asked the male flight attendant, who nodded and left. She began to relax now that she was in the cool, quiet cabin. She'd never flown first class before, and it was predictably plush. Passengers around her stowed shiny Rimowa carry-ons and slipped into Bose headphones. She was ensconced in her own walled pod, like a bougie cocoon.

Julia exhaled, counting to four. She'd white-knuckled through the Philly airport, sweating under her blazer. There'd been people everywhere, and the noise and commotion made her nervous, which she hadn't expected in the daytime. She'd thought about going home, but she'd box breathed through security, using up all the oxygen in Terminal A.

Julia took a mental inventory to make sure she hadn't forgotten anything. She'd called the prosecutor and detective to give them her contact information. They had no news on Mike's case and promised to get back to her, which they always said and never did. She'd notified her clients she was taking a week's vacation, so nothing was hanging over her head.

Julia picked up her phone, opened the StrongSign app, and checked her horoscope again.

Practice acceptance today. Remind yourself to stay flexible. Be honest and generous with yourself. Know that if you commit to a course, the cosmos will conspire to help you.

The flight attendant arrived with a mini-bottle of Brunello, a glass, and a napkin. 'OMG, are you on StrongSign, too?'

'Yes.' Julia couldn't remember the last time she had a conversation with a stranger.

'I'm *obsessed*.' His eyes lit up. 'I'm a Cap, Aquarius Moon, Rising Virgo. I'm on StrongSign, Co-Star, and Kyle Taylor Astral. Do you want to know which site is best? I have thoughts.'

'Okay, which?' Julia smiled, sensing a kindred spirit.

'Listen and learn,' he began.

It was a sunny morning in Milan, and a gleaming black Mercedes S550 picked Julia up at the airport. A uniformed driver ushered her into the back seat, pointing out water bottles and organic snacks on the center console. She exhaled, appreciating the calm after the airport's hustle-bustle. She'd gone from one bougie cocoon to another, realizing that money separated you from everybody else. Maybe all rich people were agoraphobic.

She looked out the window, trying to get her bearings as they whizzed along. Milan had glass skyscrapers, mirrored buildings, and blocky apartment complexes in a skyline that struck her as unique, even quirky. The highway was as busy as Philly, but the cars were smaller.

They approached the center of Milan, and there were people everywhere. The Mercedes navigated down the narrow Via Monte Napoleone, passing ritzy Brunello Cucinelli, Loro Piana, Bottega Veneta, and Valentino boutiques. Ferraris, Lamborghinis, and Maseratis lined the street.

The Mercedes turned the corner onto Via Gesù, passed a crowd waiting to get into Goyard, then pulled up in front of the Four Seasons Hotel.

Best. Bougie cocoon. Ever.

Julia reached her room, relieved the moment the door sealed her inside. Her clothes were damp again, and her mouth was permanently dry. Maybe she needed remedial coping strategies. She had a meeting with the lawyer and the family investigator at four o'clock today.

She slid out of her blazer and hung it on the doorknob, looking around the beautiful suite, with two rooms overlooking a courtyard of sculpted hedges and flowering vines. The living room had a flat-screen TV, a couch in a beige linen, and matching side chairs. A walnut coffee table displayed Italian magazines, a tray of designer chocolates, and a note hoping that everything was to her liking. It was.

She went into the bedroom, which had two more windows and eggshell-white walls lined with etchings of wildflowers. The king-size bed had a taupe upholstered headboard, a shiny golden coverlet, and an array of shams and pillows. She crossed to the bed, flopped down, and slid her phone from her pocket. The screen showed a notification of her horoscope from StrongSign. She'd forgotten to check it, between the change of time zone and her anxiety at the airport. She clicked:

It's not easy to unwind when you hold on so tight.
Practice letting go and learn to trust yourself and others.
The cosmos will continue to support you in surprising
ways.

Julia tried to absorb the message and resolved to let go. She exhaled, put her phone down, and shifted onto the pillow mountain. She needed a nap before her meeting. She moved one sham aside, then another, and underneath was a neck roll.

Neck rolls are better for you, Mike used to say. *It's basic anatomy.*

Julia hugged the neck roll and closed her eyes but didn't sleep. She was wondering about the surprising ways of the cosmos.

8

Julia was shown to Massimiliano Lombardi's office, and the lawyer turned out to be in his sixties, with smooth gray hair slicked back from a lean, lined face. He had milky-brown eyes behind rimless glasses and a gray mustache that coordinated with a well-tailored gray suit and patterned tie. He was trim and compact.

'Please, sit down.' Lombardi gestured to a black leather swivel chair opposite a glass desk. His manner was businesslike, if less than warm.

'Thank you.' Julia took a seat, deploying her second coping mechanism: *Ground yourself in your surroundings.* The office was large, square, and modern. Lawbooks and black binders lined glass shelves, and a floor-to-ceiling window overlooked the Milan cityscape. The only thing missing was the family investigator.

Julia asked, 'Is the investigator coming?'

'I'm sorry, no.' Lombardi sat down behind his desk. 'Unfortunately, he has Covid. But I have already contacted another investigator I know, in Florence. His name is Gustavo Caputo, and he will be more familiar with Tuscany. I made an appointment for you on Wednesday. It was his first available. I'll email you his contact information.'

'Thank you.' Julia masked her disappointment. She was dying to know who Rossi was and why the woman would leave her such a large inheritance. 'Before we get started, can I ask you about Emilia Rossi? I researched her online, but I didn't find anything, not even social media.'

Lombardi blinked. 'Of course, ask me any questions you have.'

'Do you have any idea how she's related to me, if at all?'

'No.'

'Did she say why she was leaving me so much money?'

'No.'

'What about how she knew me?'

'No.'

'Did you ask her?'

'No, and I don't typically.' Lombardi paused. 'In my practice, it is not uncommon for certain *surprises*, shall we say, to arise when beneficiaries are named. Children and lovers, relationships previously unknown, come to light. All of the secrets come out. For that reason, I make it a point not to interrogate my clients about the particulars. To do so would be to burden their disclosures to me, and I want them to have their final wishes fulfilled in every respect.'

Okay. 'How old was Rossi when she passed?'

'Seventy-seven. She died of breast cancer. I will email you the mortuary certificate when I obtain it.'

Seventy-seven. Julia realized Rossi would be about the age of her biological grandmother. 'Is Rossi her married name?'

'No, it is her name. In Italy, women keep their last names when they marry. Children take the father's last name.'

Oh. 'Was Rossi married?'

'No.'

'Divorced?'

'No, she never married.'

Julia blinked. 'But she had children?'

'No, none.'

Julia tried to understand how Rossi could be her biological grandmother, then. 'She must have.'

'None.'

'How do you know she didn't have any children?'

'She told me.' Lombardi hesitated. 'However, I do not verify information supplied me by clients.'

Oh. 'So you don't know if it's true, but it's what she told you.'

'Precisely.'

'Did you meet Rossi?'

'No. I offered, but she declined. This is not atypical, as most of my clients are older or infirm. She contacted me via phone, and I drafted the documents and sent them to her.'

'No email?'

'No.'

'Was she referred to you by another client or a lawyer?'

'No, not that I know of. She called the office, as I remember.'

'Do you know why she didn't tell me about the inheritance, when she had you draft the will?'

'No.' Lombardi shrugged his padded shoulders. 'Perhaps she tried to reach you, but couldn't, as with me.'

'No, I checked.' Julia had searched her email and spam folder. 'She had my name and address, right? Isn't that how you got it?'

'Yes, she gave me your contact information. I don't know how she got it.'

'Maybe she found it online?' Julia's name and address were in the online White Pages. Her email was on her website under Contact Me. 'But how did she even know who I was?'

'I don't know.'

'Who notified you of her death?'

'The hospital. She had already made the necessary arrangements.'

'Do you know who was at her funeral?'

'No.'

'Were you there?' Julia asked, double-checking.

'No, I rarely attend the funerals of my clients.'

'Do you know where her funeral was held?'

'In Croce, I assume. It's the town nearest the villa.' Lombardi pursed his lips. 'You may explore the family connection with Mr Caputo, when you meet. I administer only the legalities of the estate.'

Julia sensed he was over it. 'One last question. Does my inheritance include the contents of the villa?'

'Certainly.'

'Great.' Julia was thinking about Rossi's DNA. She'd researched online and learned that DNA could be found on almost every conceivable surface for years, if it wasn't contaminated.

'Now, I should mention there is a caretaker couple on the property, Anna Mattia Vesta and Piero Fano. They are the only other beneficiaries under the will.' Lombardi's spectacled gaze fell on the papers on his desk. 'They receive a bequest of ten thousand euros and they are paid through the month. They intend to retire after that and move south to be near their grandchildren.'

'Do they live in the villa, too?'

'No, in a carriage house on the property.' Lombardi raised an index finger. 'One piece of legal advice. I urge you to obtain an Italian will and I would be happy to draft one for you. You are inheriting a significant estate and you have no immediate family to inherit automatically. Here, if you die without a will, your estate would enter probate. It would lose value to the authorities, and probate would be delayed for a long time.'

'Okay, but I don't know who I would leave the money to. My best friend, I guess?'

'You should give it some thought. Likewise, consider whether you want to sell the property. I will follow up with the realtor in Chianti. I know the best one.'

'Thanks.'

'Now, perhaps I can take you through the documents I mentioned at the outset?'

'Yes, of course,' Julia answered, and Lombardi returned to his packet, which turned out to be printed versions of Rossi's will and various other documents. She signed where he asked her to, then he packed up the papers and slid a set of brass keys across the desk.

'Here are your keys.'

'Wow.' Julia picked them up, turning them in her hand. She realized she might be holding the keys to her biological family, literally.

'One final matter. I should mention that I spoke with Emilia Rossi on the phone, on one occasion. She told me she was related to Caterina Sforza, a daughter of Galeazzo Sforza and Lucrezia Landriani.'

'Great!' Julia's heart leaped. She didn't know why he hadn't said so before. 'Who are they? Can I meet them?'

'No, they're long gone.' Lombardi smiled tightly. 'They were very important historical figures who lived during the Renaissance.'

'Wait, what?'

'Galeazzo Maria Sforza was the Duke of Milan, the most powerful nobleman in northern Italy. He had many lovers, and the best-known was Lucrezia Landriani. She bore him several children, among them a daughter named Caterina, who would become Countess Caterina Sforza of Forlì and Imola.' Lombardi's tone turned professorial. 'The Duke treated his illegitimate children the same as his children born within marriage. Caterina grew into a remarkable noblewoman, legendary in the history of Italian royalty.'

Julia's head was spinning. It sounded like the History Channel. 'Are you saying that Rossi was related to *royalty*?'

'No.' Lombardi held up a cautionary finger. 'I'm saying she *claimed* to be related to royalty. I do not know if the claim was true. I have many aging clients who develop dementia and harbor common delusions, some as regards their past. Often they suspect that children or the help are stealing from them.'

Julia tried to understand the implications. 'Could she still make a will? She was of sound mind, wasn't she?'

'Yes, but she did have a peculiar, strongly held belief that she was related to Caterina Sforza.' Lombardi lifted a graying eyebrow. 'In fairness to her, it *is* a matter of historical fact that Caterina Sforza bore illegitimate children, and it is possible they went unrecorded by history. One such child could have been the beginning of a line that gave rise to Emilia Rossi.' Lombardi met Julia's eye. 'If so, then you could be related to the bravest Italian noblewoman who ever lived.'

'*Me?*' Julia laughed. She wasn't even brave enough to leave her apartment. 'Why didn't you tell me this before?'

'I like to be respectful of my clients. Yet I also felt you should know.'

Julia read between the lines. 'Do you think Rossi was… crazy?'

'I'm a lawyer, not a psychiatrist.' Lombardi rose, tacitly ending the meeting. 'You may want to educate yourself about Caterina Sforza. There is no better place to do so than Milan. You should visit the Castello Sforzesco where Caterina grew up, only a few blocks away. You should also visit the Cathedral of Milan, built by the Duke, among others.'

Julia couldn't imagine sightseeing in this crowded, bustling city. She wondered if she could drive past the castle and the cathedral in her Mercedes cocoon. She was still trying to metabolize the possibility that her biological family could be Italian royalty.

Either that, or insane.

9

Julia stood in front of the Sforza family castle, Castello Sforzesco, a gargantuan walled fortress spanning ten city blocks, with red brick walls that soared into the late afternoon sky. Huge turrets with conical roofs anchored its corners, and a covered battlement ran the endless length of its walls. It was inconceivable to Julia that she could be related to such world-class wealth and power.

Meanwhile she began to feel more and more nervous in the crowd, which she'd underestimated. Tourists teemed around the castle's arched entrances and exits, filling its open spaces. Noise, motion, sight, and sound surrounded her. People of all ages and races talked and shouted, drinking, smoking, and jostling each other. Vendors hawked souvenirs, waving Pinocchio marionettes and fake gold crowns.

Julia broke into a sweat. She had to get back to the car, which waited for her at a nearby traffic circle. She left the castle grounds and white-knuckled through the crowd heading to the rendezvous point. She looked ahead but didn't see the Mercedes. It had been parked in a line of other hired cars, and all were gone, evidently shooed away by the traffic cop. She didn't know what to do.

Her heart thundered. It was beginning to get dark. The crowd behind her pressed her forward, almost into the street. Traffic lurched around the rotary. Teenage boys crossed against the light, dodging cars and laughing. A bus driver leaned on his horn, startling her.

Julia took off. The hotel was twenty minutes away. She hurried down Via Dante, a main drag for pedestrians, lined with bustling shops, restaurants, and cafés, and kiosks vending kebabs, pizza, and gelato.

Panic tightened her chest. The moving throng was thick with noise, language, laughter, cigarette smoke, vapes, and weed. She picked up the pace. Evening was coming on, and the sky was deepening to periwinkle. Stars shone through a transparent film of darkness.

Julia hurried ahead. Fear twisted her gut. She willed herself to keep it together. The street curved, and ahead was the Cathedral of Milan, its illuminated facade of white marble bright as bones against the blackening sky. Its ornate facade came to a majestic point, its spiky Gothic towers stabbing the night.

She reached the massive piazza in front of the cathedral, lined with lighted shops and restaurants. People surrounded her, talking, laughing, and partying. She wedged her way through.

'*Mi scusi!*' a man shouted, bumping into her.

Suddenly Julia lost her sense of direction. She didn't know which way the hotel was. She was too short to see above the heads. She turned right, then left, whirling around. Everywhere around her were shadows silhouetted against the cathedral. She looked up to see its marble gargoyles glaring down at her.

'Move!' Julia barreled ahead, broke into a jog, then started running. She elbowed people out of the way, feeling like she was running for her life. Some got angry. Others pushed back.

Julia kept running.

From what, she didn't know.

10

The next morning, Julia sat in the back seat of the Mercedes, gliding through Tuscany. She was relieved to have left Milan, shaken by what happened at the castle. She'd barely slept, jet-lagged and jangly nerved. When dawn broke, she read her horoscope, taking some comfort.

Go with the proverbial flow. Don't try and control so much. The universe has agency. Let go, and go. Be of open heart and mind.

They reached Chianti province, and Julia took it in through the window, charmed by the landscape. Sunshine gilded hilly vineyards that rolled on and on, their grapes growing in neat rows against a verdant backdrop of umbrella pines and cypresses. There were magnificent stucco villas with red tile roofs and picturesque farmhouses with brownstone facades and horses grazing in small barnyards.

Julia glanced at the navigation map on the driver's console and realized they were getting close to the villa. 'Are we almost there?' she asked the driver, who had some English.

'Yes.' The driver frowned at the rearview mirror. 'But the Alfa. He follows.'

'What's an Alfa?' Julia turned around to see a dark blue sedan behind them. An emblem on its front grille read Alfa Romeo. 'Are you sure he's following us?'

'Yes. Since Croce.'

Julia felt taken aback. 'Why don't you pull over and let him pass?'

'We are at the villa, Signora.' The driver steered left into a driveway, and gravel crunched under their tires. 'Yet he follows.'

Julia glanced back. The sedan was still behind them. 'That's odd.'

The driver didn't reply, but Julia looked around, dismayed at the condition of the grounds. Broken asphalt and potholes rutted the driveway, and the Mercedes slowed to avoid them. Cypress trees, bushes, and underbrush grew together in an unruly mess that lined the driveway. They reached the end, took a right turn, and stopped in a pebbled area in front of the villa.

Oh no. Julia got out of the car, her heart sinking. The villa was an utter ruin, overrun with ivy and sucker vines. It was shaped like a long rectangle, but its crumbling stone facade peeked from the overgrowth in patches and chunks of its mortar had fallen out. Vines grew even over a window, and most of the faded green shutters were gone. A loose verdigris-covered copper gutter hung at a dangerous angle, and the roof had so many missing tiles it looked like a dental emergency. The only sign the place wasn't abandoned were two open windows on the second floor, from which muslin curtains billowed.

Julia deflated, having expected a picture-postcard Tuscan villa, given Rossi's wealth. She'd been looking forward to being in the country after Milan. Now she didn't know if she wanted to stay here a single night.

Just then the front door opened, and an older woman emerged with a smile and crossed to the car. She was short, maybe in her late seventies, with a sweet face. Her eyes were dark, close together and deep-set, and her nose curved above a mouth bracketed by lines. Her white hair, in a tight, knobby bun, looked good with her small pearl earrings. She had on a flowered housedress and black shoes.

Julia smiled, extending a hand. 'Hello, I'm Julia Pritzker.'

'*Piacere*, I am Anna Mattia Vesta.' Anna Mattia shook Julia's hand with a surprisingly strong grip. 'I am 'appy to meet you, Signora Pritzker.'

'I'm happy to meet you too. Please, call me Julia.'

'You are *Signora* Pritzker.' Anna Mattia nodded deferentially. 'Signore Lombardi tell us you come viz. We work for Signora Rossi thirteen year. I take care the villa. My 'usband Piero, too.'

'I'm sorry for your loss.' Julia felt strange saying it to someone else, instead of it being said to her.

'*Grazie.*' Anna Mattia straightened, and the Alfa driver stepped over at a break in the conversation.

'Excuse me, I'm Franco Patelli,' he said, his accent vaguely British. His smile was friendly, and he extended a hand to Julia, then Anna Mattia, and they introduced themselves. He looked like he was in his forties, with round dark eyes and brown hair in an expensively layered haircut. His suit was dark and stylish, and he wore a sophisticated striped shirt with no tie. 'Ms Pritzker, Signore Lombardi in Milan contacted me on your behalf about the villa. He arranged an appointment for you tomorrow at ten, at my office in Croce.'

'Thank you.' Julia remembered Lombardi mentioning a realtor. 'I'm surprised you followed me, though.'

'My apologies.' Franco smiled, his regret plain. 'Signore Lombardi told me when you were expected, and there's only one road in, so I kept my eye out. Real estate moves quickly here, and one has to strike while the iron is hot. I hope you will sign with me. Here's my card.' Franco slipped a hand inside his breast pocket, withdrew a monogrammed leather case, and handed her his card, which read, franco patelli, exclusive tuscan properties.

'Thank you.'

'I've sold properties all over Chianti for foreign owners. I have the most contacts, and there's no one who can get you more for this property. In fact, I can get you an excellent deal in two weeks.'

'You can?' Julia would have laughed, given the villa's dilapidation, but she didn't want to offend Anna Mattia.

'I'm very aware that this property will require a special buyer.' Franco met her eye, and Julia sensed he was choosing his words carefully. 'We'll need a buyer who will want to invest, and I know how to find them. I think Signora Rossi would be proud to have me represent her property.'

Anna Mattia interjected, frowning. 'You do not know Signora Rossi.'

Franco nodded pleasantly. 'You're right, but I know *of* her. I live in Croce, so I know she lived here forever.'

'Fifty-one year,' Anna Mattia interjected again.

'I stand corrected. Fifty-one years, thank you.' Franco faced Julia.

'I'll let you settle in now. You must be exhausted. Thank you for your time, and I'll see you tomorrow. Goodbye.'

'Goodbye, thanks.' Julia turned to Anna Mattia. 'So, should we see the villa?'

Anna Mattia nodded happily.

Julia braced herself.

It was the only time she didn't want to go Inside.

11

Julia followed Anna Mattia into the entrance hall, which was as disappointing as she'd expected. Its walls were a grimy white plaster in need of repainting, and cracks ran up and down its length. Its paint peeled in shreds, and patches revealed the gritty plaster underneath. The floor was of large red tiles, but many were broken and more than one was missing. An old brass umbrella stand stood in one corner, empty.

Julia despaired until she looked up. Remarkably, the domed ceiling in the entrance hall was frescoed with the classical astrological map of the Zodiac, a full-circle divided into twelve thirty-degree sections, each with its own sign based on a constellation and a glyph, rimming the outermost ring. Gold stars spangled a lapis lazuli heaven, and a gilded sun emanated rays opposite an alabaster moon.

Julia couldn't believe what she was seeing, given her astrology obsession. 'Anna Mattia, this fresco is beautiful. Is it original?'

'Don' know.'

'How old is the villa?'

''Undreds years?'

'And Rossi lived here for fifty-one?'

'Yes.'

Julia guessed that Rossi commissioned the fresco. It didn't look older than fifty years, and frescoes were painted into wet plaster rather than onto its dry surface, so they were embedded in the wall. 'Do you know who owned the villa before her? Did she ever say?'

'No.'

Julia made a mental note. She could get a title search done, which might tell her more about Rossi. 'Did she like astrology?'

Anna Mattia shrugged.

'When was her birthday?' Julia was already playing guess-the-sign.

'Sorry, don' know.'

Julia didn't understand. 'You don't know her birthday?'

'No, she don' like. She never say. She don' like people know her.'

'Even you?'

Anna Mattia shook her neat head, her lips pursed. 'She tell nobody not'ing.'

'How about her friends?'

'She 'ave no.'

What? 'No friends? How about people who visited her?'

'No.'

'Did she go out to visit people?'

'No, she live alone, like… ,' Anna Mattia paused, cocking her head as she searched for the word. 'Don' know in English, 'ow you say, she is… eremita.'

'A hermit?'

Anna Mattia nodded.

Julia swallowed hard, a hermit herself. She had more questions, but Anna Mattia was already motioning her into a large rectangular living room, also in disrepair. Jagged cracks ran down the walls here, too, and they bowed out in places. More grayish-white paint was peeled in patches, showing plaster. The floor was also red tile, cracked. The only saving grace was another ceiling fresco, of a whimsical Tuscan landscape. Horses and sheep danced across a bucolic pasture with oversize sunflowers, and peasants in straw hats peeked from vineyards dripping with dark grapes.

Anna Mattia waved with a flourish. 'All furnish antique from Florence. Signora love antique.'

Julia eyed the furniture, which did look antique, so it had an excuse for being old and vaguely macabre. There was a long couch of coral velvet and several mismatched chairs around a heavy wood coffee table. Ancient brass fixtures hung on heavy chains, and there were old spindly ceramic lamps on the end tables. A large stone fireplace had beautiful tan, brown, and caramel-hued stone. There were no photos, books, or other personal effects, but they could have been in storage.

Anna Mattia smiled. 'Signora love 'er villa. You like?'

Julia didn't want to offend Anna Mattia, but didn't know what to say. 'Yes, but I think it might need some fixing, right?'

'To me, yes.' Anna Mattia pointed to her chest. 'But Signora say no change, no fix. Piero want to cut vine, fix roof. Signora say no.'

'Why?' Julia asked, mystified.

'Don' know. She fix for Wi-Fi but no TV. Only comput'.' Anna Mattia gestured vaguely around the living room. 'Signora like very clean 'er villa. I make clean, for 'er.'

'I see.' Julia noticed that the tile floor glistened, the windows sparkled, and the air smelled lemon-scented. Its cleanliness was the only thing making the villa habitable, like an immaculate dump.

'Come.' Anna Mattia led, and Julia followed her into a large dining room with a heavy wood table and high-backed chairs in the same dark curved wood. There was a smaller fireplace with another stone surround, and Julia ran a finger over its rough surface.

'What kind of stone is this?'

'Alberese. Only in Tuscany.' Anna Mattia spread her arms. '*Benvenuto a casa*, welcome 'ome. Sorry, my English not so good. Signora teach.' She turned to an older man who entered with Julia's suitcase and set it down. 'This my Piero.' Anna Mattia said something in Italian that must have reminded him to smile because he did so, his dark eyes flashing from deep crow's-feet. He was so tan that his wispy white hair stood out on his dark scalp. He had a short, burly build in a baggy white shirt and long green pants, grass-stained at the knees.

'*Piacere*.' Piero extended a hand to Julia, and she liked the meaty roughness of his palm.

Anna Mattia rolled her eyes. 'Piero, speak English.'

'It's okay,' Julia interjected, smiling. 'I'm happy to learn Italian.'

Anna Mattia motioned to her. 'Come.'

Julia followed Anna Mattia into a large kitchen. It had a deep white sink of real porcelain above a window with unvarnished sills that were rotting and water-damaged. A long farm table in the center matched cabinets of unvarnished oak. The walls were dingy, the floor tiles cracked. The appliances were outdated, but clean. There was no dishwasher or microwave.

'See, bruschetta, prosciutto. Fresh. *Buon appetito*.' Anna Mattia lifted the domed ceramic lid off a plate on the table, revealing wedges of thick yellow cheese and goat cheese, furls of prosciutto, and bruschetta of tomatoes and purplish cabbage on thick pieces of crusty bread. Delicious aromas of fresh tomato, sharp cheese, and spicy meat filled the air.

'Wow, thank you!' Julia took a bite of bruschetta, loving the crunch of the bread, the tartness of the tomatoes, and the salty sweetness of the balsamic. 'This is delicious!'

'*Grazie*.' Anna Mattia crossed to a cabinet and pulled out a large glass and a bottle of Chianti Classico Riserva. She unpeeled the metal top, grabbed a corkscrew, and opened it with the skill of a sommelier. 'Chianti from local grape. Best Chianti *in* Chianti.' Anna Mattia rested a hand on the bottle, with pride. 'This Super Tuscan.'

'What's that?'

'Better Chianti.'

Julia wanted to piece together the villa history. 'So you and Piero came thirteen years ago. Was this a vineyard when you came?'

'No.'

'Did Signora have help before you?'

'Don' know. She get sick, *tumore al seno*.' Anna Mattia gestured to her breast. 'I 'elp 'er, I take care. Piero, 'e 'elp, too, 'e carry 'er.'

Aw. 'How long was she sick for?'

'Maybe five year. We stay one month more. Signora give us some money, and we go. We 'ave son in Chieti and granchildr', two boys.' Anna Mattia brightened, handing Julia a glass with a generous pour. '*Cin-cin*.'

'*Cin-cin*.' Julia raised her glass. 'To Signora Rossi.'

'*Sì*, Signora Rossi.' Anna Mattia smiled with approval, and Julia sipped the wine, which tasted amazing. She'd never been a Chianti fan, but this wine had refinement, with body, brightness, fruit, salt, sugar, and even a little earthy taste.

'Okay?' Anna Mattia asked, and her Italian accent made it sound adorable, like *O-kayee?*

'Great!' Julia answered, with a smile. She was trying to rally, but she'd need a lot of Super Tuscan to stay here.

*

Later, Julia followed Anna Mattia to the second floor, as run-down as the first floor. The walls were cracked and peeling, and most of the windowsills were rotted. There was a center hall and two bedrooms on the south side of the house, each containing a double bed with a carved headboard, a night table, and a dresser. Each bedroom had a window, and they were open, with muslin curtains billowing out in the front of the villa. The bedrooms had more ceiling frescoes, one a jungle scene with smiling tigers and toothy lions, and the other the seasons of a Tuscan vineyard, from planting to an autumnal harvest. Julia wondered how Rossi could commission such beauty, but allow such ruin.

Anna Mattia motioned her out. 'Now Signora's bedroom.'

Julia followed her to the back of the villa and a bedroom that was large and rectangular, with four windows. The walls were in terrible shape, the windowsills needed replacing, and a baseboard was missing. There was a queen-size bed covered in forest-green brocade, and its carved headboard extended up the wall, flanked by large night tables with turned legs. Arranged around the room were bureaus, armoires of dark wood, and a reclining couch upholstered with shiny brocade.

Once again, it was the ceiling fresco that caught Julia's eye, but this one was devoted to a single subject. SFORZA, she read in black Gothic script, and underneath was a massive green tree in full leaf. She realized it was the Sforza family tree, and superimposed over its leafy limbs were portraits of Duke Galeazzo Maria Sforza opposite his lover Lucrezia Landriani. Arranged beneath them in the limbs were smaller portraits of children; Carlo, Alessandro, and Chiara. In the middle, the largest portrait of all, with a body shown in full length, was Duchess Caterina Sforza.

Julia eyed the portrait up and down. Caterina was beautiful, with wide-set blue eyes, a longish nose, a pretty mouth with a somewhat receding chin. Her light brown hair was pulled back, and the blue hood of a cape draped around her head. She wore a pearl choker with a crucifix and a dark velvet gown. Underneath her, it read, DUCHESS CATERINA SFORZA next to the Sforza coat of arms, which was divided into four quadrants; two of black dragons on a gold background, and two of a coiled blue viper devouring a man on a white background.

Julia turned to Anna Mattia. 'The lawyer told me Signora Rossi thought she was related to Caterina Sforza. Did she ever tell you how?'

'No.'

'Do you know why she thought that?'

'Sorry, no.'

'Was it true? Did you believe her?'

Anna Mattia shrugged. 'Is possible. The Sforza very rich, very famous Milanese family.'

'Is that where she got her money from?'

'Yes, she say.' Anna Mattia pointed up at the portrait. 'Signora *love* Caterina. She love 'er clothes, jewel, pearl. Signora love pearl like Caterina. She 'ave many necklace, earring.' Anna Mattia touched her own pearl-dot earrings. 'She give.'

'They're so pretty.'

'Signora know about Caterina. She read *everyt'ing*.'

Julia mulled it over, resolving to research Caterina on her own. She crossed to the window and took in the view, which was even more bizarre. The vineyard was overgrown, so rows of grapevines had become mounds of underbrush, vegetation. Trees struggled to grow here and there, and patchy streaks of wildflowers and weeds shaded the hillsides between dark and thorny thatches of vines that twisted, tangled, and spread everywhere. It looked as if Mother Nature had drawn lines and scribbled over and over them, until order turned to madness.

Oddly, a large white dog slept in front of a pile of rusted wire and a black tarp. 'Whose dog is that?'

'Signora's. Is Bianco, a Maremmano, Tuscan dog. Is eight year old.'

'That trash isn't his doghouse, is it?'

'No, is for geese. Vineyard 'ave geese to eat bugs.'

'So grapes grew here once?'

'Yes.' Anna Mattia gestured to Julia's engagement ring and wedding band. 'Your 'usband come soon?'

Julia swallowed, caught short. 'Um, no, my husband passed.'

Anna Mattia's hooded eyes flared. '*Dio*, I am sorry. 'E was sick?'

'No. He was… murdered.' Julia felt a sudden wave of grief, thinking of Mike, how he should be alive, how there were no leads in his case, and how there might never be.

'Okay?' Anna Mattia asked, but before Julia could say yes, Anna Mattia took her arm and led her to the reclining couch. 'Sit. Wait. *Aspete*.'

'I'm fine,' Julia told her, but Anna Mattia had already gone into a bathroom off the bedroom, then returned with a glass of water and handed it to her. 'Drink.'

'Thank you.' Julia took a sip and flashed on her mother, getting her a glass of ginger ale, in which she had endless faith, saying, *In Canada Dry we trust.*

Anna Mattia sat down and looked at Julia with a new tenderness. 'Is wrong, 'e die so young.'

'I think that every day. I wish he were here.'

'Dead and alive 'ere. 'E is 'ere, Signora 'ere, too. Everywhere.' Anna Mattia moved her gnarled little hands in the air. 'Together.'

Julia wondered if the dead could be among the living. Oddly, she felt like she *was* the dead among the living.

'Anima. Soul. All 'ere.' Anna Mattia gestured to her chest. 'My Sofia, I lose when she is nine years.'

Oh no. 'I am so sorry.'

'After church, we come 'ome, we eat. We 'ave bread, it catch 'er throat. She choke.' Anna Mattia's hooded eyes filmed. 'I can no save, Piero can no save.'

'I'm so sorry.' Julia imagined the awful scene. A frantic mother and father, trying to save their little girl. Then she flashed on Mike, bleeding to death in her arms, his gaze heavenward. She realized it was uniquely hellish to experience the unnatural death of someone you loved, not only horrifying, but literally against nature.

'My Sofia, she 'ere now. We talk.' Anna Mattia lifted a graying eyebrow. 'You talk your 'usband?'

'No,' Julia answered, nonplussed. 'I think about him, but I don't talk to him.'

'Why no?'

'It never occurred to me.' Julia never talked to her mother, either. Maybe she would start crying and never stop.

'Ask for sign. I ask, Sofia give. It 'elp me suffer.' Anna Mattia winced. 'No, my English is wrong. It 'elp me *not* suffer. 'Ow you say?'

'It eased your suffering?'

'*Sì, certo*.' Anna Mattia patted Julia's arm. 'Sofia, she love a pink flower. Gladiolus, wild lily. Some light, some dark. Sofia pick it always. Someday, I come to my kitchen and I see on the floor a petal from this flower. She give me and Piero. A sign of love.' Anna Mattia slid the water glass from Julia's hand and set it on a side table. 'You miss your 'usband? Ask for sign. Go, now.'

'Go where?' Julia asked, confused, but Anna Mattia rose and pulled her to her feet.

'Out.' Anna Mattia led her from the bedroom, and Julia followed her downstairs to the kitchen door, then realized something. Today's horoscope hadn't made sense until this very minute.

Let go, and go.

12

Julia looked around, taking in the scene from outside the kitchen door. The day had turned grim, and gray clouds blanketed the sky, weighing the air with humidity. A rickety wooden pergola sagged with trumpet vines over a rusty tile table with broken cane chairs. A jumble of weeds, grass, and mossy stones looked like it used to be a herb garden. Beyond that was the vineyard, such as it was, curving behind the villa at a sharply lower elevation.

She spotted a narrow path down the hill and started walking that way. The ground was uneven and embedded with fieldstone. The wind dropped off precipitously, and the air smelled damp and earthy, like something decomposing.

She reached the vineyard, thinking of Mike and scanning it with his eyes. He would have loved to have a vineyard, but this neglected mess would have broken his heart. Greenish-brown vines coiled in curlicues around the underbrush, throttling tiny white wildflowers trying to find the sun. Wooden stakes meant to guide the growth had long ago been toppled by the grappling vines and swallowed up by the tangled thicket. It struck her that unlike a ruined villa, untamed nature never rested.

Mike would clear this place with his bare hands.

The thought popped into Julia's head, and she didn't try to shoo it away.

I wish Mike were here.

I would give anything if Mike were alive.

I would give all the money in the world.

I miss my husband.

Julia let the thoughts come, one after the next, and found herself not only thinking about Mike but *feeling* him, experiencing loving him as if he were still alive. She could even pinpoint the moment she fell in love with him because it happened on her birthday. They'd been seeing each other but they hadn't gotten to the I-love-yous yet, and they woke up in bed that morning.

It's your birthday! Mike had said, kissing her.

I hate my birthday. Julia didn't have to explain. He knew why.

That's about to change! Mike had jumped out of bed in his plaid boxers, then ran out of the bedroom and back in a few minutes later, wearing two giant white cartoon hands and a Mickey Mouse hat with big ears. *We're going to Disney World!*

What? Julia had asked, astonished, and Mike had pulled her from bed with his cartoon hand.

Get dressed! I packed your bag! Courtney and Paul are downstairs! Our flight's at noon! Happy birthday, babe!

Julia's mouth had dropped open. She hadn't known what to say. All she knew was what she'd felt, which was a rush of warmth, gratitude, and for the first time, true love. *I love you*, she'd blurted out.

I love you, too, Mike had said, his smile full of happiness. It was the most thoughtful thing any man had ever done for her, and so much like him, a grand gesture, a spontaneous showing that he cared, listened, and believed he could make her happy, which itself was an act of self-belief and will. Mike *tried* all the time, in every way, and she tried, too, and they had been happy together until the moment she never wanted to remember, the night he was stabbed to death.

Julia could feel grief approaching closer and closer, like a tidal wave of darkness. But this time, something told her not to hold it off. Maybe letting it come was the way to get a sign from him.

'Mike,' Julia heard herself say, looking around.

'Mike?' Julia found herself sinking to her knees, surrounded by twisting, coiling vines so thick that they formed a wall, closing her in.

'Mike, are you there?' Julia whispered like a prayer, feeling foolish but not letting that stop her. 'Will you give me a sign?'

There was no response except the faintest of breezes. Did that count? Was that him? Was that his ghost? Or a shift in barometric pressure?

'Mike, I'm sorry I don't talk to you. I should have, all this time. I never even tried.' Julia heard herself, guilty and desperate. 'But can I have a sign? Please?'

No response except the shuddering of the leaves.

'Mike, please?'

Nothing.

Mike, I'm sorry I didn't save you.

I tried but there was so much blood.

Mike, please forgive me.

Mike, please don't leave me alone.

Mike, I love you and I always will.

Julia felt tears brimming in her eyes. She wiped them away, but they kept coming. Soon she began to cry full bore, lost in emotions pent-up for days. She'd been white-knuckling through airports, flights, and crowds. Maybe even through life.

Choking sobs emanated from deep within her chest, leaving her body so racked she vomited.

It wasn't the sign she was hoping for.

'Hi, Anna Mattia.' Julia entered the kitchen from the back door, keeping her face down because her eyes were puffy and her nose leaky. She crossed to the sink to wash up.

Anna Mattia stood aside, then put a comforting hand on her shoulder.

'I didn't get a sign.' Julia rinsed her face, then twisted off the water.

Anna Mattia handed her a dish towel.

'Thank you.' Julia dried her face then hung the dishcloth on its little rack. She straightened, recovering her composure because she'd remembered something after her crying jag. She needed to go through Rossi's belongings for her DNA. 'Anna Mattia, I didn't see Signora Rossi's things. Did you store them somewhere?'

'No. All gone.'

'I know, but where? Are they in storage?'

'No.' Anna Mattia frowned with disapproval. 'Signora burn.'

Julia figured it was the language barrier. 'I'm talking about her personal belongings like her clothes, books, or whatever. All her stuff.'

Anna Mattia shook her head, frowning. 'She make Piero burn.'

'What?' Julia didn't get it. 'I mean her things, all of her things.'

'She burn.'

'She didn't burn her clothes, did she?'

'Yes. She 'ave many.'

Julia blinked. 'Do you mean she burned everything she owned?'

'Yes, sorry.' Anna Mattia nodded gravely.

'*Everything?*' Julia repeated, shocked. She'd never get Rossi's DNA now.

'Yes.' Anna Mattia frowned, more deeply. 'I say, give the church. People need. I say, sell, make money. She say no. Piero say, she is Signora. We must do.' Anna Mattia looked frustrated, gesticulating. 'She don' want people touch her things, *'ave* her things.'

'What about her laptop? Did she burn that, too?'

'Yes.'

'But *how*? Do electronics even burn? There must have been so much stuff.'

'*So* much!' Anna Mattia threw up her little arms. '*Too* much! Piero make a big, big fire. I worry trees catch to the fire.'

Julia couldn't imagine it. 'Where did you do this?'

'Come.' Anna Mattia led the way, and they went out the back door. They took a right turn and went a direction that Julia hadn't explored yet. It was a hill, its ground uneven, and they descended on a trampled dirt path. Ahead was a stone carriage house in abject disrepair, as ivy-covered as the villa. A red Fiat Panda was parked in a bay on its open ground floor.

Anna Mattia pointed at the carriage house. 'We live.'

'Very nice,' Julia said, but they both knew otherwise.

Anna Mattia continued walking, and Julia could see beyond the carriage house to an open equipment shed with stone sides and a corrugated tin roof. An old Kubota backhoe, a John Deere mower, and other heavy machinery were parked inside. They reached the shed, passed it, then kept going around the back. A vast clearing came into view, an area flattened, blackened, and scorched.

Julia felt stricken. 'When did she do this?'

'When she is sick.'

'Did she have chemo, radiation?'

'No. She say no, is too late.' Anna Mattia looked over, her hooded eyes flinty. 'She say doctor try kill her.'

'She was afraid the doctors would kill her? That's crazy!' Julia hated the term but she didn't have a better one yet. 'Was she crazy, Anna Mattia?'

Anna Mattia pursed her lips.

'Please, tell me. She *seems* crazy. She won't see the doctors. She lives like a hermit. She has no friends. She lets her villa and her vineyard go to ruin. She doesn't fix anything or keep it up, even though she has the money. Why?'

Anna Mattia nodded, cringing. '*Paranoico.*'

'Paranoid?' Julia didn't want to think Rossi was paranoid, delusional, *or* crazy, if they were blood-related. Her bewildered gaze returned to the scorched circle. On impulse, she walked over, her footsteps crunching on charred debris. Ash darkened the toes of her espadrilles, and her footsteps stirred up a residual burned odor. Seared shards, chips, fragments, and pieces of fabric and wood lay everywhere in unrecognizable pieces.

Julia stood at the center of the blackened circle, and a wave of despair swept over her. Suddenly she noticed a tiny white speck among the black. She walked over, picked it up, and brushed off the ashes, amazed to see a pearl. One side was blackened from the smoke, but the other was still white. She held it in her open palm, and it was as perfectly round as a miniature moon, with its own dark side.

Julia walked back to Anna Mattia. 'Look at this. I think it came from a necklace.'

Anna Mattia peered at the pearl, clasping her hands together. 'Signora *love* pearl. She 'ave many necklace.'

Julia felt frustrated. 'But she burned her *jewelry*, too?'

'Yes.' Anna Mattia clucked, shaking her head.

'Why?' Julia didn't get it. She'd come here for *nothing*.

'Don' know.'

'Anna Mattia, I don't know why she left me the money and the villa, either.'

'*Che*? What?' Anna Mattia frowned, stepping back. 'You are family.'

'No, I'm not. Why, did she say she had family?'

'No, no.' Anna Mattia blinked. 'I *think* you are family from America. Piero think. We *presumiamo*.'

'You presumed? You assumed?'

'*Sì.*' Anna Mattia nodded, agitated. 'She give you money, villa—'

'Right, but I don't know her.'

'*É vero?*' Anna Mattia's hooded eyes widened in disbelief.

'I don't know her at all. Did she have any children?'

'No.'

Julia felt dumbfounded. 'How do you know? Did she tell you?'

'*Sì*, yes. No marry. No childr'. Never 'ave childr'.'

'What about any sisters or brothers?'

'Don' know. She 'ave *nobody*. We think you are family from America. Signora tell nobody *not'ing*.' Anna Mattia searched her face. 'Who are you?'

Julia thought it was a damn good question. 'I'm adopted. You know *adopted*?'

'*Sì*, yes. We 'ave.'

'So if Rossi had no children, I don't know how or even if I'm related to her, at all.'

'But she give you sign.'

'What sign?'

'*Perla.*' Anna Mattia gestured at Julia's fist, and Julia opened her hand. The pearl shone like a whitish-gray moon in her palm. Anna Mattia pointed at it with her knobby index finger. 'This, a *sign*.'

'Really?' Julia wondered, rolling the pearl from its light to its dark side. 'You think it's from her? Or my husband?'

Anna Mattia shrugged.

'Where's Rossi buried?' Julia asked, on impulse.

13

The old village cemetery lay nestled in the rolling Chianti countryside, small, still, shaped like one long rectangle with several additions at the end, surrounded by a peaked stone wall. Mounted on the wall were thin headstones of grayish marble streaked with black, their engraving eroded by weather and time. Names and dates like 1825, 1821, and even 1789 were barely visible.

Julia paused on the stone footpath at the cemetery's entrance, holding a yellow iris that Anna Mattia had given her for Rossi. Her chest tightened with grief and respect for the dead, her own beloved husband and all the beloved husbands, wives, mothers, fathers, friends, and children. She'd never realized death could be so fresh, so near, and so *present*. Once you lose someone unexpectedly, you learn the truth. Death wasn't necessarily far away, on the distant horizon or at the end of some actuarial table. Sometimes it was right in front of you, in your very next step. Waiting around the corner.

Julia felt a faint breeze and for some reason, found herself glancing over her shoulder. No one was there. Piero was waiting for her at the car, and they'd driven here in companionable silence. She felt less afraid of being outside than usual, maybe because there was no crowd. In fact, there wasn't another person in sight.

Graceful cypresses three or four stories tall surrounded the cemetery. Piero had told her that cypresses were always planted around cemeteries to ward off evil spirits. It struck her that the supernatural was a given here, as if Tuscany were a different world. She carried the pearl in her wallet like a talisman.

She walked down a center path of tan gravel, surprised by the difference between a Tuscan and an American cemetery. There were headstones here, too, but the full length of each grave was covered by a long marble slab or a walled bed of mounded ivy. Each grave was different; some held a vase of sunflowers or a statue of the Virgin Mary, and others a frosted glass candle or a glazed terracotta dish.

Each headstone bore a photograph of the deceased, and Julia slowed her step and took in the pictures. Some of the men and women wore hats with net veils, since the cemetery was that old. A few of them held pet cats or dogs. She realized that each of the people was looking at a camera held by someone they loved. The mourned was in the photo, but not the mourner. The mourner was left behind, like her.

A drizzle began to fall, and Julia turned and headed toward a stone building on the right side of the cemetery, which held crypts and cremains, Rossi's among them. It had a red tile roof and was open to the air on the one side, with three archways.

Julia passed through the third arch, and the walls inside were lined with floor-to-ceiling crypts. Each bore a small brass plaque with the name of the decedent, and his or her dates of birth and death, with a photograph mounted in a gold frame. The only light came from the bulbs shaped like flames, which emitted a dim amber glow from the crypts, next to built-in glass vases that held plastic flowers.

Whoa. Julia gasped, stunned. She found Rossi's crypt instantly by its black-and-white photo of the woman, riveted by the resemblance. She hadn't anticipated there would be a photograph of Rossi on the crypt, much less that it would look like her.

Julia scrutinized the photo, double-checking to make sure she wasn't imagining the similarity. She and Rossi both had blue eyes, smallish and wide-set, and there was a slight sameness in the nose, too; Rossi's was longer, but it was small and fine-boned like Julia's. Their mouths and jawlines were decidedly different, in that Rossi's was large. Unlike Julia's, Rossi's lips were thin, and in the photo they were pursed, not showing her teeth. But Rossi looked unwell, her expression drawn, her cheeks gaunt. Her hair was pulled back, evidently gray.

Julia realized she could've been looking at the only blood relative she had ever seen. The prospect made her heart pound. She used to wonder about her birth mother and father, wishing she knew what they looked like, what their names were, and why they'd given her up.

On impulse, Julia touched Rossi's photograph.

Zzzzzzt! An electrical charge shocked her. She jumped back, dropping her yellow iris.

The electric candlelight on Rossi's crypt and all the others flickered, off and on.

What? Julia blinked, shaken. She didn't know what was going on. She didn't know why she'd gotten shocked. She hadn't touched anything but the photograph.

The candles stopped flickering abruptly, then stayed on.

Julia looked around, trying to understand. Rain was drifting inside the building, covering the tile floor with a sheen of water. She put it together. The electrical candles must've shorted out somehow, and it must've shocked her.

Julia touched the photograph again. No shock this time. The candle stayed on, burning dimly.

Suddenly the strangest sensation came over her, a tingling, an almost imperceptible vibration was conducted from Rossi's photograph to her, as if on a metal wire. In that moment, Julia *sensed* they were connected, just like the night Mike died when she *knew* something bad was going to happen. She felt she was *of* Rossi, that they shared a twisted skein of DNA, tethering one to the other over time and space.

Julia lifted her fingertips. The tingling vanished, like an electrical circuit broken. Meanwhile the crypt was darkening, and so was the sky, casting the cemetery in a premature gloom. It had begun to rain.

Spooked, Julia got out her phone and took pictures of Rossi's crypt. She picked up the yellow iris and stuck it in the empty vase. The sky had blackened to a storm, as if heaven itself had fled.

She bolted from the crypt and raced back to the car.

14

Troubled, Julia headed to the kitchen, passing a dining room table with a ceramic plate with green, blue, and yellow swirls, laid next to green goblets and bottles of Chianti and Panna water. A matching bowl held thick slices of rustic bread, next to tall golden sunflowers in a glass vase.

'Hello.' Julia entered the kitchen, where Anna Mattia was grinding fresh pepper into a small tureen of hearty tomato soup that smelled pungently of basil, lemon, and cooked onion. 'Wow, what's for dinner?'

'*Acquacotta*, soup with tomat', bean, onion, litt' bit cabbage.' Anna Mattia smiled, setting down the pepper grinder. 'You find Signora?'

'Yes, I saw her photo, too.' Julia's thoughts had churned the whole way home. 'Do I look like her?'

Anna Mattia placed a domed lid on the tureen, scanning Julia's face anew. 'Yes, a litt'. This is why I say you are family.'

Julia felt validated, which only intensified the mystery. 'Did she have blue eyes?'

'Yes.'

'And what color hair before she went gray, do you know?'

'Like you.' Anna Mattia met her eye, significantly. 'I 'ave 'er pitch'.'

'Her *picture*?' Julia asked, surprised. 'You have it? Not burned?'

'No, I keep.'

Thank God. 'When did you take it?'

Anna Mattia's face fell into deep folds. 'She ask, when she know she die.'

Aw. 'Did you take the picture on her crypt?'

'Yes.' Anna Mattia straightened, smoothing down her housedress. 'Please wash 'ands, go sit. I serve.'

'That's okay, I can help.' Julia crossed to the sink.

'*I* do, thank you.' Anna Mattia picked up the tureen and headed into the dining room, and Julia decided to accept that Anna Mattia was more comfortable serving her, a good problem to have. She washed her hands, then left the kitchen.

'Are there any other pictures of her?'

'Yes, I 'ave. Piero get.' Anna Mattia poured water into one glass and Chianti into the other. 'Please, sit.'

'Thanks.' Julia sat, enjoying the vaguely maternal vibe while Anna Mattia lifted the tureen lid and ladled some soup into the bowl, beaming.

'*Perfetto.*'

Julia had to agree. 'It looks delicious. I'd love to learn to cook these dishes.'

'Okay, I teach.' Anna Mattia nodded. 'Now, you see my pitch'?'

'Yes, please.'

'*Buon appetito.*'

After dinner, Julia sat alone in the dining room. The tomato soup had been amazingly flavorful, with the perfect touch of garlic and onion, making a full meal with the fresh Tuscan bread. She'd drunk two glasses of Chianti, which she was coming to adore. Dessert was homemade almond cookies, buttery and light, then Anna Mattia had cleared the table, done the dishes, and gone back to her house.

Julia poured another glass of Chianti, sipped some, and eyed the three photographs in front of her, which she'd arranged from the earliest to the most recent. The first photo showed Rossi with her arm around Anna Mattia in an adorably girlfriendy pose. Both women had happy grins and carefree expressions, looking directly into the camera. Rossi was wearing a yellow cotton shift that showed shapely legs in T-strap sandals. She was a head taller than Anna Mattia, which made her about Julia's height. Her build was thinner, however, and lankier.

The second photo showed Rossi frowning as she stood in the vineyard. She shielded her eyes against the sun and was alone except for a big white Maremmano, not Bianco. Her face had lengthened, and a fixed frown deepened the draping around her mouth. She was thinner and looked sloppy in a stained white T-shirt and jeans.

The third photo was downright disturbing, a close-up in which Rossi was shooing the camera away, her hand blurred. Her hair was messy, and her eyes flashed with rage, an extreme reaction to having her picture taken. She had on a white dress that looked worn and stained. Her arms and legs were like sticks. Her feet were bare.

Julia scanned the photos like an age progression from the earliest to most recent, watching Rossi descend into madness. She took pictures of the photos, then enlarged the most recent one, zeroing in on Rossi's eyes. They glittered a sharp, piercing blue, clearly unhinged, and Julia wondered if she was looking at her own future.

She felt horrified, confused, and exhausted. She checked her phone, surprised it was only 8:15 p.m. She couldn't remember when she'd slept the whole night.

It was time for bed.

Julia hesitated at the threshold of Rossi's bedroom. It was dark inside, and she felt the wall for a light switch, but there weren't any. She made her way to the bedside table and turned on a lamp with an enameled base of spiky green leaves. It had a low-wattage bulb that left in shadow the corners of the large room. She looked around for another lamp, but found none.

The windows were open, and the bedroom was cold. Outside was the chirping of crickets and a weird screeching. She went to the window and looked out, but it was too dark to see anything. Clouds obscured the moon, and the vineyard was a black blur. There were no lights or even a demarcation where trees met sky. Bianco wasn't in sight. She felt as if she were looking into a bottomless black bowl.

The air was still damp from the storm, and she tried to close the window, but it was stuck. She tried another window, but that was stuck, too. The screeching stopped, then started again.

She closed the curtains, then went to the other windows and closed their curtains. She went to the window by the bed, which overlooked Anna Mattia and Piero's carriage house. It was dark, with no lights on inside.

Julia crossed to the door and looked for a way to lock it, but there was none, only a keyhole. Anna Mattia had told her Rossi didn't lock her interior doors, which she resolved to fix as soon as possible. Julia closed her door, then told herself she was being ridiculous. She was safe here.

She went to her suitcase on the reclining couch and rummaged for something to sleep in. She undressed quickly, slipped into an oversized Eagles T-shirt, and used the bathroom, which had white tile, a porcelain pedestal sink, and a large terracotta tub. She brushed her teeth and rinsed her face, then padded out.

She set her phone on the night table and was too tired to bother finding her charger. She pulled aside the coverlet and sat down, then turned out the lamp, plunging herself into darkness.

Signora is 'ere too. The dead are always with.

Julia found herself looking around, for what she didn't know. The bedroom was Rossi's for fifty years. The woman had died in this very bed. The pillows made a faint whiteness against the dark headboard. If Rossi's spirit would be anywhere, it was here. The screeching outside burst into sound, a weird animal noise.

Julia startled, jittery. She forced herself to ease back onto the bed, then lowered until her head hit the pillow. She started to pull up the coverlet but stopped. It was one thing to sleep on Rossi's bed, and another to sleep between her sheets. She replaced the coverlet and lay down on top.

Julia eyed the Sforza family fresco on the ceiling. She couldn't see any of the Sforza family except for Caterina, because the dim outline of her figure was life-size, lying opposite her.

A wave of fatigue swept over her. It had been an endless first day. She'd drunk too much Chianti. She'd cried in a vineyard. She'd found a pearl. She'd missed Mike so deeply, acutely, painfully. She had to sleep. She closed her eyes, beginning to doze.

A chill fluttered over her bare legs.

She looked up.

Two gargantuan, enraged eyes glared down at her from Caterina Sforza's face, their gigantic irises glinting electric blue. The tree was growing bigger, its branches reaching down to her. The dragons in the coat of arms breathed fire. The vipers opened their fanged maws to eat her alive.

'No!' Julia jumped out of the bed in horror. She bolted away from the fresco.

She flattened her back against the wall. Her heart pounded. She trembled uncontrollably. The fresco roared to life before her terrified eyes. Branches zoomed this way and that, growing in superspeed, their wooden limbs sharpening into pikes threatening to impale her.

No, no, no, no.

Julia tried to scream. No sound came out. She shrieked and shrieked for help. She couldn't utter a word. She fled to the corner of the room, quivering in fear, gasping for breath. Vipers snaked from the living fresco, hissing and hissing, more and more of them, growing heads after heads after heads like hydras, whipping them around, rolling black eyes, flicking long red tongues, and opening their mouths wider and wider, their jaws positively unhinged, showing the pink of their endless gullets and the ivory of their fangs snapping as they lunged toward her, their spikes only millimeters from her face, trying to devour her.

No, no, no, help me God.

Julia curled into a ball, reduced to a quivering child, crying and praying she wouldn't be swallowed whole, stabbed, burned alive by the black dragons breathing fire into a larger and larger conflagration, spewing fireballs of red orange and gold at her, superheating her, scorching her skin, incinerating her very flesh. She screamed in pain and agony but couldn't hear herself, and a white-hot sun glowing bigger and bigger and bigger seared her eyes, blinding her, and she covered her face with her blistering and blackened hands, her skin falling charred from her flesh, praying for the end to come, praying for death itself.

End this pain, end it, kill me now.

Julia cried uncontrollably, curled as tight as she could, tortured and dying, her body torn apart by the vipers and stabbed by the pikes and burned to an unrecognizable black crisp by the raging sun and finally her last breaths leaked from the scraps of char that used to be her lungs and the breath turned into air and then into ether and then into a blue light that vanished in the night.

*

Julia woke up in bed with a start. She wasn't curled in the corner. She wasn't burned or stabbed or bitten. She blinked, wondering if she was awake or asleep.

She looked around. The bedroom was beginning to lighten. The muslin curtains were pale yellow squares, as if it was dawn. Her eyes itched like she'd been crying. Her nose was congested. She didn't understand. Had she cried in her sleep? Was that even possible?

She held her hands up in front of her. She could see them in the dim room, then fingers intact, her skin covering her flesh, her bones underneath somewhere, her body animated again. She was alive.

She looked up at the fresco. The blue eyes were back in Caterina's face, her gaze rigid and lifeless. The Sforza tree was no longer moving. Its branches and limbs were two-dimensional, painted on the ceiling. The dragons and vipers returned to the Sforza coat of arms, a Renaissance frieze.

Julia realized she must've had a nightmare. She felt exhausted even though she'd just woken up. She was drenched with sweat. Her Eagles shirt stuck to her body.

The sheets were wet with perspiration under the coverlet.

She told herself to calm down. She knew she'd had a nightmare but it had been so real. She averted her eyes, afraid to look up at the ceiling, terrified it would come to life again. She'd never had such a harrowing dream in her life.

She squeezed her eyes shut, praying for the first time in a long time.

15

It was a sunny morning in Croce, and Julia had her appointment with Franco the realtor. She'd gotten dropped off by Piero on a perimeter road that held the realtor's office, a bank, and a parking lot. She looked around nervously, but there wasn't another person on the street. The density was so much less than Milan, and there'd been almost no traffic on the country road here.

It had been all she could do this morning to shower, dress, and eat breakfast like a normal person. The nightmare last night disturbed her to her core and made her feel more anxious than usual, even a little crazy, but she was trying to get it together for the day.

She crossed to Franco's office but it wasn't open yet. She checked her phone and saw she was twenty minutes early. She was curious about Croce but didn't know if she could deal with walking around. She hated being so afraid and she had to be able to function. Plus she needed another espresso, since she hadn't slept after her nightmare. Even her horoscope this morning unsettled her:

You never know what's around the bend.
Why would you want to?

Julia slipped on her sunglasses and smoothed down her white cotton sweater, which she had on with jeans and espadrilles. She got her phone and checked Google for a walking map. Evidently, Croce was a village of about twenty winding streets, built on a hill with its town center at the top.

She headed uphill on a cobblestone walkway and into the charming village. Its scale was small, and both sides of the walkway were lined with cozy stone homes topped by red tile roofs. Most of the entrances were arched and each had a different door of unvarnished oak or a tasteful green, mauve, or tan. Over each house flapped a long, multicolored pennant that looked like it was from the Renaissance.

She followed the street around a curve, passing terracotta pots full of geraniums, small lemon trees, and jasmine, scenting the air with a natural perfume. Ivy climbed on stone facades, and palm trees sprouted here and there. Oddly, there was no one on the walkway, but she could hear people inside the houses talking. Occasionally, the aroma of brewing coffee wafted from an open window.

She walked under a beautiful arch that connected both sides of the street, then continued uphill. She passed a small statue of the Virgin Mary embedded in the wall, then noticed a silhouetted figure behind a curtain, watching her from a window.

Ahead a small sign read CAFFETERIA, and outside it two older men sat at a table under a tan awning. The glass door stood open, with a colorful line of stickers advertising LOTTERIA ITALIA, PUNTO LIS, and SEGAFREDO ZANETTI. She headed there and when she reached the store, nodded at the old men. They looked away.

She entered, looking around. The store was empty, and there was a display case that held a variety of pastries and panini. Behind the counter were stacks of M&M's, Haribo candies, and Chupa Chups next to stacks of cigarettes and Bic lighters.

She shifted over to the register and waited for a clerk. Long strips of lottery scratch-offs hung behind the counter, and there appeared to be an office to the right, but nobody came out.

'Hello? *Buongiorno?*' Julia called out, but there was no reply. She walked to the end of the counter and peered into the office. She couldn't see anybody but she smelled cigarette smoke. Somebody was there, but they weren't helping her. Maybe they were on break.

She let it go and left, smiling at the old men out front, but they looked pointedly away again. She continued uphill but the street wound this way and that, so she couldn't see around the corner. She was heading toward the village center, where the elevation was highest, and she heard voices and an engine revving up.

Suddenly a young man on a white Vespa veered around the corner. Julia sprang out of the way, but he sped past laughing, the sound echoing against the stone. She wondered where the stereotypically friendly Italians were, but maybe it was better this way, so she didn't have to make conversation.

She followed the curving walkway to a small, sunny piazza lined with houses and shops around a pretty marble fountain. Opposite was a gorgeous medieval church tower, a few more houses with rows of mailboxes, then a barbershop and a women's boutique with a colorful dress in the window.

Julia flashed on the photo of Rossi in the pretty yellow shift and on impulse, she went inside the boutique. There were no other customers, and the store was bright, with racks of summery dresses along white walls. Murano glass pendants illuminated a mirrored counter in the back, where an older saleswoman looked up from over her reading glasses.

Julia crossed the room. '*Buongiorno*. Do you speak English?'

'Yes.' The saleswoman's graying hair was pulled back into a low ponytail, and she had on a pink cotton dress. She was an attractive seventy-something, and Julia realized she would be about the same age as Rossi.

'Did you know Emilia Rossi? She passed away recently.'

'No,' the saleswoman answered flatly. 'May I help you with something?'

'Are you sure you didn't know her?'

'I am sure.'

'She must've come in shopping. I can show you her photo—'

'I am not here to look at photos.'

Whoa. 'Are you new? Maybe that's why you don't know her?'

'Signora, I am the proprietor. I am here every day we are open, for almost seventeen years.'

'Can you tell me where another dress store is, in town?'

'There is no other.' The saleswoman gestured at the door. 'If you're not here to shop, please leave.'

'Okay, sorry, thank you.' Julia turned and left, mystified. Rossi had to have been in the shop once, especially if it was the only dress shop in Croce. It wasn't likely that the saleswoman didn't know her, but Julia had no idea why she would lie. She stopped at the pharmacy, asked about Rossi, and showed the clerk the picture, but he said he didn't know her, either. She even went next door to the bakery, but the baker said the same thing, coldly. She felt like the whole town was unfriendly, for some reason.

She left the bakery, crossed the piazza, and headed down the walkway to the realtor's office.

16

EXCLUSIVE TUSCAN PROPERTIES, read the sign, and Julia entered Franco's office, which was classy/rustic, the trademark Tuscan vibe. A sleek rectangle, it held three empty desks on black easel legs with black ergonomic chairs. Architectural spotlights shone on overhead tracks, and artsy framed posters of London, Paris, and Prague lined the white walls.

Franco approached from a back room, smiling in another striped shirt and trim dark suit. 'Good morning, Julia! Great to see you! May I get you some coffee or water?'

'Water, thank you.'

'Please, take a seat.' Franco gestured her into a black chair, hustled around his desk, and sat down, pushing toward her a bottle of Panna water and a napkin. 'My colleagues aren't in yet, so we have the place to ourselves.'

'Great, thank you.' Julia opened the water bottle and sipped some.

'How was your first night in the villa?'

'Fine, thanks.' Julia wasn't about to tell him about her nightmare. 'Before we get started, I stopped in a few shops asking about Rossi, and nobody knew her, which surprised me. I get the impression people here aren't that friendly. Am I missing something?'

'No, I'm sorry. I can explain.' Franco frowned, his regret plain. 'Croce is a town of eight hundred people. We all know each other. We go to the same church, and the kids go to the same school. You saw the streets. We *live* on top of each other.'

'So they must have known Rossi.'

'Yes, or of her. We've had our eye on her property for a long time.'

'So what's going on?'

'They close ranks. They know you're the American who inherited Rossi's estate, and you're an outsider.' Franco hesitated. 'And there's another issue. People didn't like Rossi, so they don't like you.'

'Why didn't they like her?' Julia felt a pang, unaccountably defensive.

'Rossi thought she was a Sforza and acted like it. You can't behave like Milanese royalty here. She treated shopkeepers like servants. She even slapped the grocer's daughter for moving too slow.'

Julia recoiled. 'That's not good.'

'No. People are proud. They wouldn't serve her, they mocked her. It got so bad she stopped coming into town. Anna Mattia ran her errands.' Franco shook his head. 'Nobody went to her funeral Mass. I was there, and the church was empty. The only one crying was Anna Mattia.'

'You said Rossi thought she was a Sforza. Do you think she was?'

Franco cleared his throat. 'No, I don't believe she was a Sforza. I think she was crazy.'

Ouch. 'Is that what people in town thought?'

'Yes.' Franco slid a glossy brochure in front of her, opening it to an array of lists. 'These are the estates like yours that have sold in the past. I can take you through these, if you want. Bottom line, your villa and property are worth two million euros.'

'Two *million*?' Julia repeated, astonished. She felt like she won the lottery, *twice.* 'But it's in terrible condition.'

'I know. The reason it's worth two million is because of my contacts, its location, and scarcity. Property doesn't free up here. There's *no* movement.' Franco leaned over.

'I know how to find the type of buyer who can afford a villa in this condition and will spend the money to restore it to its former glory.'

Julia couldn't imagine it. 'That would cost a *fortune.*'

'Exactly, that's why you should sell.' Franco met her eye in a knowing way. 'Why burden yourself? I doubt the villa is even structurally sound, and the grounds are an absolute nightmare.'

Tell me about it, Julia thought but didn't say.

'Signore Lombardi referred you to me, so I assume you inherited money from Rossi. Of course, he didn't disclose how much.'

Good. Julia had been wondering.

'But do you want to spend the money to rehabilitate that villa? Then to *maintain* it? I have the contacts to find high net-worth individuals.' Franco nodded with confidence. 'That's who buys in Tuscany. They're from all over Europe and Asia, people with world-class wealth. That's why I can get you a deal quickly. I've already made calls. I'm getting a *lot* of interest.'

'How? They haven't even seen it.'

'I've had pictures of that place for years and I've sent them to my contacts.' Franco leaned forward. 'There are people so wealthy they buy sight unseen because the location is fabulous. They romanticize the renovation process. I swear, *Under the Tuscan Sun* still sells villas.'

Julia understood, except for one thing. 'So you're marketing the villa to foreign buyers. Why is any other foreign buyer better than I am, in the eyes of the residents?'

'I go to Italian buyers first, and they know that. The feelers I put out for your property are in Rome.' Franco slid out a sheaf of papers. 'This is a standard contract. It's exclusive and lasts six months. I can get started in earnest as soon as you sign.' He handed her a gleamy Montblanc and pointed to the line. 'Please, sign here.'

Julia felt a twinge at the idea of selling the place, even though it was a dump.

'It was her *home*.'

'True, and… ?'

'I'm not ready to sell it yet.'

Franco clucked. 'I hope you're not thinking about renovating, especially remotely. It's not just the money you'd spend, it's the trouble. You'd have to hire somebody to manage construction. There are zoning restrictions, and the permitting process is lengthy.'

'I'm sure.' Julia didn't think she wanted to renovate.

'You won't come as often as you think anyway. Nobody does. I call it second-home syndrome, I see it all the time. The villa stays closed for months. Vermin and scorpions move in. One of my clients had a viper infestation.'

Julia shuddered. She thought of the vipers on the Sforza coat of arms.

Franco's expression softened. 'I don't know if you already own a home, but every homeowner knows that things go wrong unexpectedly.' Franco frowned. 'Plumbing breaks. Hot water heaters explode. Leaks spring in roofs. I can't believe nothing catastrophic has happened already. The longer you keep the villa, the more of a chance you take. I'm the best realtor around, and if you like Tuscany, I can help you find a lovely apartment in Florence. You don't need the villa. It's a money pit. Your best financial move would be to sell the house before you have to put money into it.'

Julia mulled it over, clarifying her thoughts. She didn't want to keep the villa, she barely wanted to sleep there. But if she sold it now, she felt like she'd be severing her relationship to Rossi and giving up any chance of finding out if they were related.

Franco tapped the signature line. 'Sell. That's what I'd do.'

'Let me think it over.' Julia handed him back the pen, then she had another thought. 'But can you do a title search? I'd like to know who owned the villa before her.'

17

Julia's phone rang as soon as she and Piero pulled into the driveway, and she glanced at the screen, happy to see Courtney was calling. She pressed Accept and got out of the car. 'Hey, lady!'

'How's my girl?' Courtney asked sweetly, and Julia cheered at the sound of her voice. She thanked Piero and walked to the side of the driveway to talk, overlooking the hill that led to the carriage house, the equipment shed, and the scorched clearing.

'I'm hanging in.'

'Good for you! I'm so proud of you, going over there on your own. It's a big deal. So you're really okay?'

'Kind of.' Julia launched into a recap, telling her about Rossi and the decrepit villa, the burned belongings, and even the nightmare. She finished, asking Courtney for her thoughts.

'My *thoughts*? Jules, sell the villa! It's worth *two million* euros!'

Arg. 'But it's her home.'

'So? You'll make bank!'

'But it's not only about the money, is it?'

'Yes, well said! Exactly!' Courtney laughed. *'It's only about the money!'*

'But I'm already inheriting so much.'

'Who turns down more money? Wait, somebody wants *less* money?' Courtney laughed. 'Besides, I know it sounds like a lot, but it's not like you're set for life. Get as much as you can and invest it. Paul will help. You know he loves that.'

Julia's gaze went to the blackened circle, where she'd found the pearl. 'What if Rossi's related to me?'

'So what? What's that have to do with the villa, now that you can't get her DNA? If you sell, you can still figure out if she's related to you. You have an appointment with the family investigator tomorrow, right? Hire him like you planned. Then see Florence. Eat pasta, drink wine. Shop 'til you drop.'

Julia's chest wrenched. 'But if I sell, it breaks the connection.'

'What connection?'

'Between me and Rossi.'

'Jules. You didn't know her. You don't even know if she's related to you.' Courtney chuckled. 'If *feeling* connected to somebody was the same thing as *being* connected to them, I'd be connected to Taylor Swift. Are you in a parasocial relationship with a ghost?'

'No, it's not like that.' Julia felt a twinge. 'What if Rossi sent me a sign? The pearl? The electric shock?'

'Honey, you got a shock because you were standing in water. You found a pearl because Rossi was crazy enough to burn Mikimoto.'

Julia winced reflexively. 'Don't call her crazy.'

'But it's true, isn't it? From what I hear, she was nuts.'

Julia let it go. 'She left the villa to me. She wanted me to have it.'

'She left you the money, too. You're gonna spend it, right?'

Julia had no reply. She knew her argument didn't stand to reason.

'Are we really talking about what Rossi wants you to do?' Courtney sounded bewildered. 'Jules, I thought the astrology stuff was bad, but signs from beyond? Are you getting weird on me?'

'No,' Julia said, though she'd wondered the same thing. 'Anna Mattia thinks Rossi's soul is in the villa.'

'Do you agree?'

'Maybe,' Julia had to admit.

'So you think the place is *haunted*?' Courtney sounded disappointed, and Julia felt embarrassed.

'No, not really.'

'If you think Rossi's soul is there, that's the definition of a haunted house. Sorry, haunted *villa*.'

'I don't think of it that way,' Julia tried to explain. 'Things are different here. It's not like home, where everything is cut and dried. It's more spiritual, more mystical. Things that make sense here might not make sense at home.'

'Like what? It's Tuscany, not Transylvania.'

Julia tried to think of an example. 'Do you know they plant cypress trees around cemeteries to keep away the evil spirits?'

'My boss is an evil spirit.'

Julia smiled. 'You want a cypress tree?'

'Julia, listen.' Courtney softened her tone. 'The dead don't live with the living. That would make every house a haunted house. You don't believe that, do you?'

'No.'

'Don't you think this is happening because of Mike?' Courtney asked, sympathetic. 'I think you're grieving him. Are you wishing he were with you?'

'Yes.'

'Do you think the pearl was a sign from him?'

'No,' Julia answered, because she'd thought about it. 'Mike had nothing to do with pearls. Rossi liked pearls, and I think it came from her.' *Or even Caterina Sforza*, she almost added, but thought better of it.

'Honey, not gonna lie, you don't sound like yourself.'

'I'm just tired. I haven't slept well.'

'I'm worried about you.'

'I'm fine.'

'Should you call Susanna? I'm sure you could have a session on FaceTime.'

'I don't need one.' Julia wished she'd kept the nightmare to herself. She should've known it would worry Courtney.

'Maybe you're jet-lagged. Hydrate and get on their schedule.'

'That's probably it,' Julia said, hoping to convince her. 'I'm super tired and hungry. It's lunchtime here.'

'Is your *cook* making it for you?'

'Yes. Her name's Anna Mattia.'

'Just remember your bestie. I knew you when you didn't live in a haunted villa.'

'Very funny.'

'Boo!'

'This looks great!' Julia grinned down at a beautiful bowl of a tomato-and-bread stew with a sprig of fresh basil on the top. She welcomed eating her feelings after the conversation with Courtney.

'We call *pappa al pomodoro*.' Anna Mattia smiled, standing beside her. 'Tomat', garlic, bread, basil, salt. Piero's mother make, now me. *Buon appetito*.'

'Thanks.' Julia scooped some into her mouth, and it was absolutely delicious. The tomato was fresh and tart, with the perfect amount of garlic, and the rough bread made it chewy. 'This is so good.'

'*Grazie*.'

'Please, stay. I want to talk to you.' Julia pulled out a chair, and Anna Mattia sat down, turning to her. 'I was in town this morning, and Franco told me Signora didn't treat people well.'

'Eh?' Anna Mattia lifted a disapproving eyebrow.

'He says they didn't like her, so they don't like me. I saw it from the baker, the pharmacist, and the lady in the dress shop.'

'Leonora? A *bitch*!'

Julia chuckled. 'Still, did Rossi slap the grocer's daughter?'

'No! A lie! They are jealous 'er money. They are jealous 'er.' Anna Mattia frowned. 'They are jealous me and Piero, we 'ave money, apartment, car. When Signora come 'ome from town, she cry. They make fun.' Anna Mattia leaned closer. 'Signora, think they watch, they follow. She think they want to *kill*.'

'Rossi thought they wanted to kill her? Like the doctors?'

'*Sì*. She say they 'ave knife. At night, she see.' Anna Mattia gestured to the vineyard. 'Piero, me, we go, we look. Nobody.'

Julia tried to understand. 'She imagined they came to kill her? Here?'

'*Sì*, yes. Signora mind is wrong. They tease, so I go to town.' Anna Mattia's face fell, and Julia remembered that Anna Mattia had cried at Rossi's funeral.

'You took good care of her.'

'*Sì*, yes.' Anna Mattia nodded. 'I love.'

'I know.' Julia felt touched. 'I told him I wasn't ready to sell the villa. My friend Courtney thinks I should sell. What do you think?'

Anna Mattia shrugged. 'You decide.'

'But tell me what you think.'

Anna Mattia hesitated. 'The villa is… a lot for a woman, alone.'

'Signora Rossi was a woman alone.'

Anna Mattia frowned slightly. 'You are young, you wan' to 'ave family.'

Julia couldn't imagine that without Mike.

'*Mi scusi, aspete.*' Anna Mattia popped out of the chair and left the dining room. Julia took a few more scoops of *pappa al pomodoro* and finished the meal just as Anna Mattia returned with a ceramic bowl and a bottle of olive oil, which she set down.

'They jealous your villa, your money. They give *malocchio*, evil eye. You 'ave.'

Whoa. 'The evil eye? You think I have it?' Julia didn't know if she believed in the evil eye. She could only imagine what Courtney would say.

'I *know*, I see. I come from Abruzzo. *We* know *malocchio*. I fix.' Anna Mattia poured some olive oil into the bowl of water.

'Do I have to drink that?' Julia recoiled, and Anna Mattia motioned her into silence.

'No. Close eyes.' Anna Mattia started whispering in Italian, and Julia closed her eyes, then snuck a peek. Anna Mattia's eyes were closed, too, but she was swaying and stirring the water with her knobby index finger. Her lined face had fallen into deep fissures, and she seemed to be putting herself into a trance.

Julia closed her eyes, giving herself over to whatever was going on. She listened to Anna Mattia's words and began to sense their rhythms. They took on the cadence of a prayer, the intonations familiar from years of Masses. She put herself in Anna Mattia's hands, even in her spell, and opened her mind to a different world, a place out of time and space.

Anna Mattia kept praying, and Julia felt herself enter a deep state of calm that allowed her breathing to slow, ending only when she felt a gentle touch on her forehead. She realized Anna Mattia was blessing her with the sign of the cross.

'Signora,' Anna Mattia whispered. 'Open eyes.'

Julia opened her eyes, and Anna Mattia was beaming down at her. 'Better now.'

'Thank you,' Julia said, meaning it.

18

The late-day sun filled Rossi's bedroom with indirect light, and Julia began unpacking her suitcase and putting her clothes in the mahogany dresser. She was going to stay in Rossi's bed tonight. She couldn't let a nightmare rattle her.

She put her underwear in the top drawer of the dresser, then retrieved her T-shirts and sweaters, opened the second drawer, and put them inside. She was about to close the drawer when she noticed a white paper stuck in its joint.

She reached back and pulled it out, surprised to find it was a small, black-and-white photograph of a baby, about nine months old. She couldn't tell if it was a boy or a girl, but it had brown hair and light eyes. The baby's mouth was open, showing a few teeth, and the baby was lying on a white pad in a cloth diaper with old-school pins, its pudgy arms in mid-wriggle. One side of the photograph was a bright white, as if the light source had been nearby or the picture was overexposed.

My God. Julia didn't know enough about Rossi to know if it was her as a baby, but it could have been. Or it could have been a baby of Rossi's. She flipped the picture over. The back was blank. She examined the photo itself. It looked old, taken with a real camera, and was unusually small, maybe three by three, including a white border with scalloped edges.

Julia hustled out the door, into the hallway, down the stairs, and into the kitchen, where Anna Mattia looked up from arranging pink and purple cosmos in a glazed green pitcher. 'Anna Mattia, look what I found in Signora Rossi's drawer.'

Anna Mattia's lips parted in surprise when she looked at the photo. 'A baby?'

'Yes, do you know who it is? Is it Signora when she was a baby?'

'Don' know.' Anna Mattia shook her head, mystified.

'What do you think? Does it look like her?'

Anna Mattia squinted at the photo. 'Could be, maybe no.'

'Did Signora have any friends who had a baby?'

'Don' know.'

'What about a sister or a brother?'

'She say no.'

'Are you *sure* Signora didn't have a child?'

'She say no.'

Julia went for it. 'Anna Mattia, what if Signora lied to you and everyone else? What if she really *did* have a child?'

Anna Mattia shook her head. 'Why she lie?'

'Maybe she was embarrassed,' Julia answered, off the top of her head. 'She could have had a child but she wasn't married. Maybe she didn't want people to know, even you.'

'She *say* no childr'.'

'If she had a baby, given my age and hers, that could mean I'm her granddaughter, and that her daughter or her son is my birth mother or father. This picture could be one of my parents.'

Anna Mattia blinked.

'If we knew how old this photo was, then that would help us figure out who it's a picture of. It looks old to me. Was there a time in Italy when photographs looked like this? The shape, the size? The way the edge is scalloped?' Julia ran her finger along the bumpy side. 'Or what about the diaper? It's cloth, it has real pins.'

'Yes, is old. Don' know how old. My Sofia, we 'ave pins.' Anna Mattia's expression darkened.

'Okay, well, thank you. I'm going to take this to the investigator tomorrow.'

Night fell, and a stillness settled over the villa. Dinner had been roast chicken with lemon and *Vin Santo*, a Tuscan dessert wine that flavored the meat with honey, fruit, and hazelnut. The dish was served with roasted potatoes sprinkled with pecorino cheese and black pepper, so delicious that Julia vowed to exist only on Tuscan cuisine.

She ascended the staircase, her tummy full and her mood relaxed, thanks to two glasses of Chianti. She reached the top of the stair, then went into her bedroom, where she'd left the lights on. She slipped into her Notre Dame T-shirt, then took the baby picture and her laptop to bed.

She sat down, opened the laptop, and scrolled to her photo function. She opened her phone, took a photo of the baby picture, then navigated to the earliest photo of Rossi and set them side by side. There was a similarity of features, but also a difference in the jawline that didn't change with maturation. So, the baby in the photo might not have been Rossi.

Julia thrilled to think that the baby could have been either her biological mother or father. On impulse, she snapped a selfie, then moved her phone to the set of photos, placing it next to the baby photo and the young Rossi photo, as if they were three generations in the same family.

Julia eyed the three faces, comparing them. There *was* a likeness, a *relationship* in the eyes. The eye color was blue like hers, and their shape was roundish, set far apart. She knew she wasn't imagining it, but she didn't have any facts to go on. Her thoughts strayed to the evil eye, then to Caterina's eyes in the nightmare.

'Stop,' Julia told herself. She didn't want to get spooked before bedtime. Exhaustion swept over her, and she set the laptop on the night table. She plugged in her phone, climbed between the sheets, and slipped into bed without looking up at the ceiling. No reason to tempt fate. She left the lamp on, too. She was tired enough to fall asleep with the lights on.

And in the next minute, she did.

Then the nightmare began.

19

Julia saw a face begin to emerge from the pitch black around her. She didn't know when the room got so dark, but now it was, bottomless as space. Materializing out of its depth was a small head and she realized it was the baby in the photo, and in the next moment, the baby's face began to shift and morph and change, the cheeks pulled like taffy and the chin yanked in the opposite direction, the visage being tugged and wrenched out of shape by unseen forces, and in the next moment the baby was crying, its blue eyes losing shape and definition, constantly changing and shifting shapes.

Julia tried to wake up, but she couldn't, and she felt herself shaking in bed, turning her head right and left, trembling all over, not wanting to see what would happen next because she knew that it was going to frighten her, terrify her, scare her out of her wits. Suddenly the face turned into the stern visage of Caterina Sforza wearing a pearl necklace that she took off and handed to Julia, then Caterina's face changed, contorting out of shape, pulled and yanked in all directions, Caterina's electric-blue eyes blazing and suddenly askew, her lips being wrenched back into a hideous grimace, Caterina's white teeth turning into fangs, and then Caterina tightening the necklace on Julia's throat, making it tighter and tighter, throttling her.

Julia gasped for breath, torquing this way and that, her hands clawing her neck, scratching her own skin, trying to get off the pearl necklace, a noose strangling her, cutting off oxygen to her brain, to her body, a ligature embedding itself so deeply into her flesh that it was *decapitating* her, severing her neck in two, separating her head from her shoulders with lethal force.

Her body writhed and bucked off the bed, trying to free itself, no longer human anymore, an organism trying to survive, out of oxygen, suffocating to death in agony, everywhere was blackness, and in the next moment, Julia saw herself running out of bed and down the hall, her fingers and nails clawing at the garotte, her head wobbling as she ran, she tried to hold it on, running even though she had no oxygen left anymore, surely she was dead.

She flew out the back door and down to the vineyard and vines curled and coiled and zoomed from the ground to meet her, fastening themselves around her wrists and ankles like ropes, wrenching her back down into the earth, and she fought back, turning this way and that, fighting to stay above the ground, she would be dead if they pulled her down, it was her own grave, and she could smell the earth and the rot and the decay, and she was dead now, even as more and more vines coiled to her, whipping toward her, wrapping themselves around her neck, her upper arms, her knees, tethering every single part of her body to the earth, dragging her down, trying to bury her alive.

Julia saw herself from above, watching herself being strangled, her eyes protruding grotesquely, her mouth gaping open, her face turning electric blue, her hair writhing wild as snakes, as the vines dragged her down, down, down into the earth, yanking her through the surface all the way down to the clammy, cold, stinking decay at the black rotting center of the world.

'Signora, Signora!' Anna Mattia shook her, holding her by her arms.

'No, no, no!' Julia screamed, clawing at herself, trying to get the vines off, and in the next moment, she swallowed huge gulps of air, hiccuping oxygen, her heart thundering and her chest heaving so hard that she bucked and bucked, but she wasn't buried anymore, she was above ground, and when she opened her eyes and looked up, all she saw was a full moon like a gargantuan pearl.

'Signora, is okay, is okay!' Anna Mattia squeezed her arms. 'Is okay!'

Julia didn't know what was happening. She wasn't in bed anymore. Anna Mattia was there, and Piero stood behind her. Bianco barked in agitation, a white blur.

Julia couldn't tell if she was awake or asleep. She was lying on something rough and cold and hard. It was pitch dark everywhere except for two flashlights, their round beams like more and more pearls running over her body, plaguing her, taunting her.

She realized she was outside in the vineyard. Maybe.

She didn't know what was real and what wasn't.

She didn't know if she'd had a nightmare at all.

20

The next morning, Julia rode in the passenger seat, edgy on her way to meet the family investigator in Florence. Piero was driving quietly, but his silence wasn't as companionable as before. He'd been freaked out by the scene in the vineyard last night, and Anna Mattia had been cooler at breakfast.

Julia couldn't blame them, more shaken than ever. She had on a turtleneck because her neck was covered with scratches. Her arms and legs were cut from the thornbushes under her blazer and jeans. She hadn't slept and looked so pale she had on foundation. She'd taken the pearl from her wallet and flushed it down the toilet, never wanting to see it again. The only luck it brought was nightmarish.

Julia looked out the window, trying to collect her thoughts. She was losing her grip. She'd had nightmares at home about Mike's murder, but she'd *never* left her bed, much less her *bedroom*. Last night she'd run out of the house to the vineyard, gotten tangled in the vines, thrashed around like a freak, all while she was *asleep*.

Julia tried to let it go but couldn't. It was as if she lived through a horror and carried it with her, embodied it somehow, terrified that she was going borderline berserk. She sensed that Caterina was driving her to it for some reason, maybe even the same way Caterina had driven Rossi to it. It terrified Julia to think she'd end up like Rossi.

She told herself to get a grip. She couldn't fall apart, not today. This was her chance to see if she was related to Rossi in some way and learn about her biological family, maybe even connect with them. She glanced at her phone and touched the screen to read this morning's horoscope again, since it had been a comfort.

You are being tested in ways you never imagined. Believe in yourself. Your intuitive Cancerian nature will show you the way. Your rising Virgo will give you strength to persevere.

Julia took it in as they reached the historic district, where Piero pulled over and stopped, turning to her.

'Okay here?'

'Yes, thank you.' Julia looked out the window, newly nervous. The street was packed with cars, buses, and motorcycles. People were everywhere. She had Google-mapped the route to the investigator's office, which was along the Arno River. It was a short walk through the most congested part of the city. She told herself to persevere.

Piero held up his phone. 'You tex', I come. *Ciao*, Signora.'

'*Grazie*, Piero. *Ciao*.' Julia slipped on her sunglasses and got out of the car, acclimating herself to the scene. The streets were narrow, crowded, and rowdier than Milan, full of students with backpacks, couples with selfie sticks, and group tours in high-visibility hats.

She headed toward the Arno on a cobblestone walkway, powering through the hustle-bustle, chatter in different languages, and clouds of cigarette and vape smoke. She passed pizzerias, boutiques, a tattoo parlor, a pharmacy, and a restaurant with a chalkboard that read CUCINA TIPICA TOSCANA. Cafés lined the street, their outside tables full, and her heart pounded as she threaded her way past tourists around a kiosk selling Pinocchio marionettes, spoon rests, T-shirts, and rosaries.

Ahead the crowd spread out as Florence opened onto the Arno. She picked up the pace to get some open air and followed her map to the river. The water was a wide, greenish blue ribbon that mirrored the trees and magnificent stone buildings along its banks, but Julia felt too nervous to sightsee. Traffic was stop-and-go on the street that lined the river, and sidewalks were packed with tourists taking pictures of the ancient bridges spanning the water, among them the most popular, the Ponte Vecchio.

Julia took a right turn away from the Ponte Vecchio, hurrying along the crowded sidewalk to the investigator's address. Her steps quickened, and she felt better knowing that soon she'd be inside the investigator's office.

Julia stopped at the address on her phone. Google Maps showed the building facing the Arno, but there wasn't an office at the address, only an outdoor café. She scrolled to check the email from Lombardi, but she was at the correct address. She thought Lombardi must've made a mistake until an older man started waving to her from one of the tables. He had tinted glasses, thick salt-and-pepper hair, and a flashy suit.

'Julia, I'm Gustavo Caputo! Join me!'

Julia was surprised he would meet her at a café. She walked over, noting a large carafe of wine on his table, half-empty.

'Julia, you're even lovelier than Lombardi said!' Caputo beamed, throwing open his arms. 'If only I were younger! You could be my third ex-wife!'

Arg. Julia managed a smile. 'Nice to meet you, Mr Caputo.'

'Please, call me Gustavo! Aren't you impressed with my English? My first wife was British. She insisted I learn the language and also that I leave the house.' Caputo gestured with a flourish to the chair next to him. People flowed past them on the sidewalk, but he ignored them. 'Do sit down, Julia! Let's get to know one another, shall we?'

'Here?' Julia didn't want to discuss her family search in public. The tables were close together, full of tourists, talking and smoking. 'What about your office?'

'There's no need! Could one ask for a better view?' Caputo gestured to the Arno. 'Please, have a seat. I'm having coffee brought for you.'

Julia sat down, dismayed. She wondered if he even had an office.

'So tell me about yourself!' Caputo retook his seat. 'What's it like to be an heiress?'

Gimme a break. 'I'd rather hear about your professional services. Mr Lombardi said you were an experienced family investigator.'

'What will you *do* with that much money?' Caputo's eyes flashed behind his tinted glasses. 'If I were young, I'd take a world tour!'

Julia tried to get on track. 'Have you handled many family searches for adoptees?'

'No. I do paternity work.' Caputo took a gulp of wine as a waitress came over with an espresso, a plate of biscotti, and a menu trimmed in leather.

'Thank you,' Julia said, then the waitress left.

'Please, order whatever you wish. I'm having an early lunch. I recommend the *risotto San Massimiliano Riserva* to start. It's a delight, with cauliflower, raisins, cashews, and capers.'

'I'm not hungry.' Julia kept her voice low. 'So can you conduct a family search for me?'

'Sure, why not?'

Hmmm. 'Okay, I was left an inheritance by a woman named Emilia Rossi. I don't know if she's related to me, but she was the age my grandmother would be. However, she reportedly had no children, no known family, and never married. I wonder if you could verify that information. I assume public records would tell you—'

'Smart, beautiful, *and* rich!' Caputo poured himself another glass of wine, emptying the carafe. 'You'll be beating them off with a stick! You don't need an investigator, you need a bodyguard!'

Julia felt annoyed. 'To return to the point, the villa is near Croce, in Chianti.'

Caputo gulped his wine. 'Rosso is a very common name.'

'It's Rossi, not Rosso.'

'What's her first name again?'

'Emilia with an "E." Don't you want to write this down?'

'We need a refill.' Caputo hoisted the empty wine carafe to signal the waitress, bumping a young man in a black ballcap, passing by.

'When was the last time you worked for Mr Lombardi?'

'Ten, eleven years?' Caputo wiggled his carafe, but all of a sudden, it slipped and crashed to the sidewalk, sending glass shards in all directions. People startled at the nearby tables, and tourists jumped aside.

Julia rose. She wasn't about to entrust her family search to this idiot. 'Mr Caputo, I think we're done here.'

Julia hurried away from the café, her phone to her ear. She was calling Piero to pick her up, but he didn't answer. He must not have expected her to be finished so soon. She hurried through the crowds thronging the Ponte Vecchio, trying to get past them for open air on the other side of the bridge nearer the Uffizi Gallery.

Julia texted Piero on the way, her heart beginning to pound. She called Lombardi, hoping he would have other referrals for family investigators. She kept walking as she held the phone to her ear, covering her other ear so she could hear. The call dropped abruptly, so she tried again, hurrying along the Arno. She passed under a stretch of stucco arches, and the noise level subsided. She tried Lombardi again, and the call connected, so she ducked next to an arch, near the wall to stay out of the crowd.

'*Pronto…*,' Lombardi answered, but the reception was terrible.

'Hi, it's Julia Pritzker. I met with Caputo but he's not going to work out. Do you have any other recommendations?'

'Julia… I… can't hear… you.'

'Can you hear me now?' Julia turned around and spotted a man near one of the arches. He was the passerby in the black ballcap that Caputo bumped at the café. He turned his head away quickly. Oddly, it gave her the impression that he'd been watching her.

'Julia? Julia? I… hear… only static.'

'Can you recommend any other investigators?' Julia knew Lombardi couldn't hear her, but she didn't know what was going on with the man in the black ballcap. He had been looking directly at her, almost as if he was following her.

'I'm sorry… can you… call back?'

'No, this is a good time for me.' Julia walked away. She didn't want the man in the ballcap to know that she'd spotted him. She was wearing sunglasses, so he couldn't have seen her eyes.

'Julia… I will hang up… and…'

'No, wait, it could get better.' Julia kept walking. The call dropped again. She nodded, pretending the conversation was continuing. The arches ended, and the sidewalk narrowed on her side of the street. Traffic was stopped, and she crossed the street, still faking conversation.

Ahead was a majestic row of vaulted arches and signs to the Uffizi. Sunshine poured around the immense columns, casting long lines of light and dark. Tourists thronged on the grand stone promontory under the arches, taking pictures.

Julia headed that way, keeping her pace casual. She didn't know if the man in the black ballcap was behind her. She reached the edge of the crowd under the arches and spotted a young girl taking selfies, which gave her an idea.

She ended her fake phone call, stopped, and took selfies, selecting the widest angle to get the crowd behind her. She fake-posed and turned slowly to face the river, so she could look sideways and see if the man in the ballcap was behind her.

He *was*.

Julia's mouth went dry. He'd put on sunglasses, but it was him. He was standing at one of the souvenir kiosks looking at a scarf, but it seemed fishy. The scarf was pink, a woman's scarf, and he looked local anyway. She fixed a description of him in her mind; young white guy, average height and weight, black ballcap, skinny jeans, black sneakers.

Julia's heart began to hammer. She snapped a slew of photos, hoping they'd included him. If he was following her, she couldn't imagine why. If he wanted to hit on her, he already would have. Maybe he'd overheard Caputo say she was an heiress and he wanted to rob her. She wondered if she was being paranoid, like Rossi.

She headed toward the Uffizi, picking up the pace.

21

Julia turned left, entering the grand rectangular courtyard between the wings of the Uffizi Gallery, lined by columns with statuary on both sides. People packed the courtyard, taking pictures, laughing, and talking.

She waded into the crowd, ignoring a rising panic. French students milled under the colonnade that led to one of the entrances, shaded from the sun. She scooted up the steps, went through the group, and reached the wall, using them as a screen.

They chattered away, and she waited to see if Ballcap would follow her. In the next moment, she had her answer. He walked slowly through the crowd, his head wheeling left and right under his brim. She stayed low and spotted a ticket to the Uffizi in the back pocket of a teenager.

Julia realized there would be security guards inside the museum, and she would feel safer than on the crowded street. She slipped the ticket from the girl's pocket, feeling bad about it, but her safety was at stake. She excused her way to the front of the line, and showed the ticket. She passed through the doors and turnstiles, then entered a noisy white room packed with people buying audio tours.

Julia hurried past them, following the crowd around the corner and up a massive flight of dark stairs. She reached the top and found herself in a long, majestic hallway with a black-and-white marble floor and paneled frescoes on a coffered ceiling. To her right were the tall windows that overlooked the courtyard and on her left were rooms of paintings. People flowed in and out of the rooms, talking in groups or listening to audio tours.

Julia crossed to the windows and looked down at the courtyard. People were cheek by jowl. She didn't see Ballcap. She hoped she'd lost him but she couldn't be sure. She needed Piero to come. She called him again, but he didn't answer. She texted him again, too.

Julia's thoughts raced. There had to be security somewhere, so it was still safer to stay in the museum than leave. The crowd was flowing into the first room, and she went with them. She passed Sienese paintings by Lippi and beautiful religious art on gilded arched panels. She kept an eye out for Ballcap but didn't see him.

She followed the crowd, and the next room was the early Renaissance, then Piero della Francesca's portraits of the Duke and Duchess of Urbino that she studied in art history. Still no Ballcap. No Piero call, either.

She entered the next room, distracted by a small, dark portrait. She stopped short, recognizing it from somewhere. Its plaque read PORTRAIT OF GALEAZZO MARIA SFORZA, 1471, BY PIERO DEL POLLAIUOLO.

My God. Julia realized it was the Duke of Milan, Caterina Sforza's father. It looked like the portrait in the bedroom fresco. Quickly she snapped a picture of the portrait, lowered her phone, then froze.

Ballcap was among the throng in the hallway, but he wasn't looking in her direction. She pivoted and headed for the entrance to the next room. It was the Botticelli Room, the destination of every art tourist, packed wall to wall.

Julia entered, and people jostled each other to take pictures of *The Birth of Venus* and other iconic paintings. She hurried through them into the hallway, glancing over her shoulder.

She spotted Ballcap entering the Botticelli Room. Frightened, she looked around for a security guard. There wasn't one. She needed to stop Ballcap.

'Free money, everybody!' Julia pulled out her wallet, grabbed a bunch of euros, and threw them into the air. Bills fluttered everywhere, and the crowd reacted instantly. Some scrambled to catch the bills. Others crawled on the floor, grappling with each other. The Botticelli Room erupted in chaos, making a human roadblock.

Julia hurried down the hall to the staircase, raced down the steps, and reached the ground floor. Her heart pounded. Her breath came in ragged bursts. She hustled toward the exit and bolted out the door under the colonnade. She looked over her shoulder, but barreled headlong into a man reading his phone on a parked Vespa.

'*Che cosa*?' the man shouted, startled. He was about her age, with a headful of dark curls and an academic air. His brown eyes looked intelligent behind tortoiseshell glasses, and he had on a loose camel scarf with a black quilted jacket.

'Oh no... I'm so sorry,' Julia stammered, righting herself.

'No problem.' The man smiled, segueing into English with an American accent. He slipped his phone into his pocket. 'Are you okay?'

'I'm being followed,' Julia blurted out. 'My friend's supposed to pick me up but he didn't text me back.'

'Climb on, I'll get you out of here.'

'But... I don't know you.'

'My name's Gianluca Moretti. Don't worry, I'm a librarian. I work nearby. See?' Gianluca held up his employee lanyard. 'You can call your friend from the library.'

Julia glanced over her shoulder, terrified to see Ballcap approaching the door under the colonnade. 'Let's go!' she said, swinging her leg over the Vespa.

22

Julia perched on the Vespa's padded seat, clutching Gianluca's quilted jacket as they took off, whizzing past the Palazzo Vecchio. She didn't know why Ballcap was following her, but she couldn't think at speed. Her hair whipped around, and her teeth clenched as they bobbled over cobblestones through the historic center of Florence, cars zipping everywhere.

They wound through medieval streets, crossed a sunny piazza lined with statuary, then down streets with homes four and five stories high, with shops on the first floor. They slowed as they approached an elegant brownstone with Italian and EU flags flying from its facade. Its grand mahogany door had a large brass plaque that read BIBLIOTECA MARUCELLIANA.

Gianluca stopped in front, cut the engine, and braced the Vespa. 'We're here.'

Julia got off and raked her hair into place. 'Thank you.'

'You're welcome. I'm sorry you were bothered.' Gianluca's eyes were a concerned brown, and his smile warm. 'This is my hometown, and I'm unhappy when Florentines misbehave. What happened in the Uffizi?'

'Uh, it was nothing.' Julia wanted to change the subject. 'So this is your library?'

'Yes.' Gianluca hoisted the bike to the entrance, putting down the kickstand. 'I'm Director, a euphemism for Head Geek.'

Julia smiled. 'Your English is perfect.'

'My mom's from San Francisco.' Gianluca gestured at the door. 'Would you like to see inside? Marucelliana isn't a tourist destination, but it should be. We have forty thousand volumes, not including rare manuscripts, letters, documents, and books. You can look around, get something to drink, and call your friend.'

'Okay, thanks,' Julia answered after a moment. She felt better off the street, and he seemed nice. Plus, a librarian.

'Cool. This way.' Gianluca led her inside and up a beautiful marble staircase that wound around in several landings, complete with marble benches and ornate statuary. He gestured proudly as they ascended. 'Marucelliana was built in 1752, as part of a bequest to ensure that Florentines had access to literature. By law, every book published in the city must be deposited here. Yet we're not institutional like the National Library. That's where I was when you ran into me. Literally.'

'Again, I'm sorry.'

'I'm joking. Here, this way.' Gianluca stepped aside when they reached the second floor, admitting her to a generic reception area with fluorescent lighting, orange walls, and a long wooden desk with a plastic shield.

A young female librarian looked up with a smile. '*Ciao*, Gianluca.'

'*Ciao*, Betta. Don't mind me, I'm redeeming our city.'

The librarian laughed, returning to her book, and Gianluca showed Julia into a cramped, dark corridor that felt oddly like a secret passageway and ended in a small door of green metal, curved like a coffin.

Gianluca stopped. 'It's a weird door, right?'

'Right.'

'Wait for it.' Gianluca opened the door with a flourish, and Julia was amazed that it led to a vast, majestic room with a high, vaulted ceiling like a cathedral. Books encased in polished mahogany shelves lined all sides, extending from the floor to the ceiling, two stories high. The second floor of books was accessed by a balcony with brass ladders every four or five shelves.

Mahogany tables spanned the length of the immense room, with graceful old-fashioned brass lamps and a row of chairs on each side. Massive arched windows were embedded in vaults of cream-colored plaster. Filtered sunlight fell on a handful of young men and women working silently, their books and laptops open. The air smelled like old wood and even older paper. There was total silence, stillness, and calm, which Julia breathed in like oxygen.

'My God,' she said under her breath.

'Follow me.' Gianluca led her through the library, and she followed him into a narrow hallway that ended in a T, going left and right. The room on the left had a display of plaques and articles in a glass case, but Gianluca was heading to the room on the right. SALA RISERVATA, read its sign, and there was a velvet cordon, which he unclipped.

Julia felt like she'd been admitted to the inner sanctum. No one else was inside, and the room was small and dim, with a low ceiling of exposed unvarnished rafters. Old books lined the room, their leather bindings in dark reds, blues, greens, and tans. The balcony was wooden with an elaborately carved balustrade and library ladders. There were several mahogany tables and lamps with details in wrought iron, aglow against the wood's rich, dark grain.

'This is our rare book room, my favorite place in the world.' Gianluca smiled in the gentle lighting, and Julia realized that he was handsome, his eyes the hue of espresso, with long lashes, and a mouth that looked soft. She hadn't stood this close to any man since Mike, which threw her off-balance.

'Uh, it's beautiful.'

'Thanks. I make excuses to come here, including boring hapless visitors. Well, thus ends the library tour. Two whole rooms. We aim for quality, not quantity.' Gianluca straightened. 'Would you like a lemonade? We can have some in the garden.'

'A garden?' Julia asked, surprised. 'In a *library*?'

Julia sat at a round table amid a small, enclosed garden. Red geraniums, pink cosmos, and fresh green palms in terracotta pots lined the space, and white star jasmine like living stars covered the walls, giving off sweet fragrance. Sunshine flooded the space, but the table had a green canvas umbrella for shade. The garden's far wall was a modern brick addition that held staff offices, and Gianluca had gone inside. Its square windows were cranked open, and the sounds of rapid Italian wafted from inside.

Julia took the opportunity to get her phone and check the selfies she'd taken outside the Uffizi, with Ballcap in the background. She scrolled through, but her heart sank. Ballcap's back was turned away in them, so she couldn't see his face or identify him. She sensed it was intentional, in that he didn't want her to photograph him.

Just then her phone pinged with a text. It was from Piero.

OK? Piero texted.

Yes, she texted back, then sent him the name of the library.

15, Piero texted, which she assumed meant fifteen minutes.

Gianluca emerged with glasses of lemonade, setting one in front of her and sitting opposite. 'Here we go.'

'Thank you.' Julia took a sip, which tasted great. 'Delicious.'

'Good. So perhaps Florentines who follow a beautiful woman can be forgotten. I hope your husband would agree with me.'

Julia paused. 'My husband… passed away.'

Gianluca grimaced. 'Oh no, I'm so sorry. Please, forgive my rudeness.'

'It wasn't rude, it's okay.' Julia realized it was because of her rings, but didn't know when she'd ever take them off.

'Are you in Florence alone then?'

'Yes.'

'How long for?'

'A week or so.'

'On business?'

'No.' Julia wasn't sure how much to tell him. 'Long story short, I've inherited some property.'

'Where?'

'Outside of Croce.'

'A small village, very pretty. But I'm sorry about your loss.'

'Oh, thank you.' Julia realized he meant whoever had left her the inheritance, but she decided to be honest. Talking with him felt familiar because he sounded American, and she could use a friend. 'Weirdly, I don't know if I'm related to the woman I inherited from because I'm adopted. I have to figure it out.'

Gianluca lifted a dark eyebrow. 'That's mysterious.'

'I met with an investigator to do a family search, but I need to find a better one.'

'I can help.'

'How?' Julia asked, surprised. 'Do you have a directory or something?'

'Librarianship is about information, not books.' Gianluca slid his phone from his pocket and started thumbing. 'Tell me about your benefactor.'

'Well, her name was Emilia Rossi and she claimed to be a descendant of Caterina Sforza.'

'Amazing!' Gianluca's eyes flared as he scrolled. 'Caterina's one of my favorite characters in history.'

'You know about her?'

'Of course. She's a rock star.' Gianluca spoke without looking up, typing into his phone. 'Caterina was called a *virago*, which means a "churlish woman." Bold, brave, but ungovernable. She was the only woman ruler during the Renaissance, and very beautiful. The Borgias tried to kill her, so did the Medicis. Men were crazy for her when they weren't trying to conquer her.' Gianluca smiled crookedly. 'Some things never change, eh?'

Julia smiled, liking his sense of humor.

Gianluca paused, reading his phone. 'I found a few investigators, but most do divorce or paternity matters. There's one who sounds good for family searches, a Tancredi Ferrucci. Let me have your number, and I'll text you his information.'

'Thank you.' Julia told him her number, and Gianluca plugged it into his phone.

'As for Caterina Sforza, we do have a book or two about her in English. Would you like to see them?'

'Yes, if it's no trouble.'

'Not at all.' Gianluca was already on his feet. He left the garden and returned quickly with a large book bound in blue cloth. 'Here we go.'

'Perfect timing. My ride will be here soon.'

'Good. I could only find the one book. Other portraits of Caterina don't do her justice, but I like this one by Lorenzo di Credi in 1487.' Gianluca set the book down, opening it to a glossy portrait. 'You see, she was beautiful.'

Julia recoiled, caught unawares. She hadn't realized Gianluca going to bring a portrait, and it showed Caterina facing right, her eyes a blue that made Julia flash on the blue eyes from the ceiling fresco, chasing her into the vineyard. She masked her reaction while he continued talking.

'Her coloring is northern Italian. She was Milanese, the seat of Sforza power, but she's an integral part of Florentine history. Her first marriage was to Girolamo Riario, and they ruled a town called Forlì. If you ever get to see it, it tells you so much about her.'

Julia couldn't deny that Caterina's coloring was like Rossi's and even her own. 'Is Forlì far?'

'No, about two hours from Croce, in Emilia-Romagna.'

'I wonder if they have tours of her castle.'

'No, only a self-tour. I could take you and show you around. Tomorrow's my day off, if you're free. I swear, I'm not hitting on you.' Gianluca crossed himself. 'I'm just redeeming my fellow Florentines.'

Julia smiled. In truth, she'd love to see that castle, and Gianluca seemed to know a lot about the subject. 'Okay, thanks. I'd like to go, but not on the Vespa, right?'

'Totally, it's my sister's and I only use it in town.' Gianluca closed the book. 'I can pick you up tomorrow morning at ten. If we want to visit both locations, it'll take the day. I suggest we get an early start.'

'Okay.'

'Good, it's a plan.' Gianluca tucked the book under his arm. 'Let me show you out through our offices. There's a group of graduate students in the library, and I don't want to disturb.'

'Okay.' Julia followed him into the modern wing and a hallway lined with antique maps of Florence. They passed several offices, where women looked up from behind the desks. They craned their necks at her, and Julia got the impression that Gianluca was the library hottie.

'This is my office.' Gianluca stopped at an open door, and Julia peeked inside. His office struck her as cool, if happily cluttered. There was a big window behind his desk, and its large sill held an array of plants. Books lined both sides, and one wall held a large charcoal sketch of the library's main room, remarkable in its detail.

'That's a great drawing.'

'Thank you.'

'You drew it?' Julia asked, impressed.

'Yes. Here, everybody's an artist or thinks they are. I'm the latter.'
Gianluca smiled. 'So have I redeemed my countrymen?'

'Yes,' Julia answered, smiling back.

'Sons of Florence, I am your champion!'

Julia called the new investigator from the car, but he didn't answer.
She left a voicemail, asking him to call back. She put down the phone
and looked outside the window, relieved to leave Florence behind.
She couldn't imagine why the man in the black ballcap had been
following her, and she doubted she'd see him again.

A wave of exhaustion washed over her, and she couldn't remember
the last time she'd slept more than a few hours. 'I'm tired,' she said
to herself.

Piero motioned to her to recline the seat.

'Thanks,' Julia said, happy to obey.

But when she woke up, it was dark.

23

Julia woke up in the car, which was parked in the driveway. Piero was gone, and lights were on inside the villa. It was dark out. She groped for her phone and touched the screen. It was 6:58 p.m. She'd slept the entire afternoon in the car.

Julia gathered her purse, got out, and entered the villa, following the aroma of tomatoes, onion, and garlic into the kitchen, where Anna Mattia was putting fresh basil on top of a delicious-looking platter of *gnocchi* covered with tomato sauce. 'Hi, Anna Mattia, sorry I slept.'

'Signora, you better?' Anna Mattia frowned, concerned, and Julia decided not to tell her about being followed.

'Yes. Dinner looks great.'

'*Grazie*. Piero pick you at Marucelliana?'

'Yes, it's beautiful. The librarian's going to take me to Forlì and Imola tomorrow to learn about Caterina Sforza.'

'Good.' Anna Mattia smiled. 'Is *gnocchi* for dinner. Tomorrow, I teach you to make?'

'Yes,' Julia said, going to wash her hands. 'Tomorrow.' After dinner, Anna Mattia went home, and Julia sat at her laptop at the dining room table researching Caterina Sforza. She plugged the name into Google and to her surprise, got a zillion results. She tried the top three and realized the avatar of Caterina Sforza appeared in *Assassin's Creed II*, a video game.

Just then her laptop pinged with an incoming text, and she glanced at the preview in the upper corner. **Julia, Your table at Vetri is almost ready! Still joining us for dinner tomorrow? Press Y to Confirm or N to Cancel.**

Oh God. Julia felt stricken. It was a reservation she'd made to celebrate her wedding anniversary. It was tomorrow, and she'd completely forgotten. She couldn't believe it. She'd lost track of time.

She felt sick with guilt. Mike hadn't even been gone a year. She eyed the text, unable to press N.

In the next moment, the laptop screen flickered, pixelated, and went completely black. She glanced at the bar. She hadn't lost Internet. She didn't know what the matter was. She hit Enter a few times, but it didn't come back.

She was about to click Restart but her screen saver flickered to life, a selfie of her and Mike. Their heads were touching, and they were grinning ear to ear. He was in his white Fightin' Irish T-shirt, his freckles on full display. They'd been at the farmers' market, their Saturday-morning errand, picking goat cheese, a running debate. She liked it plain but he liked jalapeño.

Jules, try it, just once.

Is this a love test?

Of course, silly.

Suddenly the selfie began to dematerialize on the screen. The faces pixelated and then disintegrated. The screen flickered to black. The laptop slammed closed with a *smak!*

Julia recoiled, gasping. The lights in the room went off, plunging her into darkness. She tried to get up but couldn't. She tried to scream but no sound came out.

Her laptop rose into the air, levitating inch by inch in front of her.

She felt stark, cold fear. She struggled to get up and run away. She couldn't move.

Her laptop flew against the wall, crashed with a loud *bam*, and fell to the floor. She was pinned to her chair. Next her laptop opened like a huge maw, blasting intense blue light at her.

Julia tried to shield her eyes. She couldn't move her arms. The blue light enveloped her, engulfed her, drowned her in a sea of blue, seeping into her body, entering her through her eyes, its color the electric blue of Caterina's eyes, then the cobalt blue of the hoodie, then the lapis lazuli of the Zodiac fresco, and suddenly she was *in* the Zodiac calendar on the domed ceiling of the entrance hall.

She began spinning into the air, whirling faster and faster past the golden glyphs of the Zodiac signs, then the Zodiac signs themselves. She screamed and screamed to stop spinning but she only spun faster and faster, whirling around, and she put out her arms to slow herself but it didn't work, and in the next moment, there was nothing she could do to protect herself from Taurus goring her in the chest with his pointed horns, stabbing her again and again until she gushed blood from every wound, spewing all around her, spattering hot red lifeblood all over the Zodiac signs, hideously warm on her face.

A scarlet Cancer the Crab grabbed her with gigantic pincers, then suddenly there were ten crabs, then a hundred, then a thousand giant crabs plucking out her eyes, tearing off her skin, ripping muscles from her bones until she was nothing but a skeleton spinning madly on its own rotation. Leo the Lion gobbled up her bones, crunching them, swallowing her down, and the Scorpion poisoned her with his tail, pumping venom into her, then all of the Zodiac signs were whirling around her, all of their glyphs whizzing past her.

She was spinning and spinning into orbit herself, corkscrewing past the burning blazing fireball of the Sun and spiraling farther and farther away from Earth and into the blue black of the cosmos and she cried out and screamed, trying to get back but she couldn't, her own rotation was on a trajectory that couldn't be reversed, passing Jupiter, then Saturn and Uranus, expelled from the solar system beyond Neptune and Pluto and into space.

She felt the sheer terror of being so alone, all alone in the blackness and the void without depth and without end, and it turned cold then freezing and blacker and bluer until she saw Mike's eyes fix like ice and she was dying out here in the nowhere away from Earth, away from people, away from life, away from everything until she was sucked into a bluish black darkness.

Julia was running for the front door. She didn't know if she was in space or on Earth. She didn't know what was happening. She tore the door open and it flew off the hinges and zoomed into space and she raced outside into the cold dark night.

'Anna Mattia!' Julia barreled toward their carriage house and down the hill, half-running and half-tripping. She panted hard, her breath ragged from exertion and fear.

She had to keep going. She didn't know if she was spinning or running.

The lights went on in the carriage house. Piero hustled out bare-chested in his pants. Anna Mattia was on his heels, closing her robe.

'Help!' Julia ran to them and buried herself in Anna Mattia's arms, trying to hold on to something, to feel something warm and human beneath her fingers, something soft and solid, and *real*.

'Signora, Signora, is okay!' Anna Mattia rocked her like a child. 'Is okay!'

'Please, please, please, help me,' Julia said, sagging to the ground.

Later, Julia stood in the dining room with Anna Mattia and Piero, ashamed, appalled, and unable to even speak. Everything was back to normal. The lights were on. Her laptop sat on the table, intact and open. There was no blue light anywhere. It looked as if nothing had ever happened at all.

Julia was losing her mind, bit by bit. It couldn't have been a nightmare because she wasn't asleep, unless she'd fallen asleep. It felt more like a dream, a vision, a spell, but it was horrible, so horrible. She never wanted to experience anything like that again, but she feared that she would, that it was inevitable as long as she was in this house, as long as Caterina was here somewhere and maybe even Rossi, too, all of the spirits alive and dead, all of them with her, all of the time.

Anna Mattia looked down, pursing her lips. Piero stood by the wall, his face in solemn lines. He held a pistol, which Julia knew couldn't help her now.

'This has to stop,' she said, hushed.

But she didn't know who she was talking to.

24

The Tuscan night was cool and dark, and the air was filled with sounds Julia couldn't identify. She sat at the rusty table in the overgrown garden while Piero was searching the villa and Anna Mattia was closing up. They'd offered Julia to sleep at their house, and she'd accepted, but she wanted to call Courtney first. The call connected, and Julia said, 'Hey, I'm sorry to wake you—'

'Honey, what's the matter?' Courtney asked, alarmed. 'Are you okay?'

'I'm kind of upset.' Julia bit her lip not to cry.

'What's going on? Another nightmare?'

'No, I was awake, on the laptop.' Julia wiped her eyes and told her everything that happened in the dining room.

'Blue lights? Zodiac signs?' Courtney groaned. 'Jules, come home.'

'Look, I know it's crazy, and I don't know why it's happening, or what's happening to me—'

'Sell that place. Get on a plane ASAP.'

'I can't. Something's going on here—'

'Yes, you're losing your damn mind.'

I might be, I am, I feel it. 'Look, I admit I don't know what it is, but something *is* happening. I feel like this blue light is related to Caterina somehow. Remember, it came off the ceiling fresco, the portrait of her—'

'Is it a ghost? Is that what you're saying?'

'I don't know, I'm not saying it's her *ghost*, I'm saying it's like her *presence*, like it's *related* to her. And the hoodie of the guy who killed Mike, it was blue, too, and I have to figure out what's going on, I can't leave here now. You know, everybody thinks Rossi was crazy. What if the blue light came to her, whether it's Caterina or not? What if it was a vision of some kind?' Julia looked up, but there were no answers in the velvety black sky, shimmering with twinkling stars. 'It's about me somehow—'

'Jules, please. You're scaring me. These dreams, they're from PTSD. Please, why don't you call Susanna?'

'No, no, no.' Julia knew Susanna couldn't help. She didn't think anybody at home could help. It was all about her, here, and she had to help herself.

'Then come home now. Sell the—'

'It's not about the villa anymore. It's about me, finding out who I am.'

'Even if it isn't good for you?'

'It *is* good for me,' Julia shot back, but she knew it wasn't. It couldn't be. She was falling apart, maybe even going insane. She didn't know where it ended, but she couldn't stop it now, either.

'But you can't stay, it's destroying you!'

Julia's throat caught. 'It's not—'

'Of course it is! You're *seeing things*.'

'I can handle it, I'm stronger than you think. Stronger than *I* think.'

'Is this your horoscope now? Am I talking to Cancer the Crab?'

Julia shuddered, thinking of the crabs that tore her to pieces. She couldn't speak for a moment.

'Stop with that astrology crap. Listen to me. I've known you since high school, and it's a fucking *app*.'

'It's real—'

'No, it's not—'

'It is—'

'Then fine!' Courtney snapped. 'If you want to believe that, knock yourself out. You insist on believing it. Do what you want and don't ask for my blessing.'

'I'm not—'

'Then why did you wake me up?'

'I'm sorry, I was upset,' Julia answered, guilt-stricken. She never should have called Courtney. It was selfish.

'You're putting yourself in a terrible situation! You have to help yourself and the way to do that is to come the fuck home.'

'I can't, not yet.' Julia wanted to end the conversation. She had to calm down. She had to get it together. She knew she wasn't making sense. She was crazy and now she was driving Courtney crazy. It was late, and Piero and Anna Mattia were probably waiting for her, wanting to go back to bed. She'd put them through enough for one night, for two even. 'Look, I have to go, I'm sorry I bothered you—'

'Jules, really? You're hanging up?'

'I have to, I have to go to bed.'

'Okay, then go.' Courtney cleared her throat. 'I'm going back to bed, too.'

Julia swallowed hard. 'Love you.'

'Love you, too. Get some sleep.' Courtney paused. 'And Jules? Be careful.'

25

The next morning, Julia ate breakfast in the kitchen rather than the dining room. She'd spent a sleepless night on Anna Mattia's couch, and the sleep deprivation was making it hard to process what was going on. Anna Mattia and Piero looked even more concerned about her mental state than before. They were both silent, and Anna Mattia kept stealing glances at her while she scarfed down strapazzato, or scrambled eggs, and toasted rustic bread with sunflower seeds.

Julia read her horoscope again while she finished her meal.

You've heard the saying: It's always darkest before the dawn. You're entering the darkest. Stay strong. Surround yourself with those who support you, not those who restrict you.

Tell me about it. Julia worried that things were about to get worse, and her horoscope had a heartbreaking resonance after her fight with Courtney. They'd never had cross words, and it felt as if a rift was forming between them, which upset Julia at soul level. Plus she respected Courtney's opinion; it made her doubt herself.

Suddenly her cell phone rang, and she hoped it was Courtney calling back. She checked the screen, but it was Franco. She picked up. 'Yes, Franco?'

'Julia, how are you this morning?'

'I'm fine. You?'

'Wonderful! I have excellent news. We got a fantastic offer on the property. Two million one hundred euro in *cash*.'

'Really?' Julia asked, amazed. 'But how? They haven't even seen it.'

'I told you I had excellent contacts. I sent them pictures. There is a class who will buy sight unseen.'

'Do they realize how much work it needs?'

Franco hesitated. 'They want to tear it down.'

'Tear it *down*?' Julia asked, aghast. She rejected the notion, but had a second thought. Her brain was so jumbled, so were her emotions. Maybe Courtney was right, and she should sell. This place had been nothing but a house of horrors, especially after last night.

Anna Mattia scowled, turning to the sink.

Franco was saying, 'Julia, teardowns are an option for these buyers. This couple has a villa on Lake Como and they want to buy here. They intend to rebuild the villa, compatible with the region and zoning. The property will be beautiful again. The vineyard can come back. He's a wine connoisseur, he wants to dabble as a vintner.' Franco's tone turned pleading. 'This offer is excellent. Please, be reasonable.'

Julia rubbed her forehead. She couldn't *destroy* a villa that meant so much to Rossi. 'My answer is no, for a teardown.'

'But why? You said it was a ruin. It *is*.'

'I just can't do it. No teardowns.'

Franco groaned. 'Don't you want to think about it? We have time.'

'No. Now I have to go. Thank you.'

'Certainly, thank you,' Franco said, rallying.

'Goodbye.' Julia hung up, meeting Anna Mattia's eye. 'Okay? No teardowns?'

Anna Mattia smiled slightly, which was all she had to say.

Julia pocketed her phone and finished the last of her eggs. She rose, gathering her silverware, plate, and dirty napkin. She was crossing to the sink when Anna Mattia intercepted her, taking her plate and meeting her eye.

'Signora, I go church today, I pray for you. God will 'elp you not to suffer.'

Aw. 'Thank you,' Julia said, meaning it. She'd take all the help she could get.

They both turned to the unaccustomed sound of an engine in the driveway. Julia realized it was Gianluca, but seeing him was the last thing she was up for, after last night. 'That's him.'

'Okay.' Anna Mattia began rinsing the plate, and Julia went outside to find Gianluca standing with a shiny red motorcycle that read *Ducati* on the side. It was large, with a short, slanted windshield and a sleekly aerodynamic design. Its chrome exhaust pipes gleamed in the sun, and on its black leather seat rested two gray helmets.

'Didn't we agree no motorcycles?' Julia asked, dismayed.

'We agreed no *Vespas*.' Gianluca grinned, walking over and greeting her European-style, with kisses on the cheeks. 'You look great.'

'Thank you.' Julia hadn't tried to look great. It had been all she could do to get it together. She had on a white turtleneck to hide her neck scratches, a light white cotton sweater, and jeans. Meanwhile Gianluca looked handsome in his skinny jeans, black quilted jacket, and another cool scarf. But they were just friends, and it was her wedding anniversary.

'A motorcycle is the best way to see Tuscany. You're going to love it. Don't worry.'

'I *am* worried.' Julia had to come clean. 'Gianluca, if we were on a highway with a lot of traffic and a lot of people, I'd be nervous.'

'Got it.' Gianluca raised a hand. 'Then we can avoid the highways altogether. We can drive slowly and take the back roads. Truly, it's more scenic anyway. It will take longer, but that's fine with me, and if you feel uncomfortable, you let me know. Okay?'

'Really?' Julia didn't know what to do. She was too tired to fight with him and she wanted to go to Forlì.

'I promise, you'll be fine.'

'Okay,' Julia agreed reluctantly.

'By the way, I brought you some books about Caterina Sforza. My friend at another library had them.' Gianluca slipped off a black backpack. 'Here.'

'Thanks,' Julia said, grateful. She took the heavy backpack as Anna Mattia arrived at her elbow. 'Anna Mattia Vesta, this is Gianluca Moretti.'

'*Piacere*, Signora Vesta.' Gianluca shook her hand, and Anna Mattia said something to him in stern Italian, which caused him to nod.

Julia watched the exchange. 'Anna Mattia, what did you say?'

Anna Mattia wagged a finger. 'I say, Drive good!'

Gianluca brightened. 'Julia, is *this* the villa? It's *magnificent*!' He faced the villa, beaming, and spread his arms. 'It's art, it's beauty, it's history, all of a *piece*!'

'Come on, it needs work.'

'It needs *love*! Villas like this are *impossible* to come by!' Gianluca kept his arms open, as if to hug the villa. 'You should move into this masterpiece! Who *wouldn't* want this villa! You can't *buy* these anymore. Please, don't sell.'

'I might,' Julia had to admit.

'You're killing me!' Gianluca's hands flew to his chest. He staggered backward as if he'd been wounded, threw himself down on the driveway, and lay there as if dead.

Julia flashed horribly on Mike, stabbed to death. On this of all days. Her chest went tight.

'Julia?' Gianluca popped his head up, his grin faded. 'Are you okay?' He scrambled to his feet. 'What's the matter?'

'Nothing.' Julia managed a smile. 'Let's get going.'

The red Ducati thrummed along the back roads of Chianti in the sunshine, and Julia tried not to think about Mike, the villa, or last night. She felt jittery, but Gianluca kept his promise and drove slowly. There were microphones in their helmets so they could talk to each other, and the traffic was light. They passed three-wheeled farm vehicles he told her were called Aps, and a quaint mule cart that would have been at home in any era.

Gianluca pointed out the sights as they drove through vast fields of sunflowers, olive groves, and vineyards, stone farmhouses with grazing horses, flocks of sheep and goats, and cows basking in the sun. The fresh air carried the scent of fennel and lavender, like aromatherapy on wheels.

They reached a two-lane road that had more traffic, and Julia acclimated herself to the bike and was able to move with the turns. She got used to the other traffic, even picking up snippets of conversations from open windows of the cars. They passed one small white Fiat, and its mustachioed driver blew cigar smoke out the window.

She spotted a sign for Forlì and they entered the city. It was modern, unlike a medieval town like Croce, and modest homes and apartments with amber and melon-colored facades lined its circuitous streets. Shops of all types were everywhere, and traffic was brisk.

Julia saw signs for Caterina Sforza's castle, Rocca di Ravaldino, and Gianluca pointed to a massive medieval fortress ahead, which looked like a smaller version of Castello Sforzesco in Milan. It had similar brick walls, embossed arches, and round turrets, rising incongruously among the satellite dishes, as if the past were crashing the present.

They got closer, reaching wooded grounds spanning ten city blocks, occupied by Caterina Sforza's castle. Its red brick facade soared into the sky some ten stories, anchored by round, wide turrets with red tile roofs. Battlements extended around a huge wall covered by overgrown ivy, greenery, and flowers. There were several arched entrances, and each had a drawbridge over a dry moat. There wasn't a soul in sight, neither tourists nor residents.

Gianluca slowed down, heading for the small parking lot, which was empty.

Suddenly Julia experienced the strangest sensation.

That she was coming home.

26

Julia and Gianluca walked across the drawbridge to Caterina Sforza's castle, bought tickets at a retrofitted office, then entered a walled courtyard several stories high, constructed of narrow bricks that had faded to a soft orange over centuries. The castle was quiet and still, and there wasn't another tourist in sight.

Julia looked around, getting the uncanny feeling she was safe here. Her breathing was normal, and so was her heart rate. It was a relief, even if it was hard to understand. Maybe because the walls were so thick and she was decidedly Inside. After all, the castle was a fortress. Caterina's fortress.

Julia kept her thoughts to herself as they entered a dim, cavernous corridor, where it was cooler. The walls were of stone and rough plaster, crumbling in spots, and the floor was brick, set in diagonal patterns. There were no windows, but the darkness was companionable rather than frightening.

Gianluca smiled as they walked along. 'I can play tour guide, if you like. I studied for our field trip.'

'You did?' Julia asked, surprised. Her research into Caterina Sforza last night had been interrupted by a blue ghost, a vision, or whatever.

'I'm a librarian, so it's my job to be a know-it-all.' Gianluca grinned crookedly. 'I don't want you to think I'm mansplaining, as my sister says. She's a feminist, so's my mother. That's why I'm so enlightened.'

Julia smiled. 'Go for it.'

'So, to begin.' Gianluca gestured to the rooms as they walked along. 'This castle is Rocca di Ravaldino and it was Caterina's home for most of her life. As you know, she was the daughter of the Duke of Milan, came to Forlì from there, and was married at fourteen to Girolamo Riario. The Riarios were a noble family, but not as noble or important as the Sforzas. He was a power-hungry guy and takes his place in history as an organizer of the Pazzi conspiracy against the Medicis, which failed. Another noble family, the Orsis, later murdered him.'

What? Julia stopped walking, struck by the similarity to her own life. 'Caterina's husband was murdered?'

'Yes, stabbed to death.'

No! Julia flashed on Mike, falling to the sidewalk.

Gianluca paused, eyeing her. 'What? Have I said the wrong thing?'

'No, it's okay.' Julia was surprised he noticed, then decided to explain. 'Well, my husband Mike was murdered. I was mugged, and he died protecting me.'

'My God.' Gianluca recoiled, grimacing. 'I'm so sorry, I assumed it was natural causes. Please forgive me.'

'No apology's necessary,' Julia rushed to say.

'That must've been horrifying.' Gianluca's dark gaze searched her face, his expression undisguised empathy, which touched her.

'Thanks, but please, finish what you were saying about Caterina.' Julia didn't want to *trauma-dump*, a term her therapist used, but she didn't understand how that was different from confiding in someone.

'Okay.' Gianluca nodded, cautiously. 'Caterina ruled alone after Riario's death, and this castle was designed by her and built to her specifications. She was truly ahead of her time. She once said, "If I must lose because I am a woman, I want to lose like a man."' Gianluca paused. 'But she was also a mother and had a domestic side that's embodied in this castle. You'll see what I mean when we get to the top. That vantage point lets you see the part of the castle that was the most special to her.'

'Let's go,' Julia said, on impulse. 'We can start there and work our way down.'

'Good idea.' Gianluca turned around in the dim room, but there was more than one exit. 'I forget how to get to the top. You'd think they'd have signage.'

'I think it's this way.' Julia followed a hunch and ended up leading Gianluca through an archway and down a cavernous hall.

'How do you know where you're going?' Gianluca looked over, puzzled. 'I've been here twice and couldn't have told you which archway to take.'

'I'm guessing.' Julia didn't understand it herself.

'You have an excellent sense of direction.'

'Maybe,' Julia said, but she didn't. She led Gianluca down another hallway, then the route became obvious and they walked together from room to room. Each one was bare and dim, with tiny windows in thick walls and a brick floor. Their footsteps echoed on the hollow stone, and there were no other tourists at all.

They turned the corner, and Julia came face-to-face with a fresco of the Sforza coat of arms, which had the same blue vipers and black dragons as the one on the ceiling over Rossi's bed. She shuddered. 'You see this, the Sforza coat of arms? There's one in my bedroom in the villa.'

Gianluca's eyes rounded. 'Are you serious?'

'Yep, a fresco of the Sforza family tree, starting with Caterina's mother and her father. Rossi, who might be my grandmother, commissioned it.'

'So she really believed it. And if she's your grandmother, you're a Sforza, too.'

'Weird, huh?'

'No, *awesome*.' Gianluca grinned. 'I love Italian history, and you *are* Italian history.'

Julia laughed, which she hadn't in a long time.

'You know, Rossi could very well have been a Sforza.' Gianluca's eyes flashed with interest behind his glasses. 'Caterina was illegitimate and she also gave birth to illegitimate children, in secret.'

'She did?'

'Yes, after the death of her husband, she fell in love with Giacomo Feo. His brother Tomasso was the castellan here, which is like the manager.' Gianluca warmed to his topic as they resumed walking down the hall. 'Caterina and Giacomo had children together and eventually married, declaring their children legitimate much later. Caterina hid her pregnancies from the Forlivese because she would have lost her right to rule. She eventually found true love with a

Medici, who was her soul mate. He loved books as much as she did.' Gianluca smiled. 'Obviously, her love of books speaks to me.'

Me, too. 'So Rossi's claim that she was a Sforza could be true?'

'Yes, for sure. Children born outside of a marriage couldn't be claimed because of the influence of the Church. Births were recorded under new names or went unrecorded.'

Julia remembered that Lombardi had said the same thing, back in Milan.

'It's because there were so many illegitimate births in those days.'

'I guess *I'm* illegitimate,' Julia blurted out. 'I think of myself as adopted, but I was probably born outside of a marriage.'

Gianluca cringed. 'What's the matter with me today? I'm trying to impress you and—'

'No, not at all,' Julia rushed to say. 'What you said has a weird application to me. I never thought of it in a historical context.'

'Well, I majored in history and tend to see everything that way.' Gianluca smiled. 'History is about the story of human beings over time. We fall in love, and sometimes we make children. It's profoundly human.'

Julia liked his view. 'Agree. Now let's go to the top.'

They ascended brick ramps that led to one landing after the next, then climbed a cramped, narrow set of stairs, so narrow they fit one person at a time. Julia went first, reached the top, and emerged into the warm sunshine. Wind blew her hair wildly, and she looked around. There was a brick wall at the perimeter with a crenellated stretch.

Gianluca came after her, his hair blowing, too. 'Quite a view, huh?'

'Yes.' Julia scanned Forlì from above, a lively clutter of red tile roofs, a church spire, and buildings dotted with cypresses, palm trees, and umbrella pines. Closest to the castle were apartment houses, little shops, and the traffic rotary lined with parked cars.

'These are the battlements, or the ramparts, of the castle.'

'It's beautiful up here.' Julia found herself taking a few steps down the walkway, which spanned the length of the castle, with arches spaced at regular intervals. Something made her stop in the middle, for some reason.

Gianluca arrived at her side. 'This is where Caterina took her famous stand.'

'What stand?' Julia asked, not completely surprised. She'd *known* it.

'Florentine history is the story of wealthy families fighting each other for power. When Caterina became a widow, she had to defend Forlì alone. The town was valuable because of its location between Florence and Milan, and the Borgias and the other royal families wanted to rule it.' Gianluca paused. 'Caterina faced down an invading army at Rocca di Ravaldino. I mean *physically* faced, as a commander, a ruler, a *warrior*, on this very spot.'

Julia felt a tingle. The thought that Caterina herself was guiding her popped into her mind.

'The army demanded the castle in return for one of her children, whom they had captured and taken hostage. You know what she did? She famously lifted her skirt, showed them her privates, and said, "Kill him, I can make more!"'

'What?' Julia recoiled. It *felt* wrong. 'She didn't mean it. She must have been bluffing.'

'I believe that, too. It was simply the most outrageous thing a woman of the time could say, and she knew it. But that story was recorded by historians, all men, chief among them Machiavelli. He made her look like a bad mother, for all time. He did it for revenge.'

'Revenge for what?'

'Because she had previously outwitted even him. He thought she would give up her castle and tried a subterfuge to seduce her. She let him think it was working, then tricked him and threw him out. It humiliated him, since everyone knew about it, even his idol Cesare Borgia.' Gianluca's dark eyes twinkled. 'Anyway, she saved the castle, vanquished the bad guys, and got her children back.'

'Wow.' Julia could see why Rossi idolized Caterina.

'Right?' Gianluca nodded. 'She was brilliant, too. She read widely, even as a child. It's well known that she loved Boccaccio's *The Lives of Famous Women*, which was about strong women from ancient history and mythology. I personally think she modeled herself after those stories. She was completely self-actualized, and it's a testament to the power of books, if you ask me.'

Julia liked watching his face light up when he talked, his intellect engaged.

'She loved the sciences, too, like astronomy and astrology.'

'Astrology?' Julia's ears perked up.

'Yes, astrology was huge at the Sforza court. Her father employed several court astrologers. One very famous one, Cardona. She employed astrologers too, and consulted them all the time.'

Whoa. 'Do you know her birthday?' Julia couldn't resist asking.

'Historians think it's probably November 25, in 1462.'

'So, Sagittarius. That means she was bold, liked risks, and was an adventurer. Sounds right, doesn't it?'

'Totally. I'm a Scorpio. Intense, passionate, *magnetic*.' Gianluca flared his eyes comically.

Julia laughed, wondering if he was flirting, then had an odd thought. 'Was she a gardener?'

'Yes, I'll show you.' Gianluca led her across the ramparts, and Julia fell into step beside him, though she already sensed where they were going. The rampart widened, and there were other sections of the castle set off by stone walls. They kept going until they reached a smaller courtyard closest to the center of the castle, and they looked down over the wall onto a messy tangle of overgrown white and pink wildflowers, bushes, and trees.

Gianluca leaned a hand on the wall. 'This was her garden. She was an amateur botanist, too. She grew herbs and plants for salves. She became one of the foremost authorities on homeopathic medicine at the time.'

Julia eyed the garden and felt her thoughts transported. Images of flowers and herbs and plants flickered through her mind. She knew it was her imagination running away with her, but she let it go.

'Caterina designed the garden so it was the most protected place of the castle. She wanted it to be safe, and a paradise for her and her children. She called it *Paradiso*.'

'It's like the center of the castle is the heart of the woman.'

'Yes, exactly.' Gianluca glanced over with a smile. 'You have a feel for her.'

'I guess I do.' Julia realized it was the perfect way to describe what was happening. She *had a feel* for Caterina.

'Why do you think that is? Do you think you're related to her?' Gianluca eased onto the wall to listen, his head tilted. His manner encouraged Julia to answer, but she was torn.

'If I tell you, you'll think I'm crazy.'

'No, I won't,' Gianluca said softly.

'I'm starting to think I might be related to her, because I feel safe here, and that hasn't happened anywhere else.' Julia hesitated. 'I've had a hard time since my husband was killed, I don't feel safe anywhere, and now I'm having nightmares, really strange ones, and they're mostly about Caterina. One night I dreamed she came off the fresco and was chasing me. Then the next night, there was blue light from her, chasing me.' Julia watched his face carefully, but Gianluca's expression didn't change, nor did he seem to judge her. 'Then last night, I was researching her and I had a vision that a blue light came out of my *laptop*.'

'A vision?' Gianluca blinked. 'Were you asleep?'

'No.'

'Is it possible you dozed off and dreamed it? I do, when I'm working at night.'

'I suppose it's possible,' Julia answered, but she knew it was unlikely. 'The whole thing confuses me because here today, in her castle, I feel better somehow. It has to be related to Caterina, maybe she could even be guiding me. Maybe that's how I knew my way around. Is that even possible? Or am I crazy?'

'You're not crazy.' Gianluca paused. 'You're heartbroken.'

Julia swallowed hard. She *felt* heartbroken. 'I am, but what does that have to do with it?'

'It explains everything. Love is all.' Gianluca met her gaze directly. 'You're grieving a man you loved very much. You suffered a loss that broke your heart. You saw something you can never unsee and will never forget.' He touched his chest. 'That injury, it breaks your heart and your soul, too. And your sense of self. So of course, you're not yourself right now.'

Julia felt his words touch a chord. 'That's exactly how I feel, that I'm not myself.'

'So let it be,' Gianluca said, softly. 'Let yourself grieve and heal.'

'I grieve plenty, but I don't know how to heal. I have a therapist and coping mechanisms and everything.'

'Keep grieving. *Grieving* heals you. The crying, the talking, the nightmares, the memories, those things are part of grieving, and in time the grieving will be less acute, and you'll begin to feel like yourself again.'

Julia hoped he was right.

'You can't avoid the sadness. You mustn't try. Nor can you wait for it to end so you can be magically healed. There's no line between sadness and happiness, like borders of a country. Sometimes sadness leads to happiness and sometimes both emotions exist in the same space at the same time.' Gianluca spoke with feeling. 'I know how loss feels. I had a broken heart, too.'

'What happened?' Julia asked, feeling like they were making a connection, and she realized that she hadn't felt connected to anybody in a long time. Since the rift with Courtney, she'd never been so alone.

Gianluca put up a hand. 'I'll tell you, but first, please understand I'm not making any parity between what happened to you. I experienced loss but not as earth-shattering as yours.'

'I understand.'

'I thought I met the love of my life, but she gave back my ring. She decided not to marry me.' Gianluca's dark curls blew away from his face, revealing a mask of pain. 'We were together for three years, engaged for six months. She was an Australian studying here, but she decided she wanted us to move back to Sydney, and I agreed to go with her. I quit my job, sold my furniture and books, and I said goodbye to my family. I was ready to leave everything for her. I was *happy* to. Love is all. Nothing matters more.' Gianluca shook his head, smiling ruefully. 'On the way to the airport, she told me she fell in love with another man.'

'Oh no.' Julia felt terrible for him. 'That must have been awful.'

'It was, and I was a mess. I went home and cried like a small child for days. I drank, I drew terrible sketches. I reread all of Shakespeare.'

Gianluca chuckled. 'I borrowed my sister's book of his complete works, and the pages *warped* with my tears. When I returned the book, she thought I dropped it in the bathtub.'

'Ouch.' Julia knew the feeling.

'But it's behind me now. She wasn't the love of my life, and my broken engagement is another event in my personal history.' Gianluca shrugged. 'If I may say so, Italians don't deal with their emotions the same way as Americans. We don't diagnose our feelings, like illnesses. You may call your feelings anxiety or PTSD or whatever you wish, but really, simply, you're sad. You're very sad.' Gianluca held out his hands, palms up. 'Please, if you would, put your hands in mine.'

Julia did, reluctantly, and his palms felt warm and soft. She realized she hadn't been touched by a man since Mike, and somehow the skin-to-skin contact made her emotional. She didn't know what to say, so she didn't say anything.

'You miss someone you loved very much, and since he died in a terrifying way, in front of you, you're afraid to do things, to go out, to explore, to have fun, to be free. You've lost your peace of mind. It's normal and reasonable. Do you understand what I'm saying?'

'Yes.' Julia did, and it lifted her burden a little.

'We experience powerful emotions, they're as human as breathing and they change over time. They wax and wane—'

'Like the moon,' Julia interrupted him, and Gianluca nodded.

'Yes, like the moon, the tides, the seasons, all of the natural world. Your feelings will change and you'll move through sadness. It's just too soon.'

Julia's throat thickened. 'You think it explains Caterina, today?'

'Yes, that, too. I don't know why you're feeling her, but maybe you're simply *feeling* more, since you've gone through so much. Maybe you're more intuitive now. Maybe she really *is* showing you the way. You say you had a vision, maybe you're more visionary than before. Who knows?' Gianluca smiled softly. 'In my belief system, it's entirely possible that Caterina is guiding you, for a reason we don't know and can't know. So you're not creepy or crazy for feeling it, or her.' He squeezed her hands, let them go, then took a silly bow. 'End of lecture.'

Julia laughed, feeling better. 'Good talk.'

'I agree. I'm enjoying getting to know you. Sorry, I go on and on.'

Julia thought, *The gift of the gab*, but didn't say so. 'That's so Sagittarius of you.'

Gianluca laughed, then glanced at his watch. 'It's getting late, and we should move on to Caterina's other castle. It's in Imola, another town on the way home.'

'Okay.' Julia turned to go, and her gaze fell on the traffic rotary on the street. She spotted a white Fiat parked among a few other cars, then wondered if she'd seen it before. She didn't know why it mattered, but she couldn't ignore it.

'Hey, do you see the white Fiat down there?'

Gianluca squinted, shading his eyes. 'Yes.'

'We passed one on the way here. The driver was smoking a cigar.'

'That's a Fiat 500, a common car. Why?' Gianluca blinked, and Julia saw no reason to hold back anymore.

'Do you remember when I was being followed at the Uffizi? You said you thought he wanted to ask me out? I don't think that's what it was.'

Gianluca frowned. 'What do you think?'

'I don't know, but a man in a black ballcap was following me.'

'Was the Fiat driver the same man?'

'No, the Fiat driver was stockier and older. He has a mustache and smokes cigars.'

Gianluca blinked. 'So you think two different men are following you?'

Julia knew it would sound nuts, even to him. 'Maybe?'

'We'll check him out outside.'

Julia agreed, and they headed for the exit.

But by the time they got downstairs and crossed the drawbridge, the white Fiat was gone.

27

Julia stood with Gianluca in Imola, outside the grounds of Caterina's castle. It looked like a scaled-down version of Rocca di Ravaldino, but it was closed due to flooding. Sandbags and orange plastic fences prevented access to the castle and its grounds. Sand, gravel, and lumber lay mounded around the property in mid-cleanup, though there were no workmen or construction vehicles.

'I'm sorry.' Gianluca scrolled his phone, frowning. 'It doesn't say on the website that the castle is closed. I thought the flood damage would have been cleared by now. I should have called ahead. I'm a bad librarian.'

'No, you're not.' Julia didn't know if she wanted to see another of Caterina's castles anyway. The first one had been enough drama for one day, and she'd been newly nervous on the way here, keeping an eye out for the white Fiat. 'I didn't see a white Fiat, did you?'

'No.' Gianluca pocketed his phone. 'Thanks for making the best of a bad situation. For what it's worth, this castle is similar inside, but smaller. Imola's a smaller town than Forlì, too.' He perked up. 'You want to know a fun fact about Imola? Its town map was drawn by Leonardo da Vinci himself, shown from above. He made it by pacing his way around the town, then drew it as if from the air. You know, the Sforza family was a major patron of Leonardo's. Caterina's uncle Ludovico Sforza commissioned him to paint *The Last Supper*.'

'How cool is that? I have to read up, don't I?'

'Yes.' Gianluca smiled. 'But now that we have extra time here in Imola, there's something else worth seeing. We can grab lunch, too.'

AUTODROMO INTERNAZIONALE ENZO E DINO FERRARI, read the sign, or International Speedway of Enzo and Dino Ferrari. Evidently, the

Imola raceway was the site of the Emilia-Romagna Grand Prix on the Formula One racing circuit and other motorsports. Julia had been surprised to learn there was a major racetrack in this small town, but on the way here, she'd heard the roar of car engines through her helmet. Today was a practice session for a race called 6 Hours of Imola, which was endurance racing with four-man teams of the top drivers in the world.

Julia held on to Gianluca's waist, feeling more comfortable now that they'd broken the seal on touching each other. She kept an eye out for the white Fiat, but hadn't seen it, so she was trying not to worry about it anymore. Gianluca accelerated as they traveled the road to the racetrack, which wound through gorgeous parkland filled with greenery, cypresses, and, incongruously, engine noise.

They came to a large grassy field, and at the far side was a stretch of asphalt racetrack surrounded by cyclone fence with barbed wire. They reached a large parking lot filled with Ferraris, Lamborghinis, and Maseratis. Gianluca parked, cut the ignition, and they took off their helmets. Conversation wasn't possible with the engine noise, and Gianluca motioned to her and they hurried across the grass to the racetrack, where a small crowd watched from behind a cyclone fence and metal rail.

They reached the track, and it was thrilling to see sleek race cars zoom past like rockets, a streaking blur of enameled color, their deafening engines blasting full-throttle. Julia was able to lose herself in the excitement and speed, and the crowd was small and spread out enough that she didn't feel panicky. In time, the cars stopped coming, and the engine noise died off with a break in the action. The crowd at the rail started talking excitedly, resuming conversation and lighting cigarettes.

Gianluca looked over with a grin. 'Well? Do you like it?'

'Totally!'

'I come here whenever I can. It's not F1, but it's awesome.'

'Agree.' Julia thought it was cute that he was a librarian who liked to go fast. She liked the layers of his personality. There was an intriguing complexity to him, but he seemed to enjoy life, and she liked that, too.

'The cars are beautiful, aren't they? They have a Scuderia Ferrari F1 car inside the building. We can eat there, too.' Gianluca led the way past racing murals and a larger-than-life photograph of a handsome race car driver, with a plaque that read Ayrton Senna. Gianluca stopped, making the sign of the cross. 'This is Senna, one of the greatest F1 drivers ever. He was killed here in the San Marino Grand Prix in the 1994 season.'

Julia shuddered. 'Oh no.'

'He was trying to stay ahead of Michael Schumacher, who was new then. He hit the wall on the Tamburello curve, a crash at maybe a hundred seventy, a hundred ninety miles per hour.' Gianluca grimaced, pained. 'None of us knew how serious it was. They even restarted the race. Everybody believed he was going to be okay. He had to be. We loved him.'

'Were you here?'

'No, we watched it on TV. Everybody here did, even back then. Now F1 is so big, locals get priced out of the tickets. F1 fans mob the hotels and restaurants. Imola's too small to handle them. They overrun to Bologna and Florence.' Gianluca's gaze returned to the memorial photo. 'Every racing fan remembers where they were when Senna died. I was watching with my father. He cried so hard. We never thought it would happen to Senna. He was so good, so young, only thirty-four.'

'I'm sorry,' Julia said, thinking of Mike. 'It never seems possible that young people die, but they do, every day.'

Gianluca looked over, thoughtfully. 'You don't think it will happen, but it does. It's a paradox, isn't it? There's not many things like that.'

'Only death.'

'No that's not all. Let's go.' Gianluca took off, and Julia fell into step with him in the crowd past the scaffolding under the grandstand bleachers, then they flowed into a narrow tunnel of corrugated metal, echoing with chatter. They popped out on the other side, where there was a sleek complex of buildings painted Ferrari red. The gift shop had a predictably massive display of Ferrari ballcaps, polo shirts, and replica racing helmets, plus a real Ferrari convertible in flashy red, which Gianluca drooled over.

They reached a café, went inside, and scanned a display counter of panini and other sandwiches. The place was dim, with shiny black tables and chairs, smoked glass walls, and a polished concrete floor inlaid with red racing stripes. They joined the back of the line, which was all men.

Julia whispered to Gianluca, 'I'm the only woman.'

'I'm the only librarian,' he shot back, and they both laughed. In time they reached the front of the line, picked caprese sandwiches and beer, then took the food to the grandstand. They bought tickets for the next practice session and found seats near the finish line, where Julia tore into her sandwich. The *mozzarella* was soft, the basil fresh, and the tomato tart and salty, proving even café food was perfect in Italy.

She was about to take another bite when she noticed a man over Gianluca's shoulder, sitting on the far side. His profile looked familiar, then he raised a cigar to his mouth. 'Gianluca, don't turn around, but I see the Fiat driver.'

'Where is he sitting?'

'Third row from the front.'

'I'll look discreetly.' Gianluca bent over, put his beer on the floor, and glanced to the left. 'I see him.' He turned back to her, his dark eyes troubled behind his glasses. 'Maybe he's a racing fan.'

'Then why was he at Forlì, outside the castle?'

'We don't know he was. We know only that a white Fiat was parked there, not that it was his. I tell you, they're super common cars.' Gianluca searched her face, his handsome features softening. 'I'm not doubting you. I'm telling you not to jump to conclusions.'

Julia's appetite vanished. 'Let's leave and see if he follows us. Would you mind?'

'Not at all.' Gianluca drained his beer, Julia gathered her purse and trash, then they left the bleachers and went down the stairs. She forced herself not to look back because if White Fiat was following them, she didn't want to show her hand.

They headed for the tunnel, and the throaty roar of the engines resumed, obliterating all other sound. People were hurrying past them in the opposite direction, running to catch the practice session.

The tunnel was emptying. They would be alone. She didn't know if they would be safe.

'Give me your trash.' Julia held out her hand, and Gianluca gave her the trash as they approached the tunnel. She dropped it intentionally, picked it up, and quickly looked back when she threw it out. White Fiat wasn't following them.

'He's not there,' Julia told Gianluca, and they left the tunnel, headed for the parking lot, and reached the motorcycle.

Julia glanced over her shoulder. White Fiat was nowhere in sight. She wedged on her helmet, kicking herself. 'Sorry I made us leave. I guess I was wrong.'

'No worries. We should be getting back anyway.' Gianluca swung a leg over the motorcycle, and Julia climbed on after him, putting her arms around his waist. They left the parking lot and drove through the park, winding this way and that through the trees.

'Julia?' Gianluca said through the helmet microphone. He tilted his rearview mirror so she could see. 'Look.'

Julia checked the mirror. Three cars back was a white Fiat.

'Hold on tight.'

28

Julia kept her eye on the rearview mirror but couldn't see the white Fiat at her angle. The road wound through the park and ended in a larger two-lane highway with a barrage of signs. Gianluca steered onto the on-ramp.

Julia clung tightly to him. 'Is he still behind us?'

'Yes, two cars back.' Gianluca zoomed ahead, and Julia gritted her teeth. The highway widened to an overpass, two lanes going in both directions over a wooded valley. The shoulder was a skinny strip of gravel next to a metal guardrail.

'Are you trying to lose him?'

'No. Hang on.' Gianluca accelerated, and a white van in front of them switched to the middle lane, letting them pass. A narrow service road was coming up on the right. Suddenly, at the very last minute, Gianluca veered onto the service road.

'Where are you going?' Julia asked, surprised.

'Watch this.' Gianluca sped down the service road, which ran parallel to the highway. He kept looking over at the white Fiat.

The white Fiat moved ahead of them on the highway, where the traffic was faster. It was too far away for Julia to make out any details of the driver.

Gianluca raced to the end of the service road, entered the highway, and rejoined traffic. They ended up behind the white Fiat, so now *they* were following *him*. 'Boom! Turnabout is fair play!'

'Nice!' Julia felt a surge of excitement. She had a clear view of the white Fiat's license plate and tried to commit it to memory. 'I think I got the plate.'

'I do. Now let's see if he's the same driver.' Gianluca steered between the lanes and pulled up alongside the white Fiat. 'Is it him?'

'Yes!' Julia recognized him, balding with a mustache, a jowly face, and a cigar.

The Fiat driver looked over, his eyes flaring in alarm. Instantly he veered away into the right lane, then the shoulder, and down the highway.

'Follow him!' Julia heard herself say, on impulse. 'Let's see where he goes.'

Gianluca accelerated down the shoulder, chasing the white Fiat. They raced along the shoulder, spraying gravel. The guardrail was low. The overpass was high. If they skidded on the gravel, they'd fall off the overpass. The valley was a deep drop.

Julia lost her nerve. 'I'm getting scared.'

'I hear you.' Gianluca slowed, left the shoulder, and rejoined the traffic at normal speed. 'You okay?'

'Yes, thanks.' Julia watched the white Fiat disappear up the shoulder, out of sight. 'What the hell is going on?'

'I don't know but we have his license plate.'

'We should go to the police.'

'Great minds,' Gianluca said, grimly.

29

It was late afternoon by the time they pulled into Savernella, which was bigger than Croce, with bustling shops, restaurants, and modern stucco apartment buildings. Businesspeople hurried along the sidewalks with messenger bags and backpacks, talking on phones.

Gianluca drove uphill until they came to a wrought iron gate and a lighted sign that read CARABINIERI. Julia took in the police station, a well-maintained brick edifice with a stone foundation and iron bars on the windows. The front door was unvarnished, with an ornate knob in the middle, and embedded in the wall next to a call box was a marble sign engraved COMANDO STAZIONE.

They slowed to a stop, and Gianluca cut the ignition and held the bike for Julia to get off. 'Why did we come here instead of Croce?' she asked, wedging off her helmet.

'Croce's too small to have its own police force or administration. Savernella is the sister town, and this is where you file a police report. Lots of people who live in Croce work here, since there are more jobs.'

'I see.' Julia straightened, smoothing her hair into place. 'Thanks for taking me.'

'You're welcome. I'm sorry you're going through this.' Gianluca smiled, sympathetic. 'I can't redeem everybody. Misconduct abounds.'

Julia smiled back. 'Thanks. Let's go.'

They sat across the desk from a Marshal Alberto Torti, a fifty-something police captain with black-brown eyes and salt-and-pepper beard. He wore a dark tie and a starchy white shirt with a black sweater that read CARABINIERI above a red stripe. His black pants matched a Beretta in his waist holster. His office was spare and clean, with cream walls, an institutional desk, and official framed documents above gray file cabinets.

Gianluca started them off in Italian, then they segued into English, which Marshal Torti spoke in a formal way. Julia told him everything, beginning with the man in the black ballcap at the Uffizi, complete with her photos, and ending with the mustachioed driver of the white Fiat. Marshal Torti typed her statement on an old Dell desktop while she spoke, and it reminded her of the statements about Mike's murder she'd given in Philly. She felt as if they were filling out a form, not starting an investigation.

Julia signed the statement and passed it back to him. 'Marshal Torti, now that you have the Fiat's license plate, can you contact the driver and find out why he's following me?'

'We cannot.' Marshal Torti frowned. 'What he's done is not a crime.'

'It isn't? Do you have anti-stalking laws here?'

'Yes, but his conduct does not rise to that level.'

'Why not? He followed me to Forlì, then to Imola. That's stalking, isn't it?'

'We cannot be certain his intent was criminal.' Marshal Torti cocked his head. 'Did he threaten you?'

'Following me *is* threatening.' Julia tried not to think back to Mike's murder. 'I mean, it's obvious, people follow you, then they attack you. It's an ambush.'

'I mean, did he say words to you that could be considered a threat?'

'Well, no.'

'Did he speak with you?'

'No.' Julia had to convince him. 'If he didn't have criminal intent, why did he drive away from us when we caught him?'

Marshal Torti spread his palms. 'Ms Pritzker, if a motorcycle drove up alongside my car on a highway, I myself would feel threatened. I might drive away too. It was a reasonable response, not necessarily indicative of criminal intent.'

Shit. 'But what if these two men know each other or are connected somehow?'

'That is conjecture.'

'I know, but what are the odds of two men following me? That's why you have to investigate.' Julia realized he didn't know about her inheritance. 'I'm here because I inherited a lot of money. What if this is connected to that somehow?'

Gianluca interjected, 'She's right, Marshal Torti. An American inheriting a fortune? You know how word spreads out here. They could be plotting to kidnap her for ransom.'

Julia shuddered, wondering if he was right.

'I can't remember the last kidnapping we had out here.' Marshal Torti lifted an eyebrow, turning to Julia. 'If I may ask, how much money did you inherit?'

'About three million euros.'

Marshal Torti's eyes flew open. 'That's quite a sum!'

'That's our point. That's why I think you need to talk to the Fiat driver.'

Marshal Torti pursed his lips. 'No, we cannot. He would need to take a further step for us to intervene—'

'What does he have to do?' Julia flashed on the night of Mike's murder. 'I *know* stalking can turn deadly. My husband was killed about six months ago, in Philadelphia.'

Marshal Torti grimaced, recoiling. 'You have my condolences.'

'Thank you, but that's why I think this is dangerous.'

'The question is who created the danger.' Marshal Torti turned to Gianluca. 'Signore Moretti, why did you chase the Fiat driver? Driving between lanes and on the shoulder is unlawful. You know better. The danger was created by you.'

'That ignores what *he* did,' Gianluca shot back.

'It was my idea,' Julia interjected. 'I wanted to see where he went. Now you can look him up from his license plate.'

'Ms Pritzker, how long is your visit here?'

'It's open-ended.'

'Perhaps you should consider finishing your business and leaving.'

'*That's* your advice?' Julia asked, taken aback. Gianluca frowned.

'Yes.' Marshal Torti nodded. 'There is little we can do for you at this juncture. Self-help is always in order. As I said, the man has committed no illegality, and we do not harass our citizens. In addition, we don't have the manpower.'

'*You're* here. You could make a phone call.'

Marshal Torti rose, his expression grim. 'Our interview is over. I have your report. If there are any developments, you have my card. Thank you for your time.'

Not so fast. 'Can you tell me who the license plate belongs to?'

'No, such information is confidential. Now, please, I have matters to attend to.' Marshal Torti gestured to the door, and Julia and Gianluca left the office frustrated. They hustled down the steps and outside to the sidewalk, where she threw up her hands.

'I mean, what was that? Useless!'

'Typical small-town cop.' Gianluca shook his head. 'Wait. What about the family investigator? Tancredi? Maybe he can investigate and search the license plate. Or he might know someone who can.'

'Great idea, but he hasn't called me back yet.'

'Let me try.' Gianluca slid his phone from his pocket, made a call, and started speaking rapid Italian, then ended the call with a satisfied grin. 'Okay, Tancredi was supposed to call you but he got busy. There's another family investigator in his office, a British woman named Poppy Whitcomb. She can see you tomorrow at four o'clock.'

'I'll take it, thank you.' Julia felt a twinge of hope. 'What did they say about the license plate?'

'She can't run down the license plate. They don't really do that, but she might be able to give you a referral.' Gianluca paused. 'I didn't realize the size of your inheritance. That's a lot of money. Do you think you should leave, instead?'

'No, I want to meet the family investigator. Did you mean what you said about them wanting to kidnap me?'

'Yes, what you said to the cop convinced me. I can't explain the Fiat driver's actions in an innocent way.' Gianluca shook his head, his expression grim. 'I admit, I wasn't worried by him when we left Imola. I wasn't sure that you were being followed or if his intent was harmful. But when we pulled up beside him and he took off, that sealed it. If he weren't up to no good, he would have cursed me out. *That's* Italian.'

Julia smiled.

'That said, I think if you're careful and don't go anywhere alone, you'll be fine. I'll hang with you as much as you want. You'll be in Florence for the investigator, and I'd love to take you to dinner after.'

'Great, thanks.' Julia wondered if Gianluca wanted to be more than friends, but she would keep it that way. She liked him, but she wasn't ready for anything more.

It was still her wedding anniversary, whether Mike was alive or not.

30

Julia didn't get home until dinnertime, and she entered the villa and stopped in the dining room, where the table had already been set. She picked up her plates, silverware, and wineglass and took them into the kitchen, where Anna Mattia was sliding a baking dish from the oven, its top glistening with tomatoes.

'Perfect timing!' Julia crossed to her. 'What's for dinner?'

'*Polenta* with *mozzarella* and *broccoli rabe*, like *lasagne*.' Anna Mattia smiled, and Julia felt relieved that Anna Mattia wasn't looking at her funny, after last night.

'Okay if I eat in here, with you?'

Anna Mattia shrugged. 'You like Forlì?'

'Yes, but guess what?' Julia set the kitchen table and sat down. 'We caught another man following me.'

'*É vero?*' Anna Mattia's hooded eyes flared in surprise. 'What 'appen?'

Julia filled Anna Mattia in while she cut her a serving and placed it onto her plate, shaking her head.

'These men, they jealous your money!'

'That's what Gianluca thinks.' Julia forked the *polenta* into her mouth, aware she was eating her feelings. Luckily, they were delicious. The *polenta* tasted perfectly moist, like *lasagne*, only lighter. 'This is wonderful.'

'*Grazie*. The *carabinieri* no 'elp?'

'They say they can't. Not yet.' Julia ate some *broccoli rabe*, wondering if she was becoming addicted to garlic, and Anna Mattia poured Chianti into her glass.

'Very bad! You stay with us tonight?'

'No, thanks.' Julia hated to put them out again. 'I'll stay downstairs, maybe in the living room. I want to look over those books that Gianluca brought.'

'I put in living room. *Buon appetito.*' Anna Mattia went to the sink, and Julia ate more *broccoli rabe* while she picked up her phone. The home screen showed an email notification from 23andMe. It was the results of her ancestry test; she had sent in her saliva sample before she left Philadelphia. The subject line read: Click here for your results!

Gulp. Julia braced herself, clicked, and skimmed the top line: JULIA, your ancestry composition is 98.6% ITALIAN.

'Oh my God!' Julia almost choked on her food.

'What?' Anna Mattia turned from the sink, sponge in hand, and Julia scanned the results, incredulous. JULIA, YOU ARE 98.6% Italian from the Tuscany region, going back three generations. A tiny gray sliver in a pie chart showed that the remaining percentage of her ancestry was from northern Italy.

'I'm *Tuscan*! Three generations back, that's my *grandparents*! That could be *Rossi*!'

Anna Mattia frowned in confusion. 'So no 'merican?'

'I'm *Italian* American.' Julia felt a thrill, as if an electrical switch had been thrown. 'This is amazing! It means I actually have Italian blood.'

'You?'

'Yes! Now we know that I have Italian blood, *Tuscan* blood, that means Rossi could be my grandmother. But it doesn't mean she *is*. If I didn't have Italian blood, then I would know for sure she wasn't my grandmother.' Julia held up the phone, and Anna Mattia came over, peering at the screen. Julia pointed to the gray sliver of a pie chart. 'See this? Most of my blood is Tuscan, but some is northern Italian, maybe from Milan. Maybe Rossi *was* related to Caterina Sforza. Maybe *I* am, too!'

'*Mamma mia!*' Anna Mattia beamed, linking her fingers.

'What if Rossi really did have a child?' Julia returned her attention to the phone, scrolling quickly to the next section, which was LIVING RELATIVES. It read, JULIA, you have NO living relatives reported. She reminded herself it meant only that none of her living relatives had been tested and agreed to disclose their results. It didn't mean she *didn't* have any living relatives.

Julia kept reading, excited. The next section was a list of health information, and she read the highlights aloud: 'Guess what, I do not have the BRCA1/BRCA2 variants for breast cancer.'

Anna Mattia frowned, not understanding.

'I wonder if Rossi had it. I don't think everybody who gets breast cancer has that gene, anyway, so it probably doesn't mean anything.' Julia figured the implications. 'I don't think that necessarily means I'm not her granddaughter, either. It could mean I didn't inherit that gene. I have to ask the investigator.' She felt a surge of happiness. 'But I'm Tuscan!'

'Super Tuscan!' Anna Mattia clapped.

Julia laughed, giddy. She finally knew a fact about her own birth, for the very first time. It made her feel validated, too. Her father had German ancestry and her mother Irish, but even before they'd told her she was adopted, she'd never felt *of* them. She'd sensed she wasn't *theirs*.

And she'd been *right*.

Maybe she *was* intuitive, after all.

Later, Julia curled up on the couch in the living room, a biography of Caterina Sforza on her lap. Gianluca had brought her a wonderful stack of books, and she couldn't wait to read them. Discovering she had Tuscan ancestry excited her, but she was trying not to jump to the conclusion that she was related to Rossi, much less Caterina.

A bronze lamp on an end table shed a dim circle of light, and Piero had made a fire in the fireplace, which warmed the room and illuminated its far side. Julia exhaled, trying to metabolize the fact that the white Fiat had been following her. Piero had fixed the doors at her request, and she'd locked herself inside. But she wasn't worried only about external threats anymore. She worried about what was going on inside the house, even in her own head.

You're heartbroken.

Julia didn't know if that was why she'd been seeing things and having nightmares. She felt on tenterhooks, on guard against whatever was going to happen, if anything. *Hypervigilant*, as her therapist said. She even had a kitchen knife and a flashlight beside her. She didn't know what good they would do, but she was trying to help herself feel safe.

Julia opened the book, and her uneasy gaze fell on the line: *Even in her grief, Caterina forced herself to go on.* The words resonated in her heart. She and Caterina were both young widows, and Julia felt like she'd been forcing herself to go on ever since Mike died.

Suddenly the fireplace popped, and she startled. She looked over at the fire, checking because it didn't have a screen. Orange flames blazed and flickered on the fireback. Glowing sparks drifted up the chimney, rising like tiny orange suns. The fire flickered on the ceiling fresco of an idyllic Tuscan landscape and on the white plaster walls. There were pale rectangles where art had been hung, and the paint peeled and bubbled in patches. Cracks ran up and down the walls as if the villa could no longer bear its own weight.

Julia's attention was drawn to one of the cracks on the wall, beyond the couch. She blinked, wondering if she'd seen something.

In the next moment, a faint blue light began to stream from the crack, thin as a blue vein and ethereal as gas.

Julia gasped when it morphed into an electric blue.

Caterina.

31

Julia's heart pounded. The blue light intensified as it slipped from a crack in the wall, forming a sapphire stream, its beauty preternatural.

She dropped the book and backed up against the couch. She was shocked, but not terrified. Something about the blue light felt different than before. She didn't want to run. She had to fight her fear. She *wanted* the connection.

The blue stream materialized into a blue vapor hovering beside the wall, then gradually, incrementally, organized itself into a glowing blue silhouette of a woman wearing a hooded cloak, like Caterina in the bedroom fresco.

Julia gaped. She *sensed* Caterina's presence, her will, her wishes. Something told her that Caterina wanted to connect with her.

Suddenly Caterina filtered into the wall as if sucked through by an unseen force.

Abruptly, the living room went back to normal. The only light came from the lamps and the orangey fire.

Julia felt stunned, struck dumb. She didn't know what she'd just seen. She didn't know if she'd imagined it. Maybe she'd dozed off while she was reading, like at the laptop. She grabbed her flashlight, got off the couch, and went to the wall. She turned on the flashlight and stepped close to the surface, looking around for the crack that Caterina had gone through.

Julia spied a tiny, jagged crack, aglow with blue.

Caterina hovered back there, waiting for her.

Julia pressed on the crack. The wall gave way, just the slightest. She pressed again and heard a creak, the plaster breaking. She pushed again, harder. The crack widened like a seam, emitting more blue light.

Julia pressed hard, then shoved the seam with her shoulder again and again. Amazingly, she felt no pain. She felt adrenalized. She sensed something lay beyond the wall, something Caterina wanted her to see.

Julia needed something to break the plaster. She looked wildly around the room. There was a poker by the fireplace. She bolted there, grabbed the poker, and hurried back to the wall.

She whacked the wall with the poker. Once, then twice, three times, pounding on the wall. Flakes flew in the air. She broke the plaster and made a divot. She pounded harder and harder, beginning to sweat. She couldn't stop, feverish. The hole got wider and deeper. She reached old wire mesh embedded in the plaster.

She kept going, whacking away like a madwoman. Plaster chunks fell to the floor. More and more blue light shone through, electrifying her, filling her with its energy.

Julia whacked harder and harder. She felt stronger than ever, or maybe she was imagining it. She didn't know if she was sane or crazy, awake or asleep, but she wasn't stopping now.

The seam opened a hole. More and more blue light came through. She punched the poker through the hole, then used it like a crowbar, pressing it flat against the wall. More chunks fell down. The seam opened wider, cracking along its length, glowing like a bolt of lapis lightning all the way to the floor.

It was a *door*—if it was real. If she wasn't imagining it or having a vision. Or losing her mind or even entering a portal of some kind.

Julia dropped the poker, wedged her fingers in the hole, and began to yank on its side. She pulled and pulled, wrenching it open, its edges jagged. The plaster cracked loudly, and she kept going.

She opened the door partway and peered inside. She found herself standing in a shaft of radiant blue light.

Caterina hovered in the darkness a short distance away.

Julia's mouth went dry. They regarded each other, woman and *presence*.

Abruptly Caterina whooshed away, whisking down a long, dark chute. She grew smaller and smaller. Her blue form glowed as if farther away. Julia had no idea how far away or where Caterina was. Everywhere around her was pitch black.

Julia switched on the flashlight, her hand trembling. She flicked it around and watched its jittery circle travel over alberese stone and crumbling mortar. The air smelled musty and dank.

She was in a tunnel. She touched the wall. It felt cold, clammy, and scratchy, so it was real, or felt that way. It looked ages old, maybe from medieval times. She shone the flashlight on the floor, which was dirt and gravel.

Caterina still hovered in the distance.

Julia felt drawn to her, to see what Caterina wanted to show her. The notion terrified and thrilled her. She shone the flashlight ahead. It illuminated nothing, paling in intensity compared with the brilliant blue light emanating from Caterina.

Julia started walking. She flicked the flashlight right and left. She was getting closer to Caterina.

The air got colder and colder. She sensed she was traveling under the vineyard. The tunnel shot forward into the blue light.

She was almost at the end of the tunnel. Caterina's glowing form illuminated a solid metal door behind her.

Caterina vanished in an instant. The tunnel went dark except for the flashlight.

Julia gasped. She didn't know where Caterina had gone. But she *did* know what Caterina wanted her to do. Caterina wanted her to open the door.

Julia aimed the flashlight at the door. Its circle of light skittered along its rusted black metal. There was no doorknob, only a rusted metal keyhole with no key. She felt a tingle of fear, not knowing what could be on the other side. She wondered again if she was in some kind of nightmare, or a vision.

She braced herself, then pushed on the door. It didn't budge. She pushed it again and again. It gave way with effort, screeching. She shone the flashlight in. She saw vague black shapes and a back wall.

It was a room.

Julia cast the flashlight around and spotted a light switch, incongruously modern. She flipped the switch, illuminating the space.

She recoiled, horrified. It was a child's bedroom, discolored by black mold. Against the left wall was a single bed with mildewed pink sheets and a coverlet. Atop sat at a moldy plush purple rabbit, pink bunny, and giraffe. The headboard, night table, and a lamp were white but spotted with mold. On the opposite wall was a moldy child's dresser and a washbasin with a sliver of yellowed soap, a pink toothbrush, and a tortoiseshell comb. It must have been a little girl's room because so much was pink. An old-fashioned chamber pot sat on the floor.

Julia crossed to a child's desk blanketed with black mold. It held old Italian watercolor tins and brushes next to a stack of buckled watercolor paintings. She set down the flashlight and picked them up. The top one was of the vineyard, but it was thriving, its vines staked, rows pruned, and dark purple grapes hanging juicy and full. Julia guessed it had been painted by someone around eight or nine years old, but it was well done, as if the child had talent.

Julia flipped to the second watercolor, of a flock of fluffy white geese in a pen, which had to be the trashed one in the vineyard. The third watercolor was the villa itself, evidently as it used to be, clear of vines with its facade a warm amber and its shutters bright green. There was a fourth watercolor of a stone well that Julia didn't recognize, with hills in the background.

The last watercolor made her heart stop. It was of a little girl with blue eyes, light brown hair, and a tragic downturn to the mouth. A self-portrait of a child in emotional agony.

Appalled, Julia put it together. This bedroom was a prison cell. A little girl had been caged here, maybe more than once, long enough to draw pictures and need a chamber pot. Rossi had put the girl down here, and that made Rossi a *monster.*

Julia's mind reeled. She felt momentarily unsteady. She looked around, trying to get her bearings. Her stricken gaze fell on the comb next to the washbasin, and she went to pick it up.

Oh. Julia felt a tingling like static electricity. She didn't know if she was imagining that, too. She didn't know what was real and what wasn't.

She looked up and saw her own reflection in a small mirror on the wall, its backing silvered and black. Fragments of her own wide eyes and open mouth looked back at her, like moldy scraps of her own flesh.

Suddenly her reflection began to change. Her face stretched up and down, more and more distorted. Her eyes darkened and went deeper and deeper like bottomless black holes. Her mouth opened into an endless tunnel.

Julia backed up, terrified. She turned and ran from the cell as fast as she could. She scraped the wall on the right, then the left. She ran harder and harder. Her lungs burned, her thighs ached.

The tunnel seemed to elongate as she ran, stretching out like her face in the mirror. Just then she saw an orangey rectangle ahead. The doorway to the living room glowed from the firelight. She was almost there. She ran faster.

The orange glow came closer and closer. She reached the end but it zoomed away, reappearing at the end of another long tunnel.

Julia felt a bolt of sheer terror. She screamed, her wail echoing in the tunnel. She feared she'd never reach the end. The more she ran, the farther away she got. She'd be trapped down here forever, a captive of past and present.

It happened again and again, each time she got to the end of the tunnel, the orange rectangle zoomed away. Home was a fiery threshold she could never reach.

All of a sudden, she burst into the living room.

She staggered forward and collapsed on the floor.

In a dead faint.

32

Julia woke up on the floor, lying on her side, facing the fireplace. Early morning light filled the living room. The fire had gone out long ago, leaving charred splinters of wood, a pile of ash, and a burnt smell. She flashed on the little girl's cell. For a moment, she didn't know if it was real, a vision, or another nightmare.

She sat bolt upright, looking around. The flashlight and watercolor self-portrait lay beside her. So did the comb.

It was real.

Julia looked over at the wall. It was cracked and broken, revealing a makeshift door. Plaster chunks and chips were strewn all over the rug. Cold, dank air wafted from the entrance. The poker was on the floor. It was real.

Unless she was still dreaming now.

She heard shouting and banging at the back door, then realized it was Anna Mattia, locked out. She scrambled to her feet, ran to the door, and threw it open, unhinged and vaguely deranged.

'Anna Mattia, am I awake? Are you here? Is this real?'

'Oh *Dio*!' Anna Mattia's mouth dropped open. 'What *'appen*?'

'Are you here? Are you really here? Is it you? Are you *real*?' Julia reached for Anna Mattia, to see if she was real or not, to feel another human being, but Anna Mattia recoiled in fear and scurried back down the hill.

'Piero!' Anna Mattia shouted, running away.

'Anna Mattia!' Julia stepped outside, struck by the morning sun. It warmed her face. It brought her back to reality. She heard birds chirping. Bianco barking. She was awake. Everything she remembered was real.

Rossi was a monster who might be her grandmother.

That could be the worst nightmare of all.

Julia perched on the edge of the couch, sipping a glass of water. She couldn't suppress the revulsion she felt after seeing the underground cell. She didn't know if she could stay in the house another minute. The very air seemed tainted with the horror of what was underneath the floor. She'd thought Rossi was delusional, paranoid, and maybe even crazy, but she hadn't guessed Rossi could abuse a child, maybe even her own. It was *torture*.

Anna Mattia had fought tears while Julia had told her what happened. Piero stood grim-faced, listening to the account and holding his gun. When Julia was finished telling the story, Piero went into the tunnel with his flashlight, leaving her and Anna Mattia in the living room amid the debris from the wall.

'You *see* Caterina?' Anna Mattia dabbed her eyes with a tissue.

'Yes, I swear it.'

Anna Mattia made the sign of the cross, and Julia got up and gave her a hug.

'I think Caterina wanted me to see the underground cell. She wanted me to know that Rossi put the little girl in a prison.'

'Signora Rossi, no, no, why she do?'

'I don't know.' Julia's mind was already coming up with possibilities, each worse than the last. 'You saw the watercolor. It's a girl's self-portrait. Rossi locked her down there.'

Anna Mattia's gnarled hand flew to her lips. '*Madonna*, no.'

'The question is, who's the little girl? There are a few possibilities. One is that she's Rossi's daughter, so that means Rossi had a little girl, despite what she told you and everybody else.'

Anna Mattia grimaced.

'It's possible, right? She could have given birth in the villa. She could have raised the child alone. We're in the middle of the country. Nobody would know. Right?'

Anna Mattia nodded, jittery.

'Still, even if the girl was Rossi's daughter, we don't know if either of them was related to me. We look a little alike, but that's subjective. Luckily, I got hair from the little girl's comb, so we can get it tested and find out.'

Anna Mattia nodded, following along.

Julia had a darker possibility. 'But what if the little girl *wasn't* Rossi's daughter, or wasn't related to Rossi at all? What if it was a random girl? What if Rossi *kidnapped* her?'

Anna Mattia gasped, her hand flying to her mouth.

They both turned to the sound of Piero coming out of the tunnel, and he squeezed through the door into the living room, having gone pale under his tan, weathered skin. He set down the flashlight and spoke to Anna Mattia in hushed tones.

'What's he saying?' Julia asked, unable to follow.

'He say tunnel under vineyard, 'e dig to see.'

'Good, okay. Thank you, Piero.' Julia took stock of the situation. 'Look, this is a crime, whether it's Rossi's daughter or not. I mean, what if she *killed* the girl? Obviously, she didn't kill my biological mother or I wouldn't be here. But what if Rossi murdered the girl? What if she wasn't the only girl? What if she was just the *last* girl?'

'*Mio Dio!*' Anna Mattia yelped.

'Well, it's possible.' Julia crossed to the tunnel and looked down into the blackness. Cold air chilled her to the marrow. 'I'm calling the police.'

33

Julia, Anna Mattia, and Piero stood aside as Marshal Torti, two *carabinieri*, and three crime techs emerged from the tunnel, their expressions impassive. Marshal Torti was dressed in his black-and-red uniform with blue paper booties, and the techs had on white paper jumpsuits that read POLIZIA SCIENTIFICA and booties, too. They carried green metal toolboxes and flashlights, which they switched off.

Marshal Torti conferred with the *carabinieri* and crime techs in low tones. Their demeanor was professional, if hardly urgent. It had taken them so long to get here, Julia had the time to shower, change, and eat lunch. She'd even checked her horoscope, dismayed to learn that today was a once-in-every-fourteen-years conjunction between Jupiter and Uranus, one of the most intense days of the year.

'So what do you think?' Julia asked Marshal Torti. 'It has to be child abuse to cage a little girl down there. God knows how many times she was in there or for how long. She painted pictures, she slept there. That's *criminal*.'

Marshal Torti stiffened. 'At this juncture, we cannot be certain which crime or crimes were committed. We have very few facts.'

'I know, but doesn't it shock you? Clearly the child was locked in the cell. What if it wasn't Rossi's child, but somebody else's? What if she kidnapped a child? What if she even *murdered* that child? What if there was more than one?'

'I do not engage in speculation.'

'It's completely possible, and that dungeon is *not* speculation.'

'Such tunnels are not uncommon in this region. This property must have been part of a feudal estate. Perhaps from centuries ago.'

'Okay, the question is, what are you going to do about it?'

'Some additional facts, please.' Marshal Torti cocked his head in his black cap. 'How did you happen to discover it, again?'

'I noticed the crack in the wall.' Julia hadn't told him about Caterina. He already thought she was crazy.

'You had no previous knowledge of the cell?'

'No.'

'No one informed you?'

'No.'

'You started digging in the proper spot, merely by chance?'

Um. Julia swallowed hard. 'When I saw the crack, yes.'

Marshal Torti mulled it over. 'Yesterday in my office, you suggested you would be leaving Tuscany and going back to America.'

'No, you suggested I do that, but I don't want to. I'm trying to research the history of my family, and this is the best place to do it.' Julia didn't think it was his business anyway. 'Finding this tunnel proves my point. So no, I'm not leaving.'

'One would think that this discovery would support a decision to leave, rather than to stay.'

'Why?'

'You said yesterday that you were concerned about a kidnapping plot. Now you suggest that Signora Rossi may have herself been involved in kidnapping children.'

'I'm staying.'

'Fine.' Marshal Torti pursed his lips. 'We will contact the prosecutor, and he will handle the matter legally. To state the obvious, Signora Rossi is now beyond the reach of the law. Her judgment comes from God.'

'But what about the child who was put down there? She could be among the missing children. It would be from decades ago. Maybe you can find her. I'd like to find her, too. I'm wondering if she's my birth mother.'

'Ms Pritzker, we will conduct our investigation as per procedure. We will search the databases for missing children in order to determine which, if any, are still missing. It will take time, considering we do not know when the child was imprisoned. You tell me Signora Rossi lived here for fifty years, so it could have been anytime during that time span.'

'Okay, well, thank you.' Julia felt satisfied, for now. 'If you discover any names of children from the area who are still missing, may I have them?'

'No, as with yesterday, that is confidential information. If you wish to obtain such information, you would need to seek legal representation and bring the matter to court.'

Julia decided to change tacks. 'Were you able to get fingerprints from the cell?'

'No, due to the mold.'

'What about the bed or the desk?' Julia glanced at the crime techs, who pointedly averted their eyes.

'Nothing.'

'What about hair and fibers, like DNA?'

'None except for the comb that you brought out.' Marshal Torti spoke to a crime tech in Italian, and the tech crossed to the table, set down her metal case, and extracted two brown bags with yellow labels that read PROVA. She started to take the watercolor self-portrait, but Julia hurried over.

'Wait. Can't you leave that? Maybe make a copy?'

Marshal Torti interjected, 'No, the original is evidence.'

'Did you take the other watercolors from the cell?'

'Yes. We must confiscate the comb, too.'

'Hold on, please.' Julia slid her phone from her back pocket and took photos of the self-portrait. 'I'd like to take photos of the other watercolors, too.'

'For what reason?'

'They belong to me.' Julia realized they were in a power struggle and he wouldn't lose face in front of his staff. 'Marshal Torti, I would really appreciate it if you would allow me to take the photos, as a personal matter. If the girl really is my biological mother, they're the only mementos I have of her.'

Marshal Torti nodded to the crime tech. 'Fine.'

'Thank you.' Julia took photos of the watercolors, then spotted some hair in the comb's teeth and quickly slid it off. She experienced the static tingling again, but she masked her reaction.

'Ms Pritzker!' Marshal Torti snapped. 'You may *not* take that evidence. It is police property.'

'Don't worry, I left you some.' Julia was finished playing nice.

The hair tingled its assent.

After the *carabinieri* had gone, Julia stepped outside into the ruined garden to call Courtney. 'Got a minute?' she asked, when Courtney picked up.

'Yes, what? I've been worried.'

Julia sat down on the old cane chair and told her the whole story, from Caterina to the tingly hair. When she finished, Courtney went so silent Julia thought the call had dropped. 'Court, you there?'

'You think you saw a *blue ghost*?'

'I saw Caterina.' Julia thought Courtney would believe her because she had proof positive. 'You can't doubt this because she *showed me* the tunnel. I wouldn't have found it any other way. I *saw* her and I felt her presence.'

'Honey, no, *you* saw the crack, not the ghost. You were looking at the wall and the light from the fireplace.'

'I swear, Caterina showed it to me. She was pure blue light, tall and shaped like a woman.'

'The same blue light that threw your laptop at a wall? Now it's a woman, showing you around? Jules, there's no such thing as ghosts. Do I really need to say this?'

'I'm telling you she's tried to contact me, to help me, tell me about my family, the villa, maybe my own past. Anna Mattia doesn't doubt me, neither does Piero.'

'I don't even know these people, and neither do you.' Courtney groaned. 'You told me before the blue light was trying to kill you. Now she's your bestie? Which is it?'

'I know, I was wrong.' Julia struggled to put it together. 'Now I think she was trying to tell me something. Maybe she was trying to tell me to get off the laptop and get out of her bedroom. The dining room, too.' Julia realized *that* could be the answer. 'That's it! She wanted me in the *living room*. She wanted me to find the *tunnel*! She *showed* me where the door in the wall used to—'

'There's no *she*! *She* is *you*!'

Julia bore down. 'Listen, Caterina's husband was murdered, too, stabbed to death. She loved astrology and books, too. We have so much in common, and my life tracks—'

'So? That doesn't mean anything.'

'That doesn't strike you as strange? Weird? *Too* coincidental? I feel like she's here for me, I *feel* her, maybe I *summoned* her.' Julia heard her voice speeding up, her excitement gathering in strength. 'Plus I got my DNA results and my ancestry is from Tuscany and Milan, do you believe that? I'm Italian American, by blood. It makes it more likely I'm related to Rossi and her—'

'No, it doesn't, not logically—'

'—and I found hair on a comb and I'm going to get it tested and see if it's a match, like we talked about before.'

'Okay, good, at least that makes sense.'

'It *all* makes sense, not just the scientific part, I'm telling you, when I went to Caterina's castle, I knew my way around.'

'You had déjà vu.'

'Something's happening here, Court.' Julia was thinking aloud, her brain afire. 'I know this is all connected. Me, Rossi, and Caterina.'

'You don't know that, and these are three separate issues. You could be related to Rossi but certainly not Caterina. That villa is driving you crazy!'

'No, it's not. The villa is giving up its secrets.' Julia realized she was right as soon as she said it. 'They could be my family's secrets and they could lead to my *family*.'

'Oh sweet Jesus—'

'I'll tell you what scares *me*.' Julia's heart lodged in her throat. 'I'm afraid Rossi is my biological grandmother and the girl in the cell was my biological mother. I'm afraid Rossi was a monster, maybe even a murderer.'

'Murder?' Courtney scoffed. 'Girl, you're losing it. What's next, skeletons? "We're Marley and Marley, whoooo"?'

Skeletons. Julia's bewildered gaze traveled to the vineyard, where Piero was digging, next to Anna Mattia and Bianco.

'What?'

'I have to go, bye.' Julia hung up and raced to the vineyard.

34

Julia hurried to Anna Mattia and Piero, standing with Bianco, in the vineyard. Piero had been digging for some time, and perspiration dotted his lined brow and shirt. His wispy white hair blew in the breeze like filaments on dandelion seeds.

Julia touched Anna Mattia's arm. 'I think he should stop what he's doing and look around for any bones that might be buried, like a skeleton or a body—'

Anna Mattia recoiled, crossing herself.

'I know, but we have to admit it's possible.' Julia couldn't leave a stone unturned, literally. 'If we don't investigate here, no one else will. The police aren't going to do it, you heard. I want to know and I'm not going to wait.' *Caterina wouldn't*, she thought but didn't say. 'This is my villa, and it could be my family. I want to get to the bottom of what went on here. I want the truth.'

Anna Mattia bit her lip. 'Okay.'

'Maybe you can start searching for cracks inside. I have to get ready to meet the investigator.'

'When you want Piero take you?'

'He should keep digging. I can drive myself but I need a car.'

'Signora 'ave.' Anna Mattia blinked. 'She *love* 'er car. She love drive.'

'Really?' Julia asked, surprised. 'I thought she never went anywhere.'

'No, she never go in *town*.'

'So where did she go?'

Anna Mattia shrugged. 'She drive at night.'

What? 'Was this before she got sick?'

'Yes.'

'Why did she drive around?'

Anna Mattia shrugged again.

'Did she drive around in the daytime?'

'No.'

Whoa. Julia felt her stomach turn over. 'Anna Mattia, isn't it strange that she drove around, only at night? What if she was up to no good?'

Anna Mattia grimaced.

'Show me the car.'

Julia followed Piero and Anna Mattia into an open bay under the carriage house, encompassing much of its ground floor. He flicked on the lights, a line of bare bulbs that illuminated the stone walls and a floor of dirt, stone, and gravel. The wooden frames of two old horse stalls were affixed to the wall by rough-hewn nails, and a stone trough ran along one wall.

Piero and Anna Mattia's red Fiat Panda was parked on one side, and on the other was a car covered by a beige tarp, which rested on thick rubber mats. He took the cover off with care, revealing a sleek black sedan with two doors. Its side had a yellow plaque with a black prancing horse, which Julia recognized from the racetrack at Imola.

'Is that a *Ferrari*?' she asked, surprised.

Piero's eyes lit up. '*Sì*, Ferrari FF. *Bellissimo*, no?'

'Rossi had a Ferrari? Why?'

Piero spread his palms, *Why not?*

'Wow.' Julia assumed she inherited a Ferrari. 'Does it work?'

'*Perfetto*.' Piero spoke to his wife in Italian, and Anna Mattia turned to Julia.

''E take for service, 'e take very good care.'

'How old is the car? What year?'

Anna Mattia asked Piero, who answered, then she returned to Julia. '2012.'

'Where does Piero take it for service?'

'*Firenze*. Signora 'ave already when we come. Piero drive, no *ruggine*, no rust.'

'He drives it so it doesn't get rusty?'

'*Sì*.' Piero dug in his baggy pockets and handed her the keys.

'Thanks.' Julia went to the driver's side, unlocked the door, and sat in the cushy driver's seat. The interior had plush leather the color of butterscotch and matching rugs. The dashboard was matte black, and the car had a radio and a small screen near the console. The steering wheel was skinny and black, with the Ferrari plaque in the center of a red Start push button.

Julia asked Piero, 'It has a push button *and* keys?'

'*Sì*.' Piero mimed turning a key then pushing a button.

'It's an automatic, right?'

'*Sì, automatico*.'

'Where's its title?' Julia assumed Rossi owned the car outright.

Anna Mattia answered, 'Signora 'ave, gone. Burned.'

'Jeez.' Julia mulled it over, shaking her head. 'She didn't burn the car. Why?'

Anna Mattia shrugged. 'She forget? She sick, she no drive.'

Julia was struck by a revolting thought, which made sense now that she'd found the underground cell. Maybe Rossi had burned her things to destroy any evidence, like hair, fingerprints, or fibers. She could've been trying to cover her tracks and ensure that nothing remained to trace her to any crimes. Maybe she was eliminating traces of any victim's DNA, too.

Julia hoped it wasn't true. She scanned the interior for residual hair, fibers, or anything else, but it was immaculate. 'This car is so clean.'

Piero nodded, puffing his chest.

Anna Mattia added, 'Every two week, 'e clean, no dust, no dirt, no mouse. 'E worry they eat wires, so 'e keep clean.'

Arg. 'Does he vacuum, too?'

'*Sì*, Dyson!' Anna Mattia gestured to the console and side panels. ''E Dyson everywhere.'

Damn. Julia inserted the key in the ignition. The engine sprang to life with a throaty roar that filled the garage.

Piero grinned. Anna Mattia covered her ears.

Julia scanned the dials. The odometer read 56,000 kilometers. She cut the ignition. 'This car is a 2012, and you guys came in 2013, is that right?'

They nodded.

'And she got sick in 2015. Did she drive much after she got sick?'

'No, not so much,' Anna Mattia answered.

'So in two years, she put fifty-six thousand kilometers on it? That's a lot of driving for somebody who never goes anywhere.' Julia didn't understand. 'Does Piero drive it, other than for servicing?'

Anna Mattia shook her head, and so did Piero.

'How far is the trip to Florence? It's not that far, is it?'

'About forty kilometers.'

'Do you think she drove every week?'

Anna Mattia shrugged. 'More.'

'How many times a week?'

'Many. She go late, I don' see sometimes.'

'But your apartment is above. Wouldn't you hear?'

'No, she park at villa.'

Julia put it together. Rossi went driving at night, but why? For company? For protection? For a *lure*? Was Rossi driving routinely, hunting for victims to kidnap? Julia had no answers, only suspicions.

'Well, I better get ready for my appointment.' Julia got out of the car, left the garage, and hurried up to the villa. She entered the kitchen, found two plastic baggies in a drawer, and hurried with them into the living room. She made her way through the debris to the coffee table and picked up the strands of hair she'd taken from the comb.

Whoa. Julia felt the tingling again. She pulled apart the strands, divided them into two clumps, and put half in one bag and half in the other. She sealed them and left the room to shower and get ready for the investigator.

Time for answers.

35

Julia drove with an eye on the rearview mirror, worried about being followed. She kept track of the cars around her but didn't see the white Fiat. She felt edgy and preoccupied, trying to figure out why Rossi drove around at night. The awful image of the underground cell kept coming back to her, and so did the spectral vision of Caterina.

Meanwhile the Ferrari drew admiring glances, making her wonder again if Rossi bought the car for a lure. The thought disturbed her to her core. She'd imagined her biological family for so long, but never suspected they were insane, criminal, child abusers, or worse. She'd gone from hoping Rossi was her grandmother to fearing Rossi was her grandmother.

The cityscape of Florence came into view, and Julia's thoughts turned to her meeting with the family investigator. She planned to bring up the underground cell, but she didn't know if she'd mention that Caterina showed it to her.

She was tired of people thinking she was crazy.

She was starting to believe she was anything but.

Poppy Whitcomb turned out to be tall, Black, and about fifty-something, with dark eyes, a longish nose, and a chicly glossy mouth. Her hair was short and silvering at the temples, setting off hammered silver earrings. She had on a beige linen pantsuit with a melon-hued camisole, and she welcomed Julia into a sunny, tasteful office, which had a cozy sitting area of upholstered chairs and a coffee table with a tissue box, like a therapist's office.

'Thank you for seeing me on such short notice.' Julia got comfy in the cushy chair. 'It's nice sitting here instead of the desk.'

'Thanks.' Poppy smiled. 'I love my job, and doing genealogical searches for adoptees is as personal as it gets, so I prefer an informal office, too. Are you sure you wouldn't like water or coffee?'

'No, thanks, I'm fine.'

'To begin, I'd like to get to tell you what I can and cannot do, then see if that matches your goals. This is a consultation, and there's no charge for today.'

'Okay, great.' Julia liked her manner, which was warmly professional.

'All I know about you is that you are a United States citizen and were adopted in Philadelphia, Pennsylvania, is that correct?'

'Yes.'

'So you have a Pennsylvania birth certificate?'

'Yes, at home in the States.'

'And you're just beginning your search for your biological parents?'

'Yes. My adoptive parents are dead, and I knew they didn't want me to look for my biological parents, even though they never said so.'

Poppy nodded, her features softening. 'You felt like it would have been disloyal? A betrayal?'

Bingo. 'Yes.'

'I understand completely. I'm adopted, too.'

'Really?' Julia asked, surprised. 'Funny, I never met another person who was adopted.'

Poppy smiled. 'You might have, but you may not have known it. People don't always share.'

'Right, I don't.' Julia thought a minute. 'It doesn't come up in everyday conversation. It mostly comes up when they ask for medical history.'

'That's my experience as well. I'm older than you, but I didn't tell the other kids at school I was adopted. I had an older brother who wasn't, so they assumed I was his little sister. When I was growing up, adoption had a stigma, even in my mind. We stigmatize ourselves.'

'I felt it, too.'

'Most of us tend to interpret our relinquishment as abandonment, when it may not have been. We take it on, at worst. Or we fill in the blanks with supposition, projection, and fantasy, because we want it to be so.' Poppy paused. 'I always say, wishful thinking is wistful thinking.'

Julia felt it strike another chord. 'I wondered why my birth parents gave me up. I still do.'

'Yes, even terms like *give up* carry negative connotations. In my view, the quest for identity isn't limited to adoptees. It's something every individual undertakes during his lifetime, more than once.'

'That's true.' Julia thought it was an insight, and it felt good to be connecting with Poppy in a meaningful way, so quickly.

'My story is similar to yours, in the emotional bits. I had a good relationship with my adoptive parents, who were Londoners. I didn't search for my birth parents until after my first son was born. He has medical issues that made my history relevant.' A frown flickered across her lovely features. 'I eventually found my birth father, though my birth mother had passed. He was unhappy when I tracked him down.' She paused. 'Reunions with birth families may not be as we hoped.'

Julia's gut tensed. Rossi was far from the grandmother she'd hoped for.

Poppy cocked her head. 'So what brings you here today?'

'It all began when I inherited a lot of money and a villa in Croce from a woman named Emilia Rossi, whom I never met. I think she may be my birth grandmother. There is a caretaker couple there and they say Rossi didn't have any children, but I believe she lied.'

'That's not uncommon.'

'Plus Rossi thought she was related to Caterina Sforza.'

'You mean Caterina Sforza, from the Renaissance?' Poppy asked, her British accent emphasizing the second syllable.

'Yes, I know it sounds unlikely, but I think Rossi *could* have been related to Caterina.'

Poppy frowned. 'It's my understanding that if you go back ten generations in your family, your genome gets a contribution from less than half of those people. So, as a biological matter, the DNA of your biological grandmother and your DNA contain nothing of Caterina Sforza. One would not expect to find similarities in appearance or temperament, which are inheritable.'

'But I look at these pictures and I see some family similarity.'

'It's possible, but it's chance.'

'Can you trace lineage back that far, to Caterina Sforza's era?'

'*I* cannot.' Poppy held up a manicured index finger. 'It's a matter of research for a historian. They conduct such searches for clients who wish to track down their heraldic coat of arms, family crests, or the like.'

Julia felt stumped. 'So how do I find out if Rossi was related to Caterina, and if I'm related to Rossi?'

'This is what I meant by clarifying your goals.' Poppy leaned forward on her slim knees. 'I can help you with determining whether you're related to Rossi. I would begin searching Rossi's birth records in Florence and surrounding towns.'

'That would be wonderful,' Julia said, thrilled. 'And I found out from a 23andMe kit that I have almost a hundred percent Italian ancestry, from the Tuscan region and Milan, too.'

'Good.' Poppy made a note on a small pad. 'Did the results notify you of relatives in the area?'

'No, there were none who registered.'

'Okay, I can double-check other online registries. To return to topic, I'll begin the search at the Registrar of Vital Statistics here, then widen geographically and keep going. Unfortunately, Italy is balkanized in terms of provinces and local governments. One can't expect results for at least a month because bureaucrats are slow to return calls and emails. Nothing in Italy happens quickly except pasta.' Poppy smiled slyly. 'How long are you in Croce for?'

'I'm not sure, it's open-ended. Do you need me here to conduct the research?'

'No. We can communicate by email or Zoom. Very few of my clients are in the city or even in the country.' Poppy made another note. 'Do you have any relevant records or documents aside from your birth certificate? I'm sure if you search the villa, you'll find records, diaries—'

'No, it was all burned. Everything is gone.'

Poppy frowned, taken aback. 'Was there a fire?'

'Yes, an intentional one. Rossi had everything burned except her car.'

Poppy recoiled. 'So you have no documents or photos at all?'

'I do have some photos.' Julia went into her purse, retrieved the three photos of Rossi, and set them out on the coffee table. 'The only one I'm sure is Rossi is on the left. The housekeeper gave it to me.'

Poppy eyed the photos, then looked up at Julia. 'I do see the resemblance, for what it's worth.'

'Right? I also have a watercolor self-portrait that may be my mother as a young girl, but I have no proof of that, and I don't know for sure.' Julia scrolled her phone, found the photo, and showed it to Poppy.

'I see, and why do you think this is your mother?'

Julia hesitated. 'Because of where I found it.'

'How so?'

'Honestly, it's disturbing, and I think criminal. I already spoke with the police.'

Poppy blinked. 'May I know the details? I've been doing this work for twenty years. I've heard stories that would curl your hair. Learning a biological family's history may be unpleasant. One embarks on this journey with joyful anticipation, but families hide what they're ashamed of, for generations.'

'I hear you.' Julia opened up to Poppy, telling her about the underground cell and that Rossi may have burned everything to destroy evidence. Poppy listened, taking notes, and Julia ended up telling her about her nightmares, her feelings at Caterina's castle at Forlì, and her vision of Caterina last night. Julia finished, shaky. 'So do you think I'm crazy?'

Poppy met her gaze with a new gravity. 'No, but you strike me as intuitive, and it gives us an avenue to explore.'

'One last thing, I brought the hair from the comb.' Julia went into her purse and retrieved the baggie, then realized something. 'Funny, I don't feel tingling. Maybe because it's in the plastic?'

'Do you want to take it out and see if you feel a tingling?'

'No.' Julia didn't want to reduce the tingling to a parlor trick. Or maybe she was afraid it wouldn't work. Or *would*.

'I understand.' Poppy picked up the baggie. 'I have an excellent lab I use for DNA testing.'

'Great. Am I correct that if we test the hair and my DNA, we can know for a fact if the little girl was my biological mother?'

'Yes, those tests will be dispositive. Unfortunately, the results take over a month.'

Arg. 'Is there any way to hurry it, like pay a rush charge?'

'I'll inquire but I don't think so.' Poppy glanced at her watch. 'Oh no. Sorry, I lost track of time. We didn't get to discuss my fees. My rate is three hundred euros an hour, payable monthly, should you decide to engage me.'

'I would.'

'Brilliant.' Poppy smiled. 'We'll exchange contact information, and I'll send you an agreement you can Docusign. Let me know if you decide to leave the country. I will schedule collecting your DNA samples with the lab.'

'Okay.' Julia felt a frisson of excitement.

'With your permission, I'll touch base with Marshal Torti and ask him to keep me apprised of any developments.' Poppy rose, and Julia stood up, too, gathering her phone and the photos.

'Yes, thanks.'

'If I turn up anything, you'll be the first to know.' Poppy walked Julia to the door, where she paused. 'Before we conclude, I have another referral for you.'

'About the white Fiat's license plate, or the historian for Caterina?'

'No, a different referral. It's unconventional, but I recommend it in your case.'

'What?' Julia asked, intrigued.

'I know an excellent medium.'

36

Julia and Gianluca had an outside table at the restaurant, which was small, chic, and overlooking the Arno. It had a magnificent view, and they watched the sun dip below the Florentine skyline, painting the clouds gold and orange. Round amber lights glowed on both banks of the river, and the water was a liquid mirror reflecting the graceful arches of its ancient bridges and buildings. The setting was romantic, or would have been if they were in a romance.

'A *medium*?' Gianluca asked, his dark eyes flaring in surprise. His curls moved in the gentle breeze, and he had on another cool patterned scarf over a gray shirt and black blazer. Candlelight danced across his handsome features, and Julia noticed women at the other tables glancing over.

'Yes. She communicates with the dead. She's even been used by Scotland Yard. Poppy's going to see if she has time for me.'

Gianluca sipped his Chianti. 'So how does a medium help you find your family? Assuming Rossi was your biological grandmother?'

'I think the idea is that she can help me communicate with Caterina and Rossi.'

'Well, I'd go see her, totally. I'd try anything.'

'Agree,' Julia answered, though her first thought had been of Mike. 'Oops, I said the wrong thing again.'

Busted. 'No, you didn't, but why did you say that?'

'I can tell I did,' Gianluca answered softly, and Julia didn't know what to say. She felt touched that he could read her so well, but guilty that she was with him, rejoining a world that didn't include Mike.

'By the way, I buried the lede.' Julia wanted to get back on track. 'I found hair in the underground cell, and Poppy's going to get it tested for DNA, so we can see if I have any in common.'

'Incredible!' Gianluca's eyes rounded behind his glasses. 'That's, like, the answer. Where did you find the hair?'

Julia caught him up, telling him about how Caterina showed her the underground cell, and they hashed it out over a tasty appetizer of *gnocchi* with pesto and fresh mint. She opened up to him, grateful to have him to talk with, and he listened to her in an encouraging way, saving his questions until they shared an entrée of seabream with olive oil, roasted fennel, garlic, capers, and olives.

'Julia, let me get this straight. You *saw* Caterina in your living room? Like, a blue shape?'

'Yes.' Julia braced for skepticism, but Gianluca leaned forward, clearly intrigued.

'I don't doubt you. History is full of reports of visions and connections with the spirit world, even with God. Think of Mary seeing the Angel Gabriel, who tells her she will bear Christ. And Julian of Norwich, an English mystic who saw Christ. There were others, too. Locally, Gemma of Lucca spoke with her guardian angels, Jesus and Mary. Nobody says she was crazy. She was beatified.'

'But I'm no saint.'

'They weren't, either. They were normal women.' Gianluca warmed to his subject. 'My favorite account is of Saint Lutgardis of Aywières. She had a vision of Jesus, and He asked her, "What, then, do you want?" And she answered, "I want Thy Heart." Jesus responded, "I, too, want Your Heart."'

'It's beautiful.' Julia felt surprisingly validated.

'Historians read it as an expression of divine love, but I read it to mean that *all* love is divine. It elevates the notion of love itself.'

Julia listened, liking the way his mind worked. He made sense, but his rationality was bound up with emotionality.

'What is it about love that inspires legends, opera, books, poetry, and the greatest music in the world? It just can't only be earthly, like between two people in bed. It's because the emotion is bigger, and higher, than earth itself.' Gianluca spread his arms. 'Love connects us to the divine. We talk about soul mates, but I believe it, literally, and everything has a soul. That's why everything is connected, heaven and earth, all of us.'

Julia felt it strike a chord. 'That's what I like about astrology. The connection, to everything.'

'I get that. Julian of Norwich held a hazelnut, saying, "It is all that is made," meaning the entire world.' Gianluca put up a hand. 'Sorry, end of lecture, again. Want a gelato before I take you home? I know a great place.'

'Yes, but you don't have to take me home.'

'Why not?' Gianluca signaled to the waiter for the check. 'Is Piero coming?'

'No, I drove myself in Rossi's Ferrari.'

'*What?*' Gianluca asked, his eyes popping.

Night had fallen, and the sky shimmered like a Raphael-blue cupola of tiny lights. The air had a warm softness, wafting off the Arno with a pleasantly briny odor. Julia finished an icy chocolate gelato as she walked with Gianluca along the riverbank. Lovers, families, and tourists strolled the promenade, but it wasn't that big a crowd, and she let her guard down, thanks to the wine and something else. She felt safe with him.

Gianluca finished his waffle cone. 'We're going to the next bridge down. I want to show you something.'

'Great.'

Gianluca looked over, his dark eyes flashing with amusement. 'You know, my staff is abuzz about the woman I stole books for.'

Julia laughed. 'Oh no! How long can I keep them?'

'As long as you need. I run the interlibrary loan cartel.' Gianluca checked his phone. 'Here we go. Look.'

Julia leaned over to Gianluca's phone, showing a painting of a man in a red cap and a black robe, walking on a bridge over the Arno and meeting three women at the corner. The woman in the center was tall with dark blond hair, wearing a flowing white dress. 'I should know this painting, but I don't.'

'This is *Dante and Beatrice* by Henry Holiday, painted in 1884. I know it because Florentines are raised on Dante. It's the first time Dante sees his beloved Beatrice.' Gianluca stopped walking. 'See, they're meeting on this spot?'

'Really?' Julia looked around, astounded. They were standing on the same corner as in the painting. '*This* is where Dante fell in love with Beatrice?'

'Exactly.' Gianluca smiled. 'We're on the Ponte Santa Trinità. He and Beatrice were fourteen years old, and it was love at first sight. Florence is the city of love at first sight.'

Julia smiled. 'That's a love story.'

'It's *the* love story. Dante loved her his whole life and when he wrote *Paradiso*, he named her as the Angel that leads him to heaven. It's what I was saying at dinner, about love being divine. Maybe that's what love at first sight is, two souls recognizing each other.' Gianluca smiled. 'I believe it because it happened to me. I felt it the moment I saw you. I'm falling in love with you.'

Aw. Julia didn't know what to say. A warm rush of happiness suffused her, filling her heart, but her next thought was of Mike.

'I know you're in mourning, I understand that.' Gianluca gazed at her softly. 'But do you think you could ever have feelings for me? I'll wait as long as it takes.'

Suddenly a large group of men surged toward them, all wearing the same blue hoodies as the man who'd killed Mike, like a nightmare army.

Julia's heart began to thunder. Tears of fright sprang to her eyes. She was back in Philly, reliving Mike's murder. The hoodie. The knife. The blood spurting from his chest. She edged backward, trying to get away.

'What's the matter?' Gianluca grabbed her as the men surrounded them, swarming the bridge, drunkenly jostling them. He held her until they passed, searching her face in bewilderment. 'Julia, what's happening?'

'Those men—' Julia's heart pounded so hard she thought it was a heart attack. She felt dizzy, even faint.

'Let's get out of here,' Gianluca said, taking her away.

37

'm sorry,' Julia said, embarrassed. She sipped a glass of ice water, recovering her composure on Gianluca's black leather couch. His living room was lined with books and framed sketches, and its walls were a dark red. Tensor lamps on the end tables were matte black, creating a darkly dramatic interior. Two windows overlooked the Florentine night.

'There's nothing to be sorry about.' Gianluca sat on an ottoman opposite her, concerned. 'How are you feeling?'

'Better, thanks,' Julia answered, though it was only partly true. 'I guess I had a panic attack.'

'Why? What caused it?'

'Those men, their hoodies…' Julia couldn't finish the sentence.

'They were Swedish tourists. Drunk.'

'But they had blue hoodies, all of them, and that color, like cobalt…'

'It's the color of Italy's football team. Or, as you say, soccer. Our team is the Azure Blues, *Gli Azzuri*.'

What? 'You mean it's *team gear*?'

'Yes, the national soccer team. Everybody has one.'

Julia tried to understand. 'The man who killed my husband wore the exact same hoodie.'

'He did?'

'Yes.' Julia sipped her water. 'Why would a murderer in Philly have one of those hoodies?'

'I don't know.' Gianluca frowned, puzzled. 'Does it matter?'

'It's unusual at home. I've seen dozens of Eagles, Phillies, and Flyers hoodies, but I've never once seen one of those blue sweatshirts, except on that night.'

'So do you think the man who killed your husband was Italian?'

'Maybe, yes, or has been here. It might not mean anything, but still.' Julia tried to wrap her mind around the revelation, and her thoughts began to clarify. 'What if Mike's murder is connected to Italy?'

Gianluca mulled it over. 'How?'

'I don't know.' Julia blinked, mystified. 'The only thing that I can think of is my inheritance. I wonder if Mike's murder has something to do with the inheritance.' She heard herself say it, realizing it was a distinct possibility. 'I didn't think those things were connected, but what if they are?'

'How could they be?'

'I don't know that, either.' Julia couldn't deny the sense she got inside, maybe it was her intuition, so she went with it. 'But these are the two biggest events in my life, my husband's murder and my inheritance, one horrible and one wonderful, and they happened only about six months apart. Maybe they're related to each other.'

'What about through Rossi?'

'What do you mean?' Julia asked, glad of a sounding board.

'Well, you found the underground cell. A little girl was caged there, whether Rossi's daughter or someone else's. You were worried Rossi could even be a kidnapper.'

'Right, so?'

'What if Rossi was in a kidnapping or a trafficking ring? She could have been working with others. She's dead, but she may have co-conspirators who are alive.'

'A conspiracy.' Julia shuddered, trying to imagine it. 'She goes out at night to look for children. No kid would be afraid of her because she's an older, wealthy woman. She drives a cool car to lure them. But where do you find children out at night, in the countryside?'

'You find them where you live, in the poorer towns around Croce. There's kids who work in the vineyards, all year round. Migrant children, Albanians, Ethiopians, Kosovans.' Gianluca met her eye grimly. 'It's the side of Tuscany tourists don't see.'

'But what does that have to do with the man who killed Mike?'

'I don't know, I don't have enough facts.' Gianluca leaned forward. 'Begin at the beginning, would you? What happened that night? Can you tell me or will it upset you?'

'I can.' Julia bore down, despite her emotion. 'We came around the corner. The man reached for my purse. Mike stepped in to protect me.'

'Did the man have an Italian accent?'

'I don't know. He didn't say anything.' Julia thought a minute. 'Maybe *that's* why he didn't speak. He didn't want us to hear his accent was Italian. In retrospect, it's weird that he didn't say anything, not even "Give me your purse."'

'So you think it was your purse he was after? But what if it was you?' Gianluca cocked his curly head. 'What if he wanted to kill *you*?'

'You mean he was only making it look like a purse-snatching? Why?'

'What if it's connected to your inheritance? Maybe he attacked you to prevent you from getting the money and—'

'What about the *villa*?' Julia interrupted, as it struck her, horrified. 'Maybe they didn't want me to get the villa because I'd find the underground cell. Maybe they were trying to prevent me from finding evidence of their wrongdoing.'

'Yes, that could be it.' Gianluca nodded excitedly. 'If you hadn't come over and started digging, no one would have found the cell.'

Julia felt her stomach turn over. 'And they used Rossi's villa to imprison their victims.'

'And they don't want to get found out. So when they find out you're inheriting the villa, they try to stop you by killing you.'

Julia recoiled. 'That's extreme.'

'The *crime* is extreme.'

'How would they even know about the inheritance?'

'Rossi could have told them. Maybe she was close to one of them, maybe he was even a lover.'

Julia tried to wrap her mind around it. 'Do you think Rossi would be okay with killing me, if she's my biological grandmother?'

'Or, she may not have known. Maybe they kept it from her or double-crossed her.' Gianluca shrugged. 'In truth, they didn't need to kill you. Even if they only injured you, you probably wouldn't have come over. You'd have sold the villa, and nobody would've been the wiser.'

Julia shook her head. 'Wait. No, the theory doesn't work. If Rossi is part of a conspiracy, why would she leave me the villa in the first place? She'd be putting incriminating evidence in my hands.'

'Unless she didn't think you'd find the cell.'

'And I wouldn't have, if not for Caterina.' Julia's imagination began to run away with her, but she let it fly. 'Maybe that's why Caterina was trying to show me. Maybe that's why she stepped up. Maybe she wants justice for those children, whether the girl's my mother or not. Caterina was a devoted mother herself. She stepped up to save her children and her town.'

'Right.' Gianluca smiled, then paused. 'But there are two other possibilities. The first one is Rossi wanted you to find the underground cell, so that you would call the police.'

'You mean she turned on her coconspirators?'

'Yes, and it worked. You found it and you called the police.'

'Why would she turn on them?'

'Maybe she repented as she got older. *She* could have wanted them to be brought to justice, as redemption.'

'Like she regretted what she'd done when she knew she was dying? She regretted being a total monster of a person?' Julia was still disgusted. 'It's too little, too late, if you ask me. You didn't see that dungeon. I would have been terrified to be in there. I *was* terrified to be in there.'

'I know, and there's one other possibility, which is sadly consistent with Rossi.' Gianluca hesitated. 'By leaving you the inheritance, she gets you over here and puts you in jeopardy. What if she *wanted* you dead?'

'Yikes!' Julia grimaced, shocked. 'Why? She doesn't even know me!'

'She knew *something* about you. She found you, didn't she? She had your address, she left you the inheritance.'

'She wanted me *dead*?' Julia felt the hair stand up on the back of her neck.

'I'm sorry, but it's possible. She was paranoid, delusional, maybe even homicidal.'

Julia swallowed hard. 'But why me?'

'I don't know.'

Julia slumped on the couch, exhaling. 'Oh man. This is a lot.'

Gianluca smiled gently. 'Is my Ferrari finally out of gas?'

Julia smiled back. 'I'm no Ferrari.'

'Yes, you are.' Gianluca straightened. 'You should call Marshal Torti in the morning. Tell him your inheritance may be connected to your husband's murder.'

'Yes, right.' Julia finished the water and set the glass on a coaster. 'I'll call the Philly police, too. They can investigate suspects from Italy. There must be a database like that, somewhere.'

'Of course. But I think that's as far as we can take it tonight. You made progress and you should be proud of yourself.' Gianluca smiled at her. 'I don't think you should drive home. You can't be on the road the way you are.'

Julia felt fatigue wash over her, but it was awkward. 'I'll be fine.'

'Please, stay.' Gianluca put up his palms. 'I'll sleep on the sofa, you sleep in my bed.'

'I'll stay, but I'll take the sofa.'

'No, I insist. Chivalry is not dead here, my dear.'

The bedroom was small, containing a double bed, a night table, and a set of shelves with books, drawing paper, and art supplies. Moonlight filtered through a thin curtain, moving in a soft breeze.

Julia tossed and turned, trying to sleep. She felt too warm under the coverlet, even in a camisole and panties. She didn't want to sleep naked with Gianluca in the next room, and she couldn't stop wondering if Mike's murder had anything to do with her inheritance. If there was a connection, it horrified her, and she felt even more guilty for his murder. Someone had been trying to kill her, but had killed him instead.

Tears filled Julia's eyes. She stifled them, trying not to cry so Gianluca wouldn't overhear. It still felt unreal that she was in his apartment, in his bed, and she realized that before her panic attack, he had told her he loved her.

The thought filled her with happiness, and she realized she had feelings for him too, but she couldn't acknowledge them without guilt. She buried her face in the pillow, missing Mike and wanting Gianluca at the same time, both desires powerful, yet impossible to reconcile.

She couldn't stop the tears then, and she began to cry in a way she hadn't in a long time, then groped around for tissues on a night table stacked with books.

'Here,' Gianluca said softly, appearing behind her on the bed. He held out a box of Kleenex, so she tore one out and held it to her face.

'Don't look, I'm crying,' Julia sobbed. 'I don't just ugly cry, I snotty cry.'

'I can't see anyway, it's dark—'

'Stay back there.' Julia wiped her eyes. 'I really mean it.'

'I will, don't worry.'

Julia wept, grabbing another Kleenex. 'I'm sorry.'

'It's okay, don't be sorry,' Gianluca said, his voice comforting as Julia blew her nose and wiped her eyes, then went through the first Kleenex and a second, and before she realized what was happening, Gianluca had put his arms around her from behind, holding her gently. 'This okay, to hold you?'

'Yes,' was all Julia could say, heartbroken, embarrassed, and exhausted.

'Let the tears come, they will pass.'

'I don't know if they will,' Julia said, giving voice to her greatest fear, which she hadn't realized until this very moment, that she would never stop mourning Mike, that she would never rejoin life, that she didn't deserve to, that her husband died because of her and she had no right to go on. She realized she had been looking over her shoulder ever since the night Mike was killed, and the man following her was *him*.

'Julia, it will pass, but you have to let it come. If you don't let it come, it never goes away. Your heart is broken, and it will heal.'

'You think?' Julia mopped her eyes.

'I know. My heart healed, and I love you.'

Julia felt a rush of emotion. 'How? You can't.'

'Why not?'

'You hardly know me.'

'I know enough.' Gianluca paused in the darkness. 'I realize it's soon, but I know it happened. I know myself, and I think that you might have feelings for me, too, if you allow them to come.'

'They can't, they shouldn't.'

'They can and they will. The thing about a broken heart is that it's open.'

Julia felt his words reach her. She *did* feel both brokenhearted and openhearted at the same time, and she loved that he brought her to that insight.

'Ever since I met you, I find myself thinking about you, remembering things you said, or how you looked at Forlì, or how you laughed at the racetrack. How it feels to have your arms around my waist on the bike.' Gianluca's voice sounded tender as a wound in the darkness. 'I've never felt this way before, loved so intensely so quickly, with such certainty, knowing it's absolutely *right* in my *soul*.'

My God. Julia felt moved, but still. 'What if I can't love you back? I mean, I'm wearing my *wedding* ring.'

'You can wear it forever if you want to, I understand. I'll wait to see if you can have feelings for me, and until then, let my love heal you,' Gianluca said tenderly, holding her closer, and Julia found herself turning in his arms, facing him, and in the next moment, he was kissing her face and pulling her close to his bare chest. Her mouth found his, warm and soft and giving, and she felt herself lost in his kiss, the warmth of his skin, the strength in his body, this living, breathing man, who loved her.

And somewhere in this medieval city, out of time and place, Julia opened her broken heart.

38

'G ood morning,' Gianluca whispered, kissing her behind the ear, and Julia turned over, waking up drowsily. He was sitting on the bed, his hair damp from a shower and fully dressed in another cool scarf, a thin black sweater, and jeans. The bedroom was light, and she could hear traffic noise outside.

'Good morning.' Julia pulled up the coverlet. She realized she felt awkward, facing him the next morning. Or maybe facing herself. She couldn't believe she'd slept with him. She could smell the spice of his aftershave, and she liked it, which made her feel worse.

'I'm sorry, I have to get to work. You can stay here today, if you want.' Gianluca smiled, moving a strand of hair from her face. 'I can come home for lunch or sneak out early.'

'No, I've got to get home. I should call the police.'

'Okay, stay as long as you like, then. The key is under the mat. Slip it under the door on your way out. Call me when you get home, will you?' Gianluca rose and headed for the door. 'I'll come out tonight, okay?'

'Okay,' Julia answered, though she wasn't sure.

'Great! *Ciao, ciao!*' Gianluca blew her a kiss, then closed the bedroom door.

Half an hour later, Julia was back in the Ferrari heading home, her thoughts bollixed up. She kept thinking of Gianluca, the way he touched her, his whispered Italian, even their laughter and tears. But regret and guilt seeped between her thoughts like cracks that admitted darkness, not light.

She reached the highway, going against rush-hour traffic heading into Florence. She'd called Marshal Torti, leaving a message. She was beginning to feel edgy and paranoid again, the aftershocks of blue hoodies coming out of the darkness.

Fears that she was being followed crept back, and Julia took a mental picture of the cars around her, her fingers clenching the wheel. Finally, she reached the single-lane road that wound past Croce and headed home.

Julia pulled into the driveway, dismayed to see Franco's car in front of the villa. She didn't relish him witnessing her walk of shame, but whatever. She cut the ignition and got out of the car.

'Julia, good morning!' Franco emerged, grinning, from his car, in his trim dark suit. 'Wait, is that a *Ferrari*?'

'It was Rossi's.'

'My God! How does it drive?'

'Great.' Julia walked over. 'What are you doing here?'

'I'm bursting with news and I thought it would be best in person.'

Arg. 'How long have you been waiting?'

'About fifteen minutes. I knocked but no one answered.' Franco shrugged, and Julia wondered if Anna Mattia was in the vineyard with Piero.

'What's your news?'

'Well, there's been *so* much interest in your property, and an amazing offer came in last night.' Franco spread his palms. 'I feel as if *this* is the one, and it's *not* a teardown.'

'Franco, I told you, please don't solicit any more offers.'

'I'm not! Offers are coming in on their own, now that the word is out.'

'But I'm keeping the villa.'

'Don't you want to hear the offer?' Franco raised a palm. 'It's for one million, nine hundred euro, cash. It's lower because they wish to restore the villa. The wife is an artist who works in mosaics, and the husband teaches poetry at Sapienza and is preparing for retirement. They have family money, too.'

'I'm not ready to sell yet.'

'But they're flexible on the settlement date. You could stay three months, if you want, maybe longer.' Franco made praying hands. 'Please, can we sit down and talk about it?'

'No, thank you. I'm researching my birth family, and things have been going on.'

'Like what? It's a miracle that we got this offer and—'

'Come inside, you'll see what I mean.' Julia went to the front door and unlocked it with Franco on her heels. She led him into the living room, where the door to the tunnel stood partway ajar. Anna Mattia had cleaned up the plaster chunks and debris.

Franco frowned, scanning the mess. 'What *happened*?'

Julia told him, omitting the Caterina part, but Franco only shrugged, regaining his sales mojo.

'So, it's an underground tunnel and a room. Many villas have them.'

'This is a *crime scene*.'

'Did the police say that?'

'No, but—'

'So, a tunnel is a selling point to a couple like this. They want authenticity.'

'Franco, enough, I don't want to sell yet. I have to find Anna Mattia.' Julia left the living room and entered the kitchen, but it was empty. Anna Mattia wasn't there and oddly, on the table lay Piero's gun, a box of bullets, and a small white note.

Julia crossed to the table and picked up the note. It was in English, written in Anna Mattia's jittery cursive:

> Sorry we go Abruzzo. The villa have evil spirit.
> You are crazy like Signora.

'Oh no,' Julia said, hurt. She remembered how spooked Anna Mattia had been by the underground cell. 'I can't believe this. They *left*?'

Franco read the note over her shoulder. 'Good riddance. I'll ask around in town and get you some help. The villa does not have an evil spirit. If it did, I'd raise the asking. There are buyers who love haunted houses, for the novelty.'

Julia ignored him, eyeing the note. 'But I liked Anna Mattia and Piero. I'm going to miss them. They were lovely to me.' She felt a pang, then realized with a start that maybe they'd found something outside that had made them want to leave, like human bones. She set down the note and headed for the back door. 'Hold on a sec.'

'What?' Franco followed her, joining Julia as she stepped outside and surveyed the vineyard, her hands on her hips. There were no new holes, no dirt mounded anywhere. It looked as if Piero hadn't even filled in the hole he'd been digging to the tunnel. His shovel lay on the ground, and Bianco was sleeping nearby.

Julia still couldn't believe they were gone. They must have decided to go immediately after she'd left for Florence. She realized she was the only one on the property now. She wondered if that was why Piero left her his gun.

She turned to Franco. 'Do you know how to shoot?'

Back in the kitchen, Franco showed her how to load cartridges into Piero's gun, explained how it worked, and handed it to her. 'Never point it at anyone, even if it's unloaded.'

'Okay.' Julia accepted the gun, which was heavier than she'd thought. Or maybe a lethal weapon had a gravity of its own. 'Do you have a gun?'

'I have a hunting rifle, but my father has a gun. People in the country keep them to shoot rats and wild boar. You want to go outside and practice?'

'Yes, but I don't want to kill anything.'

'Of course not, but practice is very important. You should make time every day.' Franco arranged the gun in her hands. 'Hold it like this while you walk. Point at the ground, not your foot.'

'Got it.' Julia headed for the door, armed for the first time in her life. They went outside and walked down to the vineyard together. Bianco raised his head as they approached, blinking against the sun. He started to get up, looking around, and she wondered if he was looking for Piero.

'Hey, Bianco!' Julia called, and Bianco got up more slowly than usual, wagging his tail.

'I love dogs. We have a German shepherd, Yuki.'

Julia kept an eye on Bianco, who seemed to be struggling to walk. 'Something's the matter.'

'Maybe it's nothing. Older dogs are stiff when they wake up. It takes Yuki time to get going, too.'

'I don't know, this looks bad.' Julia watched Bianco take a few faltering steps. 'Hold this, please.' She handed Franco the gun and hurried to Bianco, who staggered toward her, hanging his head. She reached him, knelt down, and patted him. 'You okay, buddy?'

Bianco panted, wobbling on his feet.

Franco arrived, frowning. 'Our old dog did this after he had a stroke. I think you should take him to the vet. We use the emergency vet in Greve.'

'Okay, I will.'

'Let me call ahead.' Franco slid his phone from his pocket. 'They're very good.'

'Thank you.' Julia petted Bianco while Franco made the call, spoke in Italian to the vet, then hung up.

'They can take him now. I'll help you carry him to the car.'

39

Julia sat in the waiting room like a nervous mother. A tattooed vet tech in green scrubs had taken Bianco and whisked him behind a door of frosted white glass. She was the only person in the room, small but decidedly Tuscan. The walls were of exposed stone, the lighting recessed, and the low couch covered with a brown pleather. End tables held brochures about vaccination, microchipping, and heat stroke. On the wall hung diplomas from the University of Pisa and the University of Bologna. The air smelled vaguely antiseptic.

Julia shifted on the couch, her thoughts returning to the villa. She would miss Anna Mattia and Piero, and it stung that they thought she was crazy, like Rossi. Nor could she deny that the prospect of being alone on the property made her nervous. The Italian police hadn't called her back, and neither had the Philly detective.

Her phone pinged, and she scrolled to the text function. Her heart lifted to see it was from Gianluca.

I'm happy you got home ok. I hope you're more useful than I am today. I sit in meetings and think of you. Please tell me I didn't dream last night. It felt like one.

Wow. Julia was about to respond, but a guilty pang stopped her. She still couldn't believe she'd slept with him. She didn't know if she wanted to start a relationship with him. She both wished he would and wouldn't come over tonight. She felt pressure to respond because he would be waiting. She texted:

Bad news. I'm at the vet. Bianco is sick. Anna Mattia and Piero left.

Gianluca texted back instantly:

Oh no! Let me know how it goes. See you at 8. Until then, a kiss.

'Ms Pritzker?' the receptionist called to her. 'The vet is ready to see you. Exam room D.'

Julia entered a windowless white room that held a forty-something woman with a studious gaze behind rimless glasses and bouncy black hair. She had on turquoise scrubs and a pink stethoscope with its bulb tucked into her pocket. She stood behind a stainless-steel examining table across from black plastic bucket chairs and a cabinet with a sink. Bianco was nowhere in sight.

'Is he okay?' Julia asked, her heart in her throat.

'Yes, I'm Dr Caraccioli,' the vet said in perfectly schooled English. 'We're giving him IV fluids and a sedative that should help him sleep. You can take him home today.'

'Thank God.' Julia felt a wave of relief, then introduced herself. 'Was it a stroke?'

'*Stroke* is an imprecise term. We're uncertain as to his specific diagnosis. Sometimes older dogs have neurological events that come and go. This may happen more frequently as he gets older. We're testing his blood.' Dr Caraccioli opened a manila folder on the examining table. 'I understand you found him this way?'

'Yes, I was out last night and when I came home, he was walking funny.'

'I assume he lives outside. This breed usually does.'

'Yes.'

'So, unfortunately, they can get into anything, like animal feces or toxic plants.'

'I wished he lived inside, but he guards a pen that used to hold geese.'

'That's his job.' Dr Caraccioli smiled. 'He's fine outside.'

'Can I bring him inside if I want to? There haven't been geese for years.'

'If you want to, and for the next few days, keep him in. What are you feeding him?'

'Um, I don't know. My housekeeper fed him, but she left.' Julia worried it sounded snotty, but Dr Caraccioli didn't blink.

'I would put him on prescription kibble. We sell it here. It's easier on his stomach. I'll put it in your notes, for when you check out.' Dr Caraccioli straightened. 'So. Do you have any questions for me?'

'I'm wondering about his health in general? He's new to me. I'm not the one who takes care of him, but I will be.'

'He's doing well. His heart is fine and his hind legs are well situated in his hip joints. Do you know who his primary veterinarian is? There are several in the area. We have no records on him.'

'I don't know, but I can try to find out.' Julia hoped she could find his records or get in touch with Anna Mattia.

'Good, please let us know, and we will send your vet a report.'

'Thank you.' Julia felt unaccountably choked up. 'He's a good dog.'

'They all are,' Dr Caraccioli said with a kind smile.

Julia drove home with Bianco sleeping soundly in the back seat. She could tell she wasn't being followed because the road was narrow and most of the traffic was farm trucks toting hay bales or lumber. She'd texted Gianluca to say that Bianco was okay, and he'd texted her a heart emoji that gave her a warm rush, then made her wonder if there was a guilt emoji.

Julia knew what she had to do next, as soon as she got back to the villa.

Her villa.

Julia left Bianco sleeping in the kitchen and hurried out the back door. She had to find out if Anna Mattia and Piero had discovered something in the vineyard that scared them away, like bones or even a body.

She took a left, heading for the vineyard. The air had warmed, and sun blasted the tangled vines and unruly trees. She wondered if the little girl in the cell had been her biological mother and where she was now. Was she alive? Or was she dead, buried on this very property? The police weren't going to look, so it was up to Julia. It was a crazy thought, but she was getting used to thinking crazy thoughts.

She crossed to the hole Piero had been digging over the original tunnel. She looked down the hole and all she could see was dirt and embedded rock. The battered shovel lay in the dirt. She picked it up, scanning the vineyard. She didn't know if it made sense to go looking for a buried body, but she wouldn't sleep if she didn't try.

She got busy.

40

Two hours later, Julia hadn't found any bones or bodies, but she'd toured her property and knew it better. Her legs and arms were covered with scratches, and she was sweaty and starving, so she trudged up the hill to the villa. She entered the kitchen, fetched a glass, and poured herself water, leaning on the sink. It felt strange to be in the kitchen without Anna Mattia.

Julia crossed to the refrigerator and looked inside. Everything was organized, and on the right were grapes, strawberries, and blueberries. On the left were jars of green and black olives, fresh broccoli, and packaged lamb chops. The middle drawer was filled with cheeses, and the bottom drawers contained romaine and butterhead lettuce, potatoes, onions, and garlic.

Julia grabbed some grapes and gobbled them. She found a thick loaf of rustic bread under the covered dish, so she retrieved a serrated knife and made a cheese sandwich, while Bianco shuffled into the kitchen, still hanging his head, his walk wobbly.

'Hey buddy, how are you?' Julia went over and scratched him behind his soft ears. His round amber eyes met hers, his pink tongue lolling adorably out, then he started shuffling toward the back door. She thought he might need to go to the bathroom, so she opened it, and he trundled out and turned toward Anna Mattia and Piero's house.

Julia watched him go, then he trotted downhill and she lost sight of him. She took off, hurried down the hill toward the carriage house, then looked around. The dog had disappeared.

'Bianco!' Julia called, then heard a noise inside the equipment shed. She hustled to the shed and crossed into the cool shade next to the tractor. A plastic trash bin lay on its side, its lid off, and Bianco was sniffing soiled napkins on the ground.

'No, buddy!' Julia tugged him away by the collar and hooked a soggy napkin shred from his mouth. She realized he must've gotten into the garbage and it upset his stomach. She righted the bin, picked up the trash, and closed the lid.

Suddenly her phone rang, and she slid it out of her pocket. The screen showed the Philly area code, 215, but she didn't recognize the number. She answered, 'Hello?'

'Ms Pritzker? Detective Tom Malloy from the Homicide Division. I picked up your husband's case. I heard you called Detective Pivali.'

'Yes, is he in?' Julia walked Bianco out of the shed, holding onto his collar.

'He was reassigned, and I caught the case. I'm fully up to speed. How can I help you?'

'Have there been any developments?'

'No, I'm sorry, not yet. We have a new video from a traffic cam. We have no suspects as yet. We'll keep at it.'

Julia's heartbeat quickened. It was the first she'd heard of the traffic cam. 'What does the video show?'

'It shows the assault, but we have yet to identify the perpetrator. I will keep you posted.'

The thought that Mike's murder was recorded sickened her, at the same time it gave her hope. She led Bianco toward the hill, heading back to the villa. 'Well, I think I have a lead for you.'

'Go for it. I'm all ears.'

Julia told him about the blue hoodies on the bridge and how they matched the one that Mike's killer wore, then that it was the uniform for the Italian soccer team. By the time she was finished, she'd reached the villa with Bianco and they went inside the kitchen. 'I think that's interesting, don't you? It suggests that Mike's killer was Italian. It's an unusual sweatshirt for Philly.'

'I see what you mean. So you're in Florence now?'

'Yes.' Julia told him she was being followed by two different men, then about her inheritance and the underground cell, editing out Caterina again. 'So, Detective Malloy, you see my point? Something's going on. I'm starting to think Mike's murder is related to my inheritance or any crimes my biological grandmother may have committed. She imprisoned a child in the villa, whether it was my birth mother or not.'

Detective Malloy fell silent. 'I'm trying to understand what the villa has to do with your husband's murder.'

'Mike was killed protecting me, and now I'm thinking it wasn't a random purse-snatching. They could've made it look that way, but they were trying to kill me because they didn't want me to inherit the villa and find the underground cell.'

'You're making assumptions, Ms Pritzker.'

'I know, but it's a lead, isn't it? Don't you have a way to figure out whether there were Italian citizens in Philly last October, when Mike was murdered? What about Italian citizens with criminal records? Isn't there a database you can search?'

'This complicates the investigation.'

'How?' Julia asked, puzzled. 'I think it makes it easier. It narrows the search.'

'Here's the hitch. The Homicide Division has jurisdiction over your husband's murder because it occurred within city limits. We have access to local and state databases. We don't have access to federal or international databases.'

'Can't you get access to them? There has to be someone you can talk to.'

'Yes, but we'll have to liaise with several agencies.'

'Which agencies?'

'Immigration, for starters. Organized crime, if we're talking trafficking. Counterterrorism, too. I can get it done but it's red tape all the way down. That's how the feds are, bureaucracy on top of bureaucracy.'

Arg. 'In the meantime, can you start with your local database and see if there were any Italian citizens in it, last October?'

'That, I can do.'

'Also, as far as the Italian authorities go, I filed a report with a Marshal Torti in Savernella. He knows everything about the case. He saw the underground cell, too. I can give you his number, and you can share information.'

'Sure, go ahead.'

Julia scrolled her phone and read him Marshal Torti's phone number.

'That's a long number, huh? Looks like a bank account.' Detective Malloy chuckled. 'Look, I have to go. Call anytime. I'll keep you posted. Goodbye now.'

'Bye, thanks,' Julia ended the call, her heart sinking. She worried that the disconnect between Philly and Italy would be a problem.

She needed a friend, and one was only a call away.

Julia called Courtney. 'Hey Court, I just got off the phone with the detective on Mike's case. Got a second?'

'Sure,' Courtney answered, excited. 'Any leads?'

'Not from him, but from me, yes.'

'Wait. How'd *you* get a lead?'

Julia realized she hadn't told Courtney about Gianluca. She wondered if she could edit him out like Caterina, but it would be the first time Julia had withheld something from her. 'Bottom line, I saw a blue hoodie in Florence last night and it matched the one that Mike's killer had on, and it made me think that the killer might be Italian.'

'Really?'

'Right, and I'm thinking the purse-snatching wasn't random. Maybe they were trying to kill me so I wouldn't find the underground cell in the villa. Maybe that's why they're following me, too.'

'Who's *they*?'

'I don't know.'

Courtney groaned. 'Hold on, I have a text to deal with. Can I call you back in an hour or so?'

Julia realized Gianluca would be here then. 'No, let's catch up tomorrow.'

'I'm flying tomorrow. How about later tonight? I'll be up, I gotta pack.'

Julia braced herself. 'Actually, no, I'm having someone over.'

'To your haunted villa?'

'Yes, we're having haunted lamb chops.'

Courtney snorted. 'Is it another ghost? You got room?'

'Very funny.' Julia braced herself for a reaction. 'It's a guy.'

'Wait, *what*?' Courtney whooped. 'Hallelujah! I didn't see *that* coming. You *met someone*? Finally!'

'Are you kidding? It's too soon!'

'No, it's not!' Courtney squealed. 'Is he hot? What's he look like? Send pix!'

'I don't have one.'

'Tell me everything! What's his name?'

'Gianluca Moretti.'

'Are you fucking kidding me? Hottest. Name. Ever!'

Julia crossed to the refrigerator to see what she could make for dinner.

'This is so *great*! How did you meet him? Tell me what's going on!'

'Court, for real, I feel guilty.' Julia took the lamb chops and broccoli out of the refrigerator, then set them on the counter.

'No, why? You *should* have a romance. It's *Italy*!'

Julia's gut wrenched. 'What about Mike?'

'Look, I loved Mike, too, but it's okay. It really is. You're young and you have to live your life. Let's be in a positive space for once.'

'I'm *in* a positive space,' Julia said, defensively. She went to the base cabinet and looked for a roasting dish among the stacked pans. She found one and pulled it out with a clatter, cradling the phone on her shoulder. 'Meanwhile Anna Mattia and Piero left—'

'I so don't care. Back to Gianluca. Are you sleeping with him? Oh my God, you're sleeping with him, aren't you? I can tell.'

Julia groaned. 'I'm not *sleeping with* him.'

'But you slept with him, didn't you? The right answer is, "Hell, yes!"'

Busted. Julia couldn't bring herself to say it. She set the pan on the counter.

'Oh my friggin' God! That's a yes!' Courtney cheered. 'Tell me everything!'

'I don't have time. I have to get ready.'

'Gimme the executive summary.'

'Okay.' Julia told Courtney about Gianluca, but it wasn't as much fun as it used to be. Widows weren't entitled to joy, and romance didn't come in black.

'It really is okay to see him,' Courtney said, reading Julia's mind.

'I still wear my wedding ring. That's just weird.'

'No, it's a transition.'

'I don't want a *transition*.' Julia felt a pang. 'I love Mike.'

'But Gianluca sounds like a sweet guy.'

'He can't replace Mike.'

'He's not a Mike replacement. You're not going to marry him.'

Julia couldn't let it go. 'He was hurt before, and I don't want to hurt him.'

'So, don't hurt him.'

'I will, if I can't return his feelings.' Julia knew it was true as soon as she said it aloud.

'That's his lookout, not yours.'

'That's not nice.'

'Yes, it is,' Courtney shot back. 'He's a grown man. He has agency. Enjoy him!'

How? Julia didn't think she could enjoy Gianluca and be loyal to Mike. She felt stuck between them, neither here nor there, trapped in the interstices of her own life.

'Jules, Mike would want you to move on.' Courtney's tone softened. 'He would want you to be happy. Gianluca sounds good for you.'

'What if I'm not good for him?'

'Why don't you want to be happy?'

'What?' Julia asked, stung.

'So many amazing things are happening for you, but you turn each one negative. You inherit millions of dollars, but that doesn't make you happy. You get a villa in Tuscany, but you see ghosts. You meet a great guy, but you won't be happy. It's like you *refuse* to be happy.'

'That's not true.' Julia could hear a new weariness in Courtney's tone. 'If I could move on, I would, but it's not that easy—'

'Of course it is, you slept with him!' Courtney shot back, and Julia felt her throat tighten. A wave of shame swept over her, and she felt terrible, not because Courtney said it, but because it was true.

'I have… to go,' Julia stammered, hanging up.

*

Julia sipped Chianti in the quiet kitchen. She'd showered, blown out her hair, and changed into a white cashmere sweater with a V-neck and jeans. She hadn't brought perfume, which was good because she would have overthought wearing any.

Enjoy him.

Julia's gaze fell on the meal she'd cook when Gianluca got here. Lamb chops topped with fresh rosemary and cracked black pepper glistened in a ceramic pan, and she'd made broccoli florets, plus an endive and Bibb lettuce salad with feta cheese. She even cut shallots and thyme for a dressing of olive oil and balsamic. Mike always loved lamb chops, but she couldn't think about that now.

Her phone rang, and Julia took it quickly, expecting Courtney, calling back. But it was an Italian number. She answered, 'Hello?'

'Ms Pritzker, this is Dr Caraccioli, the vet who treated Bianco.'

'Oh yes, how are you?'

'I'm fine. How is he?'

'He's resting quietly.' Julia checked Bianco, curled up like a powdered doughnut. 'By the way, I found some garbage he'd gotten into. I assume it didn't agree with him.'

Dr Caraccioli paused. 'Garbage? How much did he eat?'

'I'm not sure.'

'Is any left?'

'No, he ate it all.'

Dr Caraccioli cleared her throat. 'I'm calling because I had some concerns when he was here. I put a rush on his blood tests, and the results verified them.'

'Oh no, what?' Julia asked, alarmed. 'Is he okay?'

'Yes, he should be fine. It doesn't change my treatment. Let me ask you, you aren't his caretaker, correct?'

'Correct. My housekeeper and her husband are.'

'May I speak with them?'

'No, unfortunately, they've gone.'

'When will they return?'

'They won't. They moved to Abruzzo.'

'What are their names?'

'Anna Mattia Vesta and her husband, Piero Fano.'

'Do you have their contact information?'

'No, I'm sorry. I only met them a few days ago.' Julia didn't understand why the vet was asking so many questions.

'Have you learned who's Bianco's primary veterinarian?'

'I haven't had a chance yet. Why do you ask?'

'Bianco's blood showed the presence of a plant substance.'

'He must have gotten it outside. The vineyard here is overgrown. There must be tons of weeds and plants.'

'No, this plant is not native to Tuscany.' Dr Caraccioli paused. 'It's the iboga plant, native to central Africa. Africa's not so far from Italy, as you may know. The drug made from the iboga plant is ibogaine. It's a controlled substance here and in the United States.'

'A drug?' Julia asked, puzzled.

'Yes. In fact, if I had a reasonable basis to suspect that you had given ibogaine to Bianco, I'd report you to the authorities.'

Yikes. Julia felt taken aback. 'I swear, I'd never do anything like that. I don't have any of that plant, drug, whatever. What does it do?'

'It's from a family of hallucinogens.'

Julia gasped.

41

Julia reeled, shocked. 'Dr Caraccioli, did you say it's a *hallucinogen*?'

'Yes. Ibogaine is a powerful psychedelic, and it can induce hallucinations in humans for up to twenty-four hours, depending on the dosage.'

'Psychedelic? You mean it makes you see colors and things that aren't there?' Julia tried to wrap her mind around it. 'So Bianco wasn't sick, he was *drugged*?'

'Yes, the drug is similar to LSD, psilocybin, ketamine, MDMA, or salvia. I can only imagine what poor Bianco experienced. We know little about how psychedelics affect animals. I'm hoping he slept through most of it. It was a small dose.'

'What does the drug do to people, in small doses?' Julia flashed on the garbage scattered on the shed floor. It was *her* leftovers. *She'd* eaten the drugged meals, too.

'In humans, ibogaine has the same hallucinatory effect. It causes an altered state of consciousness, also delusions and paranoia. By most accounts, the hallucinations aren't pleasant. They are so-called bad trips. The use of this family of drugs is highly controversial. Microdosing it and other psychedelics has been used to treat withdrawal from opiates in the United States and elsewhere. Such microdosing has mostly been discontinued for safety concerns.'

'What safety concerns?' Julia asked, aghast.

'It can cause sudden cardiac arrest and death.'

'My God!' Julia felt horrified. 'Dr Caraccioli, this is shocking. I'm trying to understand how anyone could get that drug.'

'It can be obtained like any so-called party drug. We see this sometimes in our practice. People find it amusing to give their pets drugs or alcohol. However, intentionally feeding an animal a controlled substance is inhumane under Italian law. Our practice takes animal welfare very seriously.'

'So do I, of course.'

'So please let me know if you get contact information for his previous caretakers or for your primary veterinarian.'

'Of course I will. Thank you so much. Goodbye, now.' Julia hung up the phone, distraught. She looked around the kitchen, remembering Anna Mattia cooking for her. The *pappa al' pomodoro*. The chicken with *Vin Santo*. The *gnocchi* with tomato sauce. The *polenta* with *mozzarella* and *broccoli rabe*. Had Anna Mattia been dosing her food? Or her Chianti? Giving her a psychedelic that made her see things? Become paranoid? *Hallucinate?*

Julia's thoughts raced. After her first dinner, she had the nightmare about the ceiling fresco coming alive, trying to eat her and burn her to death. After the second dinner, she'd had the nightmare about Caterina trying to strangle her and she'd run to the vineyard, clawing at her own neck. After the third dinner, she'd seen her laptop levitate and the Zodiac signs attack her, sending her running for Anna Mattia and Piero. Had she been on *hallucinogens*? Had a psychedelic produced those bad trips?

Julia tried to figure it out, testing the theory. Last night was the only night she'd eaten out, in a restaurant with Gianluca. She'd had the panic attack on the bridge, but that was real. She'd had no nightmares and slept well. Maybe there was no Caterina at all, appearing to her in the living room. Maybe she'd been drugged and hallucinated a blue ghost. But if so, how did she find the crack in the wall? The tunnel that led to the underground room?

Julia crossed to the refrigerator, opened the door, and scanned the contents with new eyes. There had been no leftovers, which now seemed odd. Anna Mattia didn't waste food, so why had she thrown away so much? And why did Anna Mattia take the time to throw out leftovers before they'd left? Piero hadn't even put his shovel away.

Julia reached the likeliest conclusion. Anna Mattia and Piero were hiding what they'd done. They'd drugged her. They *wanted* her to hallucinate. They were trying to make her think she was crazy. Or *drive* her crazy.

Her appalled gaze fell on Anna Mattia's note, still on the table.

*Sorry we go Abruzzo. The villa have evil spirit.
You are crazy like Signora.*

Anger flared in her chest. Julia had more questions than answers. What about the 'evil spirit' thing? Was that a lie? They'd sure left in a hurry. Why? Had they known the tunnel was there? Had they been lying that they believed Rossi had no children? Or were they part of a kidnapping ring, if there was one?

Julia's memories kept coming, but now she wondered what had really been going on. She remembered Anna Mattia, casting off the evil eye with her olive oil and water mixture. Talking with her upstairs in Rossi's bedroom. Saying that the dead lived among us. Telling the story about Sofia, her daughter who choked to death. Did they even have a daughter?

Julia thought back to other times she'd been suckered. Anna Mattia had told her to ask Mike for a sign. Rossi, too. Had Anna Mattia *planted* that pearl? Was the whole thing a ruse? A gaslighting scheme?

Julia felt struck by a thought, even darker. Rossi thought everyone was trying to kill her and she was related to Caterina Sforza. Dr Caraccioli had said that the drug induced paranoia and delusions. Had Anna Mattia drugged *Rossi*, too? What if Rossi's delusions were induced by the drug? If so, it wasn't heredity that both Julia and Rossi were feeling crazy. It was that they'd both been microdosed.

Julia couldn't sort it out, her mind a jumble of questions. Had Rossi really ordered her stuff to be burned? Maybe that was why Rossi never went to doctors, not that she didn't want to, but that Anna Mattia knew a doctor would test her blood and find out she was being microdosed? But why?

Julia's gaze fell on the gun, on the counter near the box of bullets, but even that baffled her. Why did Piero leave his gun? Why give her something to protect herself, after they drugged her and could have killed her? Was it part of their act? Who did they want her to protect herself from? The men following her? White Fiat? Ballcap? Were they in it together? A conspiracy?

Julia reached for the phone to call Courtney, then stopped herself. She needed to talk it over with somebody, but Courtney wasn't the right person, after that last phone call. Gianluca was en route, and he rode with an earbud so he could take calls. She couldn't wait until he got here.

Julia pressed in Gianluca's number. The phone rang, and was answered after one ring. 'Gianluca, hi, are you almost here?'

'*Ché?*' said a man's voice, but it wasn't him.

'Who is this?' Julia checked but she'd called the right number. There was a commotion and men speaking in Italian. 'Is Gianluca there?'

'*Aspete*,' the man said, and another man came on. 'Who's calling?' he asked in Italian-accented English, his voice vaguely familiar.

'This is Julia Pritzker. Who is this?'

'Ms *Pritzker*?'

'Yes, who are you?'

'Marshal Torti.'

What? 'Why do you have Gianluca's phone?'

'Why are you calling him?'

'He's on his way here.'

Marshal Torti hesitated. 'I'm sorry to say, he's been in an accident.'

42

Julia drove with tears in her eyes. Gianluca had been in an accident on the way to the villa. He'd been taken by ambulance to a hospital. Marshal Torti didn't know if he was seriously injured.

She fought to remain in emotional control. Rain screened the darkness, shrouding the road, vineyards, and farmhouses. Red lights blinked ahead. Traffic jammed in a line. It had to be the accident scene.

Julia reached the cars and joined them. Traffic started and stopped again. She craned her head and spotted black-and-white cruisers, their light bars flashing through the gloom.

The scene buzzed with official activity. Floodlights blasted the road with unnatural brightness. Uniformed *carabinieri* waved orange flashlights, detouring traffic onto the grass to the right. Smoking flares made a hazy perimeter.

More uniformed officers stood around parked cruisers, and the floodlights silhouetted their peaked caps and epauleted shoulders. Their cruisers idled, emitting plumes of exhaust. A flat-bed tow truck was parked on the scene.

Julia realized she hadn't asked Marshal Torti how the accident happened. She'd been so upset after he told her that she'd hung up quickly and left. She didn't know how Gianluca was hit or how many cars were involved.

Julia pulled over on the grass, parked, and got out into the rain. Two uniformed cops hustled toward her, but she got her phone from her pocket and called Gianluca's number to reach Marshal Torti. 'Hello, it's Julia—'

'Ms Pritzker, what is it?'

'I'm here, and I want to know—'

'Here? No, you may not breach the perimeter.'

'Marshal Torti says it's okay. Let me pass.' Julia showed the cops the phone and barreled forward, and the *carabinieri* hurried after her. She charged through the wet grass and up the embankment. She crossed between the flares, wedged between more *carabinieri*, and reached the scene.

Floodlights blasted the road like a nightmare stage set. Gianluca's Ducati lay on the street, its front end demolished and its bright red finish glistening like fresh blood. A tow truck's hook-and-chain began to drag it past her, making a hideous scraping sound on the asphalt.

No. Julia's hand flew to her mouth. She'd been on that motorcycle with him and could still feel her arms around his waist.

'Ms Pritzker.' Marshal Torti appeared beside her, holding an umbrella over her head. He looked grim under his black cap, which had a plastic cover. His raincoat was black. 'I'm sorry, I know you two were friends. Nevertheless, you are not permitted here.'

'How badly was he hurt?'

'I don't know. I wasn't here. One of my officers called an ambulance before I arrived. You must go.'

'Where's the car that hit him?'

'There was no other vehicle involved.'

'There wasn't?' Julia asked, confused. 'Then how did it happen?'

'We believe he lost control of his motorcycle, coming around the curve. He failed to complete the turn and skidded off the road. That curve, you see?'

Stricken, Julia tried to see in the rain. The curve was a sharp left turn, obscured by trees and bramble along the roadside.

'On a night like this, caution is required. You can tell how long he skidded from the mark.' Marshal Torti pointed to the road, but Julia couldn't see the skid mark in the rain.

'So how was he hurt? What injuries were there?'

'He skidded off the road and into those rocks.' Marshal Torti pointed again, and she squinted into the shadowy periphery of the floodlights, spotting large, jagged rocks on the other side of the road.

'Oh no.' Julia felt sick to her stomach.

'I don't know the extent of his injuries. I believe he sustained a head injury.'

No, no, no. 'So it's serious?'

'I'm sorry, I don't know.'

'Which hospital did he go to?' Julia asked, already in motion.

43

Julia wiped her eyes, trying to regain emotional control. Her windshield wipers beat in time with her heart. Her fingers clenched the wheel, and the Ferrari sped through the rain. There was traffic on the highway, and she had to keep her wits about her to follow the route on GPS. She didn't want to get lost or be later than she already was.

Her mind raced, full of second thoughts. She regretted not asking more questions at the scene. She grabbed her phone, pressed Gianluca's number, and held it to her ear while it rang.

'Ms Pritzker?' Marshal Torti answered, his tone surprised. 'Can I help you?'

'Yes, I'm on my way to the hospital, but I have questions. Gianluca wasn't the type to drive fast in bad weather. He was sensible. Doesn't it seem odd to you?'

'A motorcyclist going too fast is not odd.'

'It would be for him. Were there witnesses?'

'No. People are not out at night, in this weather.'

'Any CCTV cameras along the road?'

'No. Perhaps he was drinking.'

'No, he wouldn't.'

'Then perhaps he was in a hurry to get to your villa.'

'He wouldn't drive that carelessly. Could you be wrong?' Julia had a darker thought, one in the back of her mind. 'What if it wasn't an accident?'

'What makes you say that?'

'Put it in context,' Julia said, thinking aloud. 'I've been followed by two different men, and Gianluca and I chased one of them, the man in the white Fiat. What if Gianluca's accident is related to that?'

'I don't understand how it could be. There was no other vehicle involved in his accident, whether a white Fiat or not.'

'But you don't know that for sure, since there are no cameras or witnesses.' Julia felt like she was getting institutional responses, like with the Philadelphia detectives. 'The driver of the white Fiat knew what Gianluca looked like. He knew the motorcycle, too. So maybe he had something to do with the accident tonight. You have to admit it's possible.'

'Well, it's speculation, but I suppose it is possible. What is your view, then?'

'The driver of the white Fiat could have followed Gianluca and driven him off the road. He could have caused the accident.'

'But you saw the skid mark.'

'I couldn't see it in the rain, but no skid mark tells you *why* Gianluca skidded.' Julia felt horrified at the pictures flashing through her mind. 'What if the Fiat driver followed Gianluca and scared him so much that he sped up and skidded off the road?'

'I understand, but there is no evidence of that. No skid marks or the like.'

'If it happened the way I said, the Fiat driver *didn't* skid. There would be nothing to show you what he'd done.'

'Why would the Fiat driver do such a thing?'

'I don't know, for whatever reason they're following me. Please, go talk to that Fiat driver. We gave you the license plate, and I'm telling you right now, I'm suspicious.'

'Okay, we will do so. We will investigate and determine where he was tonight, as well as the reason he may have been following you.'

'Thank you.' Julia almost cried with relief.

'But I must note that I am suspicious too, of Mr Moretti's driving. If you recall, he admitted that he drove between the lanes and on the shoulder, chasing the Fiat. That is hardly the conduct of a sensible, cautious driver.'

Julia felt her stomach flip-flop. 'He did it only because I asked him to.'

Marshal Torti sighed. 'Ms Pritzker, I have decades of experience in law enforcement, and I am also a father of two sons. I will not allow them to buy a motorcycle. Do you know why? Because I have seen many motorcycle accidents and I know firsthand that young men often take chances they should not.'

Julia could hear the conviction in his voice, but she still couldn't agree. 'But what if this is tied to the villa and the underground cell? Were you able to find the names of any missing children?'

'We have just begun to investigate. We don't have the answer yet.'

'Then again, what if this is connected to the cell, the villa, my inheritance? To *me*?' Julia didn't know if she was making sense, but wasn't about to stop now. If her theory was correct, Gianluca was targeted because of her. She felt the same guilt she had with Mike, as if the worst thing she could imagine was happening all over again. 'Wait, Marshal Torti, did you get a call tonight from Detective Malloy of the Philadelphia police? In homicide? He was going to talk to you about my husband's murder.'

'No.'

'You need to call Detective Malloy. I can give you his number. You should talk to each other. These things could be related, even though they're in different countries.'

'Fine, we will do so. Kindly call me at the office tomorrow with the number. Now, please, I must go.'

'Okay, thank you.' Julia hit the gas, her gut churning.

44

*N*EUROCHIRURGIA, or, neurosurgery, read the sign, and Julia hurried off the elevator and down the hallway. She'd asked downstairs about Gianluca's condition, and they'd directed her to a waiting room on the fourth floor, telling her he was in surgery. The thought terrified her. She hustled past patients' rooms and a nurse rolling a grayish standing desk.

Julia spotted a waiting room with glass walls at the end of the hall. She got closer and saw it contained a handful of people talking and comforting each other. She realized they had to be here for Gianluca.

How can he be gone, just like that?

She recognized the voice, disconcerted. It was her mother-in-law, grief-stricken at Mike's wake, and Julia flashed back to the scene, which had looked just like the waiting room. Mike's family, lawyer friends, basketball buddies, fraternity brothers, secretaries, and other staff had come, but impossibly, he was gone. It was like a sick joke. Come to the party, where the guest of honor lies in an open casket.

Her mother-in-law said, *He looks good.*

Her father-in-law said, *They did a good job.*

Julia had said nothing. She'd avoided looking at Mike in a casket. She'd touched his hand, which felt cold and oddly tacky. His flesh-toned makeup had come off on her fingers, appalling her. She couldn't accept that he was dead, dressed in a dark suit that she remembered him trying on at Bloomingdale's.

Babe, am I partner material or what?

The tie that Mike was buried in was her birthday present to him, a blue silk Hermès with tiny horseshoes. When he opened the gift, he'd been puzzled.

Thanks, babe! But why horseshoes?

That's their trademark.

Who knew that? Everybody but you.

So it's a flex? Nice!

At the wake, Julia played the role of Mike's Widow, but inside she was horrified, utterly *horrified*, struggling to metabolize the fact that he'd been *murdered*. That he died so violently reverberated deep within her, and she overheard snippets of conversations.

If there were more cops on the street.

What's the matter with people.

They better catch the guy.

I hate the new DA.

Julia shook off the memory as she reached the waiting room and pulled open the door.

Conversation subsided as heads turned in her direction. There were eight people in the waiting room, and worry strained every face. They were all adults, and an older woman sat wrapped in a paisley pashmina, praying a crystal rosary.

Julia introduced herself. 'I'm a friend of Gianluca's. I came to see how he was.'

'I'm Sherry Borsoni, his mother,' a middle-aged woman said in an American accent, managing a shaky smile. Julia knew it was Gianluca's mother from the family resemblance. Sherry had his large eyes, but hers were blue, with thick eyebrows and almost the same mouth, wide and generous. Her hair was the same lustrous black, but straight to her shoulders, shot through with silver. She was lean, too, in a tan V-neck sweater, skinny jeans, and black flats.

'I'm so sorry this happened.' Julia extended a hand, and their eyes met with shared anguish.

'Thank you. I never would have believed it.'

'I know, it's awful.'

'He was so careful, but I know that accidents happen, and the weather was so...' Sherry didn't finish the sentence, her lower lip trembling.

'I know.' Julia let the moment pass. She doubted that Sherry knew about her and Gianluca being followed by the white Fiat, and it wasn't the time or place to air her suspicions. Meanwhile everyone else was watching them, whispering in somber tones, and she got the impression they knew who she was, which surprised her. 'I hope I'm not intruding.'

'Not at all. I'm glad you came. I've heard so much about you.'

Aw. 'How is he? They wouldn't tell me.'

Sherry sighed, pained. 'He was in surgery when we got here. The doctor said he had a traumatic brain injury, a fractured skull. There were also several broken bones, two ribs, his femur, and a bone in his arm, the ulna I believe.' Sherry's dark eyes filmed. 'He was in hemorrhagic shock when they brought him in. He lost a lot of blood. They had to transfuse him.'

'Oh no.' Julia flashed on blood glistening in the darkness, then realized it was a memory from Mike.

'They tend to the brain injury first. He's in surgery now, and they say it will take several more hours, then he'll go into the recovery room. We won't see him until dawn.' Sherry's mouth trembled at its downturned corners. 'But it's a good hospital. He's in wonderful hands. We're praying for a full recovery.'

'So what's his prognosis?' Julia blurted out, trying to get her bearings.

'We don't know at this point.' Sherry tucked a strand of hair behind her ear. 'He called me before he left. He was on his way to your place for dinner, wasn't he?'

'Yes.'

'Please, let me introduce you. My family has taken over the way we always do. We don't visit, we *invade*.' Sherry motioned to the crowd. 'Everyone, this is Julia Pritzker, Gianluca's girlfriend.'

Gulp. Julia felt mixed-up. A minute ago she was mourning Mike, now she was Gianluca's girlfriend.

'I'll introduce you, but you don't have to remember the names.' Sherry pointed out her mother-in-law, her sister-in-law, her brother-in-law, and teenaged cousins. Julia shook their hands and said *piacere* to each one. They smiled with muted goodwill, Sherry most of all. 'My son is so excited about you. I must say, I noticed the change in him, almost overnight. It's as if he was brought back to life.'

'Oh my, thank you.' Julia felt touched.

'I'd love for you to meet my husband and daughter. They went downstairs to get coffee and sandwiches.' Sherry seemed to catch herself. 'Would you like something to eat? I can text them.'

'No, thanks, I'm fine.'

'Oh, look, here they are. I'm sure they have extra, knowing my husband.' Sherry motioned to the door, which was opened by a handsome, middle-aged man carrying a tray of sandwiches, snacks, and soda. He had cool wire-rimmed glasses, a gentle smile like Gianluca's, and graying black curls. He was wearing a striped shirt with jeans and started speaking Italian when Sherry interrupted him.

'Tonio, this is Julia, Gianluca's girlfriend.'

'Hello, Julia,' Tonio said in Italian-accented English, with a teary smile. 'It's good to meet you, even on this terrible day.'

'I'm so sorry this happened to Gianluca.'

'I know, thank you. We pray for him. Julia, this is Raffaella, Gianluca's older sister.' Tonio gestured behind him to a young woman with short blue hair, funky silver earrings, and a flowery boho top with jeans. A snake tattoo coiled around her right arm.

'Nice to meet you.' Julia was about to extend a hand, but Raffaella's pierced lips parted.

'Why are you here? You're not family, and it's only family.' Julia blinked. 'They told me—'

'Wait. Are you *married*?'

Julia's mouth went dry. 'No, I'm not—'

'Then why are you wearing a wedding ring?'

Sherry's eyes flared. 'What? I didn't notice—'

'See, Mamma, this is what I mean!' Raffaella threw up her hands, turning to her mother. 'He leads with his heart, he always has. She's on her little vacation fantasy, then she goes home, leaving him in pieces!'

'No, I'm... not,' Julia said, stammering.

Everyone looked shocked, bursting into excited chatter, and Julia edged back toward the door. She didn't want to tell them she was a widow, that she was sleeping with one man and feeling married to another.

'I'm sorry.' Julia fled the room and hurried down the hallway.

45

Tears came to Julia's eyes, but she wiped them away. She got off the elevator on the first floor and headed for the exit. Her step seemed to slow of its own volition. She didn't want to leave the hospital. She wanted to be under the same roof as Gianluca, until he was out of surgery.

She spotted a ladies' room and ducked inside to compose herself. She was still getting used to the unisex European bathrooms, with a basin in a common area and private toilets. She washed her face in the sink, dried off with a section from the cloth towel dispenser, then checked her reflection. She looked haunted, which was how she felt. She left the bathroom.

She reached a large waiting area near the entrance, in which about fifty fabric chairs were arranged in an octagon, with scattered end tables. Nobody was there except for a uniformed janitor looking at his phone, his cleaning cart next to him. Beyond the waiting area was a reception desk staffed by the ponytailed woman who had checked Julia in. She was about the same age, with pretty eyes and light makeup.

Julia took a seat, flashing on the scene upstairs. She felt mortified by Raffaella's words, which cut deep because they had a kernel of truth. She couldn't shake a deeper, newer feeling, of shame. Then she realized why.

You're not family.

The words had resonated in her chest. She knew the feeling, the close-but-no-cigars of being not-quite-family. She'd had it growing up. She shared her parents' last name but she wasn't *of* them. They were on one side of the line, she was on the other. The line was drawn in blood. Everyone in the surgical waiting room upstairs was

Gianluca's blood relative. The resemblance showed in their eyes, smiles, and curls. She didn't belong there. She didn't know where she belonged. She didn't belong anywhere. She never had.

The receptionist motioned her over with a puzzled smile. 'Miss?'

Julia walked to the desk.

'Did you go upstairs? Could you not find the waiting room?'

'Yes, but I decided to wait down here. Maybe you could tell me when he's out of surgery?'

'Okay. Are you from New York?'

'No, Philadelphia, but it's near New York.'

The receptionist's eyes lit up. 'Someday I'll go.'

'We'd be happy to have you.'

'*Grazie.*'

'*Prego.*' Julia smiled, then went back to her chair, sat down, and started praying.

'Miss? Miss?' The receptionist hovered over her, and Julia woke up with a start, realizing she had fallen asleep in the chair. The morning sun was shining through a wall of windows in the front of the hospital. The waiting room was full.

'Miss, your friend is out of surgery and recovery. They have moved him to the GICU, the General Intensive Care Unit. His status is critical.'

Julia felt her stomach tense. 'Is he going to be okay? Do they have a prognosis?'

'I don't know. This is all the computer says. I must go, my shift ends at seven o'clock.'

'Can I see him?'

'You're not family, are you?'

'No.'

'Then, no. Only family members may visit GICU, two at a time. They have strict rules. Sorry.'

'I understand.' Julia tried to think. 'I'll wait here.'

'No, they won't let you. It gets too crowded in the morning.'

'But how can I find out how he's doing? What if he takes a turn for the worse, or the better?'

The receptionist hesitated. 'I have a friend on that floor. If you give me your number, I will text you. Don't tell anyone. I would lose my job.'

'Thank you so much,' Julia said, grateful. 'I won't tell, I promise.'

'Please, go now. My boss will come by soon. You cannot stay.'

'I don't understand.' Julia looked around the waiting room, which was full. 'Why can they stay?'

'They're waiting for the testing center to open. They need their results before work.'

'Testing for what?'

'Some Covid, mostly drug and alcohol.'

'Really?' Julia asked, wondering.

46

Julia entered the testing center, a small, brightly lit room barely big enough to hold a nurse at an institutional desk and a crowd of people sitting in chairs or standing along the walls, looking at their phones. There had to be thirty of them, and it struck her that even though she was in a crowd, she didn't feel as anxious as usual. Her heart beat a little faster, but she wasn't afraid. Her mouth was a little drier, but she didn't want to leave. She didn't know why the change, but she didn't have time to sort it out now.

Julia crossed to the front desk and got in line. She wanted to confirm that Anna Mattia had been drugging her. It was likely, given what happened to Bianco, but she had to make sure. She wanted to know whether her seeing Caterina was a hallucination or real. The answer felt like a question of her own sanity.

Julia waited her turn, then walked to the desk, where an older nurse looked up with a pat smile. She had a halo of gray hair and wore pink scrubs covered with rainbows. Julia asked her, 'Excuse me, how do I get a drug test?'

'Here, fill this out. It's in English. Then take a number.' The nurse reached behind her and pulled a paper from a series of black plastic trays. 'Which test did your employer request?'

'It's not for a job.'

'How will you pay, then?'

'A credit card.'

'Fine. Take a number.' The nurse gestured to a red plastic number dispenser next to the desk. 'Find a seat. It won't be long. You pay when tested.'

'When do I get the results?'

'Usually in an hour. If you can wait a day or two, it's cheaper.'

'That's okay. I'm curious, if someone took a drug two days ago, would it still show in their urine or blood?'

'What type of drug?'

'A psychedelic. Ibogaine.'

The nurse didn't blink. 'I'm not a doctor, but most psychedelics are present for one to three days after intake, at a minimum. It depends on the dosage and the individual. It would show in a urine test, and a urine test is cheaper than a blood test.'

'How long could somebody expect the effects to last? One to three days?'

'That depends on the individual, too. The effects may last longer. There may be traces in the system that are not detectable but still produce effects in the user.'

Oh no. 'I see.'

'So. Are you testing today or will you come back another day?'

Julia realized the nurse assumed Julia wanted a clean test. 'Today is fine, thanks.'

POSITIVO, read the test result, for which Julia didn't need a translation. The results of her urine test were positive for ibogaine. She stood in the waiting room, staring at the sheet. Seeing it verified shook her to her foundations. It made everything that had been happening—that she'd been followed, that Gianluca had been in an accident—so real. There could no longer be doubt. She held proof that she was being drugged. She just didn't know why.

She folded the paper, put it in her bag, and left the testing center. She headed through the hospital lobby, her thoughts churning. Sunlight flooded through the windows at the exit, and she went that way. She reached the door and left, then headed for the parking lot.

I want Thy Heart.

Julia heard a voice and stopped in her tracks. She didn't know where the voice had come from. She'd heard it clearly and recognized it instantly. It was Gianluca's. She remembered the words from their dinner, when he'd told her the story about divine love.

Julia wondered if it was just the effects of the ibogaine. If the drug could induce a visual hallucination, then it could induce an auditory one.

But she *knew* otherwise.

She just didn't know *how* she knew. Or if she was right, or drugged, or crazy.

She turned around and went back inside.

47

Julia got off the elevator and slowed her step. She didn't want to make another scene with his family, for their sake. She spotted a floor map posted next to the elevator and took a minute to orient herself, wondering if there was a way she could see Gianluca without his family seeing her. Downstairs she'd learned that his room number was three, though they wouldn't give her any other information.

She eyed the map. The floor was laid out in a rectangle, with rooms lining the perimeter. There were ten rooms in all, with three rooms on the unit's long sides and two on the shorter. In the center was a large workstation and behind it was a small room labeled SALA RISERVATA, or waiting room.

Julia figured that his family would be in the waiting room or his room. There was no way she could get in, but she felt driven to lay eyes on him. She didn't know why, but she wasn't questioning her impulses any longer.

She located room three on the map, but it was at the near end of the unit toward the elevator, the north side of the floor. If his sister or anybody else decided to leave or look around, they would see her. She consulted the map again. It showed another elevator on the south side, and if she entered the unit from there, she could avoid being seen. She hit the Down button and got back in the elevator. She reached the ground floor, navigated to the south side, and located the elevator bank and went up.

The elevator opened on the intensive care floor, and she got out, breathing a relieved sigh. She was on the far side of the waiting room, and she walked to the door, which had a window in the top half. The layout was as she suspected, and all the rooms had glass walls.

She opened the unit door to find a nurse coming in her direction, carrying a clipboard. The nurse had patterned blue scrubs, a stethoscope around her neck, with a plastic flower clip and wisps of dark hair escaping her scrub cap.

'Excuse me,' Julia said, when the nurse reached her. 'I'm here to check on Gianluca Moretti. He was in a motorcycle accident.'

'Oh yes.' The nurse smiled. 'You must be the cousin from San Francisco.'

'Yes, it took me a while to get here,' Julia said, playing along. If she had to impersonate a cousin to find out what was going on with Gianluca, that was fine with her.

'His parents are in with him. I met his mother, your aunt. She's a lovely person.'

'You mean Sherry? Yes, she is,' Julia added to establish her credibility, such as it was. 'May I ask, how is he doing? I just wanted to know what I was walking into before I saw everybody in the waiting room.'

'That's considerate of you.' The nurse met her gaze, with sympathy. 'We're monitoring him very carefully. He's in a medically induced coma.'

Oh God, a coma. 'Medically induced? What does that mean?'

'I know it sounds alarming, but it's not uncommon after TBI surgery.'

'TBI?'

'Traumatic brain injury.'

Oh no. Julia struggled for composure. 'And what's the purpose of inducing a coma?'

'It reduces swelling and inflammation in the brain. It's a state of unconsciousness that gives the brain time to rest.'

'And is it different from a regular coma?'

'Only in that it's intentional. He's given propofol and other anesthetics to stay unconscious, in a sleep state.'

Julia knew she'd heard his voice in her head, outside in the parking lot. She had to understand how. She wondered if Gianluca had communicated with her while he was unconscious. It seemed impossible, but maybe it wasn't.

Julia asked, 'If he's in a sleep state, can he *think*?'

'Yes, brain function goes on, but we can't be certain at what level.'

Julia blinked. So maybe Gianluca *had* sent her that message, somehow. She couldn't have imagined it. Unless it was drug-induced.

'The level of brain function depends on the patient. Some patients who come out of medically induced comas report having dreams and hallucinations.' The nurse cocked her head. 'Some report they heard everything said to them, but others don't.'

Julia couldn't wrap her mind around it right now. She had to know more about Gianluca. 'How long will he be in the coma?'

'I believe about two weeks.'

Two weeks! 'Do you bring him out of it or he brings himself out of it?'

'We bring him out of it. We monitor his blood pressure and other vital signs and, of course, he's on a ventilator.'

No. Julia hadn't realized he couldn't breathe on his own. 'So can I ask, what is his prognosis?'

The nurse's expression darkened. 'You will have to talk to the doctor about that.'

Oh no. 'Okay, thank you, I will.'

'I have to go.' The nurse gestured down the hall. 'You're welcome to the waiting room.'

'Thank you.' Julia walked down the hall but stopped short of the waiting room. There was a water fountain, and she leaned over and took a sip, then stood up and turned toward the room, getting a parallax view of Gianluca.

Julia's heart ached at the sight. His bandaged head lay against the pillow, leaning to the side. His eyes were taped shut, and his face was pale. A blue plastic hose snaked from his mouth to a machine beside his bed, and ports and tubes ran from both arms. The wall behind him was screens and monitors, flashing colors, lines, and numbers. His parents sat on either side of him, each holding his hand, and their faces were turned to him, so they didn't see her.

Julia wanted to be at his side with every fiber of her being, willing him to get better. Right now, horrified at seeing him so broken, she knew, in a way she hadn't before, how connected she was to him, how deep was her bond to him, even though it didn't stand to reason.

They hadn't known each other that long, but she felt he understood her, and she understood him, and they appreciated each other fully.

She remembered Gianluca saying, *The thing about a broken heart is that it's open*. She felt the truth of that now, realizing her heart had opened to him without awaiting permission from her brain, bypassing her second-guessing and overthinking that got in the way of her feelings, blocking them even from herself, burdening her every day since Mike died, maybe every day she could remember.

Julia focused her mind and her heart on Gianluca, feeling that they were connected souls, able to speak subconscious-to-subconscious, because she'd received his message *I want Thy Heart*. So she sent him the reply:

I, too, want Your Heart.

Tears sprang to Julia's eyes. It struck her that she'd fallen in love with Gianluca *and* she loved Mike, too. She didn't have to give one love up for another love. She knew that it defeated the natural law that two things couldn't occupy the same place at the same time, but that was never true of the human heart, anyway.

She turned away and walked down the hall.

48

Julia drove home and turned into the driveway. She hadn't heard from Marshal Torti or Detective Malloy, and she'd driven with an eye on the rearview mirror, making sure she wasn't followed. She hated leaving Gianluca. She didn't know if they were communicating mentally or if she was under the drug's influence, but it didn't matter now. What mattered was that Gianluca had to survive.

Julia pulled up in front of the villa and cut the ignition. The car's powerful engine rumbled into silence. She grabbed her purse, got out, and went for her keys on the way to the door, then remembered she hadn't locked up last night, having rushed out after the call about Gianluca's accident.

Damn. Julia felt nervous coming home to an unlocked house. She opened the door cautiously and looked around. The villa seemed still and quiet, and Bianco was sleeping in the center hall. Relieved, she entered, crossed to him, and gave him a pat. He roused, blinking, then went back to sleep.

She was heading for the kitchen when she heard a noise upstairs. She froze. She waited for the noise to come again. Maybe she was mistaken. Or maybe White Fiat and Ballcap hadn't followed her because they were here, waiting for her.

Bam. Julia heard it again. Someone *was* upstairs. Then she heard footsteps coming from her bedroom.

Her heart started to pound. Her mind raced, planning her next move. It didn't make sense to run back to the car. She was closer to the kitchen. The gun was on the kitchen counter.

In the next moment she heard footsteps in the upstairs hallway, a heavy tread approaching the stairwell.

She tiptoed into the kitchen and grabbed the gun.

The footsteps moved to the stairs.

Her heart jumped to her throat. She raised the gun and backed up against the back door. She tried to undo the latch behind her but couldn't. She didn't try again because she didn't want to make a sound. Whoever was upstairs must have heard the engine noise.

The footsteps reached the top of the stairs, a heavy tread. He was coming for her. She would have to defend herself.

Julia slid her finger onto the trigger. Her hand trembled. She didn't know if she could fire.

One, two, three, she counted, to the footsteps descending the stairs.

A shadow appeared in the entrance hall, cast by whoever was coming down.

Four, five, six. He was almost at the bottom of the staircase.

Julia told herself to wait. She would have to hit him with the first shot. He would be armed, too. She wouldn't get a second chance.

Julia took aim.

The figure came into view.

Julia started to press the trigger.

49

'*ourtney?*' Julia gasped. Her finger froze on the trigger. She was looking down the barrel at her own best friend.

'Jules!' Courtney's eyes rounded with shock. 'You could've *shot* me!'

'What are you doing here?' Julia lowered the gun, her heart pounding. She trembled from residual adrenaline.

'Are you crazy?' Courtney's hand flew to her chest. 'Are you really crazy?'

'No, I'm defending myself!'

'You could've *killed* me!'

'What *are* you doing here?'

'I came to bring you home!'

'Why didn't you call first?'

'I knew you'd tell me not to come!' Courtney brushed down her T-shirt, which she had on with jeans and red cowboy boots, and Julia sighed, calming.

'Since when do you have cowboy boots?'

'You said you were in the country. I got them in Jackson Hole.'

'It's Tuscany, not Wyoming.'

'But they're cute, right?'

'Totally,' Julia had to admit.

'Anyway, you could've killed me. I know you're mad at me, but this is ridiculous.'

'I'm not mad at you.'

'You *are* mad at me. And I'm mad at you.' Courtney puckered her lower lip. 'We're in a fight. Our first one ever.'

'It's not a fight, it's a disagreement.'

'Whatever, it sucks.'

'It does. It really, really does.' Julia hadn't realized how much it hurt. 'It was so nice of you to come.'

'I was worried about you.'

'I know, I'm sorry.'

'I'm sorry, too.' Courtney walked toward Julia, and Julia walked toward Courtney. They put their arms around each other, and Julia buried her face in her friend's shoulder, warm, familiar and smelling of Chanel's Chance, a perfume she'd worn forever. Courtney hugged her back. 'I was too judgy, Jules. You know how I get.'

'No, it's me, I know it is, It's just that there's so much going on… and it's crazy and… I know *I* sound crazy.' Julia felt her tears begin to flow, without knowing why. Maybe there were so many reasons they all came together, like streams into a river.

'Everything's going to be okay.' Courtney rubbed her back. 'We're going home.'

'No, I can't, Gianluca might die!' Julia blurted out, crying harder, and Courtney gathered her up, moved her to a kitchen chair, and got her a glass of water and napkins to blow her nose. In time they started talking, and Julia told her about Gianluca, including how she heard him in her mind, then she watched her best friend for a reaction.

'Go ahead, laugh,' Julia said, starting to smile. 'You know you want to.'

Courtney burst into laughter. '*Mental telepathy* now?'

'I'm telling you, I heard him!' Julia pushed her playfully, then started laughing, and they both laughed until tears came to their eyes.

Finally Bianco lumbered in, his tongue out.

Courtney looked over at him. 'He's not a good watchdog.'

'He's on drugs,' Julia told her. 'So am I.'

'*What?*' Courtney asked, her smile fading.

The *positivo* test results were on the kitchen table, and neither of them were laughing anymore. Julia told Courtney everything that happened, and her best friend understood the gravity of the situation.

Courtney clucked, shaking her head. 'This is bad.'

'I know, I tried to tell you that.'

Courtney puckered her lower lip. 'I *was* judgy.'

'I get why. I'm not a conspiracy theorist, but I'm coming around.'

Courtney eyed her, brushing back a strand of hair. 'So let's review. What's going on? Bottom line it for me.'

'Somebody killed Mike, and I think somebody tried to kill Gianluca, too, and the crimes are connected. Detective Malloy says it's a jurisdictional mess, so nothing will happen soon, and Marshal Torti is Italian, so nothing will happen soon. So the cops are useless, and two different men are following me for reasons I don't know.'

Courtney mulled it over. 'If they wanted to kill you, they would have already.'

'True, and they *could* have. The night they went after Gianluca, they could have come after me. I was home alone.'

'And the night they went after Mike, they could have come after you.' Courtney shuddered. 'And they're drugging you and you suspect that they drugged Rossi, too. So they might have manipulated her, but they didn't kill her. They might be manipulating you, but they're not killing you.'

'The question is, why?'

Courtney snorted. 'No, the question is, what the fuck?'

'Right.' Julia shook her head. 'I think it's about the underground cell and whatever kidnapping scheme was going on here, if one was. There could be conspirators still alive that don't want it to come out. I hate being here now, knowing what was going on. Rossi wasn't even drugged during that time. Anna Mattia didn't come until thirteen years ago.'

'Anna Mattia could've been in on it.'

'Maybe, but I doubt it, because it looked like the wall had been closed up for a long time.'

'No matter how you slice it, Rossi looks bad.'

'She was a monster.'

Courtney hesitated. 'What if she's your bio grandmother? I thought she was, in the beginning. People don't leave money to strangers, and she's about the right age.'

'I know.' Julia's thoughts were confused. 'Everything I've learned about her—that she let this villa fall down around her, that she was paranoid and delusional, that she smacked the grocer's daughter, that she was a hermit, had no friends, and *now*, an underground cell that she puts a *kid* in—' Julia couldn't finish the sentence. 'That's insanity, that's *criminality*, and I *pray* I'm not her biological granddaughter. I pray my anxiety isn't inherited from her, or that I end up like her.'

'Of course you won't.' Courtney frowned, sympathetic.

'Plus I don't know where she got all that money from, and I don't know if I even want it anymore. How could she have family money from the Sforzas? What the hell was she up to? Is she collecting ransoms for kidnapped children?'

'I have a question, Jules.' Courtney met her eye with characteristic frankness. 'Do you believe you saw Caterina or do you think it was the drug?'

God knows. 'I've been asking myself that since I found out why Bianco got sick. All I can say is, I don't know, but I haven't seen Caterina since Anna Mattia left. The drug should be out of my system in a week or so. So we'll know then if I see Caterina, have any nightmares, or believe I can talk to Gianluca in my mind.' Julia felt a pang. 'I wonder how he's doing.'

'The receptionist's friend was going to text you.'

'Yes, and she hasn't.' Julia felt a new determination. 'I'm going back to the hospital tonight.'

'What about his family?'

'I'll figure it out when I get there. It's for his benefit, not only mine. I feel like I could help him if I was there.'

'How?'

'I don't know. Communicate with him? Just be there?' Julia realized for the first time that she felt like she *belonged* there, with Gianluca.

Courtney cocked her head. 'Why didn't you just tell the sister you're a widow?'

'I know, I should have.' Julia had been kicking herself. 'I felt weird being there and I knew it would make her look bad.'

'And you didn't want to make her look bad even though she was making *you* look bad?' Courtney rolled her eyes. 'That's gotta change.'

'Tell me about it.'

Courtney's gaze fell on Julia's phone, which was on the table because they'd been going through her photos of the watercolors from the underground cell. 'That's cool about the hair and the DNA.'

'It was your idea.'

'I know, I'm a genius. Too bad the results take so long.'

'Agree.' Julia thought of the second batch of hair, in a baggie in the living room. When the drug was finally gone, she'd test to see if her hands still tingled. 'By the way, when are you going back?'

'Unsure.'

'What? You have work. How did you even get away?'

'I'm the boss, remember? I'm going to stay a bit and help you.'

Julia felt a rush of gratitude, plus guilt. 'Courtney, you don't have to do that. You have meetings and all.'

'I can work from anywhere. Ask Microsoft Teams. I could be in Parsippany or Tuscany.' Courtney smiled. 'I know you've been through it, but I gotta say, I give you credit. You're going out, calling cops, driving a *Ferrari*. You're more like you used to be. Like yourself.'

Julia's chest went tight. 'I still miss Mike.'

'I know, but I see a difference in you.'

Julia thought back to the crowded testing center and how she wasn't as nervous. 'I'm doing better, I guess, but I don't know why. Maybe I have to do things here and I can't let my anxiety hold me back.'

'That makes sense. Bottom line, if you do things you're afraid of, you train yourself out of being afraid.'

'Oh no, hold on, I'm afraid.' Julia almost laughed. 'I'm more afraid than ever. I'm afraid of white Fiats, black ballcaps, ghosts, and maybe losing my mind.'

'But you're not anxious.'

'Right.' Julia smiled. 'I'm not anxious, I'm insane.'

'So progress!' They both laughed, and Courtney's gaze fell on the phone, which was face up on the counter, showing the watercolor of the stone well. 'Is there a well here, too?'

'I don't know.' Julia hadn't focused on the well watercolor, preoccupied with the self-portrait. 'I didn't see one.'

Courtney eyed the picture. 'My granny's neighbor had a well. You remember, Granny Kay with the farm?'

'Yes.'

'Turns out the neighbor moved away, and the new people found a dead body in the well.'

'Wait, what?' Julia asked, aghast. 'You didn't tell me that.'

'I forgot, it happened last year. It was the body of a random guy, a drifter.' Courtney pursed her lips. 'My mother said they never caught the neighbor. He's still wanted for murder.'

'Yikes. Did Granny Kay know him?'

'Not well. The farms are far apart, and he didn't go to church. If you don't go to church, Granny Kay doesn't know you.'

Suddenly Julia found herself wondering.

'What?' Courtney asked, then her bright eyes rounded. 'Oh *shit*.'

Julia rose, grim. 'Wanna see if I have a well?'

50

Julia surveyed the vineyard. The sun was bright, the day cloudless, and she could see all the way to the hilly treeline. 'I walked the entire perimeter of this vineyard. I hacked away brush where I could, but it's incredibly thick and grown together. I didn't see a well.'

'Were you looking for one?'

'No, but how do you miss a well? I assume it would be near the villa, right? As opposed to the other side of the vineyard.'

'It's wherever the water is. I think it's as close to the villa as possible.'

'Which do you build first, the villa or the well?'

'I don't know, I'm in sales.'

'Let's look at the picture again.' Julia held up the phone and shaded the screen. 'Wait. Do you see the little bit of background behind the well?'

'Make it bigger.' Courtney leaned over, squinting, and Julia enlarged the photo and isolated the background. Behind the well was a tiny sliver that showed two hills about the same height, planted in rows.

'See those two hills next to each other?'

'Somebody needs an underwire.'

'Very mature.' Julia smiled, already scanning beyond the vineyard, but there were so many hills it was hard to differentiate them. 'Look in the distance and see if there are two hills close together like that. That could help us locate the well.'

Courtney turned toward the vineyard. 'God, this place is one big thornbush.'

Julia double-checked the photo and the tiny rows on the double hills. 'There were plantings on the double hills, probably grapes. They'd be bigger now, so we're looking for plantings, not woods.'

'Got it.' Courtney scanned the scene, then pointed to the right. 'Look. Could that be them? It looks like they might be olive trees.'

Julia turned to follow Courtney's finger. 'I see! You might be right.' She held the photo up in that direction, excited. 'Look, it matches!'

'Yay! Now what?'

'So if we hack our way in a straight line from here to there, we should find the well.'

'Wait, let's be profesh.' Courtney slid her phone from her pocket. 'There's a compass in Utilities. That would keep us straight.'

'Look at you!'

'I'm basically Magellan.' Courtney held up the phone compass. 'It's north-northeast.'

Suddenly Julia's cell phone rang, and she glanced at the screen. GIANLUCA MORETTI, it read, giving her a start. 'This must be the Italian cop.' She put it on speaker. 'Marshal Torti?'

'Julia, this is Sherry, Gianluca's mother.'

'Oh, hello.' Julia prayed Gianluca hadn't taken a turn for the worse.

'I wanted to apologize for last night. We didn't know about your late husband. Raffaella found out on your social media.'

Julia swallowed hard. She'd posted a death announcement on Instagram. 'I should've mentioned it, but I was just so thrown off by what happened to Gianluca.'

Courtney shot Julia thumbs-up.

Sherry said, 'Of course, I understand, and again, I'm sorry. Raffaella is, too.'

'No apologies are necessary, really. How is he?'

'The same.' Sherry's voice softened with pain. 'He's in a medically induced coma, but I think you know that already. The nurse told me my cousin from San Francisco was here. When she described an American who looked like you, I cracked the case.'

Arg. Julia's face went red. 'Now it's my turn to apologize. The nurse mistook me for your cousin, so I went with it because I wanted to see him.'

Courtney tugged at her collar, mouthing *Awkies*.

Sherry said, 'I understand, and Gianluca would want to see you. If you want to visit him, you're welcome.'

Julia felt her heart leap. 'I would love that. When's a good time?'

'Tonight around seven. I bet we can get you in to see him.'

'I thought only family was allowed.'

'My cousin isn't coming. So maybe we keep up the ruse?'

'Aw, thanks,' Julia said, liking her. 'See you then.'

'Bye now.' Sherry hung up.

Julia breathed a sigh. 'That's better, but I'm worried about him.'

'Of course. Sounds like she is, too.'

Julia felt her chest tighten, then returned her attention to the vineyard. She realized that she was about to try to find a well that could contain the remains of her birth mother. The prospect was so horrifying that she couldn't think about it another minute.

'You okay?' Courtney looked over.

'Does it matter? Let's go.'

51

Julia and Courtney whacked through weeds, underbrush, and overgrown grapevines using a shovel, a scythe, and a machete they found in the tool shed. Their progress was slow but steady, and every step stirred up bugs, birds, and vermin that had taken up residence.

Courtney squeaked when she saw a snake, and Julia kept it to herself when a rat raced away from them, but they kept going. Nettles scratched their forearms, and thorns tore their jeans. They were about to give up when Julia spotted a rim of an alberese stone embedded in the ground. She'd seen so much of it that she recognized it immediately.

Julia pointed. 'Is that a fieldstone or a well?'

'Get it!' Courtney answered, and they worked to clear the stone, exposing the top of a small, circular well, about four feet above ground. The stones at the rim were bigger than those on the body of the well, a decorative element, and dark green moss and slick algae covered it in patches. Sedum grew between the stones, having pushed out the mortar in chunks. They figured the earth had mounded around it from erosion.

Julia scanned the well, wiping her forehead. 'It's narrow.' Courtney looked grim. 'It's wide enough for a body.'

Julia sniffed the air. 'It smells bad.'

'The whole place does. So who's going to look first?'

'I will.' Julia braced herself, went to the well, and looked inside, but it was too dark to see anything. Bramble, ferns, and spiderwebs filled it, and beyond was darkness. 'Hold on.' She'd slid a flashlight out of her pocket, turned it on, and shone it inside the well. There was plant material all the way down, and she felt the dampness of water below, but couldn't see that far. 'In the good news department, no bodies.'

'Whew.' Courtney leaned over, looking inside the well. 'Hold on, shine the light to the right again.'

Julia did, then noticed a rusted chain. 'What's that for?'

'Probably a bucket.' Courtney scrambled to her. 'Pull it up and let's see. Go slow or the chain will break.'

Julia pulled on the chain and gathered it up. It clanked and jangled, shedding flakes of rust. Her heart began to pound. 'It's not heavy enough to be a body.'

'Skeletons aren't heavy.'

Julia halted, grimacing. She couldn't begin to think she was yanking on the remains of her own mother. 'Court, really? Are you *trying* to freak me out?'

'Sorry.' Courtney cringed. 'Don't stop.'

Julia pulled the chain, and a black box popped through the plant material. 'Thank God! It's like a shoebox.'

'Maybe it's shoes!'

Julia laughed, releasing the tension. She pulled up the box and grabbed the handle, which was rusted. The box was metal enameled black and in surprisingly good condition. 'Please tell me it's not locked.'

Courtney pointed to a keyhole on the side. 'It's locked.'

'Shit.' Julia turned the box this way and that. Something shifted inside. 'God knows where the key is. It could be anywhere.'

'How do we open it?'

'Watch.' Julia picked up the box and bashed it on the side of the well, making a dent. She bashed it again and again, until the dents distorted the shape of the box. The lid popped on one side. She turned the box around and bashed the opening, and in the next moment, the lid broke.

'Victory! Open it! Maybe there's money inside!'

'We're already rich, remember?'

'Speak for yourself.'

Julia sat on the ground, pried off the lid, and looked inside the box. There was a manila envelope with no writing. She picked out the envelope. 'I guess Rossi put it here. It doesn't look older than fifty years.'

'Hurry up! Open it!'

Julia turned the envelope over, undid the brass brad, and peeked inside. There were three white envelopes, so she took them out and set them on the ground.

'What is this? A game?'

'Hold on.' Julia opened one envelope, and it contained a thick pack of multicolored bills in a paperclip, but they weren't euros. She slid one out, and it read 1000 LIRE BANCA D'ITALIA, with an engraving of a woman. 'This is a lira, from before euros.'

'Let me find out when they changed.' Courtney checked her phone. 'Italy used lira until about 2000 or so. You were right, it's old. Open the next one.'

Julia went to the next envelope, opened it, and slid out the contents, two green passports that read REPUBBLICA ITALIANA above a gold embossed emblem, then *passaporto*. 'Italian passports.' Her chest tightened as she picked one up. 'I'm almost afraid to open it.'

'Want me to?'

'No, I got it.' Julia opened the passport to a black-and-white photo of Rossi when she was a younger woman. Her eyes were clear, her gaze direct, and she was smiling at the camera. 'This is her.'

'She *does* look a little like you.'

Julia turned the passport sideways and read the name, ELENA RITORNO. 'What? Elena Ritorno? Her name is Emilia Rossi. That's not her name, but that's her photo.'

'She's Jason Bourne.'

Julia was too tense to laugh. 'So is this a passport with a fake name?'

'It could be, or it could be her real name and Emilia Rossi is her fake name.' Courtney sat down beside her, eyeing the passport. 'See, the initials are the same. ER. People keep the same initials when they choose aliases.'

'How do *you* know?'

'From Matt Damon. Open the other passport.'

Julia picked up the other passport and opened it to a black-and-white picture of a baby with cute features, a perfectly round head, and light brown hair. Her heart wrenched. 'A *baby*.'

'Do you think it's her baby?'

'It seems likely. The passports are together.' Julia didn't see a resemblance to Rossi in the baby, but the baby's features were too unformed.

'She could have kidnapped the baby.'

'Yes, that's true.' Julia turned the passport, reading the baby's name. 'Patrizia Ritorno. They have the same last name.'

'That makes sense, doesn't it?'

'Not here. The lawyer told me Italian women don't change their last names when they get married. The babies get the father's last name. But Rossi didn't give the baby the father's last name. Maybe she never married the guy.' Julia returned to the passport, hesitating. 'Now that I know Rossi had a daughter, it kind of scares me.'

'Why?' Courtney touched her arm. 'You think the daughter's your bio mom?'

'I think it makes it more likely, don't you?'

'Not logically, but I know what you mean. Before, when we thought Rossi didn't have children, it looked like she *couldn't* be related to you. Now she *could* be.'

'Right.' Julia thought it over. 'So this baby could be my biological mother? Is the little girl in that cell Patrizia Ritorno?'

'Possibly. I think it makes the kidnapping scheme less likely.'

'So Rossi was monstrous enough to imprison her own daughter, but not someone else's. Either way, she's a monster.'

'When was Patrizia born?'

Julia checked the page. 'November 3, 1972. In Bologna.'

'May I?' Courtney reached for Rossi's passport and opened it up. 'Rossi was born in Milan. March 10, 1947.'

Julia couldn't stop staring at Patrizia's passport. She used to wonder about her biological mother all the time, and it was inconceivable that she was looking at her baby picture, retrieved from a well in Tuscany. 'But why all this mystery? Why bury passports? Why have an alias?'

'Who knows? Let's see what's in the last envelope.'

Julia reached for the third envelope, opened it up, and pulled out six Polaroid photos, buckled with moisture. She sorted through them quickly, and the images were still visible. They were photos of arms and legs with deep, purplish hideous bruises.

'Oh no, this is horrible.' Julia shook her head, appalled.

'Holy God.' Courtney groaned, and Julia picked up one picture, turning it this way and that.

'I can't even tell what body part this is.'

'It's a neck. See the jugular vein? Under the bruise?'

'Ugh.' Julia sorted through the photos with increasing repugnance. 'This is the top of an arm, bruised up. Here's another view of the neck. The bruising is worse, like somebody was *strangled*.'

Courtney straightened. 'I think this is a go-bag.'

'What's that?' Julia looked over.

'Remember when I volunteered at that women's shelter, junior year? They tell abused women to make a go-bag, which is a bag with money, car keys, ID, insurance cards, the whole nine. They're supposed to hide the bag where their abuser would never find it, not in the house or the car. Somewhere only they know and can get to if they have to run.'

Oh my God. 'Or in a well.'

'Right. They tell you to take pictures of your wounds, too, so the cops will believe you. This is evidence of a beating, maybe more than one. The neck, the arms, the legs? That's a woman who was beaten.'

Julia's stomach turned over. 'So somebody *beat* Rossi?'

'It looks that way.'

Julia stopped at the last photograph. It was a baby's arm, the elbow misshapen, pinkish, and swollen. 'Oh my God, her elbow is *broken*.'

Courtney gasped, covering her mouth. 'Somebody beat them *both*.'

'This is awful.' Julia flashed on the underground cell. She wondered if she'd been thinking about it the wrong way, topsy-turvy. 'What if Rossi *wasn't* imprisoning the girl because she was an abusive mother? What if she was *protecting* the girl, *hiding* her from an abusive man? Someone who was abusing them both.' Julia felt the revelation come over her, changing everything she thought before. 'Rossi could have raised the girl here, in the middle of nowhere. No one even knew she had a child. What if Rossi kept the child a secret, not because she was crazy and reclusive, but because she wanted her child to stay safe?'

'She could've moved here to get away from the abuser. To get them both away.' Courtney nodded, her expression grave. 'A lot of women leave when the man starts abusing the child. That's the last straw, and the mom gets them both out.'

'That makes sense here.' Julia's mind raced. 'Rossi had enough money to live on her own. Maybe she got it from him, for all we know. So she comes here to the villa. She never lets the child off the property. She puts the girl in the cell when she thinks her abuser might be around. God knows, it's still wrong, it's still disgusting, and it's still terrifying for the girl—'

'But Rossi doesn't do it because she was abusive. She does it to protect her daughter. She was a good mother.'

'I don't know about *that*.' Julia couldn't shake the horror of the underground cell. 'You weren't down there. You didn't see it.'

'I get it, but we didn't know as much about domestic violence before. Maybe this was the best she could do back then. I don't know what the law in Italy was. I doubt you could get restraining orders.' Courtney mulled it over. 'Besides, to get a restraining order, she'd have to reveal where she was. Maybe she kept to herself because she had to. She was hiding from him.'

Julia felt a stab of guilt. 'So Rossi went about it in the wrong way, but she wasn't an abuser, she was a victim.'

'I feel for her. I feel for the daughter, too.'

Julia did, too, trying to sort it out. 'If there's no kidnapping scheme, then why was Rossi driving around at night?'

'What if the girl ran away? That could be why Rossi drove around at night, looking for her.' Courtney fell quiet for a moment. 'Do you remember Scooter, that chihuahua Paul and I had? He used to get out from under the fence. We drove around at night for months. We finally got him back.'

'So Rossi was driving around looking for her daughter Patrizia, not for children to prey on.' Julia realized it was just as likely, when before she'd believed the exact opposite. 'Wait, the timing is off. Anna Mattia told me that Rossi drove around at night, so that had to have been in the past eleven years. By then, Patrizia would have been long gone.'

'Maybe Rossi kept driving around looking, anyway. Maybe she never gave up. I wouldn't. Or maybe by then Rossi had succumbed to her delusions or the drug they were giving her.'

Julia nodded, stricken. 'Another possibility is that the abuser found them and abducted the girl, then Rossi drove everywhere looking for her.'

'That could be true, too.'

Julia picked up Rossi's passport, opening it. 'If we're right about the scenario, the passport names are real. We're positing that she was with an abusive guy, runs away, and hides here with the child. She wants to hide her identity, too, so she changes her name. Emilia Rossi is a fake name. Elena Ritorno is her real name.' Julia began to process the first fact she had about her birth mother, if it *was* her birth mother. 'My birth mother could be Patrizia Rossi.'

'You're almost there, honey. I swear, you're going to find her, sooner or later.' Courtney touched her shoulder, and tears came to Julia's eyes. She had so many emotions she couldn't parse them all. She *did* feel like she was getting closer to the truth, because if she turned out *not* to be related to Rossi/Ritorno or to Patrizia, then that would be a truth, too.

'I'm going to call Poppy now.' Julia got out her phone. 'I told her to search under Emilia Rossi and now she should search under Elena Ritorno, too.'

'Look at you, Action Jackson.'

'Darn tootin'.' Julia found Poppy's number, and the call was answered after one ring. 'Hi, this is Julia Pritzker.'

'Oh Julia,' Poppy said, in her cool British accent. 'I was just about to call you. I've liaised with a colleague in the States, and she tells me that your birth certificate was amended. Did you realize that?'

'I guess so,' Julia answered, trying to remember what her birth certificate looked like. She realized she should've brought it with her. 'I assumed that was because I'm adopted.'

'Not necessarily. Amended birth certificates are permitted in Pennsylvania, among other states. An amended birth certificate should show your correct place of birth, but I found out that the agency through which you were most likely adopted was International Child Services in Bucks County, Pennsylvania, which was privately run.'

'Okay.' Julia hadn't even known the name of the agency that had handled her adoption.

'Unfortunately, it's since been shut down after litigation over fraudulent irregularities. I'm in the process of obtaining the legal papers to understand the particulars. I don't have them as yet.'

'Oh no, what does this mean?' Julia asked, alarmed.

Courtney frowned.

'It means your birth certificate was amended to state that you were born in Philadelphia, but it may not be where you were actually born. That would be the type of irregularity that would get an adoption agency shut down. In my experience, it wasn't atypical at that time.'

'So where was I born?'

'I don't know. I'll keep investigating.'

'Maybe in Italy? I have Italian blood.'

'It's quite possible, but I'll move on to my next point, as time is short. Do you remember that I was going to arrange for you to consult a medium?'

Whoa. 'Yes.'

'If you're available, she can see you at four o'clock today.'

An hour later, Julia and Courtney had showered, changed, and were leaving the house. They were going to Florence together, but Julia was going to the medium while Courtney went sightseeing.

Julia petted Bianco goodbye in the entrance hall. 'Be a good boy,' she said, then locked up with Courtney behind her.

The Ferrari awaited in the driveway.

Courtney held out her hand. 'Gimme the keys.'

52

Julia felt nervous, having never visited a medium. She entered the tiled entrance hall of a lovely Florentine home, evidently converted to apartments, and pressed the intercom button under h. davenport. 'Hello, it's Julia Pritzker.'

'Hello, it's Helen, come right up,' a woman answered, with an Irish lilt. The door buzzed, and Julia went inside and climbed a carpeted stairway to the second floor. She arrived at the landing, and the apartment door was opened by a petite, attractive older woman, with a sleek white bob and hazel eyes set close together over a nose that was small and fine. She had thin lips, and her mouth curved into a slight smile. She was fashionably dressed in a black turtleneck, leggings, and ballet flats, and she looked fairly normal, for a medium.

'Nice to meet you.' Julia extended a hand, and Helen shook it, her grip firm.

'Please come in.' Helen turned, and Julia followed her into the apartment, surprised by the decor, too. She'd been expecting incense and crystals, but this was minimalist chic, Japanese-influenced. There was a dark sectional sofa with a teak lattice table on a sisal rug. The white walls were hung with large-scale modern art with thick brushstrokes. Three windows spanned the back wall, letting in plenty of light.

'What a lovely apartment.' Julia realized she had no idea how to make small talk with a medium. *Small, medium, or large talk?*

'Thank you. Would you like tea or something else to drink?'

'Water, please.'

'Please sit down. I'll be right back.' Helen left for a kitchen off to the side, so Julia sat, brushing down her blazer, hoping she was dressed appropriately for the spirits.

'Here we are.' Helen returned with handblown glasses of water and set them down, then took a seat to Julia's right, perching on the front of the sofa. 'Have you been to a medium before?'

'No.'

'First, I will tell you what I tell all my clients. I invite the souls who will come and speak to us, but it is only an invitation. There's no guarantee any souls will come forward, and I may not be able to reach anybody. It's not a telephone you pick up and expect someone to answer.'

'Of course not,' Julia said, but that was exactly what she'd thought.

'Poppy tells me you're an adoptee seeking her birth family and that you've been having some experiences that you can't quite explain.'

'Yes, I'd be happy to fill you in.' Julia organized her thoughts, since she had so much to tell in an hour, like in therapy. 'I've been having strange experiences, like I think I saw Caterina Sforza and she showed me a—'

'Please, stop.' Helen raised a delicate hand, her fingers manicured. 'I'd rather you didn't say more. I'd prefer not to have foreknowledge.'

Oops. 'Okay. I brought some things that might help you contact people, like hair, passports, and some photos—'

'No artifacts, either. Thank you.'

'Okay.' Julia clammed up. She was flunking her session.

'Before we begin, Poppy shared with me that you recently lost your husband.' Helen's expression softened to gentle lines, bracketing a new downturn in her mouth. 'I'm sorry for your loss.'

'Thank you.' Julia's chest tightened, a griefburst.

'There is a possibility your husband may come forward to speak with you. There is also a possibility he may not. How do you feel about that?'

Julia felt like things just got real. 'I would love to talk to him again,' she answered, trying not to hope as much.

'If he chooses not to, please understand it is not a rejection.'

'Okay.'

'Let me tell you what to expect next. I am going to put myself into a trance, for want of a better expression. My eyes will be closed. I may speak, shout, or become upset, but you need not be alarmed. I will be safe. Do you understand?'

'Yes.'

'Good. I'm going to begin.' Helen shifted back in the couch, placed her hands on her lap, and planted her feet flat on the floor. She closed her eyes and began breathing deeply.

Julia swallowed hard, anxious. She didn't know if Mike would come or what would happen. She watched Helen's lips seal and her chest go up and down, as her breathing seemed to lengthen.

'My goodness!' Helen's eyes flew open.

'What?' Julia tensed.

'I've been rejected as a medium, in favor of you.'

'*What?*'

Helen looked directly at Julia. 'You have abilities of your own.'

Julia's mouth went dry. 'What are you talking about?'

'You don't need my mediumship. You don't need me to contact these souls. *You* can contact them. They want you to. They tell me they're trying to contact you.'

Julia gasped, astonished. It didn't seem possible. It *wasn't*. 'Who told you that? Who's they?'

'I don't know, but I was asked to leave.' Helen smiled, amused.

'So you're not going to contact them for me?'

'No, dear. They want you to, and you have a unique ability to receive what they're telling you.'

'*Me?*'

'Yes, you.'

'This can't be true.' Julia resisted the notion, reflexively. 'I'm not a medium, I'm a website designer. I'm a Cancer, Sagittarius Moon, Virgo rising. I grew up in *Pennsylvania*, for God's sake.'

'Yet you have these abilities. I'm an astrology adherent, too. I think we are driven by forces that we don't always understand, some cosmic in origin.' Helen shifted forward. 'Julia, have you ever had an experience in which you knew something was going to happen before it did?'

'Oh my God, yes. The night my husband was murdered. I felt like something bad was going to happen, and a man stabbed him to death.'

Helen's eyes fluttered. 'Have there been other times? What about when you were younger? Can you recall the first time?'

Julia hadn't thought about it until this moment, then it came to her. 'I knew I was adopted when I was really little.'

'Tell me. Close your eyes and try to remember.'

Julia closed her eyes, and the memory was there, as if awaiting her. 'We had a house with a back deck, and I was in a playpen.' She could visualize every detail. The white netting of the playpen. A stuffed pink rabbit she loved. The warm sun, shining. 'My mother was smiling at me, but I knew I wasn't *hers*. I knew I wasn't *of* her. I always knew.'

'Open your eyes.'

Julia did, shaken.

'You were born with this ability. Those of us who have this ability often experience it at an early age and remember that experience, just like you did. However, many people born with these abilities ignore them as they get older. They talk themselves out of them. They're seekers, but they dismiss their feelings. They see them as inconsistent with science or "the real world."' Helen made air quotes. 'In truth, these abilities are consistent with both. My mother had the gift, and she recognized it in me and nurtured my abilities.'

'You *inherited* this… ability?'

'Yes, like any other.'

Julia wondered if she had inherited it and from whom. Rossi? Patrizia?

'I regret that your mediumship comes to you in a disorienting manner. I hope you can accept it in peace. It is a gift.'

Julia felt like she was getting a diagnosis, but didn't want the disease.

'I thought I saw the gift in you when you first came in. I'm not completely surprised a soul came forward to confirm.'

Julia tried to understand. 'What about Caterina Sforza? Did I see her that night?'

'You tell me. You may have.'

Julia felt a surge of validation. 'And when I went to her castle, I felt like I knew my way around. I knew things that happened to her there.'

Helen's eyebrows lifted. 'As if you were channeling her? That is completely possible for you, too.'

'It *is*?' Julia asked, astounded. 'Look, I know you said you didn't want information or foreknowledge, but there's things you should know if we're going to talk about this. I was actually being microdosed with a psychedelic without my knowledge. I know it sounds crazy but it was put in my food. So it's possible that I don't have any ability or gift, it just could be the result of the drug.'

Helen blinked impassively. 'Thank you for telling me, but as I say, I did sense the gift in you. I saw it there.'

'But how do you know I was channeling Caterina? Does that happen to you?'

'It has, from time to time. Perhaps you were channeling her more than communicating with her, but these abilities are related. We don't know the limits, or contours, of your abilities. It's way too soon. That will be your lifelong inquiry.'

Julia reeled. 'But here's another thing you should know. I have a friend in a medically induced coma and I believe I heard him say something to me, in my mind. I believe that I communicated something back to him. Is that possible?'

'Again, yes.'

'How?' Julia asked, mystified.

'Rather than answer piecemeal, let me explain.' Helen paused. 'We think of life and death as binary, as in when you're alive, you experience things, and when you're dead, you don't. But, that is not what I have experienced. I experience a *spectrum* of consciousness. Right now we're both living, so we have a waking state of consciousness. We also have a subconscious that governs many of our actions, which hypnotherapists access to help people, let's say, quit smoking. Your friend in a coma is in yet another state of consciousness. He is kept in a state in which the brain is resting.'

'Yes, the nurse called it a sleep state.'

'Precisely. When we sleep, we are in a different state of consciousness. People who sleepwalk are in yet *another* state of consciousness. You were given a psychedelic that produced an altered state of consciousness. So these are all various states of consciousness.' Helen spread her hands. 'Death is merely another state of consciousness on the spectrum. It is the cessation of brain activity, but not of *soul* activity. In my experience, the soul lives as a consciousness, and some of us, like you and me, have the ability to access that consciousness. That is the essence of mediumship.'

'So did the psychedelic cause my seeing Caterina or communicating with my friend in a coma?'

'A fascinating question.' Helen's eyes twinkled with interest. 'I believe your gift predates the drug. However, microdosing psychedelics may open a neural pathway that preexisted, like widening a door that was already open. Science has yet to understand the effects of such drugs on the brain.'

'I guess we'll know when I'm sure the drug is out of my system.'

'Not necessarily. Not if it opened a pathway or triggered a predisposition.'

Julia didn't know whether to be horrified or happy. She didn't know if she wanted the abilities or not.

Helen smiled warmly. 'You're perplexed, and I understand that. Your goal, such as it is, would be to understand, accept, and control your abilities, so that you can use them.'

'You mean contact the souls?'.

'Yes, I could mentor you in your mediumship. I can give you instruction that can help you receive these souls. I also have books on the subject and exercises you can try at home. We can start right now.'

'Here?'

'Of course. I communicate with souls here all the time. I consider it a thin place.'

'What does that mean?'

'It's an old Gaelic notion, close to my Irish heart. It began with the belief that there are places where the veil between the material and the spiritual world is thin. Those places traditionally exist in nature, but they can exist anywhere.'

'I don't know if I want to do it,' Julia blurted out, nervous. 'What would you do?'

'Let's try something. You said you brought artifacts. Choose one for us to work with. Don't think about it, just choose. Is there one that interests you, in particular?'

'Yes,' Julia answered, trying not to overthink.

'Please get it and hold it.'

Julia opened her purse and rummaged through the baggies with the hair, the passports, and the photographs. She slid out the photo of Patrizia's broken arm, closed her purse, and held the photo. 'Should I show it to you?'

'No. I'm not the medium, you are. Now close your eyes and focus on the picture.'

Julia did.

'We close our eyes because vision requires so much of the brain's energy. When vision is foreclosed, other senses come to the fore. It's why people reflexively close their eyes when smelling a flower or listening to music. For us, it's the first step in communicating with a soul, whether alive, dead, or somewhere else on the spectrum of consciousness.'

Us? 'Okay.'

'Now. Cleanse your mind of any thoughts but the picture. Focus only on that.'

Julia obeyed her, reproducing the image of baby Patrizia in her mind. She visualized the horrible swelling at the elbow, the dark bruising.

'Now, keep your focus and breathe deeply. Open your mind to your thoughts. Don't force them to come to you. Rather, *allow* them.'

Julia kept thinking of the injured elbow. She tried to slow her breathing and allow whatever came.

'*Allow* deeper.'

Suddenly Julia felt an agonizing pain in her elbow. Her eyes flew open. She jumped up, clutching her elbow, gasping. 'Ow! My arm! My arm hurts!'

'Julia, look at me.' Helen rose, pointing to her eyes, a clear and steady blue. 'Come back now.'

'Make it stop!' Julia kept her eyes on Helen. She could hear the huffing of her own breath. She cradled her arm. The pain in her elbow began to dissipate.

'Keep looking at me.'

Julia felt the pain ebb away, then vanish. 'What just *happened*? Was that what happened to my mother? Is she dead? Did she do that to me?'

'The only person who can answer those questions is you.'

'I don't know the answer!' Julia shot back, uncomprehending.

'Please, sit down.' Helen gestured to the couch.

'I don't want to sit down! I want to understand what just happened!'

'Sit down and I'll explain,' Helen said calmly.

'I was just in pain! Have you seen anything like that?'

'Yes, it happened to me before I understood and accepted my gift. You have remarkable abilities.' Helen smiled. 'I don't have the answers. You will in time, if we go forward and work together.'

'It sounds like therapy.'

'It's not, but it may be therapeutic for you.'

'I don't know if I want to go forward.' Julia sat down. 'I might just leave it alone. It hurts, for one thing.'

'I can help you with that, too.'

'Why did it happen?'

'I think the souls wish to communicate with you, and they just did, in a way you can no longer deny.'

Yikes. 'What if I don't want to communicate with them?'

'That is your choice,' Helen answered, with finality. 'Have a think and call me if you wish to continue.'

Julia didn't know what she wanted. Her thoughts were all over the place. 'What if I'm not made for... mediumship?'

Helen met her eye with a knowing smile. 'I believe that train's already left the station, dear.'

53

Julia hurried along the cobblestone walkway, her phone to her ear. The call was ringing, but Courtney wasn't answering. They were supposed to meet in the Piazza di Santa Croce, but tourists crowded every square inch, talking, eating, and jostling each other. Tour groups filled the stone benches and thronged at kiosks selling handbags, T-shirts, and souvenirs.

Julia pressed End, anxious again. Maybe she hadn't improved as much as she'd thought. Or maybe her session with Helen shook her up. She couldn't begin to digest what she'd been told. She glanced over her shoulder, scanning for White Fiat or Black Ballcap, but she didn't see them.

Her phone rang, and she picked up. 'Courtney, where are you? I'm in the piazza.'

'Sorry I'm late but I'm here, in the Basilica. Come on in.'

Arg. 'No, let's just go. It takes time to get to the hospital. It's rush hour and I don't want to be late for Gianluca.'

'We have plenty of time. Come in, it'll take ten minutes.'

'Okay.' Julia hung up, then threaded her way through the crowd to the entrance to the Basilica, a beautiful church known as the Temple of Italian Glories because of the number of famous writers and artists buried there. The Basilica's ornate white-and-green marble facade was divided into three sections, and a soaring peaked roof with a round window dominated the center section. The largest entrance was a carved wooden door, flanked by another set of carved doors, one of which was open.

Julia beelined for it and hurried inside to the Basilica. It took a moment for her eyes to adjust to the dimness, which made her feel off-balance. It was packed, and tourists were shadows shifting in the low light. She looked around for Courtney but didn't see her.

She whirled around, getting her bearings in the immense hall. Arched vaults flanked the room on either side, and at the very end was a beautiful altar and multi-vaulted nave, its elongated windows of stained glass glowing like jewels. Statuary and massive paintings lined walls of white plaster, and tourists milled through the arches, following docents in groups. She didn't see Courtney.

Julia texted her: **Where are you?**

Courtney texted back: **Near the altar.**

Julia hurried there, crossing the hall through the crowd. She spotted Courtney in front of a statue of the Virgin Mary, lighting a red votive candle on a stand of many others, their yellow flames in flickering rows.

Julia reached her side. 'Hi, ready to go?'

Courtney looked over. 'How was it?'

'I'll tell you on the way to the hospital.'

'Don't you want to light a candle for Mike? Or did you already, like, contact him?'

'No. I'll light a candle.'

'I already paid. Just take one.'

'Thanks.' Julia took a votive candle from a box, placed it on the stand, and tried to light it using another candle, but her hand was shaking.

Courtney blinked, concerned. She took the candle, lit Julia's votive, and replaced it. 'Are you okay? Tell me about the session.'

'Let's talk in the car. I feel anxious again.'

'Aw, and you were doing so well.'

'One step forward, two steps back?' Julia closed her eyes and tried to pray for Mike, but couldn't concentrate. 'Okay, let's go.'

'This is such a beautiful church. Michelangelo and Galileo are buried here, how cool is that?'

'Cool. Now let's go.' Julia turned away, and they threaded their way back through the crowd, passing a sculpted marble figure of a woman sitting atop a marble casket, holding a portrait of Machiavelli.

Courtney pointed. 'That's Machiavelli's tomb.'

'Oh no.' Julia recoiled, remembering Machiavelli had been Caterina's mortal enemy. Was she *feeling* Caterina right now? Could she *channel* Caterina? 'Can we go faster?'

'Why?' Courtney frowned, worried. 'What did that medium *do* to you?'

'It's not her, it's me,' Julia answered, heading for the exit.

Julia told Courtney everything that happened with Helen, while Courtney drove, listening. The singular cityscape of Florence surrounded them, but neither of them noticed. When Julia finished, she looked over. 'Well? Do you believe it? That I have… abilities?'

'Yes, I believe it.'

'Why?'

'I've known you a long time.' Courtney glanced over, grave. 'Remember that night junior year, you had a dream about my father? You told me the next morning, so I called home. He'd had a heart attack that night. My mom was just about to call me. He almost *died*.'

Julia remembered, in a flash. The dream came back to her as if she'd had it last night. Courtney's father used to visit campus and take them to lunch. One night, she dreamed he appeared in a suit and a Princeton tie he always wore, and he was trying to tell her something. She hadn't been able to figure out what he was saying and she'd awakened in a cold sweat.

'You remember?' Courtney shook her head, her eyes on the road. 'You didn't think it meant anything, but I thought it was weird. So did my mom.'

'So you think your dad's soul was communicating with me?'

'It's possible, isn't it?'

'But he was alive. He lived.'

'Yes, but he was near death, he almost died, and Helen's telling you that death is an artificial line. She's saying you can communicate with the soul of the person whether they're alive or dead, even for hundreds of years, like Caterina.'

'This can't be true.' Julia glanced out the window. Florence whizzed by at a dizzying rate, but it could've been her mood.

'Why not? There are mediums in the world. They're just people, and I guess at some point they figure out they have these abilities, like you have. They have to start somewhere.' Courtney nodded, steering to the right. 'If you watch true crime, you know they use psychics. It's legit.'

'She says it might or might not be the drug. Like it might wear off, but it might have opened a pathway in my brain.'

'A pathway? Wow! Like a portal.'

'Do you think I should let her teach me?'

'Yes, I do,' Courtney answered matter-of-factly. 'You don't know where it might lead.'

'That's what worries me.'

'It's good. It might lead to your bio family. That's why you went to her in the first place, you wanted to find them.'

'No, I went because I wanted *her* to find them.'

'So, even better, you can do it yourself.'

'Is it? Do I want to be a medium?' Julia shot back, then it struck her. If she became a medium, she could communicate with Mike. She'd be able to talk to him any time and hear him talk to her. They could be together again, in a way. It would be like he was alive.

'Jules, do you realize what this means? You have *superpowers*!' Courtney's eyes lit up. 'You're like Spider-Man when he first gets his superpowers. He has to figure out how to use them. Remember?'

'I'm not *Spider-Man*.'

'It happens in Star Wars, too, with The Force. Luke has to learn to use The Force. You have *The Force*!' Courtney grinned, excited. 'Wait'll I tell Paul! He loves Star Wars!'

'No.' Julia put up a hand. 'Don't tell Paul.'

'Why not? This is the coolest thing ever!'

'I don't want him to think I'm a freak.'

'Why can't you look on the bright side?'

Why can't you be happy? Julia shooed the thought away, but it was Courtney's own words and they hit home. Why *couldn't* she be happy? If she were a medium, she could talk to Mike, and to Gianluca. What about her mother? Her father? She wondered if her gift was a blessing, or a curse. She'd be opening Pandora's box.

Courtney was saying, 'Jules, it's a gift from God, like any other talent. You're an amazing artist, remember? You used to paint all the time. Hello, you found some watercolors that a little girl did, and she might be your bio mom. Maybe your *bio mom* has superpowers, too. What if you're *both* psychics? Mother-daughter psychics?'

Julia reeled. 'I can't *begin* to deal with that, and anyway I'm not a psychic. It's not the same as a medium.'

'What's the difference?'

'I don't know,' Julia had to admit. 'I'd have to ask Helen.'

'You mean Yoda.'

Julia let it go. 'You know, she gave me an exercise to try at the hospital, with Gianluca.'

'Try not. Do. There is no try.'

54

They walked down the hallway toward the waiting room, and Julia spotted Sherry, Tonio, Raffaella, and the rest of the clan through the glass. She turned to Courtney. 'Court, you gonna be okay with the Morettis while I see Gianluca?'

'Totally. I'll hang and tell them how great you are. I'm your hype man.'

They reached the door, and Raffaella spotted Julia through the glass, glowering.

Courtney whispered. 'The sister's giving you the stink eye. Use The Force.'

Julia opened the door.

Sherry, Tonio, and everybody greeted her and Courtney, with only Raffaella keeping her distance. The family looked exhausted and drawn, all wearing the same rumpled clothes, so they must've stayed over. Sherry's eyes were puffy and bloodshot, and Tonio was haggard, his chin dotted with grayish stubble.

Julia braced herself. 'So, how is Gianluca?'

'Not good.' Sherry pursed dry lips. 'He's developing pneumonia.'

'Oh no,' Julia said, stricken. 'What does that mean? What do they do?'

'They give him antibiotics. They say it happens when you're on a respirator. We have to stay strong. It's nice of you to come, after the last visit.' Sherry gestured to Raffaella behind her. 'Raffi has something she wants to say to you.'

Raffaella stepped forward, her manner cool. 'I'm sorry,' she said in a perfunctory tone. 'I'm sorry about your loss, too. I assumed you were married because of your wedding ring.'

'Of course, I'm sorry, too.' Julia felt unguarded enough to level with her. 'I admit, it's strange, even to me, to be seeing someone so soon after my—'

'I get it.' Raffaella frowned. 'But I love my little brother and will always look out for him. I want him to be happy and find a woman devoted to him.'

Sherry sighed wearily. 'Raffi, that's not an apology.'

Julia interjected, 'Sherry, thanks, but she's entitled to her view, and I can understand how she feels.' She turned to Raffaella. 'I know you want what's best for Gianluca, but please believe me, I care for him very much, I truly do—'

'Not as much as somebody who *doesn't* wear a wedding ring.'

'*Basta.*' Tonio stepped over, raising his hands, his check shirt wrinkled at the elbows. 'We are all here for Gianluca. If he chooses Julia, that is *his* choice, and if we love him, we will choose her, too.'

Raffaella averted her eyes.

Tonio patted Julia's shoulder. 'We can only visit him for ten minutes at the top of each hour. You can take a turn this time.'

'Thank you,' Julia said, her mind racing. She wanted to see Gianluca, but more importantly, she wanted to help him.

Helen had told her how.

Julia hesitated at the entrance to Gianluca's room and though she had seen him like this before, couldn't get over the initial shock. The bandage over his head. The tape sealing his eyes. The hose snaking from his mouth.

Julia went to his bedside and sat down. She wanted to kiss his face, but she couldn't, there wasn't enough skin showing around the thick plastic seal of the respirator. IV ports were attached to his arm, and monitors clipped his fingertips. The only sound in the room was the beeping of monitors and the *shush-shush* of the ventilator, which inflated and deflated his chest to such an oddly dramatic degree that she had to look away.

Julia let her gaze travel to his face and linger there, remembering the glint in his dark eyes, his long, flirty eyelashes, his grin, so warm and wide, and the curls in his hair, blowing in the gentle breeze. She could feel her arms around his waist, and how she pressed her body against his back on the motorcycle, the two of them moving easily together. She couldn't begin to think about him in bed, especially not now, when she was on a mission to help him.

Julia remembered Helen's instructions: *Touch him and close your eyes.*

Julia took Gianluca's hand and placed her palm on top, then closed her eyes.

Clear your mind and focus only on the message you want to give him.

Julia kept her eyes closed, trying to focus on telling Gianluca that she loved him, that he had her heart, that he was going to get better and he had to fight for his life.

Gianluca, please live, for me, for all of us, Julia thought, and in the next moment, a strange sensation came over her and blackness obliterated her thoughts. An image materialized from the darkness in her mind and began to take shape. It was a round light that began to flicker in the center, then blurred into a white streak.

Julia didn't know what was happening, but she kept her eyes closed, both afraid to lose the vision and afraid of having it. The white streak morphed into a single round light, then into the headlight on a motorcycle. An entire scene materialized of Gianluca riding through the rain before the curve at which he crashed, as if a movie were unspooling in her brain.

Julia gasped, fearing what came next. Gianluca was leaning forward on his motorcycle, rain pelting his helmet and jacket, when a white van appeared behind him. The white van accelerated closer and closer to him. Gianluca sped up along the straightaway that headed toward the curve. He looked behind him, then waved the white van to pass him. It didn't, dogging him.

Julia felt her heart start to pound. She couldn't believe what she was seeing. She squeezed her eyes shut and watched in horror as the white van accelerated. Gianluca veered to the left to avoid the white van. The white van swerved left behind him.

Gianluca switched to the right side of the road. The white van tailgated him dangerously. Trees lined the road so Gianluca couldn't drive onto the grass. All of a sudden, another car sped out of the rain behind him, shooting toward him like a bullet. The car was black with a red stripe. Its side door read CARABINIERI. It was a police cruiser.

Julia's mouth went dry. She watched as Gianluca approached the curve at top speed, chased down by the police cruiser and the white van. The three vehicles reached the curve. The police cruiser and the white van accelerated to Gianluca's motorcycle, forcing him off the road. He veered directly toward the rocks.

Julia covered her mouth. Gianluca flew off his bike. His arms pinwheeled. His body flopped through the air. He landed on the rocks, tumbled over their jagged tops, then rolled over and over. He ended face up on his back, writhing in pain. Rain poured mercilessly on his visor.

Oh my God. Julia reeled, stunned and terrified. The scene vanished as abruptly as it had appeared, leaving her breathless. She realized Gianluca was communicating with her, showing her that what happened to him wasn't an accident, but attempted murder.

Gianluca, I'm so sorry, Julia said in her mind, and the next moment, she heard Gianluca speak to her, again as clearly as if he were beside her:

Julia, be careful, you're next.

Suddenly, the door opened, and a nurse in pink scrubs popped her head in. 'Time's up. You must leave now.'

Julia felt disturbed and terrified. She'd just seen Gianluca's crash, but didn't know what to do next. She couldn't risk calling the police if they were involved.

'Miss? Time to go.'

'Coming, sorry.' Julia rose, trying to get her bearings. She touched Gianluca's hand. *I love you,* she told him. She turned to go but froze on the spot.

Standing across the hall in the waiting room, black cap in hand, was Marshal Torti.

55

Julia crossed to the waiting room, her thoughts racing. She didn't know why Marshal Torti was here. She didn't know if he was the *carabiniere* who ran Gianluca off the road. Nor did she know if she could take as truth what she'd just seen in her vision. Her gut told her to proceed with caution.

Julia opened the door to the waiting room, and Sherry rallied with a smile, gesturing to Marshal Torti.

'Julia, I hear you know Marshal Torti.'

'Yes, hello, Marshal Torti.' Julia masked her emotions. 'What brings you here?'

'I wished to pay my respects to Mr Moretti's family.' Marshal Torti smiled. 'We are concerned about serious accidents on our roadways. We're putting a sign at the curve to warn that it's dangerous when wet.'

Sherry teared up. 'Good. We don't want this to happen to someone else.'

Tonio added, 'Yes, I agree.' He continued in Italian, and Julia got the gist that he was thanking Marshal Torti, who nodded.

'Well, I should go. It's been lovely to meet you both. I will continue to pray for your son's full recovery.'

'Thank you,' Sherry said, sniffling.

'Thank you again.' Tonio shook Marshal Torti's hand. 'We'll keep you apprised.'

'Yes, please do.' Marshal Torti said goodbyes all around and left the room just as a nurse wearing patterned scrubs appeared and opened the door. Julia recognized her as the nurse she'd spoken with yesterday, and the nurse spoke in Italian to Tonio, Sherry, and everyone else, then turned to Julia and Courtney.

'I'll speak English, for you. This is too many people for our unit. We've bent the rules but now we must enforce them. The only people who may remain will be immediate family. Antonio, Sherry, and Raffaella.' The nurse pointed to each in turn. 'No grandmothers, or cousins from *San Francisco*,' she said pointedly, letting Julia know she hadn't been fooled. 'Everyone else must leave.'

'Okay.' Julia knew what she had to do. 'I'll say my goodbyes, and then we'll go.'

Courtney nodded. 'Sorry, we'll go.'

'Thank you.' The nurse left, and Julia hugged everybody goodbye, but when she came to Raffaella, she took her by the arm.

'Do you think we could step out and talk a moment?'

'No.' Raffaella pursed her lips so firmly her pierced hoop twisted. 'I said what I had to say to you.'

Sherry shot her a Mom-look. 'Raffi, really?'

'Fine.' Raffaella rolled her eyes, then left the room with Julia and Courtney, and the three of them walked down the hall.

Julia swallowed hard. 'Raffaella, look, I know you don't like me.'

'I don't like you for my brother.' Raffaella pushed back her blue bangs. 'I don't think you're committed to him the way he deserves.'

'I get it, but we can discuss it another time. What I have to tell you is serious and I have to confide in you.'

Raffaella smirked. 'Oh, are we girlfriends now?'

'No, but you said you always look out for your brother, and I don't want to upset your parents.'

'What about my brother?'

'We both know Gianluca is a careful driver, right?' Julia weighed her words. She didn't want to tell Raffaella about her vision because she didn't have time to convince her it was true.

'Yes.'

'Weren't you surprised when you found out about the accident? That he'd been speeding in the rain? Driving carelessly?'

Raffaella's smirk evaporated. 'Yes. That's why I never worried when I lent him my Vespa.'

'Well, I don't think he had an accident. I think somebody ran him off the road.'

'Like road rage?' Raffaella recoiled, her eyes rounding. They were pretty and dark, almost black.

'No, it was intentional, directed at him. It was attempted murder.'

'What are you talking about?' Raffaella shot back, skeptical.

'Gianluca and I were followed by a heavyset bald man with a mustache. I'm telling you that for a description. I think somebody tried to kill him and they may try again, here. I have to leave, so you have to watch Gianluca. Don't leave him alone, ever. If you see anything suspicious, call hospital security.'

'What have you gotten him into?' Raffaella straightened, scowling. 'He told me you were being followed when you met. What *is* it with you?'

'I'm sorry, I can't explain now, and this is about him. I'm afraid for his safety.'

'Then we should tell the *carabinieri*. That marshal was just here.'

'No, I'm suspicious of the *carabinieri*, too. Gianluca can never be alone with Marshal Torti or any other cop.'

Courtney looked over in surprise, saying nothing. Julia realized Courtney didn't know about the vision.

Raffaella snorted, incredulous. 'Why would the *carabinieri* want to kill Gianluca?'

'If I'm right, they know that when he comes out of his coma, he'll say they ran him off the road. He'll point a finger at—'

'I don't believe you. You're crazy, a drama queen—'

'Raffaella, think about it. Doesn't it seem odd to you that Marshal Torti, a police captain from Savernella, would come to the hospital to see a random accident victim? Do you think that happens a lot?'

'My parents thought it was nice.'

'Did *you*?'

Raffaella didn't reply.

'Right. I believe Marshal Torti wanted to check on Gianluca's condition so they can plan their next attempt. They have more reason than ever to succeed.' Julia had to sum up because the nurse down the hall was giving her a dirty look. 'Listen, whether you believe me or not, do you want to take a chance with your brother's life?'

Raffaella lifted a pierced eyebrow. 'Gianluca is everything to me. I'd do anything for him.'

'Great, then please watch him. Protect him. Watch out for the doctors and nurses, too.'

'Are you serious?'

'Yes. What if somebody masquerades as his doctor or nurse? Again, no chances. I leave to you whether to tell your parents. I think they have enough on their plate.'

'I won't tell them.'

'Thanks.'

Raffaella turned on her heel, without another word.

Julia and Courtney turned around and fell into step going the opposite direction.

Courtney looked over. 'Why'd you say that about the police? Do you really suspect them?'

'Yes, I'll explain in the car.'

'You think they're in the conspiracy, too?'

'Yes.' Julia decided to start trusting herself and her abilities. If the police were in the conspiracy, then it was more powerful and deadlier than she'd thought. They'd done the unthinkable in trying to kill Gianluca, and she believed his warning that she was next. It shook her to her foundations.

'You think that was a good move, getting her help?'

'I had no choice.' Julia's thoughts churned. 'I wish we didn't have to leave. I'm worried about him.'

'Don't be. Nobody's getting through Raffaella. She'll watch him to spite you.'

Julia managed a smile. They reached the end of the hall and pushed through double doors to the elevator bank. 'How'd it go in the waiting room?'

'Everyone likes you except her. I couldn't sell her, and I can sell *anybody*. My mother would say, "she's on a hate campaign."'

'I'd hate me, too.' Julia crossed the bank and pressed the Down button.

'Did you do your Helen homework?'

'Yes.' Julia shuddered. 'That's the car conversation.'

'Okay, but can we get a coffee before we go?'

'Sure, I know the jet lag's tough. Thanks again for coming.' Julia looked over, grateful. The elevator arrived, the doors slid open, and they got on.

'Not at all.'

'Am I a drama queen?' Julia asked, as the doors closed.

'Of course. We're drama club, remember?'

56

Julia headed down the hall to the ladies' room while Courtney went to the cafeteria to get a coffee. She wanted to wash her face, and her head pounded after the vision of Gianluca being forced off the road. She didn't know what to do next. She certainly couldn't go to the police.

She reached the middle of the hallway and passed a line of children's drawings hanging on the wall. They had to be from an elementary school and they were crayoned pictures of smiling kids in white coats, stethoscopes, and scrubs. There were twenty or so, with Italian captions that the drawings helped her translate:

Voglio diventare la dottoressa.
I want to be a doctor.

Voglio diventare un infirmiere.
I want to be a nurse.

Voglio diventare un tecnico radiologo.
I want to be an X-ray technician.

Julia glanced at the last drawing and stopped in her tracks, stunned. The drawing was of a woman who looked like *her*, only older. It wasn't a child's drawing, but a portrait done by an adult with art talent, compelling even in crayons.

What? Julia couldn't believe what she was seeing. The resemblance was uncanny. The woman's eyes were the most like her own, blue and wide-set, though the woman's in the picture had crow's-feet. Her nose was short like Julia's, and her mouth wider, but their smiles were a lot alike.

Oh my God. Julia felt like she was looking at her *biological mother.* The woman seemed to be in her fifties, which could be the age of her biological mother. The drawing had a caption, which read, *Adoro essere un maestra,* I adore being a teacher.

Julia reeled. On impulse, she touched the picture. A tingling electrified her fingertips. She didn't pull away. She felt the connection. She *wanted* the connection.

Tears sprang to her eyes, of recognition, of validation, of sheer joy. The teacher *had* to be her birth mother. She removed her hand, and the tingling faded away.

Her thoughts raced. Her biological mother had been here with her class. Therefore, she had to live somewhere nearby.

Julia looked around for something to identify which school the children were from. There wasn't anything. The children had scrawled their names at the bottom of their drawings; Paolo, Dmitri, Elianna, and Francesco M. The teacher hadn't written her name.

Julia had to find her. She took off down the hallway and hurried to the information desk, which was staffed by an older woman. 'Excuse me, those pictures, do you know what school the kids were from?'

'We have a lot of pictures here. Which ones?'

'The ones on the way to the cafeteria. They were drawn by children. It's from a class.'

'I bring my food. The cafeteria's too expensive.'

'May I show you? Maybe you'll know?'

'No, I can't leave the desk.'

Julia tried another tack. 'Do you know the elementary schools in the area?'

'No. Call the office during the day. You can ask them. They will know.'

'Thank you.' Julia left the desk and hurried back down the hallway. She was already getting another idea. She wanted to take photographs of the drawing. It was as good as any police composite, and it could help her find her biological mother.

Julia hustled down the hallway, but stopped, shocked.

The wall was completely white. The drawings were gone, all of them.

What? Julia whirled around. The pictures had been *right* here.

Julia realized she could be in the wrong hallway. She tried to reorient herself, double-checking. The cafeteria was to the left, and the information desk was to the right. She was in the correct hallway. The drawings had been on the wall only minutes before, but they had vanished, including the one of her biological mother.

Courtney was walking toward her, holding two coffees.

Julia looked at her, unable to speak.

Courtney stopped, her lips parting. 'What'd I miss?'

57

They sped home in the dark with Julia watching the outside mirror to make sure they weren't being followed. Traffic was light, and she updated Courtney on her vision in Gianluca's hospital room and the drawing of her biological mother, which she'd seen in the hallway.

Julia was trying to process what happened. 'So the drawings must've been a vision, too. But who sent it to me? Who's trying to communicate with me?'

'Your bio mom?' Courtney sipped her coffee, holding it since the car had no cupholders.

'Maybe. Do you think she *wants* me to find her?' Julia felt old emotions coming back, darker ones she hadn't had in a long time. 'I mean, she did give me up. She didn't want me.'

'Correction, she didn't want a baby.' Courtney looked over, her expression sympathetic in the soft light from the dashboard. 'You know it's not a rejection of *you*, right?'

'I know it, in theory.'

'You know it. It's the truth.'

Julia let it go. 'I got a tingling, so it has to be my birth mother.'

'It's confirmation enough for me.'

'Do you think Rossi's daughter Patrizia is my biological mother?'

'Did the drawing in the hospital look like the self-portrait in the underground cell? Or like the baby picture on the passport?'

Julia tried to remember. She'd been so stunned that the drawing looked like her. 'A little, but mostly it looked like me. I wish I'd taken pictures.' She thought a minute. 'Then again, I doubt an iPhone can take a picture of a vision. Not even Apple can do that.'

Courtney shook her head. 'Girl, you had *two* visions tonight. Maybe you should lay off the espresso.'

'Wait, I got an idea.' Julia went to her phone, opened Google Maps, and typed elementary schools near me, with a wide search radius. The screen showed nine schools around the hospital, each with a little red droplet that reminded her of blood, a little too on the nose. 'So, there are nine elementary schools around the hospital. The next step is to research them online, then visit them first thing in the morning. It can't be hard to find where she teaches.'

'Maybe you should let the family investigator take it from here? You hired her.'

'No, I want to do it myself. I'll fill her in tomorrow. Maybe she'll have some ideas or records she can help with.'

'But what about the conspiracy? They tried to kill Gianluca. I'm worried they're going to try to kill you.' Courtney looked over, tense. 'I'm starting to think we're in over our heads.'

'You know, we have two different things going on, like two different investigations, but what if they're related?'

'What do you mean?'

'Well, we're trying to figure out what this conspiracy is up to. We think it has something to do with me and my inheritance.' Julia tried to parse their situation. 'And the other thing we're trying to do is find my biological family. Obviously, both are related to me, but there must be some other relationship between them. They're both mysteries, and I feel like if we solve one, it'll help us solve the other.'

'Why?' Courtney shrugged. 'You could find your bio mom at a school tomorrow, but it wouldn't tell us why they ran Gianluca off the road.'

Julia paused to plumb her own reasoning, then had an answer. 'I think they're related because I got the two visions together, tonight, at the hospital. I have to wonder, why did I get them back-to-back? And why at the hospital? The first vision was in Gianluca's room and it was about the conspiracy. The second vision was in the hallway and it was about my biological family. Whoever's sending me these visions sent them together, in the same place, on the same night. *That's* why I'm joining them. I think somebody's trying to *tell me* these things are connected.'

Courtney listened, driving, but Julia got excited as the notion took hold.

'Helen said there are places called "thin places." They're where the material world comes in greatest contact with the spiritual world, where the veil between the worlds is thin. They're mostly in nature.'

'Okay.' Courtney cocked her head, listening.

'But a thin place doesn't have to be in nature. It could be in a place like a hospital. It could *be* a hospital.' The more Julia thought about it, the more sense it made. 'Where else do life and death come into contact more than a *hospital*? People are born and die there every day. There's a nursery *and* a morgue.'

'Okay, I'm with you.' Courtney nodded. 'So what do we do?'

'I say we go to the schools first thing tomorrow morning and see what happens.'

'Okay, you're the one with the Spidey sense. But what about the cops in Florence? Maybe we should go to them.'

'The problem is we have no evidence. What would we tell them? I'm a rookie medium? I had a vision about a murder attempt by a conspiracy that includes a Tuscan cop? My evidence is imaginary, I can't prove anything. The only hard fact that I'm being followed is the license plate from the white Fiat, but that alone doesn't prove anything.' Julia sensed she was right. 'Plus if we go to the Florence police, it shows our hand to Torti. Right now he doesn't know I suspect him. He thinks I'm satisfied that he's investigating.'

'Agree, and I doubt the Florence police would believe us.'

'We're on our own.' Still, Julia didn't like risking Courtney's life. 'You should go back home.'

'Not without you.'

'I can't leave Gianluca. Please, go.'

'No.'

'Courtney, please?'

'No. End of convo.'

Julia tabled it for now. Edgy, she checked the outside mirror.

Courtney downed her coffee. 'Anyway, we're not *completely* on our own. We have a gun.'

'Can you shoot?'

'Sure.' Courtney shrugged. 'How hard can it be?'

58

Julia and Courtney entered the villa, turning on the lights, and the house was still and quiet. Julia closed the door behind them and turned the deadbolt, relieved she'd had locks installed.

Courtney looked up. 'I told Paul about these frescoes. They're the only nice things about this place.'

'I know. Bianco!' Julia called out, and the dog lumbered in from the kitchen, his nails clicking on the tile. His gait was steadier, so the drug was leaving his system and probably hers. She petted his soft, furry head.

'Paul wants me to send pics.' Courtney took out her phone, and Julia went to the dining room table, set down her purse, and opened her laptop.

'I want to make a list of schools for tomorrow.'

'Good idea.' Courtney took another picture of the entrance hall, then went into the living room and turned on the light.

Julia sat down, opened Word, and started a new document. It thrilled her to think she was *this* close to finding her biological mother. She paused, wondering what to name the file. 'I should title this document, "Finding Bio Mom."'

'Catchy.' Courtney took pictures in the living room while Julia navigated to Google maps and widened her search to make sure she didn't miss any schools, which added six schools.

'I have fifteen schools we need to visit.' Julia clicked the link of the first school, and its website popped into the screen, with a picture of a small brick building surrounded by cypress trees. She looked at the top of the page for an English version but there wasn't one. 'Damn. It's only in Italian.'

'The nerve.' Courtney entered the dining room, taking pictures.

Julia scanned the subject headings and guessed that *facoltà* meant faculty. She clicked the faculty link, but a blue box appeared on the screen in Italian, which she deciphered. 'Oh no, it's asking for my school ID. You can't search the site unless you're a member of the school community.'

'My nephew's middle school is like that.' Courtney took another photo. 'Schools don't post pictures of kids or faculty anymore. It's a security thing.'

'I'll just make the list then.' Julia copied the name and address of the closest elementary school and pasted it into the document.

Courtney stopped taking pictures. 'Oh, wait, the dog needs to go out, right?'

'Yes, do you mind letting him out back? Keep an eye on him.' Julia navigated to the next school's website, then copied and pasted its name and address.

'Why don't you come with? I feel nervous.'

'Of course, I'm sorry.' Julia got up. 'Come on, Bianco.'

They walked to the kitchen with the dog, opened the back door, let him out, then stepped outside. The only light came from the kitchen, and Courtney looked around. 'It's dark out here. Do they have any exterior lights?'

'No.' Julia looked around, too.

'Jules, come here.' Courtney lowered her voice. 'You need to see this.'

'What?' Julia walked over, and Courtney held up her phone, showing a photo of the astrological fresco in the entrance hall, its vivid lapis lazuli glowing in the darkness.

'See?' Courtney pointed to a tiny white fleck near the glowing yellow sun.

'Now, bear with me.' She scrolled to the photos of the living room frescoes, stopped at one, and pointed at a tiny spot again. 'There's another one. Wait.' She swiped through photos of the dining room frescoes and stopped at one, with another spot. 'See what I see?'

'What? It's a spot of plaster. Maybe some paint chipped off?'

'No. I took these with a flash. I think the spot is a reflection of the flash on glass.'

Julia didn't get it. 'There's glass in the frescoes?'

'No, there's *cameras*.'

'*What?*' Julia asked, aghast.

'Look.' Courtney enlarged the photo of the dining room fresco, and the white spot grew bigger. 'That has to be a glass lens.'

'Holy shit.' Julia felt sickened. 'Someone's watching us? Why?' Suddenly she knew the answer. 'For the same reason they're following me. They want to know what I'm doing, saying, thinking.'

'I don't know if the cameras have audio, but they could.' Courtney looked tense in the light from the kitchen. 'In truth, we don't know how long they've been here. We don't know if they're currently being monitored, either.'

'Right, Rossi could have installed the system. She was paranoid. Or maybe somebody in the conspiracy installed the cameras to watch *her*. Remember, they could've been drugging her, too.'

'I'll take some pictures upstairs and see if I find more.'

'Okay, and from now on, we can't talk about anything that matters inside.' Julia paused. 'We should leave the cameras in place, so they don't know we found them. But I'm not getting naked in front of those cameras.'

'I am.' Courtney snorted. 'I'm going to *moon* those assholes.'

59

Julia lay in Rossi's bed with the coverlet pulled up to her chest. The bedroom was dark, and odd screeches from the vineyard filtered through the curtains. A camera was concealed in the Sforza family tree on the ceiling fresco. It turned out there were cameras in the ceiling fresco in every bedroom, and she wondered who was spying on her, and why. It was scary enough to be followed, but it was creepier to be watched in bed.

Julia turned on her right side, trying to put the camera out of her mind, and her thoughts went to Gianluca. She wished she could be at his side, but she was hoping that Rossi's bedroom was another thin place. Rossi had died here, and Julia wondered now if her nightmares here had been Caterina, trying to communicate with her, before she knew how.

Close your eyes.

Julia remembered what Helen taught her about how to communicate with Gianluca. She'd done it successfully in his hospital room, where he'd showed her how he'd been run off the road, but she hadn't gotten her message to him through. She envisioned him in the hospital bed and tried to tell him how she felt in her heart.

You have to live.

You have to get through this.

You have to come back to me and your family.

Julia waited. She didn't hear Gianluca's voice. There was only silence. She saw no vision. There was only darkness. She didn't know if she was communicating with him at all. She feared the drug was out of her system and she was back to her old self. She tried to deny the thought but couldn't. Maybe she didn't have a gift, but a side effect. Maybe the drug hadn't opened a pathway, but only an illusion of one, an altered state already ebbing away. Maybe tonight was the beginning of the end.

Julia turned over, miserable. She'd gone from being terrified of the visions to missing them. She and Gianluca had shared their innermost feelings that way. She wanted that power back, for him. If she couldn't communicate with him, she couldn't help him.

Suddenly she was thinking of Mike, and guilt came back to her. She'd gotten him killed and hadn't been able to help him, either. She buried her head in the pillow. She didn't want the camera to see. She didn't want to acknowledge to herself that Gianluca could die, like Mike, because of her.

She thought about fate, and destiny, wondering if she was cursed.

60

The next morning, Julia and Courtney were back in the car, heading to the first school on the list. Julia had barely slept worrying about Gianluca and hadn't been able to communicate with him. Toward morning, she'd texted Raffaella about how he was doing but hadn't heard back. She was barely able to focus on the day ahead, as astounding as it was to be close to finding her birth mother.

The Tuscan scenery whizzed past, a blur of golden sunshine, rolling vineyards, cypress trees, and stone villas, but Julia was glued to the outside mirror, on the lookout for the white Fiat, the white van, and a police cruiser. She'd stowed the gun in the glove box, but the fact they needed it gave her no comfort.

Julia's phone pinged with a text, and she startled, checking the screen. 'It's Raffaella! She texted me back.'

'Read it to me.'

Julia read the text aloud:

My brother is doing a little worse. His temperature is up.
They continue his antibiotics.

'Oh no.' Julia's chest tightened. 'What does a "little worse" mean? I hate this. I wish I could see him. Do you think we could try at the end of the day?'

'Sure, can't blame a girl for asking.'

'Let me text her back.' Julia typed:

Thank you so much. Please give my love to your parents.
We will stop in at the end of the day.

Courtney braked at a red light, glancing over. 'Lose the "so much."
You're worse than my mom.'

'I want her to like me.'

'Too late.'

They reached Scuola Elementare di Biaggio, a small stone schoolhouse
in Biaggio, a hill town like Croce. Cypress trees screened the parking
lot from the road, and when they pulled up, Julia and Courtney could
hear children on a playground behind the school.

They parked, got out of the car, and headed for a shiny red lacquer
door. Julia pressed a doorbell in a recessed squawk box, and in the
next moment, a woman started speaking in rapid Italian.

Julia leaned close to the box. 'I'm sorry, I only have English, but
I need to come to the office. It's about one of the teachers. It's very
important.'

'Come in,' said the woman, and a buzzer sounded. Julia opened
the door, and they found themselves in a large, tiled foyer that led
to a wide hallway, an older building renovated to accommodate the
school. The office was to the left under a door that read UFFICIO.

They crossed to the door, opened it, and entered the office, which
had high ceilings, ornate crown molding, and white plaster walls.
A modern counter of blond wood divided the public area from a
staff of three women, who were working on computers in front of a
mismatched line of file cabinets. An Italian flag stood in the corner.

'May I help you?' asked one of the women, who looked up, rose,
and walked to the counter with a pleasant smile. She had dark hair in
a long braid that rested on her shoulder, and she wore a flowered shirt
with a denim skirt.

Julia introduced herself and Courtney, then said, 'I'm here on a
personal matter. I'm adopted and I believe my birth mother might be
one of your teachers.'

The woman's eyebrows flew upward. 'What is her name?'

The other women stopped working and exchanged astonished
glances.

Julia answered, 'It might be Patrizia Rossi or Patrizia Ritorno. She
may not even know her real name.'

'*Davvero?*' The woman gasped, and the other women burst into excited chatter.

'She took her class on a field trip to a hospital, I assume recently. She's about fifty-something and she looks like me. Oh, and she's a good artist.'

'Excuse me.' The woman left the desk and crossed to the other women, then they all started clacking away in Italian. The woman returned, smoothing her hair into place. 'We're sorry for your situation. We're afraid no teacher here fits your description.'

Julia's heart sank. 'Are you sure?'

'Yes. We have three teachers in their fifties. None look like you.'

'Did any class here take a field trip to a hospital?'

'No.'

Julia tried another tack. 'Do you know if any other elementary schools visited the hospital recently?'

'No.'

Damn. Julia managed a smile. 'Thank you. You've been very kind.'

'Good luck.' The woman smiled back, with genuine sympathy, and Julia felt touched. They left the office, then the school, and regrouped outside on the steps.

Julia straightened, hopeful. 'Well, we have a bunch more schools.'

'To the Ferrari!' Courtney said, raising a fist.

Three hours later, they'd visited three picturesque Tuscan hill towns like Croce, each a cluster of stone houses with red tile roofs set above valleys lush with vineyards, olive groves, sunflowers, and lavender. They'd visited three more elementary schools and met scores of sympathetic women, but they hadn't found Julia's birth mother. None of the office staff knew a teacher who looked like Julia, or a class that had gone to a hospital.

Julia and Courtney sat in the car at the parking lot of the fourth school, in another small hill town called Vincenza. They were waiting for the carpool lane to clear, since primary students went home for lunch. Adorable boys and girls streamed from the school into the open arms of happy moms, dads, and babysitters with strollers.

Julia watched them, hoping she'd get that lucky someday. She wondered if most people knew how blessed they were in a family. 'We still have plenty of schools to go, right?'

'Absolutely. We'll find her.'

Julia consulted her list, which she kept on her phone in Notes, organized geographically. The first half of the list were schools on the northern side of the hospital, and the second half were on the southern side, closer to Croce. 'At this rate, we'll get through half of them today. We'll have an answer either this afternoon or tomorrow.'

Courtney smiled. 'Exciting!'

'Totally.' Julia smiled back, rallying. She'd kept an eye in the rearview mirror the entire morning. 'I saw only a few white vans, and they weren't the same because they had windows. I saw a white Fiat, driven by an old lady, and there were no police cars.'

'So we're not being followed—' Courtney stopped abruptly, her eyes flashing with alarm.

'What?'

'Nothing.' Courtney signaled *Be quiet*, then started feeling around the dashboard.

Julia realized that Courtney was checking the car for cameras, which made sense given the cameras in the house. Julia should've thought of it herself, but she'd been too preoccupied. Courtney motioned to her to keep talking, but Julia got a better idea.

'Court, I have to use the bathroom. I'm going back inside.'

'No problem.' Courtney finished the dashboard and started running her fingers along the seam at the roof.

Julia got out of the car, closed the door, and went to the back of the car to see if it had a tracker. She felt underneath the bumper, starting on the right and moving to the middle. She didn't feel anything. She kept going to the driver's side.

There. Julia felt something hard and plastic. She slid her phone out of her jeans, tucked it underneath the bumper, and took a few pictures. She pulled the phone out and checked the photos.

Damn. There was a black plastic square under the bumper, and it looked new.

Courtney got out of the car, closed the door, and came toward her with a frown. 'I found a microphone near the visor. A bug, not a camera.'

Julia held up the picture. 'Is this a tracker?'

Courtney nodded. 'Fuck these guys.'

'My thoughts exactly.' Julia's mind raced. 'The tracker is new and that means it was put in recently. In other words, Rossi didn't do this. My guess is the bug in the car and the cameras in the house were installed by the conspiracy. We know Anna Mattia and Piero would've let them in.'

Courtney pursed her lips. 'So we can't talk in the car anymore.'

'Right, and we can't talk in the house, either. How will we live if we can't talk? We're us.'

Courtney smiled. 'Did you just joke about a life-and-death situation?'

Julia smiled back. 'I think so.'

'You're not afraid?'

'Oh, I'm afraid, but I'm not stopping.' Julia felt a new determination, deep inside. 'I didn't come this far just to come this far.'

Courtney grinned. 'That's my girl! You're back, baby!'

Julia burst into laughter, hugging her. 'I love you.'

'I love you, too. Hey, it's lunchtime, isn't it? I'm hungry.'

'Me, too. Let's go eat our feelings.'

'With fries.'

'I don't think they have fries in Tuscany.'

'They better. You know what I miss?'

'Paul?'

'No, ketchup.'

61

Julia and Courtney followed a cobblestone walkway lined with charming stone rowhouses with shutters in dark green, light blue, and mauve. Magenta bougainvillea climbed their facades, and fragrant wisteria dripped from wrought iron balconies.

Courtney began taking pictures. 'I want a garden.'

'Me, too.'

'You have a vineyard.'

'A psycho vineyard.' Julia walked along and spotted a café at the top of the street, with outside tables. They were mostly full, and she noticed her realtor Franco sitting at one with some other men. She turned on her heel. 'Uh-oh, let's go back.'

'Why?' Courtney stopped taking pictures, turning around.

'I don't want to run into my realtor. He'll start in.'

'Don't blame him, it's the sales mentality. We're about commissions, quotas, and sex, in that order.'

Just then Julia's phone rang in her purse. She retrieved it and checked the screen, recognizing the number instantly. It was Gianluca's, which meant it was Raffaella. 'Hello?' Julia put the call on speaker so Courtney could hear.

'Julia, this is Sherry, Gianluca's mother.'

Julia felt a bolt of alarm. 'Is he okay?'

'None of your business!' Sherry snapped. 'Raffi told me you think someone's trying to kill my son, even the *carabinieri*. She told me you suspect the doctors and nurses, too. I can't imagine why you would say such ridiculous things. I'm sorry we trusted you. Stay away from my family.'

Julia's heart sank. 'Wait, I can explain—'

'Raffi told me you intend to visit. Don't even think about it. I told hospital security, and they'll throw you out. Do not text Raffi anymore. Do you understand?'

'Yes,' Julia answered miserably.

'Goodbye.' Sherry hung up.

Julia pressed End, stricken. 'Damn! I'm so mad at myself. I never should've told Raffaella.'

'You were trying to help him. You didn't do anything wrong.'

'I didn't do anything right. If I could see him, maybe I could communicate with him like before.' Julia's throat felt tight. 'If I can even touch his hand, maybe the physical contact will help heal him—'

'What?' Courtney looked at her in disbelief. 'You're not responsible for healing him, Jules.'

'Why not? I'm responsible for endangering him.'

'He has doctors. This is about science, not superpowers.'

'Maybe it's not only about science. He's in a sleep state, and if I could communicate with him—'

'You can't cure him.'

'I know, but I want to do what I can.'

'Overfunction much?' Courtney took her by the elbow. 'Let's eat. You're driving yourself crazy.'

'And you, too?'

'Never, I'm ride or die.' Courtney grinned. 'Now. Think ketchup.'

The late-day sun shed a burnished gold on San Giovanni, another small Tuscan town, and Julia stood with Courtney in the parking lot of its elementary school. They'd spent the afternoon visiting four more schools, but they hadn't found her birth mother. Julia felt on tenterhooks about whether they'd succeed, and her worries about Gianluca gnawed at the back of her mind all day, too.

'Court, I think we should call it a day, don't you?'

'Yes. The offices are closing.'

Julia checked her phone. 'We've done eight schools, about half on the list.'

'Agree, let's go home.' Courtney looked at her, sympathetic. 'You okay?'

'I'm fine, but I hope Gianluca is.'

'They're doing everything they can.'

'I know.'

'There's nothing you can do, Jules.'

'Right,' Julia said, but she wasn't so sure.

She was wondering if there was one last thing she could do.

And *only* she could do.

After dark.

62

A soft, ethereal moonglow hung in the damp air of the ruined vineyard, and Julia walked among its tangled grapevines, thornbushes, and underbrush void of color, reduced to shades of black. Tonight was a special night, a full moon in Scorpio, which encouraged spirituality that she hoped would serve her first-ever do-it-yourself séance.

She turned on the flashlight and aimed it in front of her. Insects zoomed crazily in and out of its jittery beam. Birds flew squawking in panic from mounded thickets. Something flew near her head, and Julia ducked, reflexively. She tried not to think about bats, vipers, or anything else scary. Bianco trotted at her side, and she carried a brown bag, plus the gun that Courtney made her take.

Moonlight illuminated the swath they'd cut to the well, and she followed its path, casting the flashlight left and right. Her footsteps snapped twigs and leaves. Thorns scratched her ankles, and bushes snagged her shirt and jeans. She kept going until she reached its stone rim, a lightish circle.

She turned off the flashlight, waiting until her eyes adjusted to the gloom. She set the flashlight and the gun on the top of the well. She didn't know if she still had the ability to communicate with a soul, much less Rossi's, but she had to try. She was praying the well could be a thin place for Rossi, maybe more than the bedroom, because this is where Rossi had hidden her strongbox of evidence to save herself and her daughter.

Julia reached into her bag and took out the photo of young Rossi that Anna Mattia had given her. She set it down on the well. Next she took out the baby photo, presumably of her birth mother Patrizia, which she'd found in the drawer. She put it next to Rossi's. Lastly, she withdrew Patrizia's lock of hair and set it down on top of the pictures. She placed her hand on the hair to see if she felt anything.

Her palm didn't tingle. The hair communicated nothing to her, conducted nothing *through* her. It was an inanimate object, opaque to her, once again. She feared her gift was completely gone, but she kept going.

Julia kept one hand on the hair and photos, then placed her other hand on the well. Its stone felt rough and gritty under her palm, a thick and solid rock hewn from earth itself, an artifact she was going to use in her appeal to Rossi's soul.

Close your eyes.

Julia closed her eyes and slowed her breathing. She listened to the chirping and buzzing sounds until they receded into the background, then the ether. She emptied her mind of every thought but Rossi. She visualized Rossi's photograph, Patrizia's baby picture, and the hair, hoping they'd connect her somehow.

Helen would say, *Allow deeper.*

Julia's mind quieted and she found herself sinking to her knees beside the well, kneeling as if she were in church. Her thoughts echoed in her head like a prayer.

Please, Emilia, Elena, whoever you are, tell me why you brought me here.

Tell me your reason was worth the harm I caused an innocent man, lying between life and death.

Please tell me how I can reach him.

Please tell me how I can help him.

Please help him.

Please help me.

Julia waited, her eyes closed. She focused intensely, marshaling every single brain cell. She tried to see into the depths of her soul out to her very skin, desperate to plumb whatever abilities she had left, to dredge up any vestiges of her gift that remained at all.

Suddenly a twig snapped in a thicket beyond the well.

Julia's eyes flew open. A bolt of terror electrified her. She jumped to her feet. Bianco bounded past the well, barking.

A shadow flew behind the thicket. Something was running away. *Someone.*

Julia reached for the gun, but knocked it with her hand. It skidded into the well.

'No!' Julia shouted, panicky. Bianco was wedging himself into the underbrush. She ran to him, grabbed him by his collar, and dragged him away.

'Courtney!' Julia screamed, running to the villa.

63

Julia wiped her forehead, and Courtney brushed off her hands. They stood side by side in Rossi's bedroom, surveying the barricade they'd made against the door, which consisted of a dresser, an upholstered side chair, and a wooden chair. Bianco slept soundly on the bed, his white coat tangled with burrs. They were all spending the night together.

'That's good enough,' Julia said, shaken. The stakes were getting higher. They were being followed and surveilled, and now somebody was in the vineyard.

'That's the best we can do.' Courtney heaved a sigh.

'Sorry I lost the gun.' Julia hated that she'd left the pictures and the lock of hair at the well, too.

'Don't worry.' Courtney wiggled her butt, and Julia spotted two steak knives in her back pocket, their handles sticking out.

'Whoa. Ouch.'

'Dinner is served.'

Julia smiled. 'What are we having?'

'Bad guys, of course.'

After they turned out the light, Julia and Courtney pretended to sleep, close enough to talk. They'd hidden the knives under their pillows, and Bianco snored at the foot of the bed.

Courtney whispered, 'I wish we could go to the Florence police.'

'I know, but we don't have any more evidence than before. What do I say? Somebody was in my vineyard but I didn't see him? He interrupted my do-it-yourself séance?'

'We could tell them about the underground cell and the pictures of Rossi's abuse. We could task them with what Torti was supposed to be doing but isn't.'

'I hear you, but that's a risk, and it's not worth it. They'll see it as an old crime, if that, and we'll have shown our hand to Torti. I want him to think we're satisfied with whatever he's doing.'

'Okay.'

'I think we need to stay the course with the schools.' Julia couldn't believe that she could find her birth mother tomorrow, and somehow it was the second-most important thing after Gianluca. She knew there was a relationship between the two, but didn't have the facts. She felt like she was playing a deadly game, but didn't know the other players, or how to win. Right now, she was being played.

Courtney whispered, 'I have bad news. I got an email while you were outside. Things are heating up on one of my accounts. I can stay tomorrow, then I have to go. I'm sorry.'

'No worries.' Julia felt relieved to have Courtney out of harm's way.

'I don't want to leave you here, especially after tonight.' Courtney frowned in the dark, anguished. 'You sure you won't go?'

'No. Not until he's better.'

'Maybe tomorrow, we'll get lucky?'

64

The morning was hazy, and Julia drove while Courtney worked, her laptop on her lap. Traffic was congested on the two-lane road to the first school, which wound through the Chianti region. Julia's nervousness had intensified since last night, and neither of them had slept. They'd retrieved the Rossi photographs, the hair, and the flashlight from the well. They'd looked around for signs of an intruder but found none. The gun was gone for good, but they had the steak knives in their purses.

Gianluca weighed on Julia's mind as she drove. She'd called the hospital and asked about his condition, but they wouldn't tell her anything except that he was still in intensive care, in critical condition. The receptionist from the other night hadn't texted her. It killed her that she had no information about him.

Julia kept her eye on the rearview mirror. So far, so good. She spotted the first school ahead, and her spirits lifted. This could be the *one*. She could be meeting her birth mother in the next fifteen minutes.

Three hours and three schools later, Julia hadn't found her birth mother, and they set out for the fourth school. She braked at a red light on the way out of town, glancing in the rearview mirror by habit. Then she looked again.

A police cruiser was three cars behind them, the black-and-red of the Savernella *carabinieri*. They weren't near Savernella, so she didn't know why one of its cruisers would be patrolling here. She couldn't see if the driver was Marshal Torti because the cruiser was too far back, behind a VW Golf and a truck.

Julia nudged Courtney and nodded behind them, staying silent so she couldn't be heard on the bug.

Courtney understood, checked her outside mirror, and said into the phone, 'Bruce, can I call you back? Great, bye.' She hung up.

The traffic light turned green, and Julia fed the car some gas. She wondered if the cruiser was following them, then knew how to find out. The route to the next school was straight, but she steered onto a side street, then checked the rearview.

The cruiser wasn't behind them. Garages and a metal fabricating facility lined the street. She reached the corner, and just as she was about to turn, she spotted the cruiser at the far end of the block.

Holy shit. Julia turned right at the end of the street.

Suddenly the cruiser accelerated in pursuit, its siren bursting into deafening sound. Its high beams flashed, signaling to them. Its light bar began blinking.

'Whoa!' Julia steered to the curb and braked, trying not to panic.

'They're pulling us over? I don't like this.'

'Me, neither.' Julia told herself the cops couldn't hurt them. It was broad daylight in a busy Tuscan town. Heads turned on the sidewalk. People stopped and watched, covering their ears. Mechanics in soiled jumpsuits came out of the garages. Mothers hurried their children away, a protective hand on their back.

The *carabinieri* shouted in Italian from the cruiser, his voice mechanically amplified.

Julia's mouth went dry. 'We don't understand! We speak English!'

Two *carabinieri* emerged from the cruiser, in black uniforms with thick black leather belts with guns, nightsticks, and radios. The cop who was driving was tall and lean, and the other was short and wide-set. Both were young, their expressions grim under the patent-leather bills of their caps.

Julia tried to think through her nerves. 'Courtney, can you see if there are papers in the glove box?'

'No, just put your hands up.' Courtney raised her hands, and Julia did the same just as the tall cop arrived at her window.

'Out of the car!' the tall cop shouted. 'Hands against the car! Hands against the car now!'

Julia scrambled out of the car, frightened. 'What did I do?'

'Hands on the car! Now!' The cop grabbed her by her waist, whirled her around, and shoved her against the car. She caught herself just before she made impact.

The cop started running his hands up and down Julia's body. He was feeling her up, not patting her down. Horrified, she startled, pulling away.

'Stand still!' The tall cop shoved her against the car again, feeling the side of her breasts.

Julia submitted, mortified. Tears sprang to her eyes. The short cop was with Courtney, who stood across the hood of the car, distraught. The same thing was happening to her. The crowd on the street talked behind their hands.

'Go sit inside and wait!' the tall cop barked when he was finished, leaving her shaking.

Julia reached for the car door, flung it open, and scrambled inside the car. Courtney did the same, her eyes wide with fear. They exchanged looks but said nothing.

The cops cut the siren and turned off the light bar. The crowd on the street began to disperse, returning to their day. The mechanics went back to the garages.

Julia's heart kept pounding. Ten minutes passed, then twenty. Courtney didn't say anything, and Julia tried to recover.

Finally the tall cop got out of the cruiser, shut his door, and strode to Julia, thrusting a hand through the open window. 'You were speeding. Pay the fine.'

'What... fine?' Julia asked, bewildered and scared.

'Pay, *now*.' The tall cop wiggled his fingers. 'The black bitch, too.'

Oh my God. Julia reddened, disgusted at the slur. Courtney swallowed, wild-eyed. They both grappled for their purses, got out their wallets, and grabbed as many euros as they could, fumbling to hand them over as fast as possible.

The tall cop took the bills and stuffed them in his pocket. His menacing gaze shifted back to Julia, his eyes glittering under his black cap. 'Leave today, bitch.'

'*What?*' Julia blurted out, shocked, but the tall cop was turning away and heading back to the cruiser.

'Oh sweet Jesus!' Courtney said, hushed. She sniffled, wiping her eyes.

'Bastards!' Julia watched the rearview mirror, still shaking.

The *carabinieri* got inside the cruiser, took off, and passed them, driving out of sight.

'Jules, you have to come home with me.' Courtney's eyes brimmed. 'You heard him. You have to get out of here.'

'No, absolutely not,' Julia answered, a new emotion welling up inside her. She didn't know where it was coming from, but it felt like strength. 'I'm not leaving Gianluca. I'm going to find my birth mother. I own a *villa* here. I'm *from* here, by blood.'

'No, stop.' Courtney shook her head, grave. 'Be real, honey. We're so in over our heads.'

'I don't care.' Julia thought of the bug in the car, and this time, she hoped the bad guys were listening. Things were coming to a head, and she was going to fight back. 'Hey, you assholes! I'm not going anywhere! I *refuse* to be scared off!'

'Jules, what? What are you saying?' Courtney blinked with disbelief. 'Who *are* you?'

'I don't know, but I'm finding out!'

65

Half an hour later, Julia and Courtney were in the back seat of an Uber driven by an elderly man named Salvi, who spoke no English and listened to opera, humming along. It had been Julia's idea to change cars. She was over being eavesdropped on, stalked, and surveilled by thugs. She'd left the Ferrari with an astonished mechanic who agreed to store it in his garage for a few days.

She and Courtney managed to calm down on the road, processing what the cops had done to them. They talked it out, compared notes, and even cried a little together. Julia knew she wouldn't get over it completely and neither would Courtney. She felt guilty that her best friend had been victimized and she was more determined than ever to keep going.

They decided to visit the rest of the schools in the Uber, sticking with the plan to look for Julia's biological mother. They wouldn't be followed in the unknown car and they hoped the worst thing that was going to happen had already happened. So they visited the schools on the list, one after the next. They broke only for a quick lunch and another call to the hospital to see if Gianluca's condition had changed, but it hadn't.

By the end of the day, they reached Moravia, another hilltop village, and pulled into the parking lot beside the school. The sign read MONTESSORI SCUOLA DI MORAVIA.

Julia struggled to hold her emotions in check. 'This is almost the last school. What if she's not here, after all I put you through, and Gianluca?'

'We have two left. You can always widen the search and start over. Stay positive, okay? Who knows, she could be here.'

'What if this search is a fool's errand—'

'No, it's not.' Courtney touched her arm. 'Don't get carried away.'

'Okay.' Julia opened the door, and they got out of the car and walked to the school, which was a restored villa. Its stone facade looked recently repointed, and its shutters shone an enameled green. Mounded oleander in shades of pink and white flourished in sculpted beds that flanked an arched entrance of unvarnished wood.

They climbed the steps to the entrance, and Julia found the squawk box, pressing the black button. She introduced herself, then said, 'Hello, may I come in? I'm here on a personal matter for one of the teachers.'

'Okay,' said a woman, and when the buzzer sounded, Julia entered the school with Courtney. The entrance hall was posh, with classy touches like oil portraits in heavy gilt frames, ornate crown molding atop plaster walls, and a magnificent stone fireplace. There was a door on the left that read UFFICIO, and next to it an older teacher stood thumb-tacking photographs onto an old-fashioned bulletin board, under a construction paper sign that read BENVENUTO, PRIMAVERA!

They headed toward the office, and the teacher dropped some of her photographs, letting loose some flustered Italian.

'I'll get them.' Julia bent over and picked up the photos.

'Oh! You are American? I love to speak English! My name is Giovanna.'

'Nice to meet you. I'm Julia and this is Courtney.' Julia handed her the photographs. 'Here you go.'

'Thank you. I hope I don't damage.' Giovanna dusted off the top photo, a corporate portrait of a middle-aged man. 'This is Adamo Bucci. His son Paolo is here, and Signore Bucci came yesterday to present him with the award for student-of-the-month.'

'How nice.'

'Signore Bucci is considering Moravia for his new project. His wife told us.' Giovanna leaned over, lowering her voice. 'She told my friend and my friend tells me. How do you call this?'

'Telephone tag?' Julia took a guess, but she wanted to get to the office.

Courtney interjected, 'No, Giovanna, you mean dish, *gossip*. If you want to be cool, say *gos*.'

'*Gos!*' Giovanna's hooded eyes lit up. 'I am *gos*?'

Courtney shook her head. 'No, you *have gos*.'

'I 'ave *gos*.' Giovanna leaned over, again. 'The *gos* is we win. We go against Vincenza and Croce.'

'Croce?' Julia's ears pricked up. She looked again at the photo, but it seemed dark, then she remembered she had her sunglasses on. She slid them off, and Giovanna gasped, startled.

'*Madonna!* You look like one of our teachers.'

'What?' Julia asked, stunned. 'Really?'

'Yes.' Giovanna scanned Julia's face. '*Very* much!'

'Who? I'm here looking for my birth mother.'

Giovanna's dark eyes flew open. She grabbed Julia's hand. 'Come!'

66

Julia stood in the office with Courtney, so thrilled she could faint. Her heart was jumping out of her chest. Tears brimmed in her eyes. Surrounding her were Giovanna and a flock of teachers buzzing with excitement, yakking away in Italian, and smiling and pointing at her.

Julia tried to compose herself. 'Hello, I'm Julia Pritzker, I'm adopted, and I'm looking for my birth mother. Giovanna says I look like a teacher here. Who?'

'Our Fiamma!' Giovanna answered, her eyes shining. The teachers behind her chattered away in delight.

'Oh my God! Amazing!' Julia's head spun. 'Did she take her class to a hospital?'

'Yes, last year!' Giovanna answered. 'She teaches fourth grade!' The teachers burst into animated discussion. A younger teacher added, 'Fiamma arranged for her class to meet doctors and nurses in a conference room. Covid hit us very hard, and the children had negative feelings about hospitals. She wanted to reassure them so they would consider entering the medical professions.'

Julia went speechless. Her heart soared. Tears filled her eyes. She'd found her *birth mother.*

'Jules, you did it!' Courtney hugged her, lifting her off her feet, and Julia burst into laughter with sheer happiness.

'I can't believe it! We did it! Can you believe it? I can't!' Julia wiped her eyes, turning to the teachers. 'Can you tell her I'm here and see if she wants to meet me? I don't want to spring this on her but I want to meet her, so much.'

'No, unfortunately, Fiamma left for the day. She has an art show at Estrella Studio. It's opening night.' Giovanna brightened. 'You should go to the show. We give you the address. The gallery is in Florence.' The younger teacher added, 'It's in the Oltrarno neighborhood, on the south side of the Arno.'

'Thank you!' Julia had a second thought. 'Maybe I should call her and ask her if she wants to meet me?'

'Certainly, yes. We will call for you.' Giovanna and the teachers reached for phones, and a young teacher was already making the call. She pressed some numbers into her phone and gave it to Julia.

Julia held the phone with trembling hands. She could barely breathe. The call was on speaker, and the teachers went tearily silent, exchanging hushed and thrilled looks while the phone rang once, then twice. The call went to voicemail, and a mechanical message came on, speaking rapid Italian.

Damn! Julia hung up, not wanting to leave such big news on a voicemail.

Giovanna and the teachers moaned, collectively deflated.

'Oh well, thank you.' Julia handed the phone back to the young teacher. 'Now she can call me if she wants to, unless you want to give me her number.'

'Better to go see her!' Giovanna clasped her hands together. 'You should meet her in person!' The teachers broke into wild chatter. 'Yes, that's the best!'

'Go see her in Florence!' 'How exciting!' They all surged toward Julia, group-hugging her, cooing and clucking.

Julia choked up, thinking, *Tonight!*

67

I can't believe it!' Julia bounced in the back seat of the Uber, ebullient as a little girl. They were going to a gallery to meet her *biological mother*. 'We did it! We found her!'

'You found her!'

'*We!*'

'*You!* I'm so happy for you! It's amazing!'

Julia felt giddy. 'I was so excited I didn't ask any questions!'

'Like what?'

'Anything! Whether she's married, whether she has kids, whether she even put a baby up for adoption. What if she didn't?'

'They didn't seem that surprised.'

'This is so crazy!' Julia felt a rush, marveling. 'Do you realize this means the vision was *real*? The *vision* is what sent us to that school!'

'I know!' Courtney squeezed her arm. 'You legit have super-powers!'

'No, I used to, but I don't think I do anymore.'

Courtney made a sad face. 'Well, whatever, bottom line, you found your *bio mom*.'

Julia still reeled. 'Should I call her Fiamma? I'm not calling her Mom.' She flashed on her adoptive mother, whom she loved so much. 'I had a great mom, and she raised me.'

'Call her whatever you want.' Courtney grinned. 'She sounds nice, doesn't she? Taking her class to the hospital and all? That was sweet.'

'It really was!'

'Those teachers were *dying* for her to answer the phone. I think she's going to be happy to meet you.'

'I hope so.' Julia tried to process the implications. 'But I don't know. I'm crashing her life.'

'If the teachers thought it was going to go badly, they would've said something. They *wanted* you two to connect. I mean, reconnect.'

Julia felt a thrill at the thought. 'I can't even believe this. She must be a great artist to have a show in Florence.'

'She's where you got *your* art skills from. Isn't that so cool? I'm so happy for you and I'm so glad I'm here.'

'Aw, thanks for your help.' Julia blinked back tears. 'I never could've done this without you.'

'Yes, you could. You're Batman.'

Julia laughed. 'You know, I wish I had more information about her.'

'Look her up.'

'Right, I'll search Fiamma and Moravia Montessori School.' Julia scrolled to Google, plugged in the search, and got a bunch of results. She skimmed them and realized the problem. 'They're not about her. They're about the school and Adamo Bucci.'

'The guy in the picture?'

'Yes, from the bulletin board.' Julia clicked the link, and it brought her to a corporate website. She switched to the English version and read About Us aloud: 'We are the Romagna Group, the crown jewel in Adamo Bucci's suite of multinational corporations, comprising his successful entertainment, gaming, hospitality, and tourism divisions.'

'A certified BFD, huh?'

Julia read 'Upcoming Projects: Romagna Group is a huge fan of motorsports like Formula 1, Italian cart racing, and motorcycle racing. The Ferrari circuit at Imola is the most prestigious in the Romagna region.... ' Julia paused, remembering. 'I was there with Gianluca. We watched racing.'

'Cool.'

Julia read on, 'Romagna Group looks forward to developing a hospitality complex catering to those who appreciate excellence in fine accommodations when they visit Imola.' Julia looked up, remembering. 'Gianluca said whenever there was an F1 race, Imola got overrun with tourists.'

'Maybe that's the project that Giovanna meant, the one she got the gossip about.' Courtney shifted over, reading the phone. 'Jules, look, it says the project's going to cost seven hundred *million* euros. That's a lotta lira.'

'Really.' Julia scrolled down to a photo of Adamo Bucci with three other men in suits and gold lapel pins, a large *R* in a Gothic font. 'They all have the same pin.'

'Welcome to my world. Every polo shirt I own has a dancing printer. Have you ever seen a printer dance?'

Julia eyed the picture of Adamo Bucci. 'Funny, something about this guy looks kind of familiar.'

'You just saw his picture. Giovanna dropped it.'

'No, I mean he looks familiar from before, somehow.'

'Not to me. We never see people in suits here.'

'Except my realtor, Franco.' It made Julia think. 'That's it. Now I remember, from yesterday. When we were going to lunch, in Vincenza? Remember I wanted to avoid my realtor? He was sitting with men in suits.'

'Wait a minute, I might have a picture. I took some good ones yesterday, mostly flowers, but let's see.' Courtney got out her phone, went to her photos, and started scrolling, then stopped at one. 'This?'

'Yes.' Julia looked over, and it was a photo of the café at the top of the cobblestone street. There were people at the outside tables and among them was Franco with a group of men in suits. 'Can you enlarge those men?'

'Hold on.' Courtney enlarged the photo.

'Look, they have something in their lapels.'

'I'll make it bigger.' Courtney did, and Julia could see that the lapel pin was an *R*. All the men wore one except Franco, and the man sitting next to him was Adamo Bucci.

'That's interesting. Bucci and the other men were with Franco. So Franco and Bucci know each other.' Julia mulled it over. 'And Giovanna told us the gossip that Bucci's going to build something in Moravia. Remember, she said Moravia was up against Croce. So, I wonder if she was talking about this hospitality complex project.'

'She could've been. It's first on the upcoming list. What are you thinking?'

Julia tried to put it together. 'Well, I'm a landowner in Croce, a big one, and Croce's in the running for this project. My realtor Franco knows Bucci. We saw them at lunch.'

'I'm listening.' Courtney cocked her head, and Julia felt the conclusion just within reach, waiting for her.

'What if Franco is involved, somehow? What if Bucci is looking for a property in Croce? What if they're thinking about *mine*? *My* property is forty acres. That's big enough for a hospitality complex, isn't it?'

'Sure.'

'Maybe *that's* where Bucci wants to put this development.'

'I hear that. Your property looks like shit, but it's a lot of land. It has value, and it's not being used for anything else.' Courtney's bright eyes lit up. 'The fact that it's a ruin makes it better for them. You're the only owner so they don't have to negotiate with a slew of owners. They're gonna *flip* it.'

'Wait, what?' Julia couldn't follow that fast.

'They're offering you two million, but that's nothing compared to what your property's worth if Bucci wants to develop a seven hundred million euro complex there.' Courtney shifted over, newly urgent. 'Did Franco tell you there were buyers for your place?'

'Yes, a few.'

'Did you meet them?'

'No.'

'So what if they're not real?' Courtney's eyes narrowed. 'What if there is a group buying your land, like a consortium, and they're going to flip it, in other words, resell it to Bucci for a fortune.'

'So, you're saying a consortium is the real buyer?'

'Yes.' Courtney nodded, tense. '*Consortium* is corporate for "conspiracy."'

'Maybe *that's* what the conspiracy wants—my land.' Julia felt her brain catch fire. 'A project like that is so big, it would be a boon for Croce.'

'Of course, sure. It would bring tons of tourists, tons of jobs.'

'It would revitalize the town, even the region.' Julia thought of her visit to the police station with Gianluca. 'People go to Savernella for jobs, remember? It's the sister town, where the cops and administration are for Croce. Maybe that's what's been going on, all this time.'

'Croce could be bidding for Bucci's project. If that's true, then other players get involved. Not just private developers but local government.'

'It's in Savernella, that's why Torti and his thugs are in the conspiracy.' Julia put it together, and the realization horrified her. 'They want my land. They want me to sell. That's why Franco was bugging me with offers. That's why they're trying to drive me out.'

Courtney's eyes glittered. 'I bet they're under a deadline, if other towns are in the running.'

'So I guess even Franco's in the conspiracy.' Julia glanced out the window, trying to process what was going on. Rolling vineyards flew past without her seeing them. 'Franco knew that Gianluca was telling me not to sell.'

'So *that's* why they wanted to kill Gianluca.'

Julia felt her heart wrench. She struggled to stay composed. She couldn't speak for a moment, and everything made horrifying sense.

'And that's why they put cameras in the villa. They want to know what you're thinking about selling.'

Julia tried to get it together. 'But why'd they drug me?'

'They wanted to scare you away, gaslight you, make you think the house was haunted and you were going crazy—' Courtney stopped abruptly, her lips parting. 'I just had a scary thought. They need the land because the site is being chosen now, right?'

'Right.'

'I wonder what happens if you die.'

'Yikes!' Julia recoiled, aghast.

'Do you have a will?'

'No. The lawyer in Milan said if I die without a will, the estate goes to the government. It loses money, and probate takes forever.'

'Probate causes delay, and delay would put Croce out of contention for the Bucci project. That's why their Plan A was to get you to sell, fast.'

'Holy shit.' Julia felt stricken. 'And Plan B? They *kill* me?'

Courtney nodded, grim.

Julia shuddered. 'But what about the delay in probate? They don't care then?'

'If *this* much money is involved and there's *this* much benefit to the region, I bet probate gets fast-tracked. They can bribe government officials.'

'So, money talks.'

'And it speaks Italian.'

Julia's thoughts raced ahead, her gut wrenching. Something told her she was on the right track. 'I'm thinking about Mike's murder. Gianluca and I thought the guy in the hoodie was really coming after me. But what if he was coming after *Mike*?'

'Why would he?'

'Let me think out loud.' Julia tried to recall what Lombardi had told her about a will. 'If I died without a will, and Mike was alive when I inherited Rossi's property, then *he* would inherit the property. What if they wanted to eliminate Mike so the property was clear, *before* I was told about the inheritance?'

Courtney moaned. 'Oh, man.'

Julia felt a stab of grief, and bitterness. She thought of Mike and the night he was killed, then Gianluca and the night of his crash. There had been so much violence, death, and pain. Now she knew why. Money.

'Jules, are you okay?'

'Hell, yes.' Julia felt her teeth clench with anger, with resolve, with *power*. 'We have to get these bastards. We're going to the Florence police. We'll tell them what the Savernella cops did to us. We'll show them the photo of Franco and Bucci together. We'll lay the whole thing out. We'll *make* them investigate.'

'Right, agree.' Courtney pursed her lips.

'I'll call the Philly police, too. This is a break in Mike's case, finally.'

'Thank God.' Courtney nodded. 'But what about Fiamma?'

Julia's throat went thick. 'I want to meet her, first. Then, the cops.'

68

Night had fallen by the time they reached Florence, and Julia and Courtney got out of the Uber on the corner. The Oltrarno neighborhood on the other side of the Arno was quieter than the city's historic center, mostly residential rather than touristy. Tasteful four-story homes with well-maintained facades lined its cobblestone streets, many too narrow for traffic. Here and there were artists' studios and showrooms, closed now. No one was out.

'I'm nervous to meet her,' Julia said, smoothing her hair into place.

'Weirdly, so am I.'

Julia tried to get her bearings. Estrella Studio was in the middle of the block, the first floor of a home with a recessed entrance. 'Are you sure we should meet her at her show? It's essentially her workplace.'

'And you're essentially her daughter.'

'Court, she gave me up.' Julia felt a pang, an ancient pain, buried deep.

'God knows what the circumstances were.' Courtney frowned, sympathetic. She started walking toward the gallery, then stopped when she saw Julia wasn't following. 'Aren't you coming?'

'What if I'm completely wrong? What if it's just a fluke that I look like her?'

'It's not a fluke. It's real.'

'Flukes are *real*,' Julia shot back. '*I'm* a fluke. My birth is a fluke. Maybe my birth mother's a fluke, too.'

'Honey, no. You're just getting cold feet.' Courtney gestured to the gallery. 'Let's go in and see how you feel. You don't have to meet her. Let the spirit move you.'

'The spirits don't move me anymore.'

'Look, let's go in and play it by ear. If you want to leave, we'll go. If you want to speak to her, you should.'

'But what if she sees me? She'll notice the resemblance. Then I'm stuck.'

'Stuck?' Courtney flashed her a reassuring smile. 'Stuck meeting the woman you waited a lifetime to meet? You've been talking about your bio mom since *Annie* in high school. You went through hell to make this happen. You can't stop now, like you said.'

Julia got an idea. 'I know, I'll put my sunglasses on. Then she won't see the resemblance.' She went in her purse, got her sunglasses, and slipped them on. 'Better? Now we can get in and out without her knowing.'

'Great, so let's go in.' Courtney resumed walking, and Julia joined her, futilely box breathing. They reached the gallery, which had whimsical painted tiles embedded in its arched entrance, and a sign on the glass door read, FIAMMA SETTIMI TONIGHT.

'Her full name is Fiamma Settimi?' Julia had expected to see Fiamma, but Settimi came out of nowhere. 'So she doesn't use Rossi. Maybe she changed her name.'

'I wonder if Rossi called her Fiamma.'

'Me, too, so she only changed her last name. I wonder if she knows her real name is Patrizia Ritorno.' Julia hesitated. 'Or if I'm wrong and she's not my birth mother at all.'

'Why don't you ask her? That's an excellent conversation starter. Just go with, "Are you my mother?"' Courtney smiled, putting her hand on the doorknob. 'Ready?'

Julia braced herself. 'Okay, let's go in.'

'Atta girl.' Courtney opened the door to admit Julia, and they entered the gallery.

Julia's heart pounded, and she stalled, scanning the room. It was long, white, and packed with a sophisticated crowd of about seventy people in flowing dresses, unstructured linen jackets, and an array of scarves and pashminas. Everyone buzzed in clusters or shifted along the perimeter taking in the paintings, but Julia couldn't see their faces because the only illumination came from track lighting aimed at the art. Her sunglasses made it worse but she wasn't about to take them off. She didn't see Fiamma.

Courtney crossed to a placard on an easel. 'Jules, come here.'
Julia walked over and read the placard:

ABOUT FIAMMA SETTIMI

Fiamma Settimi honors us with her mesmerizing watercolors of the Spedale degli Innocenti, an orphanage for abandoned children. Babies were left on a rotating drum at its entrance, and the first such baby was a girl named Agata, relinquished on 5 February 1445. The orphanage is a Florentine landmark, designed by Filippo Brunelleschi and considered the first pure Early Renaissance building. Peruse this magnificent series of watercolors and you will understand why Ms. Settimi's work has been deemed "spectacular," "outstanding," and "profoundly moving" by art critics all over the city and beyond.

'Wow' was all Julia could say, her throat thick. Her chest tightened with emotion.

Courtney leaned closer. 'She's painting an orphanage. You know what that tells me? That she's been thinking about the baby she gave up.'

Julia couldn't hope for that conclusion. Tears came to her eyes, but she blinked them away behind her sunglasses.

'Jules, this *is* like fate.' Courtney squeezed her arm. 'This shows that you matter to her, even now. I bet every woman who gives up a child for adoption never forgets that child, ever.'

In the next moment, a compact older man in white shirt and a jeans jacket climbed onto a platform at the front of the gallery. He had frizzy gray hair and a wide grin buried in a short gray beard. 'Everyone, may I have your attention?' he asked in Italian-accented English, speaking into a handheld microphone.

The crowd quieted and turned in his direction. Julia assumed Fiamma must be at the front of the gallery near him.

'Good evening, I'm Paolo Natoli, the owner of Estrella Studio, and I'm so pleased you came to the new show by one of our favorite artists, Fiamma Settimi.' He paused for a smattering of applause. 'I'm going to introduce Fiamma, and we're going to speak in Italian, then English. Fiamma invited friends from the UK and she wants them to feel at home. So welcome everyone, even the Brits!'

'Hear, hear!' a man called out in a British accent, and everyone burst into laughter.

Paolo spoke briefly in Italian, then segued to English. 'Art critics heap praise on Fiamma's work, but I myself am the best art critic you know. Without question, Fiamma is one of the most talented watercolorists I have ever seen.' Paolo beamed, and the crowd applauded. 'Her talent is God's gift, and her creativity is inexhaustible, as is she. She teaches grade school, so there's the proof you need.'

The crowd chuckled. Julia's heart started to pound. She realized she was minutes away from seeing her birth mother, a woman she'd been wondering about her whole life.

'Many of you know Fiamma, so you know she is one of the kindest, most generous, most thoughtful, most brilliant women ever. I love her, and so do we all.' Paolo grinned. 'So without further ado, let's bring her up.'

The crowd applauded as Paolo stepped down, handing off the microphone, and Fiamma climbed onto the stool with a broad smile, a slim and attractive woman in a bohemian peasant dress.

My God. Julia stifled a gasp. Fiamma *did* look like her, or Julia looked like Fiamma. They both had wide-set blue eyes, a small nose, and the same dirty blonde hair, though Fiamma's was long and swept into a loose topknot. She looked younger than fifty-something, maybe because she had a warm and casual way about her.

Courtney whispered. 'Holy shit. It's *her.*'

Julia nodded, grateful for the sunglasses. Her heart tried to jump out of her chest.

'*Sera, tutti!*' Fiamma began speaking in Italian, smiling easily and drawing chuckles from the crowd. Her lively gaze swept the gallery as she spoke, and she turned left and right, including everyone the way teachers do.

Courtney whispered again, 'She seems so nice!'

Julia nodded, conflicted. She found herself liking Fiamma, too, which felt strange. She'd wondered about her so long and resented her from time to time, but now found it hard to stay mad at her, seeing her in person, a charming and talented woman, a teacher as well as an artist. Julia's anger began to ebb away, but questions remained, and plenty of them.

'*Grazie!*' Fiamma finished her Italian speech with a comical curtsy, provoking applause. 'And now, let me speak English for the heathens.'

Everybody laughed.

'I'm very grateful that you came tonight. I see many old and new friends here, so thank you. I adore Paolo, who does so much for local artists, even those who cannot quit our day job.' Fiamma smiled. Her English was flawless with a slight Italian accent. 'The subject of my new show is one of the most magnificent buildings in our beloved Florence, the *Innocenti*, an orphanage.' She turned to the left side of the room, where Julia and Courtney were standing. 'I love to find the emotionality and truth that reside even in the inanimate. I look for life, and light, too. History will always show both to those who are willing to see.'

Julia swallowed hard. Heads nodded around the gallery.

Fiamma continued, 'It's impossible to paint an orphanage, especially a historical one, without imagining the emotions of the orphans – their pain, love, confusion, longing, sorrow, despair, and even anger.'

Whoa. Julia felt the words grab her by the heart. She'd felt all of those emotions for so long.

'People often ask me which are my favorite paintings, and usually I decline to answer. I believe, as most of you do, that art should be interpreted by the viewer, not the artist.' Fiamma cocked her head with a sly smile. 'Also it would be like choosing between *gnocchi* and *linguini*. Both are perfect. Why ask?'

Everyone chuckled again.

'But I will admit, my favorites in this collection are the paintings of the medals, trinkets, and charms over there.' Fiamma indicated the left side of the gallery, in Julia's direction. 'I painted crucifixes, sacred hearts, and paper pictures of the saints, which were pinned to the orphans' clothes by the so-called house nannies. The charms were believed to have magical powers to reunite the orphans with their parents.'

Julia blinked. The words struck her as so pointed she wondered if Fiamma were speaking to her.

'There is so much about the Renaissance to celebrate, in painting, architecture, music, literature, and sculpture. Florence was the world's epicenter, and men like da Vinci, Michelangelo, Brunelleschi, Vasari, and Raphael gained prominence, not because they made war but because they made art. They wanted to express the struggle of man to understand himself and his times, to make sense of his place in his universe and with his God, and finally to find beauty around him, not when it came easily to the eye, but when it did not.'

Julia noticed that Fiamma stayed facing in her direction, no longer sweeping the crowd as she spoke.

'Those are the glories of the Renaissance, and we know them so well. But that doesn't mean we can ignore its underside. There is always a negative to the positive, and a dark side to the moon herself.'

Julia thought of the pearl she'd found in the scorched debris at the villa.

'The underside is, what about women during the Renaissance? They didn't experience the freedom and power of men. Even at the *Innocenti*, girls were taught only sewing and cooking, while boys were educated and taught a trade.'

Julia couldn't shake the sensation that Fiamma was looking at her, but she couldn't be sure. People nodded in the crowd.

'To be sure, there were strong women of the Renaissance, but they were exceptions and for the most part, the nobility. The perfect example is Duchess Caterina Sforza, who famously defended her family at Forlì. Caterina was a favorite of my mother's, and I grew up with stories of Caterina's bravery, intelligence, and boldness.'

Julia startled, knowing the reference couldn't be a coincidence. On impulse, she lifted her sunglasses off her face and onto the top of her head. She wanted to see Fiamma better, and she wanted Fiamma to see *her* better.

Fiamma reacted instantly. Her expression changed on the spot, as if a professional mask had dropped. She looked nakedly astonished, her eyes widening with disbelief. She even shifted on her feet, like she lost her balance.

Oh my God. Julia locked eyes with Fiamma, feeling the connection between them, as surely as there had once been an umbilical cord.

Courtney whispered, 'Jules, she sees you.'

The crowd noticed, too, craned their necks and turned to the back, wondering what was distracting her, but Fiamma seemed to forget they were even there, as she fumbled to continue.

'But the, uh, sexism of the Renaissance was worse for women… unlike Caterina… who weren't noble.' Fiamma faltered like she'd lost her train of thought, gazing directly at Julia, and her eyes began to glisten. 'When I painted… those magical charms, I imagined those women… pregnant, desperate… unable to support a child. They had no other option but to give up… their baby.'

Julia felt tears come to her eyes, too. Galvanized, she realized Fiamma was explaining, in front of everyone, why she'd relinquished her for adoption.

'And, uh, excuse me, I'm sorry… I think I see, I can't believe this!' Fiamma abruptly stopped speaking, climbed down from the stand, and vanished into the crowd, which broke into confused chatter.

Julia spotted Fiamma threading her way through the crowd toward them, making a beeline for her. 'We should go, Courtney.'

'No, she's coming to meet you. Let's stay.'

Julia was struck by a foreboding, like a child about to be disciplined by a mother she never knew. 'I'm leaving.'

'No, don't, you should meet her.'

'I can't.' Julia fled for the door, knocking over the easel.

'Jules, wait!'

Julia almost made it to the door when she felt a hand on her arm. 'Courtney, no,' she said, turning around.

She came face-to-face with Fiamma.

69

'*Chi sei?*' Fiamma asked, shocked, and Julia felt shocked, too, realizing they looked like older and younger versions of the same woman, their jaws on the floor.

'I… don't speak… Italian.'

'Who *are* you?' Fiamma asked, hushed. 'Are you my—?'

'Yes,' Julia blurted out, reeling, and Fiamma took her arm, walked her to the door, and brought her outside.

'What's your name?' Fiamma's eyes rounded with disbelief. 'What are you doing here? Where did you come from? How did you find me?'

Julia was about to answer when she spotted two men approaching down the dark street behind Fiamma, moving oddly fast. One was the Fiat driver with the mustache, and the other had on jeans and a black hoodie.

Oh my God! Julia recognized him instantly. She thought she hadn't seen his face that night, but now she knew it was him. It was the man who murdered Mike. Now they were coming for *her*.

'Call the police, go!' Julia pushed Fiamma into the recessed entrance of the gallery, then took off running. The houses were dark and shuttered for the night. No one was out on the street.

'Help!' Julia shouted, trying to rouse somebody. She raced around the corner. That street was deserted, too. She glanced back. The men were half a block away. Hoodie was fast, the Fiat driver jogged with effort. She accelerated, screaming for help. She didn't know where she was going.

She tried not to panic. Shutters opened on one window. No one came out. Ahead was a traffic rotary and a clearing. There had to be people there.

She reached the rotary. Traffic was light. She screamed, trying to flag down a driver. They sped past her. She spotted a parking lot but it was empty. A lighted sign read BOBOLI GIARDINI, Boboli Gardens.

Her heart leaped with hope. It was a tourist attraction. She could find help there. She raced toward the arched entrance, but the gate was locked. The garden was closed. No one was around, not even security. The stone ticket booth was closed too.

Julia looked around wildly in the dark. Behind the ticket office was an employee parking lot being repaired. She spotted a temporary fence of orange netting with sections lying on the ground.

She raced toward the flattened section, ran over the netting, and plowed through a sparse hedge into the garden. It was dark except for decorative lights. There were trees, hedges, bushes, and winding pathways where she could hide.

Instinct told her to keep moving. A gravel pathway bisected the garden, illuminated with bigger decorative lights. She couldn't go that way. Too visible.

She glanced behind her. The men hadn't come through the orange fence. She didn't see them anywhere else. Maybe she'd lost them.

Her mind raced. She got her phone, fumbled to the Find My Phone app, and pressed Contact Courtney. The app would show Courtney her exact location.

She took off running. She prayed Courtney would send the police. There was no time to lose. She accelerated. The elevation steepened. She started running uphill. Her breath came ragged. Her thighs burned.

She looked back. She spotted the men, their shadows racing in front of one of the lights, casting a gargantuan shadow on the hedges. They split up, going in different directions. It was two against one. They would cover more ground, looking for her.

Julia felt a bolt of terror. She prayed the police got to her before the men did. She didn't scream for help because she couldn't reveal where she was. She remembered the steak knife in her purse. She pulled it out on the fly.

She ran along the side of the garden, a hedge in front of a stone wall. Her heart thundered. She could see houses outside the wall. She looked back. She'd lost track of the men. She feared they knew the place better than she did.

She kept running along a path that wound left, then right. She lost her orientation. The garden was mazelike, bewildering at night.

She kept going up. There had to be a clearing, maybe a security guard. Her lungs burned, her thighs ached. She tripped on the gravel, then realized her footsteps were making noise.

She ran onto the grass, spotting a huge fountain surrounded with decorative lights. She'd be too exposed that way. She angled across the grass toward a line of trees, racing for cover.

Julia glanced back, terrified. They weren't behind her. She didn't know where they were. She ran past one hedge, then another, and there was a corner.

Out of nowhere, the Fiat driver barreled into her, knocking her onto her back. He landed heavily on top of her, sweating, panting, and cursing in Italian.

Julia slashed the side of his face, slicing his ear. He howled in pain. His hand flew to his cheek. Blood spurted from the wound. He exploded in rage, trying to get up.

Julia scrambled to her feet and took off. She sprinted away on a diagonal, raced over the gravel path and back into the grass. She came to a trio of winding pathways. She took the first one and kept running this way and that, trying to get away. She could hear the Fiat driver yelling behind her.

She struggled to think through her fright. If the Fiat driver was yelling, Hoodie hadn't found him. Maybe Hoodie would keep looking for her. She knew how ruthless he could be. He killed Mike without hesitation.

Julia kept going, running across the lawn, scooting around hedges on the left then to the right. The lighting was dim in the center of the garden. She could see a line of tall trees to her right, which oriented her. She ran that way, faster and faster toward yellow buildings on her left. They were dark, still, and quiet, closed. In the next moment, she heard sirens blaring.

Julia kept going. The sirens didn't sound far away. She ran through an open field, looking behind her. Hoodie wasn't following her.

She kept running up. It was getting harder and harder. She staggered and almost fell. Ahead was an open field. There was a massive bronze sculpture of a broken face, as tall as a building, illuminated in the darkness. She raced across the field at an angle, avoiding the lights.

Suddenly Julia heard footsteps behind her. She glanced over her shoulder. It was Hoodie, gaining on her in the gloom.

'No!' she screamed in terror, her legs churning. The sirens blared closer and closer. She prayed they got here in time. She had to stay alive until then.

Julia accelerated, desperate. She glanced back. Hoodie was thirty feet away, then twenty. She could hear him panting, then laughing. He was enjoying himself.

She looked around, desperate for a weapon. The face sculpture provided light. She needed something, *anything*, to defend herself with. She spotted sticks, all too thin. She spied a rock, grabbed it on the fly, and kept going.

She fought panic to plan. She would surprise him with the rock. Hit him in the face. Break his nose. Do anything to buy time.

The sirens got closer and closer. Red lights flashed in the night sky. She was losing hope they'd get here. Hoodie would kill her and get away. It didn't take long to kill somebody. He'd murdered Mike in the blink of an eye.

Julia felt a stark cold terror. The man was ten feet away from her, then six.

'No!' Julia tried to run faster, but he grabbed her by the hair, yanked her back, and hurled her to the ground.

Julia landed hard, the wind knocked out of her. She tried to get up, fighting for her life. He jumped down and straddled her, laughing and breathless. He cuffed her in the face, stunning her. Her brain rattled. She almost lost consciousness. She flailed and kicked, writhing, trying to get out from under.

He slid out a large hunting knife. Its lethal blade caught the light from the sculpture. He was going to kill her the way he killed Mike.

She was going to die.

70

Julia felt a new resolve, a *knowing* that she couldn't let him kill her. She was going to fight back and save her own life. It was another premonition, one she knew as surely as the night Mike had been murdered. The knowledge gave her a preternatural calm, even under the point of a knife.

Suddenly a faint blue aura materialized around her, enveloping her in a shimmering cerulean haze. Julia didn't know if it was a hallucination, a psychedelic, a surge of adrenaline, or even her channeling Caterina. A vibrant new energy coursed throughout her body, rushing through her circulatory system like a transfusion of something otherworldly, empowering her.

Julia marshaled every cell of her newfound strength and shoved the man off her, getting to her feet. He staggered backward, dropping the knife, his mouth agape. She didn't know if he saw the aura or if she was hallucinating his reaction, but it didn't matter now. She squared off against her husband's killer.

The man turned to get away, but Julia grabbed him by the arm and whipped him at the base of the sculpture. He stumbled toward it, losing his balance, his arms windmilling. He fell into the sculpture. His head slammed its base with a solid *thud*. He groaned on impact, then slid to the ground, writhing in pain.

Police sirens blared at the garden entrance, and Julia heard them as if from another place and time. Her blue aura began to dematerialize around her, blurring into a spangled mist that rejoined the ether and the spirits, of which she was but a part. She felt herself coming into herself again, tingling all over, nothing less than a woman in full, possessing an array of powers, a strength of her own, one profoundly human and powered by love. She was a wife, avenging a dearly beloved husband.

Sirens screamed into the garden, filling the air with deafening sound, followed by flashing red and white lights. Julia looked over to see police cruisers bounding across the grass, their high beams bouncing as they headed toward her. She waved them down, and the cruisers lurched to a halt. *Carabinieri* jumped out, shadows racing to her and her attacker, who was still groaning at the base of the sculpture.

Behind the police ran Courtney and Fiamma.

Julia's heart soared, and she ran toward the women. All three opened their arms, meeting and hugging each other. Julia managed not to cry, feeling an outpouring of gratitude for a best friend who was closer than any blood relation, as well as a blood relation who was a total stranger, but who somehow, in that moment, felt like the most remarkable of everyday miracles.

A loving mother.

71

Julia and Courtney sat across the desk in the office, a bright white room lined with framed official certificates and group photographs of *carabinieri*. They'd been taken to the *Comando Provinciale*, the Florence police headquarters near the Arno, and Julia had given a complete statement to Marshal Vernio, a sixty-something precinct captain with refined features and wavy gray hair. His white shirt was crisp even at this late hour, and he looked born into a navy jacket trimmed in red around the epaulets.

Julia told him everything, starting with her husband's murder, going through her vision of Gianluca being run off the road, and ending with how she was attacked by White Fiat and Hoodie in the Boboli Gardens, even about her premonition, being microdosed with psychedelics, and the blue aura that she thought may have been Caterina, if it wasn't a hallucination.

Marshal Vernio lifted an eyebrow as he typed on his desktop computer, and Julia felt her anxiety coming back when he questioned her further, about the night that Hoodie murdered Mike in Philly. When she was finished, Marshal Vernio checked his desktop screen. 'Now, Ms Pritzker, I have your statement, and its gravamen is that you believe there was a conspiracy to buy your property in order to resell it to Adamo Bucci and the Romagna Group, to develop into a hospitality complex. You believe that your realtor Franco Patelli was part of the conspiracy and that your housekeeper Anna Mattia Vesta and her husband Piero Fano were also involved, drugging you in order to make you think you were crazy or that the villa was haunted, so that you would sell it and go back to America.'

'Right. When it looked like I wouldn't sell, or at least not fast enough, they upped the ante.'

'I understand.' Marshal Vernio nodded. 'You believe that Marshal Torti and two *carabinieri* from Savernella were also involved. The conspiracy, and at this point we are unsure who in the conspiracy, attempted to murder Gianluca Moretti because he didn't want you to sell the house and because you and he were beginning a relationship that might incline you to stay in Tuscany. Then, when they saw they could not convince you to sell, they attempted to kill you, which was their motive for the attack tonight in the Boboli.'

'Yes.'

'So, both the attempted murder of Gianluca Moretti *and* the murder of your husband Michael Shallette were in furtherance of the conspiracy. Is that your belief?'

'Yes,' Julia answered, though it was hard to hear. She felt a wave of guilt that she knew would never go away. 'What are your next steps, if I may ask?'

'Obviously we will investigate these allegations starting tonight, via many means. Our goal is to identify the bottom rung of the putative conspiracy and hope we gain confessions and cooperation to indict whoever is giving orders at the top rung.' Marshal Vernio checked his phone. 'I will share with you that we now have the name and identification of the two men who assaulted you in the Boboli. The man you call White Fiat is Bernardo Vitali and Hoodie is Ciro Nardini.'

Julia felt her chest tighten at the name of the man who killed Mike, and Courtney looked over at her, sympathetic.

'Both men are in custody at the hospital. Vitali is in stable condition. Nardini's condition is critical but he is expected to survive. He sustained a skull fracture and a broken collarbone.'

'I hope he's in pain,' Julia said, meaning it.

Courtney interjected, 'He will be if *I* run into him.'

'Both men have criminal records and are known to us as thugs-for-hire. We will endeavor to identify the third man, whom you call Ballcap and who followed you at the Uffizi, as soon as possible. We have your photos, and I have sent them on to my officers.' Marshal Vernio gestured at the photos on his desk, which he'd printed from Julia's phone. 'I will send a team to Savernella to meet with Marshal Torti and another team to Croce to meet with your realtor Franco

Patelli. We will also be paying a visit to Anna Mattia Vesta and Piero Fano in the near future. They should not be too hard to find.'

'Good.' Julia thought it sounded thorough. 'What about Adamo Bucci of the Romagna Group?'

'We will visit him, as well.'

'Can I ask another question? How does that work, with Ciro Nardini being charged with my husband's murder? The murder took place in Philadelphia, so you don't charge him with that here, do you?'

'No.' Marshal Vernio frowned. 'I will liaise with Detective Malloy of the Homicide Division in Philadelphia in the morning. They have jurisdiction over the murder of your husband, and they will be in charge of that investigation and prosecution.'

'Which case goes first? Or do they run at the same time?'

'We go first. This matter involves crimes on Italian soil perpetrated by Italian citizens. We will get it sorted with law enforcement in Philadelphia, and you will be kept informed, as you are integral to both prosecutions.' Marshal Vernio's face fell into grave lines. 'However, our investigation does not happen overnight. Were you intending to return to the villa from here?'

'Yes,' Julia answered, nervous at the thought. 'Do you think you could put a police car in front of the house? Others in the conspiracy may still come after us.'

'Certainly, that was my concern, too. I will send you home tonight with two officers, and I will make sure there is protection for you until we have apprehended all of the suspects.' Marshal Vernio nodded, in a final way. 'I will kindly ask you to keep our discussion confidential, and not to post about it on social media.'

'Of course not. Thank you.'

Courtney interjected, 'Marshal Vernio, I'm supposed to leave Italy tomorrow. Is that okay?'

'Yes. Please give me your contact information, in the event that we need to follow up.'

Courtney looked at Julia. 'Jules, are you still okay with my going?'

'Totally. Please, go. I'll be fine.'

Marshal Vernio cleared his throat. 'Ms Pritzker, I have two points I would like to clarify about your statement. You believe that Gianluca

Moretti was run off the road on his motorcycle because you saw this in a vision, which took place in the hospital?'

'Yes.'

Marshal Vernio frowned. 'I cannot file charges on that basis, for obvious reasons.'

'They're not obvious to me,' Julia shot back. 'When you investigate Marshal Torti, Nardini, Vitali, and whoever Ballcap is, I guarantee you'll be able to substantiate charges for what they did to Gianluca. Maybe they'll turn on each other, like you say. One way or the other, whoever did this has to be charged.' Julia worried about Gianluca, even now. 'No one loves this city more than he does. He deserves your full force—'

'I have your point.' Marshal Vernio raised a hand. 'The other part of your account I would like to clarify is what happened in the Boboli, between you and Nardini. How did you *really* get away from him and inflict those injuries on him? It cannot be the account you told me.'

'It is, I swear. I managed to get him off of me and send him into the base of the sculpture. It could've been adrenaline, or the psychedelic, or even the spirt of Caterina, empowering me.'

Marshal Vernio pursed his lips. 'The *ghost* of Duchess Caterina Sforza?'

'Look, I know what I saw, but I admit, I'm not sure if Caterina was really there or not. She could've been because, evidently, I have abilities as a medium. I thought they'd gone away, but maybe they haven't, completely. If you want to verify what I'm saying, contact Helen Davenport. She's worked with Scotland Yard.'

'I have heard of her.'

'So then you know I'm telling the truth.'

Marshal Vernio clucked, shaking his head. 'So Duchess Caterina Sforza herself, dead for hundreds of years, enabled you to throw an adult male against the pedestal of the sculpture.' Marshal Vernio mulled it over. 'Em, Ms Pritzker, I wonder if, perhaps, you misremember.'

Julia blinked. 'I don't. It just happened.'

'Reconsider the matter. When one is under threat of mortal

danger, one's perception may be faulty and one's memory may be, too.' Marshal Vernio cocked his head, his manner deliberate. 'Here's what I think happened. I think Nardini was chasing you and trying to catch you, but just as he reached you, he accidentally slipped and fell against the pedestal, injuring himself.'

'No, that's not true.'

Marshal Vernio smiled gently, his manner newly paternal. 'Ms Pritzker, this incident will arouse great public interest. The media is already gathering outside. Residents heard the sirens and saw police action. The Boboli is a major tourist attraction, known worldwide. Do you understand?'

'Yes,' Julia answered, but she didn't know where he was going.

'So, if I file your account in your official statement, it will attract the press and the media, perhaps from all over the world. That will result in reporters, questions, stories, and headlines about you, for years to come. The notoriety will upend your life.' Marshal Vernio opened his palms. 'Therefore, I suggest that I draft a statement for your signature, which will set forth the above version of the incident, with Nardini accidentally falling.' Marshal Vernio paused, expectantly. 'Will you… ?'

'What?' Julia asked, puzzled. 'Sign?'

'Yes, and will you also… ?'

Courtney interjected, 'She'll shut up, Marshal Vernio.'

Julia looked over. 'Shut up about what, Courtney? That's not what happened.'

Courtney smiled, amused. 'He knows that, Jules. He needs a pitch for the media. This way, they get their headlines and clicks, and you won't be "The Crazy American Who Turned Blue in the Boboli."'

Julia caught up. 'Oh.'

Courtney winked. 'Welcome to sales, honey.'

Julia left the marshal's office with Courtney and one of the officers. He led them to a waiting area filled with people, among them Fiamma, who rose, her eyes full of concern.

'How nice of you to wait.' Julia crossed to her, happily surprised, but Fiamma's manner seemed tentative, after the Boboli.

'Of course. How did it go?'

'Fine, thanks.'

'I thought we might talk, but you're probably too exhausted tonight. You've been through an ordeal.'

'No, I'm fine.' Julia was dying to talk to her. 'Let's talk. This officer is going to take us home.'

'Okay, where are you staying?'

Oh no. Julia realized that she had no idea if Fiamma knew Rossi had passed. 'Uh, I'm sorry to tell you, but your mother—'

'I know she's dead,' Fiamma said matter-of-factly.

Okay. 'Well, I'm staying at the villa you grew up in.'

Fiamma hesitated. 'I'll meet you there.'

Julia climbed into the back of the police cruiser next to Courtney, but before they left Florence, she called the hospital to check on Gianluca. His condition hadn't changed, but that didn't come as any relief.

The cruiser took off, gliding through the dark night with two cops in the front seat. A faint greenish glow emanated from their laptop, and a perforated barrier divided the front from the back seat, which were bucket seats of hard black plastic. The air smelled like stale cigarettes.

Julia turned to Courtney, since it was the first time they'd gotten to speak, just the two of them. 'Court, I can't thank you enough for what you did.'

'Please, I love you, I'm so happy you're okay. How are you, honey?' Courtney eyed her with sympathy, in the lights from passing traffic.

'I'm okay.' Julia was trying to get calm. 'I'm glad it's over.'

'I bet, that must have been so scary in the garden.'

Julia shuddered. 'It was, but I'm glad they're going to put those guys away. I want them locked up for good.'

'They will. I liked Vernio. I have confidence in him.' Courtney hesitated. 'Are you really okay with me leaving tomorrow? I could squeeze in another day.'

'I'm fine. Go home, you've been amazing.'

'Girl, *you* have. Give yourself some credit, okay? I heard you tell the whole story to Vernio. You stayed alive until we got there. You stayed away from *two* killers, not just one. You kicked Hoodie's ass, and you saved yourself from a bad guy with a *steak* knife.'

'Like you said, we served bad guys.' Julia smiled. 'Thanks for calling the police so fast.'

'I didn't,' Courtney shot back. 'Fiamma did. She didn't know why you ran away from her at the gallery, but she didn't hesitate. She said you told her to call the cops and she took over.'

'What happened?' Julia asked, surprised. 'You used Find My Phone, right?'

'Yes, I found you on the app, but she was already on her phone with the cops. She kept them on the whole time we were running and told them exactly where you were.' Courtney nodded, excited. 'She got the cops superfast because she knew who to call and spoke Italian. If it weren't for her, I don't know when they would've gotten to you. I don't know *what* would've happened.' Courtney shook her head, wide-eyed. 'Fiamma was so worried about you. She wanted to run into the garden herself. The police had to hold her back.'

Aw. 'You think she really cares?'

'Of course she cares.'

'It's probably because she feels guilty.'

'Don't be that way. Anyway, so what if she feels guilty? It doesn't mean she doesn't care.' Courtney frowned, sympathetic. 'Listen, you guys have a lot to talk about. When we get home, I'll go upstairs. I have to pack anyway.'

'No, don't, you can hang with us.' Julia couldn't imagine being alone with Fiamma, even though it was a meeting she'd waited so long for.

'You're just worried, but don't be. You'll do fine. Just talk to her, tell her what you feel.'

Julia's chest went tight. 'It's not that easy.'

'Sure it is, she wants to talk to you.'

'But I don't know what she knows. Like, does she even know about the inheritance?'

'I have no idea. We didn't get to talk. It all happened so fast.'

Julia was about to talk it over but the police radio burst abruptly into loud static and the cops started talking, making conversation impossible.

Courtney took her hand and held it, all the way home.

Julia smiled, realizing that best friends didn't always need words.

72

Julia was opening a bottle of Chianti when she heard Fiamma's car in the driveway. She popped the cork, smoothed her hair, and hustled from the kitchen, stepping over the sleeping Bianco. She told herself to stay calm, that she'd faced ruthless murderers tonight, so she should be able to deal with her *bio mom*.

Julia went outside and waved as Fiamma parked her car next to the police cruiser. The two officers nodded in acknowledgment, since she'd told them to expect a visitor. Fiamma drove a vintage maroon Karmann Ghia, so evidently Rossi wasn't the only one with the car fetish.

Julia crossed to the car, managing a smile. 'Thank you for coming.'

'Of course, thank you for having me.' Fiamma got out of the car with a smile that vanished when she scanned the villa. 'My God! How did she let it get like this? This is shameful. I thought maybe it was only the driveway, but the villa, too? This is terrible. How did she live in this *ruin*?'

'It's clean inside,' Julia said, unaccountably defensive, whether of Rossi or the villa, she didn't know. Maybe both.

'If you had seen it before, you would understand. This used to be beautiful, a *magnificent* villa.' Fiamma shook her head, aghast. 'It had so much charm, and the grounds were stunning. She let it fall down around her.'

'You get used to it,' Julia said, surprised at the words leaving her own lips.

'What? How can you *stay* here? You must have been shocked when you arrived.' Fiamma looked at her, directly. 'I guess you figured out my mother was crazy.'

Arg. 'Let's talk it over inside.' Julia led the way to the villa, and

Fiamma followed her, entering the villa and frowning at the cracked walls, peeling paint, and broken floor tiles in the entrance hall.

'My God, this is madness, pure madness.'

'I like the frescoes,' Julia blurted out, awkward.

'Yes, true, there's that.' Fiamma looked up, unsmiling. 'I remember when she commissioned them. She planned every one.'

'How old were you?' Julia asked, but Fiamma was already heading into the living room, stopping at a distance from the broken wall to the underground tunnel.

Oh no. 'I'm so sorry.' Julia went to her, feeling a rush of sympathy.

Fiamma seemed rooted to the spot, her expression agonized as she confronted a childhood horror. She didn't speak for a moment, then said, 'So you know.'

'Yes. I found the… room.'

'She had the entrance plastered over?'

'I guess so, yes.'

Fiamma shook her head. 'It used to have a door.'

'I can't imagine what it was like.'

'I can't forget what it was like.' Fiamma spoke quietly, her voice pained. 'She put me down there for a few days every month, sometimes a week, and it *terrified* me.'

Julia shuddered.

'Sometimes she would stay with me until I fell asleep, but then I would wake up, even more afraid because she was gone. I would scream but she didn't let me out.'

Julia touched her arm. 'Let's go to the kitchen. We can have some wine.' She walked that way, and Fiamma followed her. They entered the kitchen, and Julia poured Chianti into their glasses while Fiamma looked around with disapproval.

'This kitchen used to be so wonderful. This is sad.' Fiamma's expression changed when she noticed Bianco, still fully asleep. 'This must be her dog. She adored this breed.'

'His name is Bianco.'

'I know. She names them all Bianco.'

'Really?' Julia almost laughed.

'I'm telling you, she was crazy.' Fiamma bent down and stroked Bianco's head, smiling. 'But she loved animals, I'll give her that.'

'Here we go.' Julia handed Fiamma her glass, picked up her own, and hesitated, thinking of a toast. 'To the future?'

'Yes, perfect.' Fiamma managed a smile, they clinked glasses and took a sip, and Julia never needed alcohol more than this very moment.

'Anyway, thank you for everything tonight. Courtney told me you called the police and they wouldn't have gotten to me, if not for you acting so quickly.'

'It was the least I could do.'

It kind of was, Julia thought but didn't say.

'Why were those men after you? What's going on?'

'I'll tell you, but first I want to say I'm sorry about crashing your opening night. I never meant to ruin it for you.'

'The show?' Fiamma dismissed it with a wave. 'I called Paolo and my friends to apologize. Don't worry.'

'I didn't know if I should come.'

Fiamma smiled. 'I'm glad you did. It was brave of you.'

'Thank you,' Julia said, pleased, which struck her as pathetic. She was seeking the approval of a mother she didn't know.

'I've dreamed about meeting you, and here we are.'

Aw. 'That's how I feel,' Julia said, relaxing a little. 'When you spoke at the gallery, I was wondering if you were speaking to me. Were you?'

'Oh my goodness.' Fiamma sipped her wine, thoughtfully. 'I have to say, I had the strangest feeling all day. I knew something wonderful was going to happen tonight, something really wonderful.'

Whoa. Julia wondered if Fiamma had the gift but didn't interrupt her.

'I assumed the feeling was about the show, so I thought it meant I would sell some pieces. I didn't intend to talk about the orphanage but when I saw you, I realized *you* were what was wonderful, not the show.' Fiamma averted her eyes, as if she were thinking aloud. 'I kept saying to myself, who is that girl, she looks like me, I wonder how old she is, I wonder if it's *her*, my *baby girl*.'

Julia's throat thickened, but she stayed silent.

'I have to say, I think of you all the time.' Fiamma met her eye, sadly. 'On your birthday, on holidays. You were always with me.'

'Thank you,' Julia said, feeling Fiamma's words resonating in her chest.

'So at the gallery tonight, I found myself saying what I did, knowing how those mothers must've felt so long ago because it was how I felt when I relinquished you, which is what they say instead of abandoned.' Fiamma's eyes filmed. 'But I *did* abandon you. I felt I had to, and it was the hardest decision I ever made. I've never made peace with it, and then there you were tonight. Before I gave you up, I memorized your face, every detail. I *knew* exactly who you were, somehow.' Fiamma wiped away a tear. 'I thought I was doing the right thing, for you. I knew I couldn't support you, I was so confused then, at that point in my life.'

'Is that… what happened?' Julia felt tears in her eyes but held them off, and Fiamma's anguished gaze traveled around the kitchen.

'I guess we should begin way back. I was so unhappy here, so miserable, with my mother. I tried to run away again and again when I was young, as young as thirteen, but she'd drive around until she found me, obsessively looking. She was *obsessive*. Anyway I got away from her for good when I was seventeen. I started drinking and partying, I made it to London, then back to Bologna and Padua.' Fiamma's lower lip puckered. 'I became pregnant with my boyfriend, your father. You were born in Padua. He taught mathematics at the University.'

My God. Julia couldn't believe she was finally hearing her own life story. She tried to stay in emotional control. 'What was his name?'

'Roberto Colapinto. He was from Siena.'

'That's not far, right? I think I've seen signs.'

'It's in Tuscany.'

So, Tuscan blood. Julia tried to process Roberto Colapinto. 'What did he look like?'

'Tall, thin, good-looking. We were so in love.' Fiamma smiled. 'I think your nose is like his, I can show you pictures another time.'

'Great,' Julia said, trying to keep up. 'What was he like?'

'A kind man, a brilliant man, but too serious-minded.'

'I'm serious-minded,' Julia blurted out. 'Is that bad?'

'No, but that wasn't why we didn't marry. I didn't feel that I was ready to become a mother, given the way I was raised. I just didn't know if I could be a good mother to you. I just didn't know what a good mother was like, and he was too insecure to raise you on his own. We both decided that you would be better off with a solid family, one more established.' Her smile faded. 'I'm sorry, I am. I placed you with a very good international adoption agency and I trusted them. Were they good people, who adopted you?'

'Yes, a couple with no other children. My mother was wonderful, but I always wondered where you were.' Julia hesitated. 'And when I got a letter about an inheritance from an Emilia Rossi, I didn't know who she was, so I came to find out. Did you know about that?'

'The inheritance? No.'

Julia felt awkward. 'I don't know why she left it to me and not you. Of course I'd split it with you, or you can have it. You lived with her, you deserve it more.'

'I don't want her money, not any.' Fiamma frowned. 'No, thank you.'

'But the inheritance alone is around three million euros, and the land is worth much, much more. That's what tonight was about, people are trying to get it and resell it for a hospitality complex that will be seven hundred million—'

'You keep the money, all of it,' Fiamma said, more gently. 'I want you to have it, it's your legacy. You're her granddaughter, and it doesn't surprise me that she left it to you.'

'How did she? I don't even know how she knew about me, or where I lived, or anything.'

'That's because you didn't know my mother.' Fiamma's eyes narrowed, and hostility edged her tone. 'She claimed she was a Sforza, which was a wealthy royal family from the Renaissance.'

'I know, I heard, and there's the bedroom fresco.' Julia wasn't about to tell her that Caterina saved her in the Boboli and showed her the underground cell. Not yet, anyway.

'Oh, right, I forgot, that monstrosity of a family tree. My mother was obsessed with her own heritage, especially with Caterina.'

'Was she related to Caterina? Am I?'

'I believe we are, and I know she believed it, and the resemblance is there. She always said the Sforza family was where our money came from. She never worked a day in her life, so I think it's true.'

'I think it's true, too. I *know* it's true, in my heart.'

'That said, where I differ with my mother is what it means to be descended from the Sforzas.' Fiamma pursed her lips. 'My mother was obsessed with Caterina, always looking back to the past. It made her snobbish, and she built her identity around it, you see from the frescoes in this house.'

'Right.'

'Me, I've learned to look forward, not past. I believe that as an artist, my job is to create myself.' Fiamma's blue eyes calmed like a sea. 'I think we're all artists, and we create ourselves. The past does not create you, the *present* does, and in return, you create the future. Your future.'

Julia thought it was a wonderful sentiment. 'I get it. If Caterina stood for anything, it was that.'

'Yes, she invented herself. She was ahead of her time.'

'So, how did your mother know where I was?'

'I'm sure she kept looking for me. She hired people. I always suspected she knew where I was and that she knew about your adoption, or even had a hand in it.'

'How?' Julia asked, surprised.

'The agency I used was a private charitable organization in Bologna. They handled me with kid gloves. I always wondered if she'd made a secret donation. You would never believe what my mother got away with because she was rich.'

Julia couldn't ignore the bitterness in Fiamma's tone.

'She knew I would never speak to her again, but I believe she kept track of you. She would have found out where you went, who adopted you, all the things I couldn't bear to know.'

It hurt to hear, but Julia understood.

'I understand how, and why, she left you her estate. She couldn't have known where I was. After I gave you up, I left Italy, I went into a depression, missing you. I experienced grief, I couldn't shake it.' Fiamma looked at her plaintively. 'I hope that doesn't sound self-indulgent.'

'No,' Julia answered, since it struck an uncomfortable chord.

'I traveled through Scotland and Ireland. I didn't have any address, I was staying with a series of artist friends. "Couch-surfing," they call it now. Even my mother couldn't have found me.' Fiamma straightened. 'Losing you became my turning point, and I went back to Italy, changed my name, and got back to school.'

'Why do you think she didn't go after you, try to meet with you?'

'Because I'd run away again. She knew I didn't want to see her.' Julia's mind raced. 'Maybe she left me the estate because she hoped I would find you, and we would find each other.'

Fiamma blinked, as the revelation dawned on her. 'She was trying to reunite us?'

'Yes, exactly. She couldn't find you, but I'm not hard to find, even in the US. She found me and sent me *after* you. She willed us back together again.' Julia felt a lump in her throat. 'It's lovely, isn't it? She wanted to reunite us, and here we are, because of her.'

'Ha!' Fiamma smiled, her eyes shining. 'I guess that's true. She put us together.'

'Kinda smart, huh?'

'She was something.' Fiamma shook her head, amused. 'I guess I have to hand it to her.'

'Me, too.'

Suddenly Fiamma's expression darkened, lapsing into angry lines, like a lithograph etched with acid. 'And so my mother, ever the master manipulator, did one good deed in her life.'

Ouch. 'Really?'

'What? Should I forget that she locked me in a cell? Never let me off the property? Wouldn't send me to school? Wouldn't let me have friends?'

Julia's heart broke for her. 'Do you know why she did all that?'

'Yes,' Fiamma shot back. 'She wanted me to herself. She conceived me to fill her own needs, to be her constant companion, her confidante, her best friend. She lived alone so she manufactured company. Me.'

Arg. 'Are you sure?'

'Of course.'

'Sit down, would you?'

Julia sat opposite Fiamma at the kitchen table, and between them lay the three photographs of Rossi's deterioration, the two passports, the strands of hair, and the Polaroids of Rossi's abuse. Julia told Fiamma about her visions, about how she was drugged and maybe Rossi had been, too, about how Caterina showed her the underground cell and how she found the watercolors, the well, and the strongbox. She held back the Polaroid of the broken baby arm. She didn't know if Fiamma could handle it, since the other photos had shaken her.

Fiamma blinked tears away, holding the Polaroid of Rossi's bruised neck. 'You say you found this photo in the well?'

'Yes, in a go-bag. I think your mother was protecting herself from her abuser. I think that's why she used a false name and put you in that cell, too.'

'My God,' Fiamma said, anguished, her eyes filmed and her expression drawn. Her topknot had fallen to the side. 'So she was beaten?'

'Yes, almost strangled.'

'She was protecting me?'

'Yes, I believe so.'

'I used to say to her, what did I do, what did I do?' Fiamma rubbed her forehead, leaving pinkish streaks. 'It wasn't because I did something wrong? Like a punishment?'

Julia felt a stab of pain for her. 'No, not at all,' she answered, comforting her mother as if she were her child.

'Do you think it was my father who abused her?'

'I don't know. What do you know about your father?'

'Nothing, only that she hated him. She never wanted to talk about him, so I never asked again.'

Julia understood, only too well. Her parents never wanted to talk about her birth mother or father, so she'd never asked, either. She wondered if every family should start talking about the things they were afraid to discuss, to start saying the unsayable. Keeping secrets hurt people, but so did keeping silence.

Fiamma picked up her passport and opened it to her picture. 'And this is me? This is my real name? Patrizia Ritorno?'

'Yes, I believe so. What did she tell you your name was?'

'Felicia Rossi. I started calling myself Fiamma Settimi after I ran away. I wanted to hide from her, and reinvent myself.' Fiamma set the passport down, shaking her head. 'You know what is so awful about it all? The most awful?'

'No, what?'

'That my mother suffered such physical abuse, but then she inflicted it on me.'

Julia blinked. 'What?'

'It's true. I didn't want to tell you, but she broke my elbow, when I was just a baby.' Fiamma gestured to her right arm. 'I've had four operations. It still aches sometimes. I think of it every time I paint, with every stroke. I hate her for it, I always will. Of all the things she did to me, it was the worst.' Fiamma shook her head, her eyes glistening anew. 'To break the arm of a *baby*? She was *sick*.'

Oh no. Julia braced herself to reveal the truth. 'What if *she* wasn't the one who broke your arm? What if it was *him*? Look.' She set down the Polaroid of the baby with the broken elbow. 'I got this photo from the strongbox, too. I think this is you.'

Fiamma gasped, looking down at the photo. Her hand flew to her arm. 'That's where my break is.'

'What if she didn't do it?'

Fiamma shook her head, stunned. 'The doctors told me it happened when I was a baby, and she was the only parent I had.'

'But she wasn't the only adult around. Her abuser was there, too, at some point.'

'I didn't know that.' Fiamma moaned. 'I didn't remember him, I *don't* remember him.'

'I really think *he* did it.'

'You do?' Fiamma looked up, her eyes unmistakably hopeful. 'Why?'

'Look at the photo, in context.' Julia gestured to the photos and passports from the go-bag. 'He must've abused her, and then, when he started abusing you, she left with you. She took pictures of her injuries and yours, for evidence. She bought a villa in the middle of

Tuscany and hid you both away. She changed your name and hers. She kept your passports in case he found you and you both had to run. She did everything she could to keep you safe. That's why she kept you inside. That's why you couldn't go to school.'

'No, no, this can't be, no.' Fiamma's hand went to her cheek, her fingers trembling. 'But why the cell? Why that?'

'For protection? Maybe when she heard he was in town or was looking for you?' Julia puzzled it out, considering what Fiamma had just said. 'Maybe he was a powerful man with a lot of money. Maybe he hired investigators to find *her*, just like *she* did to find *you*. Just like *I* did, to find *her and you*.'

'Oh no.' Fiamma's glistening eyes flew open. 'I had it wrong? I had *her* wrong, all this time? How could I?'

'You can't fault yourself. You couldn't have known.'

'Why didn't she tell me about him? Why didn't she say why she was putting me down there?' Tears filled Fiamma's eyes. 'She could have explained everything, I would have understood.'

'It's not the kind of thing you tell a child, is it?' Julia kept her tone gentle. 'If I were in her position, I wouldn't tell you, either. I would just protect you.'

'I suppose.' Fiamma nodded, wiping her eyes. 'It was a terrible decision, but she must have been so desperate, so frightened.'

'Yes, and she wanted to keep you alive.'

'I wish I had known, I wish I had understood it. I never gave her the chance to explain it when I got old enough to understand. I so wish I had, while she was still alive.'

Julia watched guilt and regret wash over Fiamma. 'I'm sorry.'

'When she wasn't putting me down there, we were happy. She read to me, she taught me to read, and to draw and paint. We played with the dogs and the ducks. We picked grapes and pressed flowers in books. She loved me, she was loving to me.' Fiamma smiled sadly, at the memories. 'She could be so much fun, so delightful really, but then she would put me down there, I couldn't understand why. I thought she was crazy, truly *crazy*.'

'Who knows what that means, Fiamma?' Julia asked, speaking from the heart. 'We throw that word around all the time. I do, too, it comes too easily, but who says what's crazy and what's not? Who says what's normal and what's not? I've experienced so much here, I've changed, and what I think is real or crazy or normal has changed, too. It's grown, it's *expanded*.' Julia realized the truth of her words. 'I don't know if she was crazy when you lived here, all I know is that she loved you enough to keep you safe. She imprisoned herself, too. For *you*. Is that a mother's love? You tell me.'

Fiamma's eyes filled with tears.

Julia had another thought. 'Are you and your mother so different? You let me go because you wanted me to have a better life. She *kept* you because she wanted you to have a better life. You're mother and daughter, just as you and I are mother and daughter. We're the same and different, both at once.'

Fiamma picked up the photo of a young Rossi, and a sudden sweetness softened her smile. 'Mamma?' she whispered, a tear rolling down her cheek.

'Yes,' Julia said, trying not to cry.

Mamma.

73

Julia couldn't sleep, tossing and turning all night. She'd called the hospital to check on Gianluca, but his condition was still critical, which worried her sick. She could only pray he survived and that the authorities arrested whoever had tried to kill him. She wondered if they were watching her right now, through the cameras in the ceiling, which the police had decided to leave in for the time being.

She'd been processing everything that happened, and the fact that the conspiracy and Mike's killer would be brought to justice gave her a grim satisfaction. It wouldn't bring Mike back, and she knew she'd mourn and miss him forever. She would settle for putting Hoodie and the rest of them behind bars.

Julia tried to quiet her mind, but the thoughts kept coming. She still couldn't believe she'd found her birth mother, and Fiamma turned out to be a lovely person. Julia took comfort in knowing why Fiamma had relinquished her, a truly unselfish act that enabled her to find her wonderful adoptive mother. She felt gratified that Fiamma knew the whole, if complex, truth and hoped that eased her pain. She and Fiamma both wanted to continue getting to know one another, and Julia couldn't have been happier.

The bedroom began to lighten, and she realized it was almost dawn. On impulse, she threw off the coverlet and left the room, padding downstairs in her Eagles T-shirt. She went through the kitchen to the back door, unlocked it, and stepped outside, taking a deep breath. The air smelled fresh and sweet, and she felt drawn to see first light over the vineyard.

Julia walked through the wet grass in her bare feet and headed down. It was a cool, foggy morning, and a bluish gray mist enrobed the vineyard and obscured the cypress trees and hills on its horizon.

The fog shrouded the details of the vines, weed, and underbrush. Birds burst from the thicket, calling and flapping their wings. Bees and insects buzzed around. A flurry of gnats swirled on a windy whirlpool. Julia found a flat rock and sat down, breathing in. The sky was a massive expanse aglow with a transparent cerulean hue, growing infinitesimally brighter and warmer as the sun rose behind the hills, burning away the fog and washing heaven in gold, as if a painting were coming to life before her eyes.

Julia spotted patches of clarity here and there as the fog evaporated over the cypress trees, then the hilltops, and in time vivid colors began to announce themselves in the tangled vineyard, the yellows and whites of the wildflowers, the bright green of the younger vines, the darker browns of the tree limbs, and the rich black of the bark.

Suddenly the trees at the horizon became more and more clear against the brightening sky, and in the next moment the sun rose like a white orb emanating light and warmth everywhere.

Julia felt tears come to her eyes for a reason she couldn't understand, or maybe so many reasons she couldn't parse them all. It was the start of a new day, but felt like the dawning of the next part of her life, her own rebirth.

The sun began to rise slowly, slightly, incrementally but inevitably, shedding more and more light, and in the next moment, the light intensified, burning white and cleansing the sky with the most pristine purity.

Julia gasped, not understanding, then from the light emerged a form, the figure of a man whom she knew in her heart, the one she had married, and in the next moment, the lightness revealed the details of Mike's face, his freckles coming into the faintest focus, and he was smiling at her, then reaching out an ethereal hand.

Julia found herself on her feet, reaching out to him, and she heard him say:

I love you forever, babe.

I love you forever, too, Julia told him, tears brimming in her eyes.

Mike squeezed her hand to say goodbye, then he faded away bit by bit, rematerializing as if in a dream into Gianluca, sleeping in his hospital bed, his bandaged head resting on the pillow.

Julia watched spellbound, and in the next moment, Gianluca's dark eyes opened, his irises the rich brown of the earth against the sheer whiteness of heaven's light.

Gianluca smiled at her.

Alive.

The courtroom was spacious, sleek, and modern, with a witness stand, jury box, and a wooden judge's dais flanked by an American flag and the blue flag of the Commonwealth of Pennsylvania. The overhead lighting was harshly bright, and the air-conditioning so cold that Julia felt tense all the time, though it was more likely her state of mind. Ciro Nardini was being tried for Mike's murder, at the Juanita Kidd Stout Criminal Justice Center in Philadelphia, and the jury foreperson had just sent word they'd finished deliberating. They'd reached a verdict, and court was about to reconvene.

Julia willed herself to stay calm, stiff in her tailored navy pantsuit and alone in the smooth wooden pew. The two years of legal jockeying between Florence and Philadelphia were almost over, but she felt no relief. Today mattered most to her, even though the Italian prosecution had ended in convictions across the board. The coconspirators had turned on each other and pled guilty for lesser sentences. Anna Mattia and Piero Fano implicated realtor Franco Patelli, who confessed to paying them to drug Julia, to gaslight her so she'd sell. Anna Mattia claimed in a sworn statement that she'd never drugged Rossi, but Julia would never know the truth. After all, she herself had signed a sworn statement that wasn't exactly the truth. She'd learned that not everything was knowable, whether for good or for ill.

The conspiracy plot in Italy started to unravel after Franco was arrested. He implicated the kingpin Maksim Tsarovich, a double-dealing executive at the Romagna Group, who'd hatched the scheme behind Adamo Bucci's back. Tsarovich had known months in advance that his boss Bucci was looking for a property in Tuscany, so Tsarovich approached Franco, recruited him, and together they targeted Julia's property while Rossi was dying, planning to buy it as a consortium to mask their true identities. Tsarovich's plan was then to flip Julia's property, make a fortune on the resale to Bucci, and quit the Romagna Group.

It turned out that Ciro Nardini and Bernardo Vitali pointed the finger of guilt at Marshal Torti, who'd hired them to do the dirty work, and Torti turned in the two *carabinieri* who'd harassed Julia and Courtney. Marshal Torti also implicated two public officials in Savernella government and one Tomasso Lino, aka Black Ballcap, who'd followed Julia at the Uffizi and driven the white van that forced Gianluca off the road. All eleven coconspirators were currently serving various sentences in Italy, according to their crimes.

Julia wasn't satisfied because the job was only half-done. Nardini had to account for killing Mike, and she'd fought hard to get him extradited to the US for this trial. If he were convicted today, he'd serve his Pennsylvania sentence after the one in Italy. She hoped he'd be locked up forever.

The courtroom began to fill up as administrative personnel returned for the verdict. The uniformed bailiffs resumed their posts next to the dais, then a female law clerk trundled in and sat down at her desk. The court reporter bent her coiffed head over her steno machine. Someone coughed, the sound breaking the silence and echoing in the cavernous space.

Julia was only one of a handful of people in the gallery. She'd expected the proverbial packed courtroom she saw on Netflix, but that wasn't real. Sadly a homicide trial in a major American city wasn't front-page news, but Mike would always be a headline to her. Courtney had come to watch when Julia took the stand but couldn't make it today. Mike's father had passed last year, and his mother had gone into memory care after an Alzheimer's diagnosis. Julia was the keeper of Mike's memory now.

A female police officer entered through the side door, which led to the secured hallway where Nardini was in custody. Julia struggled to stay composed. She went to Zoom therapy from time to time and had even seen Helen once or twice, but got too busy with the legal proceedings. She felt as if the rest of her life was on hold, in suspended animation until after the verdict.

She assessed the chances of Nardini's conviction, going back and forth in her mind. She didn't know whether the jury would find Nardini guilty, and the prosecutor said their chances were fifty-fifty. Nardini hadn't confessed in Italy to Mike's murder and didn't take the stand here, so the American prosecution stood on its own. Julia had testified as the prosecution's main witness, but she'd been impeached on cross because she hadn't identified Nardini in her statement on the night of the murder and even stated that she *couldn't* identify the killer. The prosecution offered the traffic cam video, arguing that it showed Nardini killing Mike, but the defense countered that the image wasn't clear enough. The prosecutor had warned Julia as much, but she'd left the courtroom every time they showed the video. It was the last thing she wanted to see, ever again.

Worst of all, the prosecution was dealt a blow when a cranky Judge McAfee excluded the evidence that Nardini was convicted of Julia's attempted murder in Croce and his participation in the conspiracy there, deciding it would be too prejudicial. It was a technical ruling that meant the Philly jury knew nothing about the Tuscan conspiracy. Julia thought law was supposed to lead to justice, not thwart it, but she'd learned that the opposite could be true. Today, Nardini might get away with murder.

The side door opened, and two Philly cops entered the courtroom, leading Nardini in a suit and tie, handcuffed and shackled. Julia shuddered at the sight of him, mostly from righteous anger rather than residual terror. He'd lost weight in prison, so he looked almost harmless, though he was anything but. She knew he was a sadistic killer because she'd seen him kill Mike, and he'd tried to kill her. She'd learned there was evil in the world, and sometimes it wore a tie.

The cops escorted Nardini to the defense counsel table, where he pointedly avoided Julia's eye as they took off his handcuffs and leg shackles, then sat down. They stood behind him as defense counsel Matt Ivrez strode in, a notoriously pricey criminal lawyer with a dark beard and shiny black manbun, who always wore a flashy suit.

In the next moment, the female prosecutor hustled up the aisle, flashing Julia a tense smile. Her name was Valerie Nakata-Simons, and she was an attractive forty-something with a short haircut and a slight build in a no-nonsense black pantsuit that comported with her somber, dogged, and dedicated manner. She'd been kind to Julia, though she'd avoided showy emotionality. If they lost today, it wasn't for lack of trying.

Another law clerk entered the courtroom through the front door near the dais, mounted the steps, and set some papers down. It meant that the judge would be out any minute, and Julia straightened in her seat, as the lead bailiff straightened, saying, 'All rise for the Honorable William R. McAfee.'

Everybody stood up, including Julia, though she felt weak in the knees. Judge McAfee was older, making a stooped figure as he swept berobed up the stairs of the dais to his black leather chair. He was painfully thin with wizened white hair and wire-rimmed glasses that slid down his bony nose. He hadn't showed much personality during the trial, except that he was a stickler for any technical detail, though as far as Julia could tell, his rulings disadvantaged both the prosecution and the defense at times. He had a reputation for fairness, but she wasn't seeing a lot of heart. She resented him for his evidentiary ruling against them, but now it was all up to the jury.

'You may sit down,' Judge McAfee said, nodding, and Julia did, turning expectantly to the side door behind the jury box as another bailiff entered and the jury began to file in behind him.

'Hey, sorry I'm late,' Gianluca whispered, appearing at the end of the pew and making his way toward her. His hair had grown back but he'd lost weight, looking undersized in his wool jacket and scarf. He moved with difficulty, still in physical therapy after the motorcycle crash. His rehabilitation had been slow and painful, requiring him to relearn walking as well as fine-motor skills like painting, which killed her.

'It's okay. They're just about to come back.'

'The jury was in the men's room, so they wouldn't let me in.'

'No worries,' Julia said, as Gianluca sat down, raking back his curls. Psychologically his recovery had been hard on him, too, because he hadn't been able to return to work yet. He and his father were talking about helping her restore the villa if she chose to stay in Tuscany permanently, but Julia's plans were up in the air. She'd been with Gianluca every step of the way during his rehab, taking him to his various appointments and cheering him on, and he'd been with her every step of the way during these cases, meeting with the prosecutors and translating on the Italian side. But they both knew that they hadn't had a fair chance at a normal relationship. In a way, they were in suspended animation, too.

Both turned to watch the jury come in, and Julia knew that Gianluca was feeling as tense as she was. He took her hand, and held it, and she gave him a squeeze back but they didn't exchange a word. He'd been such a support during the trial, but he shared the prosecutor's fear that the verdict could go either way.

Julia watched the jury shuffle into the box, twelve faces that she had come to know from watching them while testimony came in. There were seven men and five women of all shapes, sizes, and races, and they'd been remarkably attentive during the trial. But none of them made eye contact with her as they came in and sat down, which worried her. The courthouse lore was that if the jury didn't look at you when they entered, they were going against you.

Judge McAfee turned to the jury. 'Madam Foreperson, have you reached a verdict?'

'We have, Your Honor,' she answered, her expression impassive. She held out a sheet of paper, which the bailiff accepted, walked to the dais, and handed it up to the judge.

Julia held her breath, trying to read his expression, but she couldn't. Gianluca's hand tightened around hers.

'Mr Nardini, will you please stand and face the jury.' Judge McAfee handed the verdict back to the bailiff.

Nardini and his counsel stood up. So did Valerie, at counsel table.

The bailiff brought the verdict to the foreperson, who accepted it, read it, and stood tall, as if to shoulder responsibility for what she was about to say.

Julia held her breath, her heart pounding. Gianluca placed his other hand on top of hers, joining them as if they'd be stronger that way, better able to absorb the impact together.

The jury foreperson cleared her throat. 'In the Common Pleas Court of the County of Philadelphia, in the Matter of the *Commonwealth of Pennsylvania vs. Ciro Nardini,* Case Number 25-9383. We, the jury, in the above-entitled action, find the Defendant Ciro Nardini guilty of the crime of murder in the first degree, upon the person of Michael Aaron Shallette, pursuant to 18 Pennsylvania Crimes Code Section 2502(1).'

Julia's hand flew to her mouth. She wanted to shout for joy and relief. Gianluca gasped, putting an arm around her and hugging her close, and she could feel his body shudder, as if he was experiencing everything she was at the very same moment, sharing it with her completely.

Julia buried herself in his chest, feeling an overwhelming sense of gratitude that the jury had done the right thing, that Nardini would pay for his crime, that all the trials, proceedings, statements, and investigations were over, and that the horror that had begun on a cold October night, when her husband had been cut down before her very eyes, was finally ended, and every day of the struggle since then had been worth it, because it had all come down to this:

Justice.

EPILOGUE

It was a superhot afternoon, or maybe Julia just felt that way because she was extremely pregnant. They were in the nursery, which used to be a guest bedroom but was now one of the few rooms completed in the restoration of the villa. She sat with her feet up and watched her vision come to life, but it wasn't like the ones she used to have. She met with Helen off and on, but she was still too busy to develop her gift, though she'd learned to trust herself and her feelings, at least most of the time.

Gianluca, now her husband, was sketching on the nursery wall, drawing a mural they'd envisioned together, their unconventional version of a family tree, which included all the people they loved and wanted their baby to know, whether alive, dead, or somewhere in between. Its branches would be green, leafy, and full, containing portraits of Mike, then Julia's adoptive parents Melanie and Martin, and Gianluca's late grandparents Letizia and Raimondo, and even Caterina herself. Courtney and Paul would be depicted, too, as well as Fiamma and Julia's biological father Roberto. She'd reached out to him, and he'd been delighted to get to know her. She'd come to like him and didn't find him too serious-minded. On the contrary, she thought her wacky and wonderful family could use adult supervision.

She sipped her water, happy to watch Gianluca, who was back to himself after a long rehabilitation, which included clearing the vineyard with his father. He worked on the mural next to Fiamma, Sherry, and Tonio, while Raffi told them all what they were doing wrong. Julia loved belonging to a family of artists and had already finished her portraits because she didn't leave everything to the last minute like these Florentines. Plus she had a baby to deliver. Next week.

Whoa. Julia felt a sharp pain in her belly and set down her water glass. She'd had Braxton Hicks from time to time, but this was stronger. It was early for a real contraction, but it sure felt like one.

'Julia?' Gianluca turned around, alarmed. 'Are you okay?'

'Um, I don't know.' Julia tried to breathe through the contraction, but it wasn't helping. The hospital was over an hour away. 'I think—'

'It's time? My God!' Gianluca rushed to her, and everybody exploded into talk and action. Fiamma helped Gianluca get Julia to the door. Sherry ran for Julia's purse, Raffi for her hospital bag, and Tonio for the Fiat Panda. Only Bianco stayed put, raising his head, determining he wasn't needed, then going back to sleep.

Julia made her way to the stairs, where Raffi met her with the hospital bag. Gianluca supported her one arm, and Fiamma the other. They descended the stairs, and Sherry met them with purses and water bottles.

Julia had another contraction in the entrance hall and stopped, clutching her belly and glancing up at the astrological fresco. *It's a Leo!* she thought, delighted. The baby would be fierce, loving, passionate, and creative. Basically, Tuscan with a splash of American.

Gianluca helped her to the idling car, gentled her into the back seat, and got in beside her, holding her and counting her breaths like they'd learned in class. Fiamma locked the house and jumped in beside him. Sherry climbed in the passenger seat, and Tonio hit the gas. They took off with Raffi jumping on her Vespa, zooming ahead like a police escort.

Julia tried to breathe through her contraction, listening to Gianluca's calm voice amid the loud and animated chatter in Italian and English, everybody excited to be adding new life to an already lively clan. Tears sprang to her eyes, not from pain but from happiness, and she realized *this* was her dream, not a painting of a family tree but a flesh-and-blood family, filling a tiny car with noisy love for a baby they had yet to meet but already adored.

Julia felt flushed with joy and wonderment, about to become a mother to a daughter of her own, a little girl named in honor of the mother who was always there for her.

Melanie Pritzker Moretti was about to enter the world.

Taking her place among the stars.

ACKNOWLEDGMENTS
AND AUTHOR'S NOTE

First, thank you very much to my readers. I'm grateful every day that I make a living in books, and when I'm writing, I always wonder how my reader will respond. I not only read the reviews that people post online, but I practically memorize them. I'm grateful because no story is complete unless it is heard by another person, namely you.

I believe in research, especially if it involves a place as gorgeous as Tuscany. (Nice work if you can get it.) I traveled to Milan, Florence, Forlì, and Imola and visited places that served as settings for the story, like the Cathedral of Milan, the Uffizi Gallery in Florence, and Caterina's castle at Forlì, as well as off-the-beaten track locations like the historic Marucelliana Library in Florence, which should be on any book lover's tour of the city, and Casa Emma vineyard in Chianti for amazing Chianti tasting. Many people helped me along the way, and they deserve thanks here:

Thanks to vintner Noemi Veltro, who explained the process of making Chianti and took me on a tour of an aromatic array of casks. Thank you to Roberto Cresti, the very kind owner of the lovely B&B Del Giglio in the lovely town of San Donato in Poggio, who spontaneously welcomed me into his beautiful home and answered all of my questions about village life in Tuscany. Thanks to Marco Morandini, who took me everywhere, including a Tuscan graveyard. Even though the novel tells a darker story, I hope you nevertheless get a flavor of the magnificent vistas, vineyards, wines, and delicious foods of this magnificent region.

By the way, I filmed videos of the various locations in the novel and posted them on my website. They make a wonderful companion to the novel, and I've heard they help book club discussions a great deal. I'm one of those people who look things up while they read, and if you're like me, let yourself get crazy. In addition, there's even an interactive map of Tuscany on my website, so you can see where actual scenes are located. Some of the towns in the novel are fictionalized, like Croce and Moravia, but they are based on what I saw and learned.

Thank you to Elana Vitali and Anastasiya Voloshyna of the tourism office in Forlì, IAT HUB, who helped so much with my research of the life of Duchess Caterina Sforza and my self-guided tour of her castles. Those who wish to learn more about the remarkable Caterina Sforza may enjoy the following: DeVries, *Caterina Sforza and the Art of Appearances: Gender, Art, and Culture in Early Modern Italy* (2010); Breisach, *Caterina Sforza: A Renaissance Virago* (1967); Lev, *The Tigress of Forlì* (2011); Azzolini, *The Duke and the Stars: Astrology and Politics in Renaissance Milan* (2013); Ray, *Daughters of Alchemy: Women and Scientific Culture in Early Modern Italy* (2015); and Klapisch-Zuber, *Women, Family, and Ritual in Renaissance Italy* (1985). As a child, Caterina herself devoured Bocaccio's *On Famous Women,* a groundbreaking work because it featured the lives of famous women rather than men. That she became so powerful herself is a tribute to the power of reading.

I love astrology, which really was the rage during the Italian Renaissance, especially among the nobility. If you want to learn more about the subject, you might enjoy Garin, *Astrology in the Renaissance: The Zodiac of Life* (1983); Whitfield, *Astrology: A History* (2001); and Niccoli, *Prophecy and People in Renaissance Italy* (1990). On astrology in general, I love these beautiful books: Richards, *Astrology* (2020); *Parkers' Astrology* (2020); and for fun, Roob, *Alchemy & Mysticism* (2021). By the way, I assigned to Julia my own birthday and zodiac sign, Cancer the Crab, and though the horoscopes herein are fictional, the cosmic positions referred to are absolutely true to the date.

On more earthly territory, huge thanks to my dear friend Nick Casenta, Esq., formerly Chief Deputy District Attorney of the Chester County District Attorney's Office, for his legal expertise. Thanks, too, to Jorge Figueroa of Ferrari Philadelphia, who helped me research this amazing car.

Huge thanks to my genius publishers at Grand Central Publishing, a terrifically energetic team led by the great Ben Sevier. Thanks to Beth deGuzman, Karen Kosztolnyik, and my amazing editor Lyssa

Keusch. I am so grateful for Lyssa's editorial insights, humor, and kindness during the writing of this book. Thanks, too, to Danielle Thomas, who keeps Lyssa and me on task.

Thanks for innovative marketing to Tiffany Porcelli and Quinne Rogers, and big hugs to Matthew Ballast for his efforts and expertise in publicity. Thanks to Albert Tang for a sensational cover, and thanks to my old pal Ana Maria Allesi in audio. Lots of love and gratitude to Lauren Monaco and the sales reps who took me on with such energy and enthusiasm.

Thanks and love to my terrific agents Robert Gottlieb and Erica Silverman of the Trident Media Group. Finally, thanks to their assistant Aurora Fernandez, who has been so helpful. Thanks to Debbie Deuble Hill and Kyle Loftus of Independent Artists Group for all of their efforts in Hollywood.

Finally, lots of love and thanks to my bestie and assistant Laura Leonard, who supports me every day in every conceivable way. Thanks and love to Nan Daley and Katie Rinda, who help with every kind of support. Thanks to all of my amazing other gal pals, Franca, Paula, and Sandy.

Thanks and big love to my amazing and brilliant daughter Francesca Serritella, a novelist in her own right. I've been writing about family all my life because that's what matters most.

Love you, honey.

ABOUT THE AUTHOR

Photo credit © Jeff Wojtaszek

Lisa Scottoline is a #1 bestselling and Edgar Award-winning author who also serves as president of the Mystery Writers of America. A former trial lawyer, she has written thirty-seven novels in addition to nine humorous memoirs she co-authored with her daughter, novelist Francesca Serritella. Lisa has over 30 million copies of her books in print and is published in over thirty-five countries. She also reviews fiction for the *New York Times*, the *Washington Post*, and the *Philadelphia Inquirer*. She graduated magna cum laude from the University of Pennsylvania and cum laude from its law school, where she taught Justice & Fiction, a course she developed. She lives on a farm in Pennsylvania.

Scottoline.com
@LisaScottoline